Shaken Free

Shaken Free

Sequel to Shaken Loose

Ilana DeBare

HYPATIA PRESS

Published by Hypatia Press in the United Kingdom in 2025

ISBN: 978-1-83919-661-4

www.hypatiapress.org

For my parents, whose faith was placed in people, including their three children.

CHARACTERS

Annie Maple: Twenty-nine-year-old San Francisco college dropout who died and was immersed in Hellfire, then inexplicably "shaken loose" into the deserts of Hell. She returned to life through a portal that opened between Hell and Earth.

Ben Maple: Annie's older brother, a celebrity atheist pundit.

Mary: Baby whom Annie miscarried when she was nineteen, and whose soul she rescued from the marsh of Limbo in Hell. Annie returned to Earth pregnant with Mary.

Callie and Herb Maple: Annie's parents.

Melanie: Annie's roommate in San Francisco.

Billie: Young mother from 1963 Alabama who was shaken loose from the fire like Annie and went through the portal back to Earth just before Annie.

Trua: Fourth century Hun tribesman who was shaken loose from the fire like Annie and chose not to go through the portal.

Henry Mwango: Kenyan engineer who was shaken loose and chose not to go through the portal.

Ifechi: Pre-colonial Igbo farmer who was shaken loose and killed by marauders.

Dev: Hindu boy who was shaken loose and killed by marauders.

Chen Haisheng: Student radical from 1927 Shanghai who was shaken loose into a devil city built by enslaved wraithlike souls.

Ishaq Abu Daoud: Twelfth-century Syrian merchant and companion of Haisheng.

Eiko: Japanese woman who was a companion of Haisheng and Ishaq in their safe house in the devil city.

Oudine: Medieval French woman who also stayed in the safe house.

Kezia Parker: Widowed accountant from Brooklyn.

Satan: Ruler of Hell, formerly the angel called Lucifer.

Baphomet: Young girl devil in love with Satan.

Ardat: Devil who used to be a harpist in Heaven.

Zarphan: Devil leader trying to supplant Satan as ruler of Hell.

Beelzebul: Another devil leader trying to supplant Satan.

Turael: Zarphan's chief of intelligence.

Michael, Urielle, Raphael, Gabrielle: Archangels.

PART ONE

Apart

CHAPTER ONE

Annie

Annie Maple had been back from the dead for a week before her brother Ben came to visit.

The first few days were a hospitalized blur, loopy from painkillers. Now she sat in her childhood bed at her parents' house with the shades drawn, eyes closed, earbuds on, listening to *Clair de Lune* on looping replay. Before that, it had been Pachelbel's *Canon*. Before that, Chopin nocturnes.

Soft chords echoed, arpeggios rippled, but Annie was listening for the single notes and the silence around them. Pure note followed by pure silence. In those moments it was as if the world had halted all movement. The ache in her arm and the pounding in her head melted away.

The doctors at San Francisco General said it was a miracle she had come through the deck collapse with so few injuries—concussion, broken arm, assorted cuts and abrasions. But the doctors were talking about medical miracles. Annie had no idea how to tell people about the other miracles, which sounded crazy even to herself.

I'm pregnant even though I didn't have sex.

I'm pregnant with a grey orb I was carrying around in the deserts of Hell.

I'm pregnant with the baby I miscarried ten years ago who was returned to me by a girl devil who is a lovestruck assistant to Satan.

The arpeggios swelled, blossomed, faded. A single note hung in her earbuds like a drop of rainwater on a leaf.

Silence.

Through the hammering in her head, the beauty of it all overwhelmed her. How a single finger on a single key of a piano could produce a sound of such clarity. How someone, somewhere, had invented the piano. How someone, somewhere, had invented musical notation so that the sounds in Debussy's imagination could be documented and reproduced a hundred years and half a world away. How engineers had figured out a way to turn sound into signal, and then into bits and bytes, and then miniaturize it all so that a palm-sized rectangular device could hold all the music conceived and notated by a thousand Debussys.

Before, Annie had loved the beauty of nature. Now she felt raw to the beauty of human creation—of everything.

And so much of it would end up in the fire.

No. Don't go there. Listen to the piano, its single notes glistening like icicles. Focus on those. But would Debussy be in Hell? Would Chopin? They were Christians, so maybe not. But didn't Chopin have an affair with George Sand? Was that a sin? What would Hellfire do to a pianist's fingers? What would it do to a composer's ears?

No. Breathe deep. Breathe with the notes. Think about nothing but breath.

She calmed. Annie removed her earbuds to better hear the sweep of her own breath. The bedroom door cracked open and her mother peered in.

"Sweetie. I have a surprise for you."

Not more flowers? Her room looked like a greenhouse with all the plants people had sent. Or ice cream? Annie used to binge entire pints of Ben & Jerry's but since the accident had no appetite. She made a halfhearted effort to look excited. Then her mother vanished and a tall, skinny figure appeared in the doorway.

"Ben!"

The dim room felt suddenly aglow. Her brother had taught her reading and Monopoly and the physics of paper airplane flight. He'd broken the news to her that there was no Santa Claus and then, when she wouldn't stop crying, made up for it by using the Christmas tree lights to show her the difference between serial and parallel circuits. These days she saw him only two or three times a year, when he came back to the Bay Area for holidays or a book tour or a speaking gig.

"Got here as fast as I could. I told you on the phone, right? There was the conference in Brussels and then that panel in Amsterdam. I hopped on a flight the same day I got back to New York. Just had to change my underwear."

He grinned, his old multi-layered grin that boasted that Ben Maple could do no wrong, acknowledged that this was of course bullshit, and then touted his superiority for acknowledging that. Someone could write an entire PhD thesis deconstructing that grin. Annie smiled too. She no longer cared that it had taken him a week: he was here.

Ben set down his briefcase and carry-on bag, positioned himself on the edge of the bed, and squeezed her hand.

"How you doing, Anna Banana?" He hadn't called her that in fifteen years. "You look pretty good for someone who had a near-death experience."

"I don't feel so good."

He nodded. "Fracture, should take four to six weeks. Concussion, anywhere from a week to six months. Those cuts will be better in no time. You were damn lucky."

You have no idea, she thought but remained silent.

"Want me to sign it?" He gestured at the cast on her arm. So far it was blank, but she held it up and he reached in his briefcase for a pen. "Hmm." He thought for a minute, then wrote. *Our greatest glory is not in never falling, but in rising every time we fall.* The black letters skittered like spiders across the white plaster.

"Most people think it's Confucius. But it's actually Oliver Goldsmith, writing under the alias of a Chinese visitor to London in the 1760s. A classic device, using the perspective of an outsider to critique one's own society."

He paused, then touched the pen tip to her cast again.

—*Oliver Goldsmith, via Benjamin Maple*

"So. Did Mom tell you where I was when she texted me? On the runway at JFK waiting to take off. Good thing the flight was delayed, otherwise I wouldn't have found out until we landed. As it was, I was able to call her back right away. Called Peter Neuman, too, San

Francisco mayor's office. You can be sure they're taking this seriously. Whoever screwed up that deck—the builder, or the owner, or whoever—isn't going to get off easy."

"Thank you."

"The guy right across the aisle from me was Raymond Doyle. Excuse me, the *Most Reverend* Raymond Doyle, Archbishop of Hartford, who was going to Brussels too. He overheard the call and offered to pray for you. I told him you needed antibiotics, not prayers. And single-payer health care."

This was a laugh line, but for once she felt excused from smiling.

"Ben. Can you close the door? The light makes my headache worse."

He shut the door, returned to the bed, and looked around the room. "You okay here? Mom said you asked to go back to your apartment."

"I didn't want to feel like I was twelve years old again. But the doctors said this would be better. Just for a while."

Ben nodded. He was skinny as a post, but six feet and two inches added up and his mass created a valley on the left side of Annie's mattress. She reflexively shifted her weight to the right so she wouldn't roll in. Her attention was sunk into one question: should she tell him?

Antibiotics, not prayers. That was classic Ben, whose book jackets described him as "America's Most Famous Atheist." Ben was a fierce culture warrior who loved skewering the religious right on Fox News. But he was also the big brother who used to read Lyle the Crocodile

5

to her behind the hydrangea bush on summer evenings when she was supposed to be in bed.

Annie put a protective hand over her belly.

"Ben. Can you listen without interrupting if I tell you something weird?"

"Sure."

"When the deck fell, I died. Really died. And then came back to life."

"That's—"

"No, stop. Don't interrupt, okay?"

He nodded.

"I went to Hell. At first I was in this sea of fire. But then somehow I was popped out onto the land. There were devils. I met Satan—"

"Annie—"

"*Don't interrupt!*" She never spoke this sharply to him. She continued but the words of her story jumped out of their own accord, disjointed and disordered. Psychopaths in the desert...a devil civil war...a marsh of dead babies...a portal to Earth through a rock arch. She knew it made no sense.

"Annie, you were delusional. You'd been knocked unconscious and concussed. It's normal in that kind of situation to have hallucinations."

"It wasn't a hallucination."

"Did you have a feeling of floating above your body?"

"No."

"A tunnel with light at the end?"

"No."

"Things happen to the brain in a state of near-death. Hypoxia. Hypercarbia. Dysfunctions of the temporoparietal junction. What you experienced was a normal response to brain injury. The key thing is that you're recovering. You're going to be fine."

"It wasn't a brain thing. It was real. The fire, the desert—that was all real."

She thought of Trua, the Hun tribesman whom she had come to trust and then love, and their one truncated kiss in the desert before Hell lurched them into retching. That had been real too.

"The people were real. And I was there for a long time. Months—"

"Annie. You were unconscious for a few minutes, lying under the deck the whole time. It may *feel* like months, but that's the way the mind works. Think about when you dream. You feel like you're in Paris or Japan but it's only a few minutes and you're in bed the whole time."

"This wasn't a dream. It was real."

Ben sighed, stood up, and paced across the room. Annie readied herself for a barrage of arguments. *Hell was fiction; Hell was a myth left over from the days before science; Hell was an ideological construct designed to control fearful, uneducated people.* She'd had this exact argument with herself, over and over, when she first arrived there. She prepared herself for his steel irony, his slashing rhetoric.

But Ben didn't argue. He sat back down on the bed looking sad.

"Don't worry about any of this right now," he said. "Just focus on getting better."

"I'm not *worrying*. I'm trying to tell you what *happened*."

"Give yourself time. The best thing is to avoid stress. You've got music, right?" He gestured at her earbuds. "Hey, Anna Banana. What're you listening to?"

How infuriating: he wouldn't even argue with her. She was too pathetic to merit an argument. And this was Ben, who in high school used to pick political fights with the U.P.S. delivery guy, who needled the Salvation Army ladies collecting toys outside the supermarket.

Her head pounded with a clanging, metallic pain.

"It was real," she muttered, but he just patted her hand as if she were a child with an invisible playmate.

CHAPTER TWO

Trua

*burningburningburningburningburningburningburningb
urningburningburningburningburningburningburningbu
rningburningburningburningburningburningburningbur
ningburningburningburningburningburningburningburn
ingburningburningburningburningburningburningburni
ngburningburningburningburningburningburningburnin
gburningburning—*

Flame beyond flame. Char beyond char. The hottest
cookfire is barely an ember next to this, the biggest
grassfire hardly a spark. Fire around you. Fire inside
you. Your guts are on fire, your throat is on fire. Each
hair on your head a burning brand, each scar on your
cheek a river of flame.

*burningburningburningburningburningburningburningb
urningburningburningburningburningburningburningbu
rningburningburningburning—*

No sight. No breath. No thoughts. Only fire.
Flames take your toes. They blacken and crumble,
then burn again. Flames eat your soles, your heels, lick
up to your ankles—*ankles? your ankles?* and just for a

9

moment you remember someone talking about touching your ankle, you remember laughter, you remember a name, *Annie*—and then that too is gone, lost, burnt away with everything else that is not fire and pain and fire and pain and fire and pain—

burningburningburningburningburningburningburningb urningburning—

* * * * *

The fire was gone.

Rocks and gravel pressed into Trua's side. Silence filled his ears: had he gone deaf? His forehead throbbed and, touching it, he felt a scabbed lump. Hands, legs, feet were all there: he was unburnt and alive. Or whatever "alive" meant in this place. He wanted to lie back and spread his arms and bask in the non-existent sun. Then with a gush of panic everything came back to him—the ambush, the Roman bastard, Annie on the clifftop by that rock arch. Trua jerked into a sitting position but the ridge above was empty, just the black arch and reddish-gray sky. The Roman lay on the canyon floor barely a horse-length away, neck at a strange angle, head crusted with dried blood. And just past the Roman, the body of Henry Mwango.

"Henry!" he rasped, crawling across the gravel.

The old man wasn't breathing. This wasn't the trancelike, temporary slippage back into the fire that happened after a shock or injury. Henry lay curled as if trying to comfort himself, but his torso was cold and limbs stiff.

10

Trua tried to sort out the chaos of those last moments. The three attackers had jumped them from behind. The Roman killed Henry, or at least that's what Trua had thought. Then he pinned and bound Trua while the other two men scuttled up the cliff wall after Annie and her friend Billie. When Annie pulled the men through the arch with her, Trua used the distraction to rip through his ties and lunge at his captor. The Roman slammed him with a rock.

Then the fire.

That was all he remembered; the rest was guesswork. Henry must have stayed alive long enough to stagger over and kill the Roman, then curl up nearby and truly die. A small dry lakebed of brown blood extended from beneath Henry's head.

And Annie? Again he glanced up at the empty ridge. The cliffs hovered like vultures, craggy and black against the red-grey sky. Now he noticed sounds in the silence—wind on the cliffs, and the gurgle and sizzle of lava fountaining into a pool on the far side of the canyon.

Trua didn't know if the deserted arch was a good or bad sign. Gingerly he stood and began the climb to the ridge—tough under any circumstances, but even more so with stiff legs and an aching head. On top, he looked out and saw only more black mountains—no Annie, no Billie, no marauders. The opening of the arch no longer shimmered. He tossed a pebble through and it clattered into the gravel on the other side. The magic gateway had closed. Annie was really gone. But where had she ended up? Had the marauders captured her?

He tossed another pebble and it clattered through too.

Gods of the plain, keep Annie and her baby safe, he thought, and then remembered that his people's gods were fiction.

He turned and edged his way down the cliff, back to Henry's body.

* * * * *

The clear glass disks that Henry used to wear on his face lay shattered on the rock floor. Henry could barely see without those disks, he was old and lame, and yet he'd given his life to save Trua's.

Trua pondered what to do with Henry's body. At home on the Great Plain, Huns buried the dead together with their most valued possessions. Romans burned or buried their corpses. There were people in the North, he'd been told, who sent their dead out to sea.

Henry had recounted sliding the body of another victim of the marauders, Ifechi, into a fire river. So Henry wouldn't view that as disrespect. Trua gathered the remnants of those glass disks and slipped them inside Henry's shirt. He lifted the old man—so light, so insubstantial—and carried him across the canyon. Heat slammed his face, evaporating his sweat even before it could form droplets. He pushed through the heat, dropped Henry into the lava pond, and retreated.

Safely away, he scoured the ground for a sharp stone. *One for his head of clan Eskam. One for his father. One for his uncle.* Annie had asked him about the scars on his cheeks, and he'd explained how Huns honor their most important dead by drawing their own blood. *Now one for Henry.* Henry wasn't a member of his clan—he wasn't even a Hun—yet like Annie he was now family to Trua. But at home there were metal blades. Here there was just rock. He moved across the gravel floor, fingering shards, looking for the sharpest.

He chose one and wiped it with one of the rags Billie had left for Henry. He clenched his jaw, gripped the rock, and willed his hand to be steadfast. The skin gave way with a burst of pain and he plowed the rock across his cheek. *Henry, my uncle. You thought you were a coward, but you were not.* The cut was rough and messy—shredding, not slicing. He threw the rock down as soon as the gash was long enough and bristled with angry defiance.

I spit on that Jesus Christ god.

So what if his own gods were fiction! So what if everything he'd believed about the afterlife was wrong! Henry Mwango would not be forgotten: Trua at least would remember him. The scar would see to that.

He waited in the canyon for an appropriately respectful amount of time, then packed up Billie's collection of rags. In this world of nothing, rags mattered: they could serve as rope, blanket, bandages. He threw a final look at the rock arch and glanced across the canyon at the Roman's body, which lay untouched and exposed. He resisted the urge to kick it.

Trua set out walking for the devil city, the last place that he'd seen other humans. He'd promised Annie that he would try to eliminate the fire before she and her baby might ever have to come back here. Trua wasn't sure of the way to the city, but he was sure of his goal.

If he were lucky, he'd find other shaken-loose humans who could help him fulfill that vow.

CHAPTER THREE

Annie

By the time Ben returned to New York, Annie understood that she'd have to keep Hell a secret. But then
there was the other secret of her pregnancy.

Annie had lost this baby a decade ago, when she ac-
cidentally became pregnant and miscarried during her
freshman year of college. She'd blamed herself for both
the pregnancy and the miscarriage—subsumed them
within the other failures of that disastrous year—and
never told her family. She dropped out of college, carried the failures home with her, and silently let them
bind her.

Now Hell had given her a second chance at both
motherhood and life. Resting in bed, Annie touched her
belly and treasured each muffled kick. At the hospital,
she'd clawed through the medicated haze to ask the
doctors not to tell her parents she was four months
pregnant. But she was living with her parents, at least
for now. They'd find out sooner or later. Annie hesitated
for days—*would they see this as yet another fuck-up by
their disappointing daughter?*—but eventually steeled
herself to tell them.

They were sitting at dinner. "That's...unexpected,"
her father said, then broke into a fit of coughing and

excused himself to get some water. But her mother was terrific.

"Oh sweetie," she said, eyes moist, and enfolded Annie in a hug. "I've always wanted to be a grandma. I'd been losing hope with your brother. This is wonderful." She came home from work the next day with a copy of *What to Expect When You're Expecting*, a giant bottle of prenatal vitamins, and a tiny cotton onesie festooned with ducklings. "The first of many," she said. "What colors do you like—pastels? brights? Once you're better, we'll go to Target together and start picking things out."

Annie felt liquid with relief. Before, she would simply have concluded she was lucky. Now she consciously channeled that gratitude towards God. Annie had never felt God; she'd seen no evidence in Hell of a just or caring God. But she was determined to do whatever it took to keep herself and her baby out of the fire.

Thank you, God, for giving me this mother.

Thank you for second chances.

As her injuries gradually healed, Annie emailed her boss at Ocean Allies and asked to be reassigned from her tedious desk job to work outdoors with kids as a coastal educator. To Annie's amazement, her boss agreed without hesitation.

Pity for the deck collapse victim? Or did they find someone better at her job while she was out? Never mind. She would seize the opportunity and try not to second-guess herself, a lesson carried home from Hell.

She took slow walks around Mill Valley, her parents' suburban town, and paid attention to small, beautiful things: anise swallowtail butterfly zigzagging through stalks of fennel. A mountain of firm, red cherries in the produce bin outside Whole Foods. Graffiti that appeared overnight near the high school, in striped pink and white like a candy cane, "Julio rules." Who was Julio—teenager? adult? Over what did he rule? She pictured a 16-year-old boy in a hardware store, perusing spray paint colors, and in defiant exuberance deciding on pink.

In one of her last conversations with Trua, he'd growled that such joy in the details of life wouldn't last.

You'll sit on the grass one day, two days. But then you'll have things to do. The grass will be something to feed goats, nothing more. You'll forget about it.

"I'm not forgetting," she told him fiercely in her mind. "See? I'm not."

She wished he were there in person to argue with. She imagined how he might react to the 21st century. Buying ice cream, she pictured Trua opening and closing the glass case to figure out how winter could be compressed into a box. In the elevator to her doctor's office, she imagined Trua lurching in shock as it lifted up, then realizing he could control it and pressing all the buttons to see what they did.

Thinking of him at these times made her smile. Her senses felt heightened. Lights were brighter, foods were sweeter and spicier, the redwoods of nearby Mount Tam were taller and the cars on the freeway faster when she viewed them through his eyes. He would be so delighted, surprised, curious. The world felt magical to her then, and even alone she was happy.

She was less happy thinking of him at night. Annie lay in bed wondering what had happened to him and the others who had been shaken loose from Hell's fire— the young revolutionary Haisheng, the Syrian merchant Ishaq, plus Eiko, Oudine, Henry Mwango. Her last glimpse of Trua had been at the bottom of the canyon in the hands of a man who hated him. He might be dead. He probably was dead. But imagining him back in the fire was horrific. She should never have left him and climbed up to the portal with Billie. She should have stayed, made a life with him there in the desert, and helped overthrow the oppressions of Hell.

No. She was right to come home and give her baby Mary a chance at life.

She was wrong to come home with Mary.

She was right to come home with Mary.

Annie had no idea if she'd made the right or wrong decision. All she knew, lying in bed and listening to the occasional car rumble up the hill beside her parents' house, was that she missed him terribly. She was terribly frightened for him. But there was nothing she could do, and no one she could tell.

* * * * *

She decided to find Billie.

Billie was a thief and a racist. Trua claimed she was a liar and murderer too. But she was also the only person alive who would understand what Annie had experienced. Annie didn't remember Billie's last name or town, only that she'd died in a traffic accident on a bridge in Alabama shortly after Kennedy was shot. Annie did web searches, skimmed Alabama history sites, bought a membership in an online newspaper archive. Nothing. She searched during the day while her parents were away at work, and again at night after she and her mother finished perusing *What to Expect*.

Finally she struck gold on a page of newspaper head-lines.

TRAGEDY ON THE THOMPSON BRIDGE
A family visit turned into tragedy on Tuesday when a 1955 Chevrolet driven by Mrs. Billie Masters of Sweet Valley ran off the Thompson Bridge.

Yes! With exhilaration, Annie recognized the name of Sweet Valley. Everything fit. This was "her" Billie. Was it wrong to feel so happy reading about a car crash? She clicked to view the rest of the story.

Mrs. Masters was hospitalized and her three children, Katherine, Natalie, and Kenneth Jr., were killed.
State police attributed the accident to heavy rain. County Coroner Samuel Davis reported the cause of death as drowning.
"By the time the police got there, those children were long gone," Davis said. "It's a miracle that Mrs. Masters survived. The only consolation is that those little souls are with the angels now."

Annie's exhilaration vanished. Billie had said a truck ran her off the bridge, but the newspaper didn't mention a truck. Billie insisted that her babies survived the accident, but her children hadn't survived. Their souls weren't with any angels. They were in the marsh of Limbo where she'd found Mary.
Billie had taken one look at that marsh and fled. Damn all her talk about trying to get home to her babies! Billie ran from those babies; she was *haunted* by those babies. She might even have killed those babies.

18

Oh Trua. You were right about her all along.

Was Billie even still alive? Over 50 years had passed since her car went off the bridge. With a last name now, Annie found wedding notices and property records: Billie had remarried, twice, and today owned million-dollar mansions both in Alabama and on the Florida coast. She had apparently moved up in the world in her second-chance life. Annie pushed aside moral judgment and dialed.

Ringing. At least it wasn't disconnected.

Someone picked up. Annie held her breath.

"The Crenshaw residence. May I ask who's calling?" The voice was female, with a southern drawl. But it wasn't Billie.

"My name is Annie. I'd like to speak to Billie, please."

"Let me see if Mrs. Crenshaw is available."

Annie waited. Finally, amazingly, a familiar voice emerged through the digital ether. It was flatter and less musical than she remembered, but it was Billie.

"Hello?"

"Billie, this is Annie. Annie Maple. Do you remember me?"

A pause on the other end of the line. Then it went dead.

Annie stared at the reflective glass of her phone. She'd feared Billie might not remember her or might not want to talk about Hell. It hadn't occurred to her that Billie would just hang up.

She tried again, and this time the housekeeper blocked her.

"Mrs. Crenshaw is not interested in what you have to sell. Please don't call here again."

Annie threw herself onto the bed and throttled her pillow. *Oh Trua,* she thought, and for the first time shared his impulse to hurl rocks and smash things.

CHAPTER FOUR

Haisheng

It took Chen Haisheng some time to understand where he was. Hard ground under him, shadowy dimness all around. And no fire—*truly no fire*? His nerve endings still shrieked but in a diminished way like the afterburn of a hot pepper in your mouth. Then he noticed that the dimness contained walls and a ceiling. He heard a deep, restrained voice—somehow familiar—

"Praise Allah. You have returned."

Ishaq's voice! He was in the safe house!

The last thing he remembered was a chaotic battle in the middle of the devil city—swords slashing, winged bodies hurtling, fireballs exploding. Now everything was still. Somehow the safe house was intact and the Syrian merchant, who was old enough to be Haisheng's grandfather, had managed to haul his unconscious body here.

He pushed himself up to a seated position. The room swirled. His voice came out raspy.

"How long was I...gone?"

"Perhaps weeks. Perhaps months. You were hit by a ball of fire."

"What about the others?" Eiko, Trua, Annie, and Oudine had been close behind him in the chaos. "Where are they?"

"In the hands of Allah."

"Did they survive?"

"I do not know."

"You haven't looked for them?" Anger swamped Haisheng's relief. What in the world had Ishaq been doing all this time—hiding like a frightened mouse? Praying mindlessly in the back room as always? Ishaq was the first human Haisheng had encountered in Hell, and they'd created the safe house together, but Ishaq was useless—conservative, passive, superstitious.

"I was keeping watch over you," the Syrian said, which was hardly an answer.

* * * * *

Once he could stand without wobbling, Haisheng set out to look for the others. The devil city had always been grim, but now it was a wasteland. Rows of black stone buildings had collapsed into rubble. Alleys dropped off into craters. Crossing the central square meant clambering over chest-high chunks of rock, remnants of the palace that had once stood there.

And it was deserted. The square used to echo with the clamor of iron against stone and the barked commands of devil overseers. The streets used to channel columns of filmy gray wraiths—human souls plucked from the fire to be the devils' slaves, hauling stone from the mountains. Now the devils seemed to have fled. The wraiths were gone too, perhaps herded away by their devil masters, perhaps destroyed during the battle. Haisheng found no trace of the other humans.

Ishaq urged him to stop searching. "They are gone," he said. "Anything you find in this city will be evil. It's better to stay here, inside."

"Forever? In this room?"

"We can go to the mountains. With Allah's help we will find caves that are safe."

"So hide in a cave instead? Doing nothing?"

Haisheng kept searching, but the silence left a watery space inside him. He imagined footsteps. He imagined wispy grey figures slipping behind rubble. He yearned for the clamor of Shanghai—its crowded markets, shouting dockworkers, roaring industrial machinery. The clatter of rickshaws against the growl of automobiles. The shoulder-to-shoulder rallies of laborers and students chanting in a single voice for revolution. Here in this ruined city there were no noisy crowds, only ghosts that taunted him.

How do you lead a workers' revolution when all the workers are gone?

* * * * *

Haisheng hadn't always been a revolutionary. Once he'd been a dutiful schoolboy, working hard to justify the sacrifices his parents made to enroll him in a school run by English missionaries. At university, he fell in love with poetry and decided to become a poet like the great Du Fu. He wrote verse after stilted verse about wild geese and moonlit fields that were completely outside his own experience.

Then he met Xinghua, an intense young Marxist from a wealthy land-owning family in the countryside. Xinghua knew everything about China's politics; he moved with leonine smoothness from university lecture halls to Shanghai's straw-hut shantytowns. Haisheng had never encountered such a mixture of hot and cold—blazing passion for justice married to steel-cold political analysis. He threw away his poetry books and followed Xinghua into the Communist Party's youth organization.

When first shaken loose from Hell's sea of fire, Haisheng had been befuddled by this land of black deserts and winged demons. Why had he been sent here? What was he supposed to do? He remained off-balance until he saw the grey wraith-slaves stumbling under the batons of their devil masters. Oppression was something Haisheng understood. The wraiths were the proletariat of Hell: organize them and you could overthrow the devils. Hell could become a utopia—humans and wraiths united, building a new and just society.

Now the city's devastation left him as unmoored as when he first arrived. *If only Xinghua were here to make sense of it all.* Wandering the empty streets, he thought longingly back to their late-night meetings. They used to gather in the dim backroom of a printing company—him, Xinghua, Xinghua's beautiful girlfriend Liang-li, and a dozen other student cadre. The acrid smell of printer's ink filled the room. Others would talk but it was Xinghua who mattered. He led the discussions, dissecting and reassembling the latest political developments with a cigarette dangling casually from the side of his mouth. The orange glow of the tip always seemed like a secret code, the heat hidden inside Xing-hua's cool.

Alive, Haisheng used to picture taking the cigarette from his friend's lips...and then what? He didn't smoke. He had no purpose for a cigarette. It was a half-finished thought, now as then.

Haisheng let it slip away and turned the corner onto yet another ruined street.

CHAPTER FIVE

Annie

Billie's rebuff didn't cause Annie to question whether she'd truly been to Hell. Nothing could do that—not when she felt Mary's small kicks inside her. She made resolutions and wrote them in a notepad that she hid in her underwear drawer:

I won't question my sanity.
I will do whatever it takes to keep myself and Mary out of Hell.
I will go on with my life and appreciate every minute of it.

She started work as a coastal educator and loved it— leading school groups on outings to urban creeks, wetlands, and shoreline. Some of the kids had never been to the Pacific Ocean before, although they lived barely two miles away. All of them were ecstatic to be outdoors, hunting for salamanders or starfish.

"You're a natural," one of the other educators said as Annie helped a third-grader empty sand from his sneakers. She smiled and wiped her hands on the big shirt aimed at masking her growing bulge.

Two months had passed since Annie's return to life, and she was now six months pregnant. She felt those damped-bell kicks every day now; her breasts had grown from a C to a double D and were starting to leak colostrum. Naked in the shower, she ran hands over her belly and marveled at its sleek, firm roundness. She'd imagined pregnancy like flab—loose and jiggly—but this was nothing like that. This weight was purposeful, powerful.

Great gods, you're beautiful.

Trua had said that, staring at her shirtless in the wide desert. If only he were here now.

The advancing pregnancy made her loneliness worse. Annie was used to keeping secrets: in ten years, she'd never said a word to anyone about her miscarriage. But this was so much larger. She woke at 3 a.m. from nightmares about Hell and couldn't tell her parents why she was exhausted. She watched her students happily gathering seashells and couldn't help thinking how the non-Christians among them were destined for Hellfire.

Annie wondered if she might feel less alone moving back in with Melanie, her flatmate in San Francisco. Mel had held Annie's room open and clearly wanted her back. But Mel also kept pressing her on how she got pregnant and who the father was. Annie's claim that it was just a random hook-up didn't satisfy her.

"Look, we need to talk," Melanie said one weekend afternoon, visiting over chips and guacamole in Annie's mother's garden. "You're my best friend. I don't get why you're shutting me out about the baby. I feel like you don't trust me anymore."

27

There was pain and love in Mel's voice. And Annie needed so badly to connect with someone. She took the risk.

"This is a weird response, I know," she said. "But during the deck collapse I died. Just for a few minutes, I was dead."

Melanie nodded and reached for a chip.

"I went to Hell—real Hell. Not a dream. That's where I found Mary."

A bee buzzed around a bright red penstemon. Somewhere in the distance, a dog barked. The garden felt suspended in the golden warmth of Bay Area autumn.

"I know it's hard to accept," Annie continued. "I wouldn't have believed it myself. But I need your support. There's no one else I can tell."

The bee flitted away. A second dog joined the barking, then a third and a fourth. It was a Vienna Boys Choir of unhappy canines. Melanie put her uneaten chip down on the table and leaned forward. She spoke as carefully as if her words were crystal stemware.

"Annie. I know the doctors said you're over the concussion, but you need to see somebody. Like a therapist. Someone who specializes in PTSD or maybe brain injuries. At the very least you should get another CAT scan."

* * * * *

Annie decided to give up the apartment and stay with her parents, who didn't ask as many questions. She packed up her belongings—just a few boxes of books and clothes, shockingly little for someone who was almost 30—and drove them out of San Francisco across the Golden Gate Bridge. It felt like crossing an ocean between her life before and her life now.

No more trivia contests with Melanie at bars. No more getting stoned and baking fruit pies at midnight. Annie had no idea if beers and weed were sins meriting an eternity of Hellfire, but she couldn't take chances. She needed to become a practicing Christian.

Christianity as insurance policy. As get-out-of-jail-free card. As entry ticket to the most exclusive after-hours club.

She knew that wasn't the right attitude. Annie ordered a Bible from Amazon and resolved to read a little bit every night, starting with Matthew. Given how much she didn't know and how urgent the need was, it seemed best to skip all the Jewish parts and jump straight into Jesus.

She read in bed stealthily, feeling like an underground Christian in the early Roman Empire. Some of it was familiar, stories she had inhaled like air from the surrounding culture: birth in the manger, the three wise men, the golden rule. Other parts were perplexing: the endless stream of healings of lepers, paralytics, the blind and maimed and mute. In her previous life, she would have assumed that all those miracles were fiction. Now she accepted them as real but wondered about their meaning. Was it fair that people lucky enough to encounter Jesus were healed, when other sufferers a few miles away had no such opportunity? Did God even care about fairness or did God only value faith? Annie shared the outrage of the older son when his prodigal brother was feted and rewarded; she chafed at the parable where vineyard laborers who worked for an hour received the same wage as those who sweated for a whole day. She didn't know how to reconcile the Jesus of "turn the other cheek" with the Jesus who came with a sword to turn sons against fathers, daughters against mothers.

She needed help. Skimming the web, Annie found a church near her parents' house, a friendly-sounding place with a top-rated preschool and a rainbow flag over its front door. Of course she was nervous. Her only experiences inside a church were weddings of distant cousins, tourist sites in Europe, and a carnival as a child when she tossed ping pong balls into jars of water and won a goldfish that died four days later. She'd never actually spoken with a minister or priest.

"You must be Annie. I'm Pastor Pullman, but call me Mike. What can I do for you?"

A slender man with greying sideburns, he met her in a small office with walls displaying a photo of Marin Community Food Bank volunteers, a calligraphed quote from First Corinthians, and a wooden cross with brightly enameled images of Latin American *campesinos*. His desk held a bobblehead of Giants pitcher Tim Lincecum, which felt weirdly reassuring.

They chatted and he described the church's programs, its community service opportunities, and its preschool. It all sounded good—upbeat, progressive, not so different from the world Annie knew. She asked about baptism.

"For you, we'd set up a program of Bible study and reflection. For Mary, baptism would come when she's nine or older."

"Nine?"

Annie had assumed infants were baptized immediately. Wasn't that the reason for all the frilly white baby outfits in Mission Street clothing stores?

"Some denominations like the Catholics do infant baptism. But we believe baptism is only meaningful if someone can consciously choose it. So we wait until our young people are old enough to understand their choice."

"But...what if something happens to Mary before then?" Her voice quavered. So much could happen in nine years—car crashes, earthquakes, epidemics. Zombie attacks and alien invasions. Killer bees and killer sharks. Collapsing decks.

"She's in good hands, the best hands. God loves children. Your daughter doesn't need a baptism to be with Him."

The minister spoke with the generous confidence of an oncologist reporting that your margins were clear. But he had never witnessed that desolate acid marsh, its smell of sulfur and overripe peaches, the keening of a million unbaptized babies. He'd never met the rambunctious Hindu boy Dev, only eight or nine years old, condemned to eternal Hellfire for not being Christian.

"You're wrong. She does need baptism."

"What makes you think that?"

Annie hesitated. Ben and Melanie had dismissed her. But this was a minister, someone who not only believed in God but had built his life around God. Suddenly the enamel cross on the wall felt more reassuring than the Giants bobblehead.

"I was in Hell. I know it sounds crazy, but I was."

He listened carefully. When she finished, he paused. It was only the slightest pause, but she sensed him calibrating a diplomatic response.

"That sounds disturbing," he said. "No wonder you're worried about your daughter's soul."

"Yes, but do you believe me?"

"I believe you experienced a very dark and frightening vision of the afterlife. I believe those experiences are true for you."

"But do you think they really happened?"

"I can't speak to 'real' or 'not real' in the sense of whether this desk and chair are real. I *can* say that if you believe them, they're real for you. And that's the place we need to start from."

"What do you mean by 'start from?'"

"I'd like to re-introduce you to God. The God I know is very different from the one you describe. He's loving and merciful. He doesn't abandon any of his children. Once you get to know Him, you'll have a very different view of the afterlife."

Annie shook her head. "This isn't about my *view* of the afterlife. It's about the *reality* of the afterlife, which is horrible."

"Annie, none of us know what the reality of the afterlife is. That's part of the human condition. We know our life here on Earth, and the rest we have to take on faith. My faith tells me there is a compassionate, loving God who takes care of His children, both here on Earth and afterwards."

"So you don't believe me."

"I believe you experienced something disturbing—"

"It's not just disturbing, it's *real*. As real as this chair. As real as this desk!" Her voice rose. If a minister didn't believe her, who would? "It's horrible. It's like nothing you've ever imagined—"

"I know it's real for you—"

"Not just for me! For all of us! For everyone on Earth!"

"Annie, calm down. It's okay—"

"It's not okay! Everyone on Earth who isn't baptized is going to Hell! And I'm not making it up and I'm not crazy and I don't need to see a shrink!"

His sunny complacency infuriated her more than Ben's pity or Melanie's suggestions of PTSD. It was hopeless; no one would believe her, no one would understand. Annie blurted a goodbye and fled from the church, its bright rainbow flag snapping back and forth as the afternoon fog surged across Mount Tam onto the waiting valley.

CHAPTER SIX

Kezia

Kezia Parker stared across the vast expanse of Tupperware and wished she were at the cemetery.

The big round bowl held Shawna Cook's coleslaw: you could always tell from the bits of red and yellow pepper that popped like fireworks in the mayo. The rectangular casserole was Ivy Washington's mac and cheese. The blue tub was her friend Donna's potato salad, the same dish Donna had been making for church potlucks for decades. The potatoes were capped with a yellowish crust, and Kezia wondered if it came from sitting in plastic all morning or sitting in Donna's fridge since last year's picnic.

Uncharitable. But she really did not want to be here.

Kezia zipped up her jacket against Brooklyn's October chill. Today would have been her husband George's 60th birthday. Sixty! They should be growing old together, doting on grandchildren, taking long road trips where he could fish and she could pretend to be interested. They should be celebrating with a party in the backyard of their old brownstone—all those hypothetical grandchildren running around, their son Jeremiah manning the grill, a daughter-in-law bringing out the cake.

34

Instead, no party. No grandchildren. No daughter-in-law.

No Jeremiah.

Just George in the cemetery, where she'd gone every October tenth for the past 26 years.

Kezia glared at the potato salad and made plans for after the picnic. Stop at the Foodtown for flowers, then take a taxi. It would be dusk by the time she got to George's grave, but she didn't care: she'd go in the thick of night if it came down to that.

Wind slapped the nylon of her jacket. She reached for a fork and—checking to make sure Donna wasn't nearby—scraped the crust off the potatoes. She stripped plastic wrap from casseroles, plunged serving spoons into salads. She stacked paper napkins and weighted them with pebbles so they wouldn't blow away.

"Kezia!"

Pastor Leland emerged from a cluster of congregants and strode towards her—*Young Pastor*, as she still thought of him even after four years. Her real minister would always be Pastor Ron. He'd baptized her as a girl, married her and George, baptized Jeremiah. Of course he'd done George's homegoing too. But Pastor Ron had grown old, and the church needed new leadership, and things changed. Too many things changed, and never for the better. Pastor Leland had gotten rid of the Usher's March, added lights like a Broadway theatre, and now folks were showing up in jeans and t-shirts instead of good church clothes. Outside the church too: Kezia's latest TV remote was incomprehensible, and QuickBooks seemed to introduce new versions every six months, which put her accounting clients into constant turmoil, and the subway was worse than ever, and hurricanes from climate change—

George. Maybe it's good you didn't live to see this world.

"Kezia! Now this is a feast!" Young Pastor waved an arm over the picnic table as if he were multiplying loaves and fishes. "They told me that Brooklyn Missionary Baptist was the best-fed congregation in the city, but I didn't believe it until I came here. You do an amazing job with these potlucks."

This new pastor had no idea it was George's birthday. He had no idea who George was, or Jeremiah, or how many troubles she'd seen: first the death of George, a firefighter, when Jeremiah was an infant. Then raising their son alone. Then Jeremiah's problem. His running away. Spending money she didn't have on private investigators to try to find him, and selling the brownstone to pay those bills. And still, ten years along, Jeremiah never being found.

Through it all, Kezia's faith and her church had kept her going. Not that this baby-faced minister knew any of that.

"Mmm." Young Pastor reached for an open bag of potato chips and plunged one into onion dip. "Tasty. By the way, I need your counsel on the budget. How to amortize the new boiler. Can we talk sometime this week?"

"Of course. How's Tuesday or Wednesday?"

"Kezia Parker, you are a pillar of this blessed community. And oh—remember. There's a fellow coming by later I want you to meet."

The pastor stepped away. Kezia slammed a stack of paper cups onto the table. She opened a Coke bottle but it geysered, leaving little globes of brown sugar-water on the salads and casseroles. *Lord, give me patience.* She didn't want to meet any "fellows." She was a one-man woman, and she would reunite with her one man someday in Heaven. Her friends had learned long ago not to try matchmaking. That darn Young Pastor—

"Auntie Kee!"

LaQuan, her friend Donna's eight-year-old grandson, ran up to her.

"Where's Grandma?"

She glanced around: Donna was off under a tree, changing the diaper of one granddaughter while another tugged on her jacket.

"Busy. What do you need?"

LaQuan looked down. "The football. It went in the bushes." He glanced toward a thick bramble patch near the edge of the lake.

"Well, then, you just go in those bushes and get it."

"But there's homeless people in the bushes."

LaQuan suddenly sounded younger than eight. Kezia peered across the lawn and indeed saw a shopping cart piled with old clothes and who-knows-what next to the bushes. Might be junkies, crazy people, even child molesters.

"Okay, I'll get it. But don't lose it again, you hear me? Where exactly did it go?"

LaQuan pointed to a spot within the bramble and Kezia trudged across the field, glad she'd worn sneakers. The bushes were larger and deeper than they looked, stretching for about forty yards along the lake. *Here's hoping it didn't go in the darn lake.* She kept far away from the shopping cart and looked for an opening.

Finally she spotted an area where the branches weren't too thick and pushed her way through.

No football.

She made her way deeper into the thicket and found a small clearing. Still no football. The wind had ceased and the air was weirdly shimmery, like over hot blacktop on a summer day, although it wasn't hot out at all. She peered across into more branches: maybe in there. She took a step into the clearing, then another step.

Everything changed.

The thicket was gone. The lake was gone. The picnic area and the park and all of New York City were gone. Kezia stood on a barren plain, with black gravel under her feet and black jagged mountains marking the horizon.

Was it a stroke? Nuclear disaster? And where was the picnic—Donna, LaQuan, the others?

"Hello?" she called tentatively.

No answer. Nothing stirred on the gravel expanse.

"Pastor Leland! Donna! Anyone!"

The sky held no sun, just reddish grey haze. The air was hot and dry and reeked of rotten eggs. It was nothing like any place Kezia had ever been, and yet the hot air and barren desert were somehow familiar.

Then Jesus was led up by the Spirit into the wilderness to be tempted by the devil.

Dread pierced her.

"Jesus! I don't want to be in this place. I don't know what kind of place this is, Lord, but I don't want to be here—"

A hand touched her back. Kezia spun around and gasped.

It was the Devil himself. Rows of scars lined both his cheeks, black dirt caked his olive skin, and he wore filthy, ragged animal hides. He was evil made flesh.

"Get thee behind me, Satan!" she shouted, backing away.

"Quiet! Be quiet!" The Devil waved his hands in denial.

"Get away! I'm a child of the King—you have no power over me—"

"Shut up!"

The Devil rushed toward her, grabbed her, and clamped a hand over her mouth. Kezia flailed and kicked and bit, but he was too strong.

"Grandmother," he panted, struggling to hold her. "Listen to me—you can't pray here—"

She kicked and wriggled. *George, help me. Lord, help me.*

"You'll bring demons—"

Lies and trickery! Pretending he wasn't a demon himself! Kezia continued to flail but was getting tired. She would resist the Devil until Judgment Day, yes she would, but right now her arms were jelly and her heart was beating like it might burst and she couldn't kick any more...

"Grandmother—I'm trying to help you—"

His voice was hoarse and jagged. Kezia stopped kicking and his grip on her loosened. It was still hard to breathe with that hand over her mouth. The Devil eyed her warily.

"No praying."

She nodded as best she could and the Devil removed his filthy hands. She tried not to look at those frightening scars.

"Who are you?" he said.

"None of your business. I'm a child of God—a child of the King—"

"Did you just come from the fire?"

Fire? Kezia's mind lurched reflexively to thoughts of George. There had been so many fires. She always worried. Then there was the *one* and all her fears were realized.

"You leave me alone! I trust in the Lord Jesus—"

The Devil looked exasperated. He peered at her.

"Are you from Africa?"

What trickery now? Crazy thoughts raced through her head: the Devil was a racist, the Devil was a birther. She straightened her shoulders and assumed her most authoritative tone.

"I was born and raised in Brooklyn. My parents and grandparents were from Brooklyn. I'm a God-fearing Christian and an American—"

"America?" The Devil's eyes widened. "Do you know Annie Maple?"

"No. Now get your hands off of me. You're hurting my arm."

He let her go. The power dynamic between the two of them had inexplicably shifted. He seemed almost beseeching.

"Annie Maple is from America too," he said quietly. "From the city of San Francisco. Annie Maple. The daughter of Herb."

"No. I told you I don't know any Annie Maple, daughter of whoever. Now get out of here, Satan. But first take me back to Prospect Park."

Somehow, miraculously, she had conquered the Devil. *Thank you, Jesus.* Kezia straightened her windbreaker and prepared herself to return to the picnic. But the Devil didn't do anything. He just stood there looking sorrowful, like a dog someone left out in the rain.

"I can't take you back."

"What do you mean?"

"I'm trapped like you. There was a gateway, but it closed. I left there"—he paused as if trying to calculate, then gave up—"a long time ago. Walking. You're welcome to come with me. I'm going to a city where there are other humans. I hope. But there are also demons. It's dangerous."

"Wait. You want me to go to a city of demons?"

"Only if—"

She'd dropped her guard too soon. He might look sorrowful but he was scheming. "Get out of here!" Kezia shouted. "Satan, I bind you in the name of Jesus!" This time she knew better than to kick or bite; there was only one way to defeat the Devil. She clasped her hands together.

"God, I need you now. Father God, in the name of Jesus, show yourself strong—"

"Don't!" the Devil sputtered. He grabbed her shoulder.

"Jesus, give me strength—"

"Don't do this!"

"God, help me—"

The Devil jerked his hand away. "You're on your own then. I warned you." He turned from her with angry, stomping steps. She prayed louder and he broke into a run, heading toward the craggy black mountains.

"Hallelujah!" Kezia exclaimed. *Resist the Devil, and he will flee.* "Thank you, Jesus. Now show me how to get out of here—"

She halted. Foreboding flooded her as if something terrible were about to fall from above. She glanced up into the grey sky and saw nothing. She looked across the plain and saw only the tiny, receding figure of the Devil, still running.

Then it came—winging across the desert, heading straight towards her, a huge dark body with dark bat-like wings.

Kezia's prayers froze on her tongue. Her feet froze on the black dust. Whatever this was, it was a thousand times more powerful and dangerous than that pathetic demon she'd sent fleeing across the plain.

"Jesus, save me," Kezia managed to gasp, and the thing was upon her.

CHAPTER SEVEN

Trua

Trua flattened himself against the gravel, heart hammering the dirt.

Don't let it find me.

His breath sounded loud as a storm and his legs felt like stone weights. He hoped he was still invisible to the demons, as all the shaken-loose humans seemed to be. Across the plain, the woman shrieked. He heard the scuffing of gravel and the clap of wings. A gust of cold wind sliced his back.

They were gone.

He knew it without looking up. The air lost its chill; his legs started to feel like legs again, chafed by the gravel, twitchy. He still felt weighted down but now it was with despair. The woman was the first human he'd seen since Annie had vanished, and now she was gone.

He pushed himself up and headed back toward the spot where the woman had appeared out of nowhere. Was there an invisible door like the one that took Annie? He stepped cautiously. There was no rock archway here, but maybe you didn't need an archway. He reached for a handful of gravel and, piece by piece, tossed it in a semi-circle ahead of him. None of it vanished. He took a few steps forward and tossed another handful.

Nothing seemed amiss. No sense of magic or difference. The plain stretched black and desolate. Trua grabbed another handful of gravel, tossed more pieces—

Yes.

One piece seemed to disappear before hitting the ground. He threw a larger stone in that direction and this time clearly saw it vanish in mid-air. He stepped back, fixed his gaze on the spot, and detected a faint shimmer. His heart leapt: this could be a path home.

His sister Damla during shearing season, arms piled high with clouds of wool.

The laughter of his brothers around the fire pit on a cold night.

His horse's flanks pulsing against his thighs, the two of them flying faster than any other wingless creature on the plain.

A family.

Alive, Trua hadn't felt any particular urgency to marry. Here in Hell, marriage and children seemed more precious than gold, an embodiment of everything he'd lost. He'd have two, three, four sons and just as many daughters. He'd teach them to ride and hunt and herd. Small children would jump on him when he woke in the morning, and big children would ask him questions: What does the sea look like? Where does the sun go after it dips below the plain? He wouldn't scoff like his own father; he'd have answers for them, and if he couldn't find answers, he'd encourage them to go look for themselves.

That had been the hardest part of his decision to stay behind when Annie left—giving up the family he had not yet had. Would never have.

Trua tossed another rock and watched it vanish.

A wife. Children. Someday grandchildren. Just a few steps and he could be home, surrounded by human voices and faces, bustle of the tents, bleating of the flock. No longer alone.

But the same questions held him back. What if, instead of taking him home, the magic shimmer dropped him somewhere worse than Hell? Even if it took him home, what would happen after he died? Wouldn't he and his family and tribe—everyone he cared about—eventually end up back in the fire?

The thought of Damla and his brothers burning was unbearable. Maybe if they all became Christians they could avoid the fire. But there were no Christians on the Great Plain, and Huns wouldn't be welcome in a Roman garrison town. And truly, how could he bow down to a god who created something as evil as the fire?

He tossed another pebble. It vanished.

Maybe the gateway would take him to Annie. He imagined her back on Earth, holding her baby, feeding it from her beautiful breasts. In his mind she stood in front of his family's tents since, despite her descriptions, he had no idea what her home might look like. A life with Annie: waking entwined every morning, raising children together. He might risk eternity in the fire for that.

No. That was reckless thinking, the result of walking alone for too long. He'd made that pledge to her about eliminating the fire.

Trua turned away from the shimmer and resumed his trek—however long, however futile—to the city.

* * * * *

One set of black mountains gave way to another. Trua had crossed more ranges and basins in Hell than he could count, but this trek was his first alone. He breathed songs from his tribe to himself. He catalogued the name of every ancestor he could remember, every kinsman, every girl his age with whom he might some-day have had a family. The image of Annie and her baby at home bolstered him. Instead of all this dust, they would be standing on grass. Instead of barren rock, they'd have rivers and trees. Knowing all this allowed him to keep walking.

At least walking was better than the fire. But the si-lence and isolation broke him down in a different way. At one rest break he started arranging stones into a pile—a wall, a tower, a city, something to show he was here. He spent the equivalent of perhaps a day doing this. It was a magnificent little city of rocks. Then he remembered that staying unnoticed was his path to survival. Trua knocked the piles down and swept them flat and kept walking.

He grew careless, tripping on a hillside of loose rock and slicing his calf open. One of his cousins had gouged his calf playing stupid games with a spear when they were young. The leg had turned yellow with pus, then black; his cousin babbled about imaginary monsters, shrieked when Damla tried to apply poultices, and fi-nally, still babbling, died.

Trua wrapped his wound with one of Billie's rags. The bleeding stopped, but his calf swelled and reddened and hurt when he walked.

When he heard singing, he assumed he was hallucinating.

It was a man's voice, hearty even at a distance, billowing with enthusiasm. It wasn't a song he knew. It was coming from craggy mountains just ahead of him.

Trua halted. He tried to banish the imaginary voice but it wouldn't leave. Panic rose in him: he didn't want to die a raving, putrid death like his cousin.

Curse that wound. Curse my carelessness.

But what if the voice were real? He felt an urge to run towards the sound but resisted. Growing up, he'd heard stories about herders who left their flock to follow the song of a mysterious, invisible woman and were never seen again.

Still, another person...

He moved cautiously toward an opening in the cliffs that seemed to lead towards the voice. Foreboding rippled through him: the marauders had made their camp in a narrow passage like this.

The singing grew louder. He made out some words:

Noble horsemen of the table rou-ound, drink and see if the wine is good—

Horsemen and wine, that was reassuring! The voice echoed off the canyon walls. Whoever was singing had no concern about being heard by demons. But what if the voice *was* a demon? A drunken demon?

Trua picked his way up the canyon, favoring his wounded leg and looking around for possible assailants. He turned a corner.

A bald, obese man—human, not demon—sat on a large flat-topped rock waving a stone in the air and singing joyously.

Drink and see – yes yes yes

Drink and see – no no no

Drink and see if the wine is goo-oo-ood—

He saw Trua and stopped singing.

"Hello, my friend. Join me for a drink?"

Trua stared. There were no drinks here, only rocks.

"Come now. Have a seat. Have a drink." The man gestured at a flat rock across from him and proffered a stone. Dumbly, Trua took the stone and sat down.

"What's your choice? A hearty red Bordeaux or some Spanish sherry? Perhaps some good whiskey from those sons of whores in England?"

"Who are you?"

"Come now. Choose your poison. Wine, sherry, brandy? We've got absinthe too and barrels of beer from Alsace Lorraine. A magnificent cellar."

"Who are you?"

The man picked up a long, almost cylindrical stone and tipped it to touch the one Trua was holding. "All right, then, the Bordeaux. My personal favorite." He set the cylindrical stone back down and raised his own smaller stone. "To our health!" He held it to his lips, pretended to swallow, and resumed singing.

Noble horsemen of the table rou-ound, drink and see if the wine is good—

Drink and see – yes yes yes

Drink and see – no no no

The man's vast flesh seemed to drip down his torso like wax from a candle. He wasn't a Hun and he wasn't from any of the other horse tribes either. Alive, Trua

48

would have scorned him as a soft city dweller, even an enemy. Now, he saw a fellow human.

"What are you doing?"

"Tasting. Celebrating. Enjoying. For good drink is the essential companion to good food. I prepared only the best food for the Count of Harcourt. And the Count of Marsan. And the Duke of Lorraine. A *confit* for the counts. A *daube* for the duke. If only I'd been in the employ of a marquis I could have made *macarons* for the marquis. *Marrons* for the marquis."

"You were a cook?"

"Cook. Chef. Patissier. Master of cellars. Master of bottles. A lifelong chef and an occasional husband. In fact, it's better to be a chef than a husband. With a haunch of beef and bottle of wine, any of the scullery girls can be yours for the night. Then when the bottle is gone, so is the girl! To our health!"

He raised his stone and pretended to drink again. Trua placed his stone on the ground.

"You're making too much noise. The devils will find you."

"To the devil with the devils!" The chef started singing again, a different tune.

Drink a little cup, it's pleasant
Drink a little cup, it's nice
But there's no need to roll around under the table

"Be serious—"

"My young friend, I am serious. What's more serious than our daily bread? And if someone has the talent to make that daily bread into something magnificent, so much the better. Even our Lord God didn't settle for one loaf of bread and one fish, he multiplied them into a banquet. There was one banquet for the Count of

49

Harcourt—or was that the Count of Marsan?—where we made beef *a la daube* and roasted sheep tails and fried artichokes and braised partridges—now those were exquisite, such savory little birds, sauté them with butter and bacon and simmer them in a rich broth, garnish with truffles and mushrooms and sautéed asparagus—and of course there was strong brandy, always brandy, we rolled the barrel of brandy into the chicken house and lived off it for days. To our health!"

"Would you stop!" Trua's leg throbbed. If the man pretended to drink that stone one more time, he would shove it through his teeth. "Look. You're alone here. It's not safe. Come with me and we can find other humans. We'll keep each other company."

The man looked thoughtful. "Company is good," he said. He paused and then grinned. "That's why I never drink alone!" He launched back into song.

A little cup, la la la la

A little cup, it's nice

The man's voice cracked and wobbled but he barreled on with glee. His cheeks and nose were as red as Trua's brothers' after a long night of celebration. Might he truly be drunk from stones? This was, after all, a world where demons flew and the dead weren't really dead.

Trua picked up his stone and weighed it in his hand. It felt like a normal stone, but how wonderful to drink something, anything: mare's milk, wine, water. He'd be thrilled to drink muddy water from a ditch. Even more wonderful if it were something that would get him drunk...

Trua touched the stone to his lips. He tried an awkward swallow.

Nothing. Just the hard mass of a stone on his lips, and his own leather tongue in his mouth. He wanted to strangle this moron of a chef.

"You're crazy!" he shouted. "You're not drunk! You're dead, man, and you're in the Christians' Hell. Are you too stupid to realize that? What kind of idiot are you?"

The fat man stopped singing. He placed his stone carefully beside him, cocked his head, and narrowed his eyes at Trua. He now looked completely sober.

"I'm in Hell but I'm no idiot," he snarled. "The Lord Jesus Christ saw fit to take me out of the flames. But I know I'm going back there. Maybe now, maybe tomorrow, maybe the day after tomorrow. So I am going to be drunk, whether or not there is any water or wine in this godforsaken shithole. If you don't want to join me, get your piece-of-shit face out of here."

He started singing again, the same melody as when Trua had arrived, with the same gusto, but with different words.

The moral-e of this stoo-ry is to drink – before you die
Is to drink – yes yes yes
Is to drink – no no no
Is to drink, before you die-ie-ie

Trua lurched up, hurled his stone against the wall of the canyon, and stalked away.

Let the demons take that lunatic. With him making noise like that, they certainly will. He's no concern of mine.

Later, limping down the far side of the mountain range, he started to wonder if the fat man had been crazy or wise or both. The man's tune had lodged itself in his head and he couldn't stop hearing it:

Is to drink – yes yes yes

Is to drink – no no no
Is to drink, before you die-ie-ie
It played over and over, a plague and a reproach.
He kept walking.

CHAPTER EIGHT

Kezia

The demon hoisted Kezia under its arm like a sack of groceries. She'd never liked heights—used to hate thinking of George on those telescoping firetruck ladders—and now she was hundreds of feet in the air with nothing under her.

She held herself still to avoid being dropped, but the creature carried her effortlessly. It was larger than life, one and a half times the size of a human, its limbs and tunic a splotchy greenish-black like tarnished silverware. Its wings heaved the air as steadily and surely as a woman beating out a rug.

They flew over black mountains and black sandy basins. They skirted the shore of an orange lake of fire. As improbable as it all was, Kezia had no doubt this was Hell.

Please, God, don't let it drop me. Tell me what I need to learn so I can go home. Give me strength, God. Don't let me fall...

The trip seemed endless. Then, crossing yet another plain, the demon veered towards a lone black mountain—volcano-like, immense. They landed on a ledge with a black iron gate, where a dozen demons with swords and armor breastplates converged around her.

One poked her belly with a finger, then jerked back as if surprised.

"What is it?"

"A human out of the fire?"

"Why isn't it—"

The largest guard demon pushed the others back and gestured authoritatively towards the gate. "Take it to Zarphan. Now."

Inside, another guard demon escorted them with restrained, small flaps down a sloping corridor lit by sconces of lava. Dark passageways forked off like New York subway tunnels. They veered into a windowless antechamber and waited. Finally an iron door opened and revealed a new devil, smaller than Kezia's captor but with the same blotchy tarnish. His red eyes blinked rapidly as if bothered by allergies. A tall, angular female demon stood behind him.

"Your highness Zarphan." Bowing to the blinking demon, her captor sounded nervous. "I found this on the plain."

Zarphan—as the blinking demon was apparently called—frowned. "No 'highnesses.' No bowing either. We don't do that here. What do you know about it?"

Her captor started to bow again, then stopped himself. "Nothing. It was praying. With its hands together, that human way."

"Where did it come from?"

"I don't know."

"Why isn't it a wraith?"

"I don't know—"

Zarphan folded his arms and glared. "You didn't find out where it came from? You didn't check if it were a trap? You brought it here—"

"I'm not an 'it!'" Kezia couldn't stop herself. "I'm a person!"

Zarphan looked her in the face for the first time, blinking. He turned back to her captor. "You can go." The demon hesitated as if he'd been hoping for something more. "Go," Zarphan repeated. The angular female devil nodded, and the demon spun away and winged down the corridor.

Zarphan turned back to Kezia. "Where are you from?" His voice was flat. She already regretted her outburst.

"The sea of fire? Beelzebul's city? Pandaemonium?"

She remained silent.

"Or Heaven? Earth? You must have come from somewhere."

Lord, give me strength.

"Were you a slave? You just demonstrated you can talk, so there's no point in playing mute."

The female devil leaned close to Zarphan and said something that Kezia couldn't make out.

"Your...pockets." It took him a moment to find the word. "Show us what's in your pockets."

Kezia's hand slipped protectively over the front pocket of her jeans. Yes, there were things in her pockets, but nothing valuable: A dirty tissue. A cough lozenge. Thankfully, her keys and wallet were in her purse back under the picnic table. She wriggled her hand in and pulled out the tissue and lozenge.

"All your pockets."

Oh no. How could she have forgotten?

"Do it. Now."

Reluctantly she reached into her back pocket for her phone. All that time being hauled through the air: could she have called for help? She pressed the button but the phone didn't light up. Blank, dead. She handed it over with the tissue and the lozenge.

Strangely, Zarphan seemed equally fascinated by all three items. He started with the tissue, uncrumpling it, fingering it, tearing it to scrutinize the fibers. He went on to the lozenge, rolling it in his fingers and then unwrapping it. He handed the lozenge off to the female devil and honed in on the plastic wrapper, tugging it gently, folding and unfolding it, then holding it up to the lava sconce and peering through it. Finally he turned to the phone, rotating it in his hands, pushing buttons that did nothing. He looked up at her again, blinking.

"What's the function of this?"

She didn't answer. No way would she help the devil.

"From Earth? You brought it from Earth?"

Still silent.

"How did you bring it here? How did you get here?"

His wings slapped together. She felt his anger rising, a pot on the stove that could easily boil over. But his face remained blank except for that blinking and his tone remained flat.

"You can't win," he said. "You're human and we're immortal. We can keep you here forever. You're nothing. Dust made out of dust—piteous, feeble, stupid. We'll find out everything eventually, so you might as well tell us now."

"Let me question her," the female devil said. Kezia looked closely at her now and realized she was beautiful—high cheekbones, a slender neck, and sinewy legs. If not for that blotchy, tarnished skin she could have been a supermodel.

"No," Zarphan said. "Take her to a cell. She could be a spy."

The female devil handed the lozenge back to Zarphan, wrapped an arm around Kezia and, surprisingly strong, lifted her up. She flew a confusing route through several corridors to a barred and windowless chamber.

"We'll talk later," the devil whispered. "Don't despair. I'll be back."

Metal thudded against stone and an iron latch clanged into place. The cell was smaller than Jeremiah's old bedroom. A lava wall sconce that provided enough reddish light to make out shadowy forms was the only furnishing. You'd think a dungeon inside a mountain would be cold and dank, but this had the same dry warmth as the desert.

Please, Lord, take me back to the park.

The picnic seemed like a different lifetime. Why had she been so irritated with Young Pastor? Maybe this was God's way of telling her to stop fretting the small stuff. Were they all looking for her now, posting flyers with her photo in shop windows? What if her purse got left in the park and someone stole her credit cards? What about her clients' tax extensions that were due on the 15th?

What if God healed Jeremiah and she weren't there?

Lord, I've learned my lesson: Don't judge the little things. I'm ready to do Your will, if you'll just let me know what it is.

Now can I go home?

CHAPTER NINE

Haisheng

Haisheng was searching near the fire river on the edge of the city when something moved in a doorway. It was just a hint of movement, fast and slight—probably another figment of his imagination, but still worth checking. He padded cautiously up to the door and peered inside.

The interior held rough stone walls and a black dirt floor like the safe house. Part of the ceiling had caved in and created piles of rubble. A gray form huddled in the darkest corner, shifting like folds of fabric, barely visible in the shadows.

A wraith? Alone?

Until now he'd seen them only in large groups herded by devil overseers. He inched forward. *Be gentle. Don't scare it.* He squatted down to its level and spread his hands to show he was unarmed.

"My name is Haisheng. I'm human. I'm not going to hurt you."

It was as frightened as a sparrow, but sparrows could fly away. This creature just pulled further into itself. From a distance the wraiths seemed faceless but here, close, he made out crevice-like black eyes and a faint crease that passed for a mouth. Its limbs were hidden beneath gauzy grey folds and layers. It trembled like leaves in a late fall wind.

"You're not safe here." He gestured at the gaping roof. "I know a better place."

It shrank further into the corner.

"Here. Touch me. You can see I'm human. I want to help you."

He reached out a hand. The wraith stared with those eerie pupil-less eyes. It seemed incapable of decision or even movement.

"Please. Trust me."

The wraith pulled back even further.

"Can you hear me? Can you understand me? Say something!"

Damn it. The thing was beyond reach. Ishaq said they were soulless and evil, and maybe Ishaq was right. Or maybe he was just inept. He'd failed as a militia leader when he was alive; now he was dead but still failing. Damn his own ineptitude, damn this city, damn the wraith—

"Get up!" he shouted. "*Now!*" He grabbed a chunk of rubble and lifted it in anger. "Get up, damn you, or you'll end up back in the fire—"

He halted, mortified. Yelling at the creature would just scare it further. Xinghua would never lose control like this. A real revolutionary would never let his emotions take over—

The shape in the corner shifted. It rippled and elongated. Haisheng's breath caught.

An arm emerged from the billowing grey, then a leg. The wraith stood up.

* * * * *

Haisheng led the wraith back to the safe house, brandishing the chunk of rubble to keep it moving since it
seemed to respond only to threats. Once inside, it fled
to a corner and collapsed into a trembling grey heap.
Ishaq of course was furious. He called the wraith evil,
insisted it be sent away, and threatened to leave himself. But Haisheng knew it was an empty threat and
they reached a standoff. The wraith stayed and Ishaq
also stayed, grumbling.

Haisheng set about trying to communicate with the
wraith.

"What's your name?" he asked it. "We can make up
a name if you don't have one. How about Hope? Or
Dawn? Or Freedom?"

"How about Accursed," Ishaq muttered.

When the wraith didn't respond, he decided to call it
Hope and consider it a female. He asked Hope if she
could remember her life before she died and was condemned to the fire. At the word "fire," the wraith made
a keening wail and collapsed in on herself. He tried a
different tack and told her about his own childhood—
his father's small grocery store, his mother's dressmaking, his younger sisters. The wraith just cowered.

"You have perseverance, which is admirable," Ishaq
said grudgingly. "My son Daoud had none of that.
Whatever struck his fancy he would pursue...for a day
or two. Perhaps I made life too easy for him as a child."

"My father was fixated on an easy life!" Haisheng
couldn't keep the irritation out of his voice. "All he
wanted was for me to become a clerk and be

comfortable. He didn't care about the suffering around us. He didn't care if children were dying of starvation."

"He wanted to ensure that his own children would never starve."

"That's not it. You don't understand."

"I do understand. I've been both a son and a father, while you are still only a son. There are some kinds of understanding that Allah only brings with time."

Allah again! The old man always brought things back to his god. "If Allah's so wise and powerful, how'd you end up here?" Haisheng snapped. "And you're wrong about the wraiths too. Hope's listening, even if she doesn't show it. It's just taking time. She's going to respond, wait and see."

* * * * *

Finding that first wraith was like opening a spigot. Soon afterwards Haisheng came upon a dozen gray shadows quivering in a half-destroyed building. Then he found a second cluster, and a third, and a fourth. The fourth group was crouched behind a roofless wall—easily visible by any devils that might return to the city—so he herded them back to the safe house. Hope melted into the huddle, her grey folds indistinguishable from the mass of others.

Ishaq stood on the far side of the room, eyes narrow in fury.

"Chen Haisheng."

Haisheng stared. Ishaq had never called him by his full name before. He hadn't thought the Syrian even remembered it.

"This is a line too far. You will not bring a hoard of those things into this house. They will destroy you. They'll destroy both of us. I will not allow it."

"They need protection. And it's not your decision, anyway—"

"You're making a grave mistake. Even a sin."

"Who cares about sin! We're already in Hell! The real sin is how they're oppressed by the devils. If you don't want to be around them, just go. You said you'd leave when Hope came. Why'd you even stay?"

"I stayed for you. But you have chosen. If you insist on bringing those creatures here, I will leave."

Ishaq straightened his robe with as much dignity as one could muster with a garment that was a tattered, dusty memory of fabric. He stepped across the room and into the street. Haisheng didn't bother to follow. The old man would be back soon enough: where else did he have to go?

* * * * *

The wraiths weren't all as cowed as Hope: a few were willing to inch out of their huddle when coaxed. Haisheng moved from one wraith house to the next, reassuring them and trying to win their trust. If he moved too abruptly, they retreated into the indistinguishable jumble of grey. If he stayed away too long, they forgot who he was and he had to start all over. It was exhausting.

"Come. Take this," he said to a wraith that had reluctantly edged forward from its group. He proffered a piece of iron from a mangled door. "Just touch it. You don't need to take it. Just touch it."

The wraith quivered. Haisheng waited. If he could get them to wield batons, they could defend themselves. They could form an army. And this time—unlike the workers' militia unit, he'd been assigned to lead when alive—he would not let his charges be slaughtered in an ambush.

"Touch it," he repeated harshly. "Do it now. That's an order."

A filmy grey arm reached out and touched the metal.

Progress! The slight pressure on the shard was as exhilarating as the biggest rally he'd ever attended. If only there were someone he could tell: Xinghua would be best, but Trua or Eiko would be good too. Even Ishaq would be fine.

The old Syrian had never returned, though. Haisheng pictured him hidden in some distant cave, praying all the time, oblivious to the suffering of the wraiths.

Let him stay hidden. A brigade of wraith fighters was worth more than a dithering bourgeois merchant.

The iron shard quivered as the wraith jerked its arm away and melted back into the jumble of grey.

CHAPTER TEN

Annie

Annie's mother joined her for childbirth classes and then for the birth itself. Her father offered too, but Annie and her mother looked at each other and simultaneously burst out laughing. "Herb, you did it twice and that's plenty," her mother said, and he looked relieved.

In the delivery room, while the contractions were still mild, her mother read aloud from the police blotter in a nearby small-town newspaper:

FOREST KNOLLS: At 11:20 a.m. a farm stand owner reported receiving an anonymous letter criticizing his high prices.

MUIR BEACH: At 11:31 a.m. three men in suits were knocking on doors, asking if people spoke French.

FOREST KNOLLS: At 5:15 a.m. someone had been listening to a dog bark for an hour.

Annie laughed so hard she forgot the pain. She'd thought her mother was nuts to bring the newspaper, but it was a brilliant distraction. And then she looked at her mother—*really* looked, the way daughters rarely look at their mothers until they become mothers themselves. Her wavy brown hair had turned gray during one of those years when Annie wasn't paying attention. The smooth skin bracketing her eyes now showed wrinkles, thin and delicate as spun sugar. There was nothing pretentious about her—no dye for the grey hair, no Botox for the wrinkles. Her mother had paced and breathed and pushed in a delivery room like this twice before. Now here she was again. There was something mystically circular about it, a mother giving birth to a daughter and now helping that daughter give birth.

But oh. The contractions were getting worse. And worse.

She forgot about the police blotter. She forgot about mystical circularity. She gripped the sides of the bed and tried to do the deep breathing they'd taught in childbirth class. "Annie, you're doing great," she heard her mother say from a great distance but then she couldn't hear her mother at all. The pain wracked her and each contraction seemed longer and steeper than the one before and she gripped the bed harder and arched her back and the pain was terrible but it was NOT AS BAD AS THE FIRE! The realization arrived with the tinsel and glitter of presents on Christmas morning. This was not the fire! This pain was nowhere near the fire, it was timid and puny, just a scraped elbow in comparison with the fire, and the most wonderful thing about this pain was that it was finite, it would end, she could watch each contraction rising and falling on the monitor by the bed, and eventually there would be pushing and doctors and then at the very end she would have Mary. This was pain with a purpose! She felt elated. She felt empowered. She wanted to spring out of the bed and dance around the room, but the nurse and her mother were telling her to hold on, to ride the contractions, to breathe.

Afterwards, groggy, she held Mary close to her chest. Her mother kept a gentle hand on her arm and beamed. The chief of obstetrics stood at the foot of the bed smiling too. Annie's mother was vice president of community relations for the hospital; the entire staff knew her.

"Callie, your daughter is something," he said. "I've never seen anyone shrug off the pain like that. And the way she laughed when I asked if she wanted morphine." He shook his head. "She's something else."

"I laughed?" Annie asked. She didn't remember much except for the police blotter.

"What are you naming her?" said a nurse with a digital tablet. "Full name, for the birth certificate."

"Mary," her mother said. "Mary Maple."

"Wait," Annie said. "There's a middle name too."

She shifted the baby against her chest, a tight warm bundle. Mary must have had the longest gestation of any child in history—ten years in that acid marsh, then weeks as a little grey sphere, then months more in her womb. The birth certificate would leave the name of the father blank, but Annie imagined things differently. It seemed ungrateful, but she wished it were someone other than her mother touching her arm and beaming at the baby.

So soft and warm against her chest. Alive. Every baby was a miracle, but this one was a miracle squared, a miracle cubed, a miracle to the nth power.

"Her middle name is True," Annie said. "Mary True Maple."

Mary had ten nubby toes like tiny pink erasers and fists smaller than lychee nuts. Sometimes she closed a hand around one of Annie's fingers while nursing, and it was too small to encircle the entire finger.

She nursed easily with light, persistent tugs: this was a baby that had no doubts about living. Her breath came out in soft puffs that tickled Annie's neck. *Thank you, God,* she thought, nursing in the wooden rocking chair her mother had bought when they converted Ben's old bedroom into Mary's room. But even with the baby's determined suckling and steady breaths, she worried.

The flimsiness of the line between life and death was frighteningly apparent once you'd been to Hell. What if Mary stopped breathing? It might happen in the depths of night while Annie slept, or in bright daylight when she stepped away to shower. Or even here, now, on the breast. The two of them couldn't be physically closer, yet Mary's heart could fail, her lungs could fail, her tiny kidneys could fail.

And then, because she hadn't been baptized…back to the marsh.

Or worse, into the fire.

"Is everything all right? You seem anxious," her mother said one morning, packing her attaché case for work while Mary napped upstairs and Annie crammed down a bowl of cereal. "Are you worried about going back to Ocean Allies?"

Yes, she was anxious. Yes, it was about returning to work. But it wasn't what her mother imagined. Halfway through her twelve weeks of parental leave, Annie knew she should have lined up child care by now. She wanted—no, *needed*—to go back to work. Giving up her apartment, sleeping in her childhood bed, she already felt unmoored from adult life. Without work, she'd be lost in an eddy of endless nursing, diapering, rocking, and worries about Hell. Yet she couldn't stand the prospect of leaving Mary. Beyond the normal maternal fears—illness, accidents, neglectful day care workers— she worried about the devil. Like in an old folk tale, Satan might show up and snatch Mary to fulfill a bargain. Annie didn't remember signing any kind of pact in Hell. But maybe she'd done so without realizing it? Certainly the devil didn't need a thumbprint by a notary public.

"Stay home," her mother said firmly. "You know that's fine with us. And you're not paying rent, so you don't need the money."

"No, I'm going back. I want to go back."

Annie pushed clumps of granola around in her bowl. Her mother set her attaché case aside and sat down across the table. "She's terribly young, Annie."

"You've said that before."

"The first year is so important. Bonding. Trust. It influences how a person relates to the world."

"Mom, I get it. I've read the parenting books too."

"No, I don't think you get it. Mary needs the attention of a single loving adult at this stage. Someone holding her, talking to her—"

"Mom! Stop already!"

"Honey. Hear me out. This isn't easy to say."

Her mother paused. Annie looked up from her bowl. Callista Maple—captain of to-do lists, commander of PowerPoints—was rarely at a loss for words.

"I stayed home with Ben until he went to preschool. By the time you came along, we had a mortgage and I had my job at the hospital. I couldn't afford to stay home with you. I've always wondered if..."

Her voice trailed off.

"What?"

"Honey. I don't want this to come out wrong. Ben's gifts. His confidence. While you...you never really found yourself that same way. I've always wondered if..."

"If I turned out stupid because you didn't stay home with me?" The words spurted out, venomous.

"No! You know I don't think that. You're so far from stupid, darling. You're brilliant in your own way. You've just never seen yourself for who you are—"

"Stop it, Mom! I don't need to hear it. I'm over it, okay?"

It was the theme song that played through her whole childhood: Ben the brilliant, Annie the amiable. Sidekick, supporting actress, the underwhelming second act. She wanted to cover her ears like a five-year-old and slam doors like a teenager. She wanted to storm out of the house and stomp up Mount Tam—jump on a bus and move back to San Francisco—

"Annie!" Her mother's voice turned sharp. "This is about Mary. And you. I don't want you sitting here in 20 years having regrets. Feeling like you let your daughter down—"

A wail from above. Annie hurled herself out of the kitchen and up the stairs. Damn her mother. Damn Ben. Damn this whole family—why did she have to be part of it—

Nursing calmed her, as it always did. Crisp winter sunlight filtered through the window. Annie sank into the rhythm on her breast and let the outside world fade away, leaving only Mary's need and her fulfillment of that need. She'd never done anything perfectly in her life, and now she could do this. The tiny mouth tugged on her nipple, the tiny body rested on her arm.

What would it be like to feel that you'd failed your child?

That moment in Hell when she first heard Mary's voice, one strand among millions of bereft voices in the marsh: it had been a sledgehammer to her gut. She'd never meant to get pregnant, and of course she didn't mean to miscarry. Yet there was her baby—*hers*—floating alone for eternity in an acid marsh. She was responsible.

Was that how her mother felt about her?

Mary pulled back from the breast and Annie burped her against a shoulder, rocking from foot to foot. Afterwards she padded downstairs and found Callie in reading glasses, typing on her laptop.

"You didn't fail me," Annie said gently. "I'm okay. I really am."

Her mother smiled sadly over her glasses.

"I appreciate it," Annie continued. "Your advice. I really do. But it took me so long to find a job I love. I don't want to quit—"

"Annie." Her mother sounded exasperated now. "I'm not suggesting you quit your job. I'll stay home with Mary. You won't have to send her to day care. It will all work out."

Annie stared. Her mother had worked at the hospital for as long as Annie could remember. The story of how she started as a secretary and rose to vice president was family lore. She served on state panels and national commissions; she *lived* for her work. Only her garden came close as a passion.

"I'd been thinking of retiring in a couple of years anyway. This just moves it up. Mary will get as much attention as she needs and I'll get a chance to spend time with her." Her mother smiled, and the thin lines around her eyes unfolded and bloomed into smooth skin. "I missed so much of both your and Ben's childhoods, working all the time. This is a chance for me to make up a little of that."

"Mom."

Annie couldn't say anything more, words clumped in her throat. *Callista Maple, devil slayer.* Her mother was the only person in the world who could defend Mary as fiercely as Annie would.

Baby Mary, patron saint of do-overs and second chances.

"Is that all right with you?" her mother asked.

"Oh Mom." Annie reached across the table and gripped her mother's hand, thin and starting to dapple with brown but still, forever, so strong. "Of course it is."

CHAPTER ELEVEN

Kezia

The female devil returned to Kezia's cell.

She flew in, shut the iron door behind her, and lowered herself onto the floor. She squatted, stood, then settled awkwardly into a cross-legged position.

"You've been sitting like this?" Her tone was accusing, as if it were Kezia's choice. "We need to get you a seat."

Kezia didn't respond.

"What's your name?"

Kezia stayed silent.

"All humans have names, don't they? You said that you're a person, not an 'it.' I'd like to be able to call you by your name."

Names had power—power to define, to command. One of the first things Kezia had learned as a young, Black, female accountant was to introduce herself to clients as Mrs. Parker, not Kezia. She refused to give these demons any more power over her than they already had.

"My name's Ardat," the female devil continued. "Ardat means wind. A certain kind of wind that exists in Heaven. I don't know how to describe it in human terms."

"Heaven?" Kezia's astonishment swept away her caution. "You've been to Heaven?"

"A long time ago. We all used to be angels."

Of course. She should have remembered that.

"I was a harpist." Ardat held up her hands. Her fingers were long and graceful, yet also solid. The nails glistened like dark mother of pearl.

"In the celestial orchestra. You have orchestras on Earth, don't you? I was the best harpist. There were thousands of us, but no one else came close to my tone. They all sounded hollow next to me, empty. But they never let me solo. Can you imagine? The best harpist in Heaven. I was prepared to play the most magnificent solo in the cosmos, all for the glory of God, but they never gave me a chance."

Ardat looked at Kezia, waiting for a response.

"I suppose you think that's arrogant. But it's not arrogance. It's the truth."

Her tarnished wings fluttered restlessly in the silence.

"Do you even have music on Earth? Do you have the slightest idea what I'm talking about?"

Kezia remained silent. Ardat clapped her wings and rose.

"All right, don't answer. I'll be back. And I'll see about getting you a seat."

* * * * *

Some time later, the door to her cell opened and a guard devil hauled in a large flat-topped rock, just the right size for a bench. Kezia paced. She sat. She curled up, tried unsuccessfully to sleep, and then stood and paced some more.

She prayed silently. She talked to George.

Her husband had died rescuing a family of six from a blazing apartment when Jeremiah was a baby. For almost three decades Kezia had pictured him in Heaven, in some divine bandstand where it was always a springtime Sunday afternoon and he was always 34 years old, playing the blues harmonica he loved so much, maybe *Mystery Train* or *Mannish Boy*, only now with angels on guitar and bass instead of the guys from down the street. It was a silly image, she knew: Heaven must be grand beyond imagining, not cluttered with mundane, mortal objects like harmonicas and band-stands. But still the image gave her comfort.

She'd talked with George whenever life felt too heavy to carry—the abyss right after his death, the chronic money worries and home repair crises, the stumbling efforts to be both a mother and a father. The failed efforts to be both a mother and a father.

Most times, he didn't answer her with words. But she always felt his watchful love.

George, are there orchestras in Heaven? I just met a fallen angel who played the harp. Tell me what to do, George. Tell me what I need to do to get home.

Ardat returned with more questions and Kezia stonewalled again. Ardat talked more about Heaven. When Kezia didn't respond, she left. This happened multiple times. Kezia found herself looking forward to the rush of cold that signaled Ardat's arrival.

No. Don't let them get to you. They're not your friends.

But she couldn't stop herself from listening, and gradually she learned more. Zarphan had been a harp maker in Heaven, a master craftsman who'd built Ardat's harp and many others. He had ideas about how to make harp-building more efficient: break the process into separate steps and assign some angels to shaping the golden frame, others to weaving the strings, still others to assembling the parts. But his ideas were spurned, just like Ardat's offer to solo. He was told God wanted it this way, each angel artisan making one complete harp at a time. But why? No one gave him any good reasons. It was inefficient, slow, cumbersome. It infuriated him. So he joined Satan's rebellion.

"So...Zarphan isn't Satan?" Kezia's curiosity got the better of her. She had assumed that the authoritative blinking demon was the leader of all the devils.

Ardat smiled. "No. Not yet."

"Then who's Satan? Where is he?"

Ardat's seamless face folded into a sneer. "Mouldering in his palace. He's done nothing for us. It's time for a new Satan, one who will get things done."

Time stretched and thinned between Ardat's visits, like dough rolled out to the point of tearing. Kezia turned the past few months over in her mind, trying to figure out if she'd been sent here as punishment. She'd been judgmental about the pastor. She'd coveted Donna's intact family and flourishing grandchildren. She'd told a client his tax return would be done within a week when she knew full well it would take longer, and when the supermarket cashier undercharged her for groceries she saw the error at once but kept the $4 anyway.

Plenty of shortcomings. Even added together, though, they didn't seem enough to justify Hell. And on top of that there were all these demonic rivalries and rebellions. This place was more like Washington D.C. than the afterlife. Did the Book of Revelation talk about devil civil wars? There was the Harlot of Babylon and the Beast and all sorts of disasters, but she couldn't remember anything about devils fighting each other.

"You don't look well," Ardat said on one of her visits. "You're worried. Maybe about someone back on Earth?"

Jeremiah, of course. She'd never stopped worrying about him, even after all these years. But she refused to mention his name to these fiends.

"You need a break from this cell. Why don't I take you on a tour."

The devil ferried Kezia up corridors and around corners until they reached the mountain's gate. Kezia squinted: even without a sun, the reddish-grey sky dazzled after so much time underground.

They crossed plains and mountains. Kezia was so delighted by the light and the broad horizons and the wind on her face that she forgot her fear of heights. Then she glimpsed something orange in the distance. Ardat touched down on a rocky promontory.

"Look," she said.

An ocean of fire stretched to the horizon. Tendrils of orange flame whipped up from the surface and danced in the air. Hot wind slapped Kezia's face.

"No. Look *down*. Listen."

Kezia shifted her gaze down and her breath caught. What she'd thought were churning waves was in fact a sea of people on fire. Heads bobbing and arms flailing. And screams: now that she was listening, the voices battered her skull. They shrieked, begged, wailed. It was like standing next to the siren on George's fire engine. She was obliterated. She couldn't piece together a thought.

"I can't—" she sputtered. "They—"

Ardat nodded and lifted her up. They hovered higher, where the voices were fainter.

"Do you know people in there?"

"No. Nobody."

She didn't know anybody in there, right? Not George, of course. And her parents were certainly in Heaven. Her grandparents too. And George's parents—they'd always been so kind to her, never a minute of that wife-versus-mother-in-law thing—Heaven. Her family were all good church people. Her friends were church people, all of them. Except...

Jesus! No! Help me!

Her only child, Jeremiah.

* * * * *

Jeremiah had been such a good baby. Sure, there was crying and tantrums and potty problems but that was all normal. Kezia barely remembered any of that. What she remembered were his fat cheeks, like a squirrel storing nuts. How as a toddler in the bathtub he used to sing "wait in the water," having misheard the lyrics in church. His talent for drawing. His smacky, wet kisses when she was feeling down.

When did the troubles start? Maybe elementary school, when he didn't want to play sports like the other boys and refused to fight back against schoolyard teasing. George would have taught him to shoot hoops and defend himself, but George wasn't there. Kezia did her best—judo lessons, basketball camp at the Y—but those efforts invariably ended in tears. She became a sterner version of herself, scolding Jeremiah to act like a man and turning her back when he cried. After multiple conferrals with Pastor Ron, she moved him to Catholic school, hoping that uniforms and structure and male teachers would help.

They didn't. Jeremiah went to and from school as if punching a time clock. Sometimes he came home with unexplained bruises. Things finally looked up in tenth grade when a new boy arrived and became a friend: they shared music playlists, shot wacky videos, rode the subway into Manhattan to see classic black-and-white movies. They even took up running together—not to the point of joining the track team, just laps through Prospect Park, but at least it was something athletic.

Then Kezia came home early from work to find them naked and kissing.

Blood rushed to her head. Her heart felt like it might explode. "Out! Get out of here!" she shouted at the other boy, who scurried away like an insect in the light. There had been incidents before—an M2M chat room on the computer, a smutty magazine in a dresser drawer—but this was worse than anything Kezia could have imagined.

"Put your clothes on and stay there," she ordered Jeremiah, then ducked into her bedroom and rummaged through the dresser for George's old leather belt. Kezia had vowed never to use such a thing but clearly she'd been too soft. The devil had snuck his evil ways into her very own home.

She returned with the belt in one hand and her cell phone in the other. Her heart was still pounding. Jeremiah, in sweatpants now, stared at the floor. Kezia couldn't see his face. "First I'm calling that boy's parents," she said. "And then we'll deal with the devil in you."

"Don't!" Jeremiah jerked his head up in alarm. "His stepfather'll do stuff to him. Really bad stuff. Mama, don't call them. Please."

"What?"

"Punish me instead. Whip me. Do anything to me. Just don't tell them." He turned around and bared his buttocks. He was crying now. "Please, mama. We'll stop. I promise. Just don't tell them. Please."

Kezia considered. She put away the belt.

She called the other boy's parents.

Lying in bed that night, the house ragged with estranged silence, Kezia accepted that Jeremiah's problem was beyond her ability to handle. She talked to Pastor Ron and he agreed. So she pulled Jeremiah out of school and sent him to stay with George's sister's family in Alabama—solid church people with good morals, a strong father figure, fresh country air and an equally fresh start.

He ran off.

They couldn't find him.

It was incomprehensible to Kezia. How could a child simply disappear? George's family was clueless and the Alabama police were dismissive. The police in New York wrote a report and buried it in a file. She spent tens of thousands of dollars for a private detective who came up with nothing. Bitterness was a sin, but Kezia knew that a white child would never be allowed to disappear like this: there would be milk carton photos, *60 Minutes* episodes, all-point alerts. They'd never let a white child simply vanish.

Of course she prayed. Ten years of conversations asking God to drive out Jeremiah's devils and bring him home. But all those prayers were about healing the living Jeremiah. She'd pictured him struggling with his urges, mastering them, and finally walking through her front door—safe, healthy, cured. With a girlfriend in tow, maybe a wife, maybe even babies.

Through ten years, Kezia had never allowed herself to accept the possibility that her son might be dead.

* * * * *

"Nobody?" Ardat echoed smoothly. "Let's take a closer look."

She wanted to see and she didn't want to see. The devil flew down, skimming slowly over the flames, and Kezia gaped with panic. *There, that bobbing close-cropped head? Or over there, those long skinny arms reaching up in despair?* It seemed like every tenth figure could be Jeremiah. Heat and screams joined forces to assault her. Yet another head emerged, and another set of beseeching arms, and then they too were gone. Might be her son, might not. She hadn't seen him in so long.

Jesus! Help him!

Here was another head, burning and shrieking. Big ears and wide cheeks like his, but he slipped beneath the waves before she could be sure. More heads. More arms. Kezia couldn't wait for certainty. She'd just have to assume one of them was Jeremiah and do whatever it took to save him.

"Ardat!" she gasped. Her skin was tight with the heat. Sweat rolled down her body and dripped into the flames. "Can you get him out? My son—"

The devil swooped up and away from the fire. She seemed unfazed by the heat. They headed back to the promontory and kept going.

"Wait—we can't leave him—" Kezia called, but the wind swallowed her voice and the demon kept flying until they reached the mountain complex.

* * * * *

Back in the cell, Kezia sank onto the stone bench.

Ardat squatted and looked at her directly. "We can rescue your son. But first you need to help us. Tell us how you got here. And about life on Earth."

"What...for?" The words came out as a croak.

"It's hard for us to visit Earth. A few of us used to go, but not very often. Answer our questions and we'll rescue your son from the fire. Then we'll return both of you to Earth. I promise you."

She was making a pact with a devil. Kezia couldn't believe it, but she nodded. This was for Jeremiah, not for herself. Did that make it less of a sin?

Oh George. Don't hate me for this.

She swallowed with a dry throat and slumped on the bench.

CHAPTER TWELVE

Ardat

"I've cracked her," Ardat said. "Finally."

Zarphan looked up. He was squatting on the floor of his private chamber, perusing a complicated diagram in the dust with a stubby-winged female devil who was one of his top engineers. It looked like a set of interlocking wheels, but that was about all Ardat could tell. She respected Zarphan's strategy of designing more advanced weapons—that was why she'd thrown her lot in with him—but she had little interest in it herself.

"It took you long enough."

Ingrate. He could never have won over the human himself, and he knew it.

"Do you want to see her now?"

"Yes." Zarphan stood up, blinking. "Bring her and tell Turael to join us."

Ardat set off through the mountain's maze in search of Turael, Zarphan's chief of intelligence. "Good for you," he said pleasantly when told that Kezia would finally talk, although she knew he didn't mean a word of it. Turael only valued information that he controlled; anything else was a threat. "I'll be there as soon as I'm done. In a quarter of a flow," he added, referring to a system of timekeeping Zarphan had designed based on the speed at which lava flowed through a stone culvert at the center of the mountain.

A quarter flow. She wouldn't need to fetch Kezia right away. Ardat opted for a quick detour—out the gate and up the face of the mountain to a narrow notch between two jutting sections of rock. There were no guard devils here, and the wind often blew through in a way that made a reedy, high whistle.

She flapped against the wind, settled lightly down on the rock beside the notch, and listened.

There it was, that whistle.

If you closed your eyes, you could pretend it was a flute. Not the crystal highlights of a flute solo, but the breathy parts where the music faded into air. Ardat swayed back and forth ever so slightly, imagining strings welling up behind it. The sound used to fill Heaven's concert halls: flutes, violins, amber depths of the cello. Her fingers twitched. She was thinking of one particular composition right now, where harp melodies had darted in and out among the flutes and the two sets of instruments seemed like the front and back of a single hand. She'd practiced those sections over and over, long after the other harpists stopped in satisfaction. She played them backward and forward and inside out, with time slowing down as her fingers sought each isolated note, and when she was done the melodies came back together and flowed like one of Heaven's fountains. Even after all these eons, she could hear them in her head, feel them in her fingers.

The wind whistled.

Her fingers twitched.

The wind sang.

A quarter of a flow.

83

Ardat silenced the music in her head. She needed to arrive in Zarphan's chamber before the others did. She pushed herself up from the rocky ground, leather wings working to gain purchase in the wind, and leapt on an eddy to coast back down to the mountain's gate.

* * * * *

They sat on a stone bench facing Zarphan and Turael. Ardat had arranged the seating so she would be by Kezia's side, both literally and figuratively: the human would be more forthcoming that way. And if Kezia provided useful information, Ardat would get the credit. It would move her up a notch in the hierarchy, closer to taking Turael's position.

"Start at the beginning," Zarphan said. "How did you get here?"

Kezia told them about walking through a bush and finding herself in the desert. Turael snorted in disbelief, and Zarphan pressed her on it repeatedly, but she insisted that the unlikely story was true.

"So what is this device?"

Zarphan proffered the small rectangular object they'd confiscated when the human first arrived. His metalsmiths had examined it but couldn't make it do anything.

"A cell phone," Kezia said.

"A telephone of some sort," Zarphan mused. "But without wires?"

"You know about phones but you don't know about cell service?"

The human was feisty. She'd recovered from her emotional breakdown at the sea of fire and seemed almost eager to spar with Zarphan. Lucifer and Beelzebul wouldn't have tolerated such audacity, but Zarphan's drive for knowledge outweighed his ego. It was another of the reasons that Ardat had followed him.

"We visit Earth rarely," he was saying. "That's why your information can be so helpful."

"I'm not telling you anything if you're going to use it against Earth."

"I have no intention of doing anything to Earth. It's probably hard for you to believe, but I couldn't care less what happens to Earth."

"If I answer your questions, you have to save my son. Like she promised." She nodded in Ardat's direction. Ardat remained expressionless. She'd told Zarphan her game and trusted he would play along.

"Yes. Of course. Now let's get going. Tell me how you use this device, and how it transmits voices without wires. And then we need to know more about this gateway from Earth—what it looked like, where it was, how you found it."

* * * * *

Ardat returned to Zarphan's chamber after ferrying Kezia back to her cell. As she'd expected, Turael was dismissing Kezia's account.

"Walking through a bush! A human child could come up with a better story. She could at least have made up a magic carpet, or a giant cloud, or a flying chariot."

Ardat fluttered smoothly onto the stone bench. "She's telling the truth."

"Oh, suddenly you're the great reader of human minds? As if they have much mind to read anyway. The

85

question is who sent her, Lucifer or Beelzebul. And how she plans to communicate with them. We need to know if she has co-conspirators here in the mountain."

"She wasn't sent by anybody. She really did end up here by accident."

Turael smiled in a way that was both taunt and threat. "A co-conspirator *would* say that she came here by accident."

"Stop it, both of you." Zarphan stood and paced, his wings tight in concentration. "I'm inclined to believe her story. Not least because if it's true, we have a remarkable opportunity.

"A direct route between Earth and Hell that doesn't involve flying through Chaos. And allows the transport of human objects like that telephone of hers. Think about it. Humans may be mortal and small-minded, Turael, but they're prodigies when it comes to technology. They've harnessed electricity and steam and they mass-produce steel. They convert oil into plastics. They use radio waves to communicate across oceans. We've heard about all this, but we've never been able to replicate it.

"This kind of gateway would let us access human inventions. Their devices, their processes. Their blueprints and manuals. We could build an industrial infrastructure. No more shoddy handwork by slaves. And what it means for weapons..."

Ardat's pulse quickened. She'd guessed that Kezia would prove valuable but hadn't pushed the scenario this far. Now she pictured vast factories of human-style weapons—guns, cannons, whatever powerful devices humans used for war. Lucifer and Beelzebul would beg for mercy. Zarphan would absorb their followers, create one united devil army, and turn that industrial arsenal on Heaven.

At the root of it all would be her success in cultivating Kezia.

She forced her face to stay blank. Why settle for chief of intelligence? She deserved to be Zarphan's chief deputy—and when they took Heaven, his prime archangel.

"Agreed," Turael was saying. Even he could see the possibilities. "But I'm still keeping an eye on her in case this is a trick."

"Of course you should. That's your job," Zarphan said brusquely. "But I want a massive search to locate this portal. There may be other portals too. Put every available devil on this. Look for disruptions, displaced humans, artifacts from Earth, anything that might signal an opening.

"And Ardat, keep her talking. Let her rest and then bring her back for another session. We need to find out everything she knows about human technology and weaponry."

"My pleasure," Ardat said. She pulled back her shoulders and stretched her wings. She hadn't felt such satisfaction in eons. She was successful, important, and on her way to a position commanding thousands of other devils.

It was nowhere near playing the harp, but it was better than anything else she'd experienced in Hell.

CHAPTER THIRTEEN

Trua

Trua hauled himself up the last few vertical feet onto the ridge—yet another barren ridge like all the others—and saw the city.

Hallucination? Real? He didn't care. With a reckless whoop, he ran down the slope, rocks clattering before him. He raced past the broken city walls, leaped over rubble in the streets, and reached the safe house. It was still standing, its iron door fully closed, not hanging askew or crumpled in the street like so many others.

That was good. Encouraging. He cracked open the door, eager for a human face—ideally Haisheng or Eiko, but even Ishaq. Even Oudine.

Grey shifting forms filled the room where the humans had been.

Trua slammed the door and hurled himself behind a pile of rubble in the street. Had the humans all died in the devil battle? Had they survived, only to be killed by wraiths? He'd always found the creatures unsettling but now they seemed monstrous. And what was he to do now? He'd come all this way—but no one was here—he might be the only shaken-loose soul left in all of Hell—

Footsteps whispered down the street. He tensed, peered around the broken stones, and could have shouted with relief.

"Trua!" Haisheng exclaimed, breaking into a grin.

His impulse was to grab Haisheng in a giant hug. But physical affection made you violently ill in Hell; he'd learned that the hard way with Annie and didn't intend to test it again. So he just grinned back.

"Come in, come in!" Haisheng called.

"But there are—"

"Yes, yes, it's fine. It's more than fine. I'm making great progress with them. You'll see. Just come in!"

* * * * *

They exchanged stories. Trua told Haisheng everything, even details he'd previously withheld like his and An- nie's visit to Satan's palace. He couldn't stop glancing at the mass of wraiths huddled across the room, min- gling like smoke, flowing into each other like troubled water. It was hard to imagine they had once been hu- man.

"Hope! Sun! Dawn!" Haisheng called. "Come here. This is a friend. He won't hurt you."

The mass swelled and ebbed. Finally one wraith sep- arated itself. It was shorter than Haisheng, even shorter than Trua.

"Sun. This is Trua. Say hello to him."

The creature shrunk back.

"I've told you, you're allowed to speak here. Part of being free is speaking your mind. Tell Trua your name. That's an order."

"I am...Sun."

Trua had imagined the wraith's voice would whistle like night wind across grass, but it creaked like a slowly breaking tree limb.

"Wonderful, Sun! Now tell Trua you're pleased to meet him. When you start coordinating with other comrades, that's what you'll say."

The wraith was silent.

"Tell him."

"I'm...pleased to meet you."

Trua's cheeks flushed: the creature was obviously not pleased at all.

"Thank you, Sun. Trua's going to help with your training. So you can defend yourselves. Can you say his name? Trua."

The wraith didn't answer.

"Say it." Haisheng's voice sharpened.

The filmy grey folds quivered and leaned away, back towards the huddle.

"Say it," Haisheng repeated. He raised an arm ever so slightly.

"Trua," the wraith rasped and collapsed back into the shifting mass.

* * * * *

They scavenged the city for debris that could be turned into weapons—iron bars that could become clubs, sharp stones that could be daggers. When they weren't scavenging or visiting the wraith houses, they sat in empty buildings and talked. Haisheng floated strategies for building an army and mused about freeing more wraiths from the mines in the mountains. Trua was skeptical but didn't argue; he was grateful to be

90

around another human, and in fact had no better ideas for how to transform Hell.

Occasionally Haisheng turned silent and distant—maybe remembering his life on Earth, or maybe thinking about Ishaq. Trua was shocked that he'd let the Syrian leave, but Haisheng didn't voice any regrets.

"Do you love Annie?" Haisheng asked at one point.

Trua was taken back. The question came from nowhere and was something his sister Damla would have asked.

"Yes. I suppose. Why?"

Haisheng scuffed his foot back and forth in the dust. "How do you know if you love someone? Not like a brother or sister, but the other way. The difference between 'like' and 'love.'"

He'd never thought about this. Trua pictured the girls he'd known at home, all marriageable, some with smiles bright as the sun, a few who'd been more than satisfactory lovers. Then he thought of Annie. The feeling was different but he couldn't describe how. He shook his head.

"You think about them more than other people?" Haisheng said.

He nodded.

"You think about them...physically?" Now Haisheng reddened. "Not *that*, I don't mean that. Or yes, that. But also other parts of their body. Their hands, maybe? Their mouth?"

Trua nodded.

"Even if they're not suitable? If it's not possible?"

"Especially if." Now Trua grinned. "So tell me, who was the girl?"

"No girl. No one. Well, maybe someone. But in any case, that's all past. It doesn't matter. Let's go check on the wraiths."

* * * * *

They worked on getting the wraiths to wield clubs, which was harder than it seemed. Yelling at them helped. Threats helped. After numerous efforts, a few particularly brave wraiths were willing to hold a bar. Swinging it would be a whole new challenge, but Trua had some ideas about how to work on that.

Then Haisheng told him he was leaving.

They slouched on the broken wall of a warehouse along the fire river, tearing and knotting Billie's rags to make sheaths for daggers. Now Trua jerked upright.

"Leaving for where?"

"I'm going to find Satan."

"Why?"

"You remember how he called on the devils to join him in a mass suicide?"

Of course Trua remembered. They'd all been trapped in the central square during the battle between devil factions. Suddenly Satan had appeared overhead—not the depressed, world-weary Satan he and Annie had encountered at the palace, but a gleaming, incandescent one. He'd called on the insurgent devils to stop squabbling and join him in a mass suicide—a slap in the face to God.

This is the ultimate denial, Satan had declaimed. *If we destroy ourselves, there is no longer anyone to punish human sinners. We destroy Hell. We destroy God's plan.*

"Think about it," Haisheng said. "Hell without devils could become a paradise—no overseers, no slavery. I'll go to Satan and offer him an alliance. Our army of wraiths will help him defeat the other devil factions. In exchange, he'll free all the souls in the fire. And then when he carries out his suicide, we'll have this world to ourselves—wraiths and humans together."

"That's crazy."

Trua had so many objections that he hardly knew where to begin. Satan would never listen to a human. The wraiths would never become fighters. Devils would never free humans from the fire, and the Jesus Christ god who created this place would never let any of this happen.

"How would you even find Satan?" he said, gesturing at the desolate city around them.

"I'll go to his palace, of course."

"You have no idea where it is."

"But you do." Haisheng grinned. "You've been there. You can give me directions. And while I'm gone, you'll continue training the wraiths. Really, Trua, you've made this all possible. Thank you. I could never do this if you hadn't come back."

"No," Trua said. "It's crazy. Everything about it is crazy."

But Haisheng insisted. He talked up his plan when they were training the wraiths, and he talked it up when they were surveilling the city, and he kept talking about it when they were resting by the fire river.

"Look, if you don't give me directions, I'll go anyway," he said finally, when Trua demurred for maybe the twentieth time. "I can walk for years if I need to. I can walk for decades."

"You don't understand. It's hard out there. It's terrible."

"I don't care. I'm going."

The endless black expanse, the isolation, the exhaustion: Trua had barely survived the desert, and he'd grown up on the Great Plain. There was no way a city dweller like Haisheng could make it without help. Trua didn't remember details of the route from Pandaemonium—the girl devil Baphomet had flown him and Annie from there to the city—but at least he knew the general direction.

"I'm going to find Satan, whether you like it or not," Haisheng repeated.

He told Haisheng what he could remember, and Haisheng set off into the desert, and Trua was left alone to oversee the wraiths.

CHAPTER FOURTEEN

Annie

Annie's thirtieth birthday passed quietly. Ben, busy with some conference at Harvard, sent her a text with a mathematical formula that apparently resulted in the number 30. Her co-workers bought a chocolate cake that they ate with messy hands along Ocean Beach. Her parents made a toast over dinner with a bottle of chardonnay.

"You're a survivor. A fighter," her mother said. "We're so glad you're here with us. We're so glad you brought Mary into our lives."

Her mother had made the shift from high-paid executive to unpaid nanny without a hitch. Now she spent her days in jeans and Crocs, her attaché case replaced by a diaper bag. One day Annie returned home to find a box on the kitchen table with three fluffy yellow chicks.

"We'll build a coop for them in the backyard," her mother said. "When Mary's bigger, she can gather the eggs. You know, I always wanted chickens, ever since I was a little girl."

Her mother? Chickens? Her garden consisted of meticulously planned compositions of color. Annie never would have imagined her mother with messy, scratchy chickens. Yet here they were, pecking on the kitchen table.

Everything was going smoothly—work, home, Mary. But the very smoothness made Annie uncomfortable.

The grass will be something to feed goats, nothing more. You'll forget about it.

She was leading two lives—one inside her head that included Hell and the other outside, where Hell had never happened. In Hell, she had feared forgetting her life on Earth. Now she feared forgetting Hell.

It would be so easy just to live—to limit her worries to work and diapers and whether Mary was putting on the right amount of weight. But she needed to get Mary baptized. She needed to figure out what God wanted from her.

She missed Melanie, with whom she'd barely spoken since moving out.

She missed Trua.

When Annie lived in one of her lives, she felt like she was denying the other. So she really didn't live anywhere at all, except those minutes in the rocking chair with Mary tugging on her breast, hungry and determined.

* * * * *

April was the start of wildflower season on Mount Tam. Annie normally spent all her non-working time with Mary, but the allure of the mountain was too strong. One Saturday morning she left Mary with her parents and took a shuttle bus to the Steep Ravine trailhead.

The creek was full and loud. Annie climbed down off the trail and sat by the water on a mossy, fallen

96

redwood. She had conjured this trail so many times in Hell that it was no longer simply a beautiful spot in nature; the air itself was thick with a history of longing and hope and despair. She had thought of this place when the endless black desert overwhelmed her. She had imagined bringing Trua here. She had imagined bringing Mary here. There were times she was sure she'd never see it again, and other times when the need to return helped her persevere beyond anything she thought was possible.

She imagined Trua with her now. They could hold hands and watch the water. Such a simple kind of physical contact that you took for granted: she'd held hands with Ben as a toddler crossing streets, with best friends in elementary school, with her students now when they pulled her to see a crab or a washed-up jellyfish. But she'd never held Trua's hand.

She had no idea what he was doing now or even if he was still alive. She composed imaginary messages to him: *Please be well. Be safe.*

They wouldn't reach him. None of her prayers ever sparked a response from God; why should a silent message to a dead human do any better?

The stream burbled over its rocks. Above her, leaves rustled where some small bird hopped in the foliage. Annie ran her hand along the spongy trunk, pressed her fingers into the moss.

Soft. Moist. Alive.

She breathed deeply, took in the spiced scent of bay laurel and manzanita, and tried to set aside her anxieties—work, Mary, Trua, Hell. Just breathe and be grateful. Reading alone late at night, Annie had moved on from the gospels to Psalms, and finally found one that spoke to her own experience. She summoned it now.

Bless the Lord, O my soul, and forget not all His benefits...who redeems your life from the pit.

* * * * *

Annie hopped off the bus from Steep Ravine and trotted up the street to her parents' house, refreshed and eager to reclaim Mary. But neither of her parents' cars was in the driveway. She glanced at her cell and saw a half-dozen attempted calls and a bunch of texts from her father.

Call ASAP

Call me

Where are you?

Call urgent

Meet me at the hospital

Oh God. Something terrible had happened to Mary while she was blithely traipsing through the woods, out of cell range. Medical emergency? Car accident with both Mary and her mother?

Satan?

In her family, there was never a need to specify which hospital. When her father's phone went straight to voicemail, Annie called a ride-share and rushed to the hospital where her mother had worked, the same hospital where she'd given birth.

She shouldn't have taken the hike. She should have taken Mary with her. She should have called the pediatrician about that runny nose. She should never have gone back to work...

The recriminations were crazy, overwrought, but that didn't stop them. Like shuffling a deck of cards, her mind flipped over and over through possibilities: Choking. SIDS. A fall—could her mother have dropped Mary? Fever? Car crash? Deviltry?

At the hospital, her father was pacing in the lobby. He wore old jeans and a T-shirt, his usual weekend garb. She sprinted over.

"What happ—"

"Thank God you're here."

He nodded towards a couch, and there was Mary's plastic car seat. Mary lay cozily tucked under her blanket, asleep. She was all right, then? Cured of whatever it was? But her father didn't sound relieved or happy.

"She's in surgery. They're doing something called a burr hole."

The realization struck her like a bat to the head.

"Mom?"

Her father's face was grey. Sweat formed dark continents on his white shirt.

"A cerebral aneurysm that burst. In the supermarket with the baby. She had a headache and went straight to the manager's office. Such a smart woman. She blacked out before the ambulance got there."

"Will she be okay?"

"They don't know. The surgery's supposed to release some of the pressure on her brain. They got to it fast, which is a good sign."

The two of them paced, and sat, and paced. Eventually a surgeon emerged and reported: the procedure had gone smoothly but the bleeding was immense and continuing.

They moved her mother out of surgery and into a dark, quiet room. Her father texted updates to Ben. They took places beside the bed with Mary's car seat at their feet. Her mother lay still, eyes closed, an IV in her neck and a respirator tube in her mouth and little cardiac stickies under the pale blue gown on her chest. The last time Annie had been here, she'd been the one in the bed and her mother had been reading the police blotter. This was completely different. This was completely wrong.

Mary woke and nursed. They waited. Her father talked with Ben. The gaps between the jagged bumps on the electronic monitor grew longer. The doctors counseled patience but did not sound encouraging. Various hospital administrators came and went, taking her father out of the room for quiet conversations. Her mother looked newly small and frail, almost a stranger, a grey-haired old woman hooked up to machines.

No one said this, but at a certain point Annie realized they were no longer waiting for recovery but for death. "Please, God, no," she prayed silently. "She's only 63. Please give her more time." And then Annie's own heart seemed to stop for a moment: her mother had never been baptized.

"Can I have some time with her?" she asked, and her father nodded. She left Mary with him in the hall and huddled as close to her mother as possible.

"Mom, I hope you can hear me," she said in a whisper. "You need to give yourself up to Jesus. Tell him with your heart, even if you can't speak. Tell him that you accept him as your Lord. You have to do this, Mom. You *have to*. Just do it, Mom, I mean it. Please."

The woman on the bed lay still. The room was silent except for the monitors' steady electronic beeping.

"Mom. You've got to. *Please.* Just accept Jesus. Ask him to forgive your sins. If you don't—"

Her whisper gulped into a sob. It wasn't working. Her mother couldn't hear her. She spoke louder.

"Mom. Accept Jesus. Please. Tell him you believe—"

Time was passing. Her mother could die any minute. The stakes were as large as eternity. Annie didn't know what to do.

"Please, Mom—"

She was sobbing now, loudly, and gripping her mother's hand.

"Mom, you've got to. Please. Accept Jesus. Ask him to take your sins away. Mom, please. Tell Jesus you repent for your sins—"

It was at this point that her father opened the door. Annie was sobbing too loudly and huddled too closely to see his face cloud over and his sagging shoulders straighten in fierce, protective anger as he took in her words.

"What the Hell are you doing to your mother?" he shouted.

CHAPTER FIFTEEN

Annie

The memorial service was unbearable. It took place in the chapel of the funeral home where her mother was cremated, with thick burgundy carpet and dark wood paneling that felt like a strip-mall attempt at a Central European castle.

Annie's father made all the decisions. The hospital would hold a public memorial later; this would be a small service for family and close friends. It was perhaps overstating things even to call it a "service." There were no prayers, no hymns, not a single mention of God. Ben emceed the program and read a poem about starlight and death. The hospital CEO talked about Callie Maple's friendship and wisdom and how her personal advice had helped save his marriage. Annie's father started telling the story of how they met in college, but he became too choked up to finish.

Annie had made a feeble push for some Christian content. Perhaps a minister? Perhaps they could at least sing "Amazing Grace?" But her father shut that down, and Ben shot her a look that said she'd lost her mind.

It was Mary who got her through the service. Annie sat in the first row, cradling her daughter, and every time her mind veered into thoughts of the fire she cuddled Mary tighter. There were so many words: *Callie Maple was generous, Callie Maple was compassionate, Callie Maple was that rare path-breaking executive who always made time to mentor younger women...*Those words were meaningless air. They made her want to scream at everyone in the room. The words were true and might make everyone feel better, but they had nothing to do with the fate of Callie Maple's soul. All that compassion and generosity and mentoring were probably sizzling this very minute, burning and re-burning, charred black yet still on fire...

No. Hold it together. Hold Mary.

When the program was done, she stood in a line with her father and Ben and numbly accepted people's condolences. What a strange phrase, "accepting condolences:" did anyone ever refuse a condolence, like refusing a package? She greeted her parents' close friends, their neighbors, what seemed like the entire board of directors of the hospital. And then, at the very end of the line, there was Melanie.

"Oh Annie, I'm so sorry," Mel said, her brown eyes glistening. They fell into each other's arms, crying and hiccupping together, and Annie finally let her grief overflow. How, she wondered when the sobs subsided, had she let Melanie slip away? Here she was reading Bible passages about loving your neighbor, yet she'd allowed Heaven and Hell to drive her apart from her closest friend in the living world.

*****

That night, after their father had gone to bed, Annie and Ben sat at the kitchen table. The house felt wrong and empty, like a favorite sweater that had stretched in the wash and was now too big. Annie was limp with exhaustion. She asked Ben about the poem he'd read, and he handed her a neatly folded printout.

There are stars so far away that we only see their light long after the star itself is gone.

There are people whose memory lights the world after they themselves have departed from it.

These are the lights that, even in the darkest of nights, illuminate our path.

"It's by a Jewish woman who died fighting the Nazis. A little sentimental but it seemed fitting for Mom. Plus I had to decide between something uplifting and something more stark. If it were just me, I'd have gone with Auden, 'Funeral Blues.' Or St. Vincent Millay, 'I do not approve, and I am not resigned.' Or even *The Tempest*. But there was dad to consider."

"Of course," echoed Annie. She had no idea what he was talking about.

"It's a good thing you're living here now," he continued. "He's going to have a rough time. Not just cleaning out her stuff, but living alone. It'll be good for him to have you and the baby around."

"I'm thinking about quitting my job."

The idea had swum up through the murk of her shock. She suddenly had no child care. If she stayed home, she could take care of Mary and also be available to her father.

"Probably a good idea," Ben said. "But look. There's something we need to talk about."

"Now?" Annie could barely put a sentence together. Her arms ached from holding Mary through the service and the reception. The past three days seemed to have gone on forever.

"Yeah, now. My flight home is tomorrow."

"Okay."

"Dad told me what you were saying to Mom in the hospital. And then you wanted to have a church funeral for her—"

"Not church. Just a little spiritual stuff."

"Were you trying to torment her in her last hours?"

"Of course not!"

"Because that's what it sounded like. Telling a dying person they're a sinner and need to repent? That they're going to go to Hell?"

"I didn't say anything about Hell."

"Well, you sure implied it. You know, the idea of talking to someone in a coma is to encourage them. To tell them you love them and you want them to recover. Or didn't that ever occur to you?"

"I wasn't—"

"This is left over from your accident, isn't it. The idea that you went to Heaven and saw God, or the devil, or whatever. Annie, you've got to get over this. You're going to need to be extra strong for Dad. If you're hearing voices, there are medications. They're better than they used to be. They can calibrate them to your exact condition. But you've got to see a doctor. A psychiatrist."

"I'm not crazy. I don't need a shrink."

"Just give it a try. Things will look completely different once you're being treated."

"No!" Annie's jaw was tight with fury. This was precisely why she'd never mentioned Hell again to him. There was no winning an argument with Ben, even if it was about your own brain.

"So tell me, what is it that you believe exactly? That you went to Heaven and met God?"

"I went to Hell." She spat out the words grudgingly, the bare minimum.

"Okay, Hell then. I suppose it was underground and there was fire and devils?"

"More or less." Annie didn't want to have this conversation, especially now. But Ben could pull answers out of her like a dentist pulling teeth.

"Annie, the Earth is 8,000 miles in diameter. It's got a solid crust. Then the mantle, which is semi-molten rock. The outer core, which is liquid, and the inner core, which is solid iron and under pressure that's more than 3 million times the pressure of our atmosphere. Where exactly do you propose to locate this kingdom of devils?"

"I don't know."

"And this Hell is purportedly the destination for all sinners, from everywhere on Earth."

"Yes."

"So tell me exactly which Hell you were in? Did you visit all the 28 different versions of Hell that people go to in Hinduism? There's the hungry-bird Hell where vultures pluck out the eyes of hosts who mistreat their house guests. There's the cooking-pot Hell where people who eat animals are cooked alive in boiling oil. There's the sexual Hell where men who make their

wives swallow their jism are thrown into a river of se-
men and forced to drink it—"

"Ben, stop it!"

"Maybe you visited one of the Hells that people go to
in Buddhism, like the one that's so cold your skin blis-
ters and bursts. Or did you see the Zaqqam tree with
heads of demons as its fruits? That's in Jahannam,
which is Muslim Hell. Did you see the giantess Hel,
daughter of Loki, who rules over the Norse under-
world—"

"Ben!"

"How about Cerberus, the three-headed dog at the
gates of Greek Hell. Did you run into him? Or Anguta,
the Inuit god who carries the dead down to the under-
world to sleep with him for a year—"

"Goddamn it, Ben! Stop already!"

"You didn't see all these Hells? It sounds like you
didn't get your money's worth."

"You're not being fair."

"What's unfair? I'm just pointing out that there are
a lot more versions of Hell than you even know. Those
other versions have a lot of believers too. If you add up
the world's Hindus and Muslims, they easily outnum-
ber Christians. So why should your Christian version
be correct? Annie, you're a product of your society. You
were raised in a predominantly Christian culture and
so the parts of your mind that are misfiring draw on
imagery from that culture. If you were a Viking, you'd
be having delusions about visiting Valhalla. It's all just
mythology. Sure, there's a universal impulse to create
stories about life after death, but they're just stories.
They're not real."

"Ben, enough already."

"Even Judeo-Christian doctrine is all over the map. The Pentateuch doesn't talk about Hell, just a shadowy place called She'ol. And modern Christian theologians—"

"Ben! It was our mother's funeral today, okay? Can we just go to bed?"

Annie was shivering from exhaustion. Everything Ben said was correct, but it didn't matter. Hell was real. She'd been there. And she wasn't going to start doubting her own memories. *That* would be a path into mental illness.

She dragged herself up the stairs. Ben closed himself in the bathroom to wash up. They'd temporarily moved Mary's crib into Annie's room so he could sleep in his old bedroom. Annie straightened Mary's blanket and dropped into her own bed like a stone.

She was on the verge of sleep when a thought hurled her upright.

A nearly full moon glinted through the cherry tree outside her window. The house was silent. Annie threw on her bathrobe, fumbled into unlaced sneakers, and padded back downstairs.

In the backyard, free of branches and clouds, the moon became a spotlight. Her mother's blue delphiniums, golden coreopsis, and red penstemon were all bleached to the same shade of spectral white. Annie reached for a thigh-high bag stacked against the house with other garden supplies. For three days, no one had remembered to feed her mother's chicks.

She opened the door of the new wooden structure in the corner of the yard and heard faint peeping. She tossed a handful of feed and saw small shapes converging in the black. Sound, movement, hunger. At least something of her mother's was still alive.

She latched the door carefully, wary of neighborhood raccoons and cats, and picked her way back across the ghost-pale yard to bed.

CHAPTER SIXTEEN

Kezia

Kezia found the interrogation sessions puzzling. Zarphan didn't ask who the president was or which countries were at war with each other. He didn't ask about religion or if people still believed in the Lord. Maybe, she thought, the devil could figure out religion and politics on his own without her help.

He mostly asked about technology—how oil was refined into fuel and turned into plastics, or the various techniques for generating electricity. She gave answers worthy of a second grader, and for the first time in her life saw her technical ignorance as a blessing: *If I don't know, I can't tell them.*

Zarphan asked about weapons. This was an area where she was particularly grateful to be ignorant. He asked how many bullets a machine gun could fire without reloading, and she didn't have an answer. He asked about explosives and she mentioned hand grenades, land mines, and IEDs.

"What are IEDs?"

"Some kind of explosive they used in Iraq."

"But what are they?"

"I'm an accountant, not a soldier."

"What's the most powerful weapon humans have?" a heavyset devil named Turael asked. He attended most of the interrogation sessions, while Ardat attended all of them.

"Atom bombs."

"What are those?"

Kezia hesitated. These devils knew about radio but not TV, land lines but not cell phones, dynamite but not nuclear weapons. Their last contact with Earth must have been before World War II. She didn't want to be the person who introduced the devil to atomic bombs.

"What are they?" Zarphan repeated.

She couldn't refuse to answer, but she could say the bare minimum.

"Bombs that can destroy a whole city. Houses, people, everything."

Zarphan leaned in. "How do they make them?"

"I don't know."

"What are the materials?"

"I don't know. Atoms. I told you, I'm not a scientist!"

Turael snorted in contempt. Ardat looked pained.

"That's all for now," Zarphan said, and motioned for Ardat to return Kezia to her cell.

* * * * *

The interrogations became fewer and farther apart. Time dissolved in the dimness of Kezia's cell and she floated on waves of memory. Jeremiah's infancy was more vivid than her last client meeting; her own childhood felt closer than that fateful picnic in Prospect Park. Sometimes she panicked and feared spending

111

eternity in the cell. Then she'd grip onto God and remind herself that He never abandons any of His children. But through it all, she couldn't escape the image of those souls in the orange fire—their shrieks, their flailing. Did anyone's sin warrant that? Did Jeremiah's sin warrant that?

She asked George. She pictured him across from her on a stone bench, legs spread wide in his weekend sweatpants, leaning forward like when she used to vent about problems at work.

"George, is Jeremiah up there with you? Maybe that wasn't him in the fire. Maybe he was saved and he's with you."

George shook his head. "Can't say."

"You're not allowed to tell me? Or you don't know?"

He shook his head again.

"I always thought he was alive. I prayed on it so much. Even when the detective gave up, I believed he was alive."

"Kee, you don't know. Maybe he is."

"But ten years! You see these kids on the street. They get trafficked, boys as well as girls. They get addicted to drugs. They get AIDS. He was such a sweet child, he wasn't street smart. He couldn't protect himself—not from bullies, not from Satan. He was no match for the devil. George, I'm so afraid that's him in the fire."

"Kee, you got to have faith."

"I do! I do! I know the Lord kept an eye on him. I know the Lord reached out to him with an outstretched hand. I have faith in the Lord. I just don't..."

She silenced herself before the words could leave her mouth.

She had faith in God but not in her own child.

"What, Kee? Were you saying something?"

"No. Nothing. Nothing at all."

They fought! For the first time in 26 years, they argued.

George leaned against the opposite wall, now in the yellow flannel shirt and jeans he wore for fishing and hiking. "Kezia," he said. "Maybe you should have let Jeremiah be."

"What?" She'd been slouching on the stone seat but jerked upright.

"You know what I'm saying."

"Let him be? Let him be *what*? Are you saying I should have just stood aside and let him end up here?"

"Maybe it's not such a sin."

Impossible. She stared at her husband. Up there in Heaven, and he'd forgotten Scripture? *God made man and woman. Sodom and Gomorroh. An abomination.* Pastor Ron had preached on it numerous times: *no place in the Kingdom of God for idolators or adulterers or homosexuals.*

George shook his head. "You ever talk to Pastor Leland about it?"

No. Of course not. Why would she? But now that she thought about it, the sermons about homosexuality had stopped after he took over. Young Pastor didn't say outright that it wasn't a sin. But he talked about every person being made in God's image. And last year he'd recruited a flamboyant gay man with a beautiful tenor voice for the choir. That was another thing she hadn't liked about him.

"The world's changed, Kee. It's always changing."

"Yes, and for the worse. But wait—you never even met Pastor Leland. How can you talk to me about

Pastor Leland? How can you talk about the world changing when you've been gone for 26 years?"

"Our son was a fine boy, Kee. You should have let him be himself."

"He was *not* fine if he was violating God's laws! And what do you know about him anyway? You weren't there. You were gone—you left us alone—"

"Kezia Parker! Watch your mouth! How dare you say I wasn't there? After all those years at your side?"

"If you were there, why'd you let this happen to him? Why'd you let the devil sneak in?"

"Kezia Parker. You tell me who's the one who made a deal with the devil."

"That wasn't for me! It was for Jeremiah! Everything was for Jeremiah—"

A chill breeze pricked her arms. Kezia glanced towards the door and saw a guard devil flap past.

When she looked back, George was gone and the cell stood dark and empty.

CHAPTER SEVENTEEN

Ardat

Ardat heard the excited voices from far down the stone corridor. She flapped into the council room and saw a tight knot of wings—Zarphan, Turael, and a half dozen other senior devils peering at something in their midst. She pushed her way into the circle and found two human artifacts on the stone meeting table.

The objects had long, narrow cylinders, hand grips, and a bulging attachment. She'd never seen a gun but instantly understood this was what they were.

"You found a gateway?" she blurted. "And brought those through?"

Turael shot her a tight-lipped smile of satisfaction. "My agents did."

"No one told me?"

Zarphan tried to sound conciliatory. "We couldn't be sure until they came back. It could have been a false opening, or they could have been trapped there."

"She was *my* source! I should be in the loop!" Her voice rose; they would think she was emotional and weak. She forced herself to calm down. "Never mind," she murmured. "It's a great breakthrough. It's exactly what we need."

* * * * *

Thousands of devils fanned out across Hell. Ardat heard them grumbling about getting trapped on Earth if a gateway closed. But soon they found more portals—only a handful, but sufficient to accommodate whole teams of devils. Zarphan listed items to bring back: industrial blueprints, tools, batteries, plastics, lubricants, computers, and of course weapons. He also asked for some surprisingly primitive items—paper and pencils.

"You can't build an industrial infrastructure from diagrams in the dust," he said, blinking.

He set aside several chambers in the mountain for human artifacts and Ardat fetched Kezia to explain how they worked. The human was annoyingly useless: she had no idea what went on inside the black box called a router, and when asked how batteries were manufactured could only answer "in factories."

Even more annoying, few of the transported objects seemed to work in Hell. Anything electronic was dead as rock, even when plugged in to a battery. Zarphan had the most luck with things that required no electricity—solvents, hand tools, a manual typewriter, handguns.

At one point, Ardat found him peering into a device through a cylinder just wide enough for his eye.

"It's called a microscope." He looked up, beaming. "Unbelievable. You can see the building blocks of Creation. It gives you the eye of God."

"Do you want to talk to Kezia?"

He shook his head and returned to the device. "We've gotten what we needed from her."

116

Ardat stood idly, eyeing the piles of documents, devices, and inscrutable metal objects that filled the room. So much human *stuff*, all of it beyond her comprehension.

"Do you think…" she murmured.

Zarphan looked up. "What?"

"Could they bring back a harp?"

He eyed her appraisingly. Finally his mouth stretched into an ironic grimace.

"Like I used to make," he said. "The human ones wouldn't be anywhere near as good."

* * * * *

Turael became unbearable, lording it around the palace as if he himself were the next Satan. Zarphan barely paid attention to Ardat anymore. She gave it one last try.

"Think hard," she barked at Kezia in the cell. "You must know things about human technology—how computers work, how plastics are made, anything like that. You've got to know *something!*"

"I told you, I'm not a scientist," Kezia said for what must have been the hundredth time. Did humans always repeat themselves like this? Didn't they realize how tedious they were?

"You used all these things. You must know how they work."

"I don't!"

Worthless human. Ardat couldn't understand how God had taken pleasure in their creation. She reached for the cell door to leave.

"Wait—"

Ardat pivoted. Maybe not worthless after all?

"Can we go see my son—it's been so long—"

"Certainly not!"

She slammed the door and flapped away. Kezia had been the one thing of value she'd possessed since leaving Heaven, and now her value was gone. Ardat wasn't about to discard her in the sea of fire—who knows, the human might prove useful again somehow—but she certainly wasn't going to waste more time on her.

Let her sit there in her stubborn ignorance and rot.

* * * * *

Ardat was patrolling the outside of the fortress when Zarphan summoned her to one of the storerooms. She found him unrolling and examining large sheets of paper with diagrams on them.

"Blueprints. They're more useful than the actual objects." He set the papers aside and eyed her speculatively, blinking. "Ardat, your work made this all possible. I haven't forgotten that."

He flapped to an alcove at the back of the storeroom and returned with a human artifact—a triangular frame that was almost as large as she was, and bulky enough to make flying awkward. Its color was an unfamiliar warm brown.

He held out his arms and handed it to her.

"A human harp," Zarphan said, and for once smiled.

Her heart raced as she flew through the tunnels hugging the human instrument close. It was bigger and clumsier than a heavenly harp, something you wrestled to carry rather than tucking under an arm. And it was wood instead of gold—so easy to crack or break. She held it carefully as she pushed open the door to an empty chamber.

Ardat settled the instrument on the floor beside a stone bench. She was both eager and afraid: it had been so long. And the thing had pedals, which were new to her. It stood on its own while angelic harps were built to be cradled in your arms.

She ran a finger along the top of the curved frame, which was already covered in black dust, ripped off a piece of her tunic, and wiped the wood. There: clean. Not sparkling like her old harp, it would never sparkle, but that didn't matter. Through millennia of dust and humiliation and boredom and anger, she had never forgotten those words: *your fingers could make a scrap of copper sing.*

* * * * *

They had been rehearsing the newest symphony of praise—a swirling, barreling composition for some 20,000 instruments that included 3,000 harps. Music swelled through the ether, so thick and lush that you could almost reach up and touch it. In the meadows of Heaven, angels picking flowers for garlands stretched and swayed to the rhythm of the orchestra. In front of God's palace, angels polishing the golden doors tapped their feet against the crystal pavement.

Ardat sat in the front row of harpists, the instrument's gold frame pressed against her shoulder. She moved in unison with the others—fingers plucking, torsos anchoring, as if they were one vast multi-limbed musician. So much beauty. So much praise. And such a God, who had created all of this and was so deserving of that praise. Ardat felt like God had given her 20,000 ears. She could distinguish each individual harp, each viol, each flute, and she could hear how they all melded together. One instrument, though, emerged more clearly than the rest—her own. So rich. So clear. So utterly perfect for praising God.

Ardat prayed with her fingers that she be given an opportunity to solo. She prayed with her biceps. *Choose me, God*, the strings said with every note, and *Here I am, God*, they said with every chord. She had no doubt that God—through Sandalphon, the orchestra conductor—would hear and choose her.

Sandalphon chose someone else.

An inferior musician. Even now, she refused to say his name. His chords sounded hollow. His stops were too abrupt. Sometimes he even played a half-note flat or sharp.

She approached Sandalphon after rehearsal. "You should have picked me," she said, and the conductor opened his eyes as wide as if she had cursed the name of the Creator.

She talked to other harpists. "Didn't (the name she refused to speak) sound a little off-key today?" she'd say in a low voice. "Don't you think they could have chosen someone better?" But the other harpists turned away, and soon she found herself alone within the crowd.

Ardat redoubled her practicing. She poured herself into the music. And still she went unchosen, unpraised, unrecognized. Then, one day, during yet another frustrating rehearsal where she was forced to listen to (name unsaid) butcher the most simple chord transition, she felt warm eyes upon her.

120

Someone was listening.

Someone heard her virtuosity.

Lucifer flapped down beside her after rehearsal was over and nearly all the others had flown away. Of course she knew of Lucifer, but he'd never spoken to her before.

"That was magnificent," he said.

"Thank you. We're getting better. The violins were wonderful this time."

"Not the orchestra. You. You're outstanding."

"With a good conductor, every musician sounds outstanding. Or perhaps you were noticing my instrument. It was made by Zarphan, who does such fine work."

"Cut the crap." Lucifer's golden angel-eyes flashed and in those eyes, for the first time, she saw a reflection of her own righteous anger. "We both know it's not the conductor or the harp maker. It's you. You're an incredible musician, and they're burying you. They're trying to make it so no one can hear you."

"That's not true!" The denial sounded feeble even as she mouthed it.

"Ardat," Lucifer said, and she was amazed that the prime archangel knew her name. "It's you. Your fingers could make a scrap of copper sing."

* * * * *

This human harp wasn't even copper, but it would sing for her.

Determined now, Ardat lunged her hand forward and plucked the C string. Too forceful. Too brassy. But—oh Creation—how it did feel good. She plucked it again, more gently and nuanced this time. Better.

She played a D, an F, an A. She experimented with pressing the pedal to get an A flat. Her hands and her feet slipped into motion together as if harps always had pedals.

Don't rush. One note at a time. Remember the form before getting fancy.

She played a C scale—once, twice, twenty times. She played a D scale. Forward, then backward. Again. Again. Again. At first the wooden frame felt flimsy against her shoulder, a twig that might snap if she played too hard, but soon she settled into it and discovered that she liked its suppleness. The sound had a mellow warmth that gold lacked. The vibrations poured into her chest and nourished her body. It had been so long.

Again.

The familiar push and pull. So much torque on each string: it took all your strength to make the most delicate sound. She was out of shape, out of form. Back then, when she had practiced a piece enough, her body took over and her thinking mind flew away and she played intuitively, meditatively. Now she had to struggle for each individual note.

She halted her scales and returned to single notes, first with her right hand and then with her weaker left hand.

C.

Too brash, too buzzy.

Stay focused. Keep trying.

Over and over, C.

Finally, as if she were working a lump of clay, the note began to assume a shape resembling what she wanted. All was not lost! She was so excited that she played a set of triplets—C-A-F— and the notes gamboled up from her fingers like the winged horses in Heaven's meadows.

More triplets. They were a treat, a reward, a delight. She frolicked through them. She launched recklessly into an arpeggio and the sound was imperfect and sloppy but magnificent.

Again.

Ardat closed her eyes, and the dim cell and dusty desert and torturing fire vanished, and she was somewhere above—not Heaven, not that unjust and oppressive place, but somewhere light and airy and free and suffused with music.

Again. Again. Again.

She lost herself in the music and continued playing—*more, more, more*—until she noticed a slick of black on a string. Ardat peered closer and saw that it came from her own fingers, cracked from millennia without practice, now seeping blood.

CHAPTER EIGHTEEN

Haisheng

Haisheng hadn't understood distances in Hell until now. When Trua had warned him that the palace was far, he'd imagined far in human terms. *Far* was the other side of the devil city. *Far* was the day-long journey by ox cart from Shanghai to the village where his father was born. Here distances were geared to creatures that could fly. Haisheng trekked across basin after basin, all empty and sulfurous. The openness made him nervous. The only times he'd been outside of Shanghai while alive were New Year's visits to his father's village, and one trip to Xinghua's family estate.

He and Xinghua had sat by a pond, throwing grain to the ducks. They lay back in the grass and imagined patterns in the clouds. For once Xinghua seemed to forget about politics and let himself play, and for once Haisheng felt like he had his friend's undivided attention. It was wonderful. Those had also been open spaces—grass and pond and sweeping sky—but they were Xinghua's childhood home and thus felt welcoming, even revelatory.

Here nothing revealed itself. And certainly nothing welcomed him.

He watched the sky for wings. He stepped carefully up the hillsides to avoid dislodging noisy rocks. Sometimes his chest seized up with so much dread that he couldn't breathe. All the political manifestos he'd read did nothing for him then; he found himself clinging to lines from the poets he'd repudiated.

Afoot and light-hearted, I take to the open road

Walt Whitman was better than any of the classical Chinese poets for bolstering his spirits—the voice of the common man, of action, of a vigorous democratic future. Even translated into Chinese, the cadence was optimistic.

> *Henceforth I ask not good-fortune, I myself am good-fortune,*
> *Henceforth I whimper no more, postpone no more, need nothing*

His steps quickened. For a little while he would dance across the plain. And then he would run out of verses.

As much as he tried, he couldn't invent more.

* * * * *

He thought about Ishaq. Now that Haisheng understood the immensity of the desert, he feared for the old man. Ishaq had saved his life and he'd repaid him with disrespect. That wasn't revolutionary; it was childish. He scanned for a silhouette bent in prayer behind boulders or a robed figure in the canyons. It was more of a hope than a search. Hell was huge, and the Syrian could have gone in any of a thousand directions.

He thought about love, and that conversation with Trua. Had he ever loved anyone? What was love and what was friendship? Eiko had been a ray of sunshine in the safe house but he'd never felt desire for her. Liang-li, Xinghua's girlfriend, had the still beauty of a painting with perfect brush strokes. The only time he felt heat was imagining her and Xinghua together—the two of them caressing in the dark of Xinghua's room. Was he perverse? He'd heard of such things in the brothels—two men and a woman, or two women and a man—but he didn't want that. He would never go to such a place.

Perhaps he wasn't made for love. Perhaps it was just as well he was here, slogging through Hell, free to direct all his energy into liberating the wraiths.

Henceforth I whimper no more, postpone no more, need nothing

Haisheng stumbled down a ridge into a basin that was rougher and more jagged than the others. He fell onto a pile of crystals and slashed his leg. Pain shot through his side and he cried out.

Don't make noise. Don't attract demons.

Hell had no clouds, no sun that could dim, but the plain felt darker. He needed Ishaq. He needed Trua. Why was he out here alone? Xinghua and Liang-li had each other and all the other cadre. Right now they might be planning the final uprising. Or the revolution might already have happened—Annie had told him that the communists won—and they would be celebrating with the masses in the streets of Shanghai.

Banners! Firecrackers! Songs and jubilant slogans!

The plain felt emptier than ever. Haisheng tried to stand and his leg buckled. *Keep going. Reach the next ridge.* Again he summoned Whitman but the boasts about needing nothing now felt hollow. The only poet who responded was from centuries ago—his old hero Du Fu whom, like Ishaq, he had tossed away.

The solitary goose does not drink or eat,
It flies about and calls, missing the flock.

CHAPTER NINETEEN

Annie

Annie's father was a wreck. His usual endearing absent-mindedness metastasized into a broad inability to function. He forgot to shave in the morning. He backed the car into a fire hydrant on a trip to the drugstore. One of his colleagues at the high school called Annie and said he was spending lunch hours in the men's bathroom crying.

Annie didn't know what to say to him. Her father was never comfortable with emotional talk. She made dinners for the two of them—really just microwaving the mountain of casseroles delivered by her parents' friends—and sat nearby as he graded papers. While he was at work, she cleaned out her mother's closet and drove black garbage bags of clothes to Goodwill.

Even if he'd wanted to talk, she felt unable to console him. Whatever he was feeling, the reality was so much worse. Annie had no doubt that her mother was in the fire.

Fingers that had stroked her forehead, charring into black flakes.

Knees that knelt in damp garden soil, exploding like kindling.

Those lovely, thin wrinkles along her eyes—burning.

Annie's gut rebelled with massive diarrhea. She had never known that grief could take such a physical form. She sat on the toilet, head in hands, wishing she could shit away the past weeks, the past year, everything.

It was her fault. That was the worst part of it. If she'd warned her mother about Hell, Callie might be in Heaven now. Annie had almost told her once or twice but backed off—afraid of conflict, of being dismissed as crazy, of becoming that disappointing second child again. Focused on saving herself and Mary from Hell, she hadn't paid attention to the risk to anyone else.

She read Paul in bed at night: *How shall they hear without a preacher?*

And Mark: *Go home to your friends and tell them how much the Lord has done for you, and how He has had mercy on you.*

She'd done no preaching and no telling. She'd chosen the easier, safer path. Because of that, her mother was burning in Hell.

* * * * *

Annie determined to try church again. This time she sought out a conservative church, one that seemed more likely to believe in a fire-and-brimstone Hell, and drove 30 minutes on the freeway to a campus whose parking lot was bigger than her high school's football field. She lugged Mary in her car seat to meet with the minister, a rotund, blue-suited figure who looked more bureaucrat than prophet. He too had a bobblehead athlete on his desk, although his was Steph Curry.

She steeled herself for skepticism. But this pastor didn't scoff or suggest that Hell was real "for her."

"You've been blessed," he exclaimed, eyes bright across the desk. "Praise the Lord! Annie, your return to life is a miracle. You've got to share this message."

"I don't have a message," Annie said. For months she'd wanted to find someone who believed her. Now she had, but his enthusiasm was unnerving. "I just want to save my mother."

"You can save many more souls than your mother, Annie. Think about it! Millions of people, non-believers like you used to be, whose hearts remain closed to Jesus Christ. When they hear your story, their eyes will open. Their hearts will open."

"But first I need to help my mother," she said. "Are there things I can do? Aren't there churches that baptize your ancestors?"

"The Mormons." The pastor frowned. "They profess to be Christian but follow false prophets. No, Annie, your mother's soul is in God's hands now, not ours. You need to trust that He'll do what's right and just."

"I didn't see anything right or just in Hell."

"His ways are beyond us, Annie. His justice is greater than we can understand."

"But how can that kind of torment be just? If there's some bigger plan, why can't he let us see it?"

"Faith, Annie. It's a test of our faith. *We are saved by hope; but hope that is seen is not hope.* You have a story that will bolster people's faith and hope. That's a gift from the Lord. It's why you were returned to life. Think of the souls you can save, millions upon millions. The Lord returned you for a reason, Annie. You have a mission to share the good news of Christ risen."

A mission. Until now, it had never occurred to Annie that God might have restored her to life for a reason.

130

Her return was too arbitrary and chaotic—cosmic glitch, not divine plan. She herself was too confused to be any kind of a messenger; all she wanted was to protect her family. But what if this round-faced minister were right? All these months she'd been straining to hear something—anything—from God. Perhaps her presence here on Earth was God's response and she had been staring right past it.

And if so...

A vision of the future spread before her. The minister would guide her. He would answer all her questions, explain the inexplicable. Annie would stand at his pulpit telling her tale to a rapt congregation. She'd share her story—a cautionary one of fall, redemption, and renewal—not just with this one church but with national conventions of believers. She'd appear on Christian radio shows and Christian TV. Her face would shine forth on glossy book jackets, her journey tidied up by a devout and talented ghostwriter and filed on bookstore shelves beside *The Five People You Meet in Heaven*. For the first time, she would be as famous as Ben. In fact they would be a TV producer's dream: *Atheist brother faces off against born-again sister!* She would be radiant, lauded, and secure. Her path would be clear and the world would make sense and her soul would be safe and Mary's soul would be safe...

But sharing "good news of Christ risen?"

Annie had only bad news. She'd seen nothing of Christ, risen or otherwise. She had only seen eternal suffering for people who didn't deserve it—the little Hindu boy Dev, devout Ishaq, sunny and generous Eiko.

Henry Mwango. Trua. Her mother.

"I don't know—" she began but the pastor cut her off.

"You *do* know, Annie. Your heart knows. But the devil is planting doubts that hold you back. You bear a wonderful gift for the world, but first you need to secure your own faith. Are you ready to accept the Lord's wisdom and justice? To give yourself up to His will? Are you ready to accept Jesus as your personal savior?"

Her chest tightened. Her heart pounded. She couldn't accept but she couldn't refuse. Her tongue filled her mouth like Styrofoam and her body grew heavy as mud. Indeed, she was tempted. The most compelling part wasn't the fame but the welcome—how finally she would be believed, accepted, safe. Her worries about eternity would vanish. But that would mean justifying the fire and accepting all those millions of souls tortured for eternity. It would mean praising a God who condemned her mother to the fire—a God who levied an eternity of unrelenting pain on people who screwed up, sometimes unwittingly, during the minuscule speck of time that was a human life. Annie had read the story in Matthew about Jesus on the desert mountaintop, viewing the kingdoms of the world and rejecting Satan's offer of them. Here was her own mountaintop. She wanted to be like Jesus! She did! But which was the kingdom she was supposed to reject? Where was the temptation and where was the truth?

The minister beamed with encouragement. She couldn't speak. Mary saved her, yet again. A mew wafted out of the car seat and thickened into a wail and then a holler.

"The baby—need to change—" Annie sputtered, and fled yet another church.

She was crying so hard she couldn't drive. In the back seat, Mary was wailing—wet or hungry or both. Annie pulled off the freeway into a gas station and called Ben. She knew it was a mistake even as she tapped his number.

"I can't deal with it," she sobbed, hunched over the steering wheel. "I keep thinking about Mom in Hell. It's my fault. You don't know how bad it is. And I just visited this church but I can't do it. I can't. I don't want to be on the mountaintop—"

"Annie. *Stop it.* Stop it with all this Hell stuff. Where are you?"

She gulped and snuffled. She could hardly hear him over Mary's wails. "A gas station. Off of 101." Her breasts were aching and her face was swollen. Annie contorted herself to reach into the back seat and fumbled with the car seat straps.

"Okay. Listen to me. Calm down. Then go home. Wait for Dad to get home from work. But write this number down first, okay? Hold on one minute."

Clicks from his keyboard. Mary still hollering. Faint odor of gasoline through the closed windows. She managed to pull Mary over the back seat and onto her breast.

"Write this down. I'll text it to you too. North Bay Community Mental Health. (415) 921-4500. Write it down. Are you listening?"

"Yeah. Okay." The old reflex: listen to Ben, follow Ben. Cradling Mary with one arm, she groped in the diaper bag for a pen. Her fingers touched a cylindrical object, but when she pulled it out, it was a lip balm.

Her mother's lip balm. Buried in the diaper bag, the $4 stick had outlived its user.

"Call them. Make an urgent appointment. You hear me? And call me afterwards. I'm going to make sure you get the best professional help."

Annie uncapped the lip balm. It was stubby and uneven, slightly melted, used. Slowly she slid it across her own lips. But there was only a lemony, waxy flavor—no taste of her mother, no smell of her, nothing.

She ended the call, closed her eyes, and slumped back in the driver's seat until Mary finished nursing.

CHAPTER TWENTY

Annie

Annie didn't phone the mental health center. She didn't answer Ben's repeated calls. She managed the drive home, made dinner for her father like any other night, and sat with him while he went online to close the last of her mother's credit card accounts. After he went to bed, she threw feed to the chickens, checked on Mary, and shut herself in her room. The lip balm now seemed like a sick joke—protection against pale springtime sun for lips that were destined for eternal Hellfire.

God, save my mother, she thought, kneeling by her bed. *Please, God. I don't know who else can help me.*

She'd made this plea a hundred times already. It was no good. She wouldn't get an answer. Annie flopped onto the floor and buried her face in the shag carpet, nylon fibers worming against her cheeks, dust chafing her nostrils. If only she could dissolve into dust. She had wanted to dissolve into dust in Hell too, lying in gravel by the marsh of limbo, unable to rescue Mary. And remembering this, she realized she was wrong. She *did* know who could help her.

Or at least respond to her. Maybe.

Annie peered into the hallway to make sure her father and Mary were asleep. The house was silent. She closed the bedroom door tight.

"Satan."

The name, whispered, slicked her tongue like syrup.

"It's Annie Maple. I met you at your palace before I came back to life. Satan, can you rescue my mother from the fire? I'll give you my soul. I'll do whatever you ask, as long as it doesn't hurt other people. But please, can you save my mother?"

Outside her open window, wind rustled the cherry tree. Inside, everything remained silent.

Idiot! She had just thrown away any slim chance of Heaven. Annie waited for a thunderclap of doom, a flash of divine fury, *something*. But nothing happened. When she'd called on Satan by the marsh in Hell, a low-level devil named Jomjael had responded. But now there was nothing. Neither God nor devils cared. She was truly alone.

Limp with exhaustion, she let her body drop into bed.

* * * * *

A nightmare: *She'd locked Mary in the car at the gas station and lost the key.*

Annie lurched awake in the dark, heart racing, but her panic collapsed into relief. It was just a dream, and a normal, maternal dream to boot—nothing about fire or devils or Hell. She peered at her bedside clock—4:45—and hoped for another couple of hours of sleep before Mary would wake.

She heard a soft, leathery scraping.

136

Annie bolted upright. There, at the foot of the bed, stood a slender winged silhouette, dark against dark.

She groped for the lamp on her night table and nearly knocked it over.

"Baphomet?"

The girl devil watched her, wide-eyed, wings brushing lightly against each other.

"You came. You heard." Annie could hardly believe it.

"This is...your home?"

Annie nodded.

"So soft." Baphomet reached out and fingered the comforter on Annie's bed. "It's filled with soft things." She glanced toward the window. "But your world is so dark. Like it's all a cave."

"It's nighttime."

"Ah. I know about night. I thought it would be more...limited. Like smoke from a volcano. Coming and going."

"No, it lasts for about 12 hours. Then it's daytime."

"Hours?"

"A division of time. Never mind. Can you help—"

"I can see you."

The devil was eyeing her, up and down, and Annie remembered that through her entire time in Hell, she'd been invisible to devils.

"You're pretty. I didn't think you were. I thought you would look like the slave-humans, only more solid. But you have skin and hair and eyes. And you're such a strange pale color. Not shiny or dark. There were flowers like that in Heaven. I can't remember their names, though..."

"You heard me calling?"

"Oh." Baphomet shook herself out of her reverie. "Not me. The Great Satan heard and sent me here. It's my first time, you know." She beamed with pride.

"Thank you. Thank you both. So he'll save my mother?"

"Oh, he didn't say *that*."

"Well, what *did* he say? Will he help?"

"He wants me to bring you back. So he can talk to you in person."

"I can't." Dread gripped her. Annie had imagined pleading with Satan—groveling, offering her soul—but doing that right here in Mill Valley. "I have a baby now. I can't leave. What if you just take him a message?"

"No." Baphomet looked insulted. "I'm not a messenger. I'm a *lieutenant*. That's new since you were there. Things are much better now." Baphomet's wings fluttered. "You're lucky to be summoned, you know. And if you're summoned, you have to go. "

"My baby—"

Baphomet shrugged. "Your baby doesn't matter. Let's go."

Annie's chest tightened. Appeals to compassion had never worked with Baphomet. Calling on Satan was a terrible mistake. Could she negotiate?

"He can have my soul, but not now. When I'm old—like in fifty years—fifty years is nothing compared to eternity—"

"Now."

"How about thirty years! When my daughter's grown up!"

"Stop delaying." Baphomet leaned forward. "*Now*. Or I'll take your baby too."

138

"Okay! Now! But..." Annie groped for a response. "You have to bring me back immediately. As soon as I've spoken to him. Promise to bring me back. And promise that I can stay on Earth long enough to raise my daughter."

Baphomet narrowed her eyes.

"Maybe. If the Great Satan agrees."

Annie's chest loosened ever so slightly. *Think. Push. Press for more.*

"And I need time. I have to find someone to take care of Mary while I'm gone. My baby. Remember her? You saved her from Limbo for me?"

"How much time?"

"A week? That's seven times the change from day to night."

"No. Too long. We're leaving now."

"Three days—"

"No."

"One day then! Give me one day! And you...you could explore Earth! You said this was your first visit, right? Wouldn't you like to see what Earth is like during the daytime? You could see forests, oceans, cities. You could fly all over, do anything you want."

Baphomet's wings fluttered. She was wavering. Finally she pursed her lips in a pout.

"All right, human," she said. "I will explore Earth. But no tricks. And one day only. Nothing more."

139

CHAPTER TWENTY-ONE

Baphomet

The hard part was the crossing.

Baphomet had worried she might not be able to find the ancient passage that led through Chaos to Earth. But Satan gave her detailed directions, which she took pains to memorize. It was a long flight that involved navigating multiple mountain ranges and passing through the dense fumes of a spewing volcano, but she could tell when she'd arrived. Above the far rim of the volcano, a patch of sky glistened—trembling, almost alive—and she knew that was it. She herself began trembling. The route through Chaos was the sole path to Earth: only Satan and his most trusted aides knew its location, and throughout the millennia, only they had crossed.

You had to be strong. Centuries ago, she had listened to senior devils trading stories of how the trip nearly tore them to pieces. Back then she would never have imagined herself on such a mission. But since Satan's miraculous revival, she'd been secretly training to strengthen herself. She launched herself off cliffs and forced herself to stay aloft using only the tips of her wings. At the bottom, she'd flap her way back up using only the left wing or only the right. She sought out secluded desert canyons where she loaded herself up with large rocks and flew back and forth until her arms felt liquid. She was determined to play a useful role in Satan's renewed ambitions. Still, until he tapped her on the shoulder and said carelessly, "You. Bathmat. I've got a job for you," she never dreamed he would send her to Earth.

Perhaps he was finally noticing her.

The entry to Chaos glistened and shimmered against the volcanic haze. Baphomet heaved her wings and threw herself in.

It slammed her. She felt herself pounded from all sides. It was just wind, but it felt solid. She braced herself in one direction only to be dragged in another. Torrents of wind, landslides of wind. A universal hubbub filled her ears—shriek of metal, roar of volcano, screams of the damned, all in one. She closed her eyes against the wind and forged ahead. Whirlpools of wind. Steer between. Wind pressed her backwards but she counter-attacked. Forward. She feared her wings would be ripped away. Forward. Her mind was in fragments. Forward. Wind hurled her up like a piece of dust and threw her down like a clatter of stones, and through it all she just kept pushing on. Forward.

Finally she emerged into stillness.

She hovered in calm air, stunned by the emptiness. Everything was black. No, not quite everything: small dots of light hung in the sky above her. The air felt shockingly thick. She heard a low rhythmic sloshing and looked down and realized she was hovering over an ocean—not the familiar orange ocean of fire, but a black ocean of what must be water.

Baphomet flapped gently—effortless, frictionless, compared to the crossing—and let her heartbeat slow. She'd done it. Satan would be pleased. Maybe even proud? But she had the rest of the mission to fulfill, including the return where she'd have to drag that human Annie through the crossing. Don't get cocky.

She knew exactly where to go. Satan had known from Annie's prayers, and all he had to do was touch her forehead to pass that on. She had no idea how a dead human like Annie could have returned to Earth, but that wasn't her problem.

Baphomet's wings still felt like puddles of melted ore, but she gave a flap and headed towards the shore and the home of Annie Maple.

* * * * *

A full day on Earth!

Baphomet now eyed the human Annie and wondered if this were a trick. What if she returned from exploring and Annie had fled? There were no limits to human guile and betrayal; she had learned that from centuries of listening to the senior devils. But thanks to Satan's touch, she had the ability to find Annie anywhere.

So escape was not a problem, and Satan hadn't given her a deadline. This would be just one rotation of the human Earth. If anyone asked, she could say that with her unripe wings, her undersized limbs, the crossing took longer than usual.

She fingered the bottom of the fabric covering Annie, thick as a half dozen tunics yet so light it could have been filled with breath. So many textures in this world. Under her feet another kind of fabric, soft and tickling like the grass she vaguely remembered from Heaven. Even the walls seemed warm and giving, almost alive— so different from the stone and gold of Pandaemonium.

Yes, she'd spend a day on Earth.

"Be here when night returns," she ordered, trying to deepen her voice to sound as menacing as the senior devils. "If you're not, I'll find you. I can find you anywhere."

She turned to the window where she'd entered. Already the black sky was giving way to streaks of rose and orange. She hunched to lift off.

"Wait!" The Annie human gestured her to halt. "You can't just fly around out there looking like that. People will go nuts. They'll call out the police or the army."

"So?"

"They'll try to capture you. They have weapons. Even if you're immortal, it'll make a big mess."

Human souls in Hell were powerless, pathetic things, and Annie's living form didn't seem like much of a threat either. Still, she had a point. Satan's ancient visits to Earth had always been discreet. She didn't want to disgrace herself.

"What do you suggest then?"

Annie frowned. "I could lend you clothes. Maybe you could tuck your wings inside a jacket. We could fix your skin with make-up, but it would look weird...Wait, can't you shape-shift?"

"What do you mean?"

"Take on a different form. Didn't Satan become a serpent in the garden of Eden? Doesn't he take on a human appearance when he comes to Earth?"

Again Annie had a point. It had been so long since Satan or any of his aides had been to Earth that

Baphomet had forgotten about assuming human form. She knew it could be done, but she'd never seen anyone do it.

"I...don't know how." The admission felt shameful.

"Maybe you should just wait here then."

No. This might be her one chance in all of eternity to see Earth! If she'd managed the crossing, she could manage this. Baphomet turned away from Annie and concentrated. How did Satan and the more powerful devils do things? Flying came naturally to her—she had flown as long as she could remember—but there were other kinds of power. Satan touching her forehead to pass on Annie's location. Devils' ability to hear human prayers. There were never any special tools or totems, just concentration. So she quieted her mind and focused every part of herself on becoming a human like Annie. Wings falling away. Talons into toenails. Skin blanched and roughened, pocked with bumps and hairs and wrinkles.

There!

She looked at her hands and they were pink. Horrible. Legs pink too. She reached behind her back and the space where her wings should be felt empty and vulnerable. She was grateful that Satan couldn't see her like this.

Annie stared, stunned. That was satisfying enough to make up for the awful transformation.

"Well," Baphomet said. "Now you can give me some of your clothes."

* * * * *

She couldn't fly; she had to walk.

144

Annie had ushered Baphomet out of the house and pointed her in the direction of town. Red and orange streaked the sky just above the horizon, while the upper regions melted from black into a deep blue. Trees lined her path—not the symmetrical gold and silver trees she'd known in heaven, but unruly, massive trees of green and brown with branches fighting each other every which way. She stopped to touch a trunk and found it rough and ridged, both cold and damp from the air but also warm from the life pulsing through it. She pulled off a piece and brought it to her lips and had a disturbing urge to eat it. Eating! That was such a human weakness. She had eaten manna in heaven, although the point hadn't been taste or texture or even hunger, but communion with God. She tossed the chunk of bark to the ground and kept going.

Walking was slower than flying but it allowed more time to experience things. The sponginess of the ground alongside her path. The piles of damp leaves with a soft, multi-layered smell that seemed to curl in on itself. Was this what humans meant by rot?

And so much water. It was everywhere. She'd realized that was what made the air feel thick, but it was also inside the tree trunks and the dead leaves, it pooled and trickled below the straight hard path, it beaded on the glossy metal roofs of the wheeled vehicles resting along the path. If Heaven was the realm of God, and Hell was the realm of fire, then Earth was surely the realm of water.

The orange streaks had vanished and the sky was now a pure light blue. The sun formed a brilliant orb, white as the light of Heaven. This place was brighter than Hell and more richly colored than Heaven.

Baphomet might not be able to fly but she gave a little skip. The human world had come awake and cars darted past, stopping abruptly at a red sign and then lunging forward. A human woman approached her, running at a moderate pace, a blank look on her face, thin cords hanging from her ears. Baphomet tensed for some kind of reaction—the "going nuts" that Annie had feared—but the woman simply kept running, and she realized with glee that her transformation was successful.

She gave another little skip. Annie's shoes had some kind of lightweight cushion in them that made you bounce. It was fun, but nothing like flying. Poor frail humans. She skipped again and saw a crack in the path where tree roots were pushing their way up so she hopped over that with her right foot, and then saw another spot where the path had chipped away so she hopped over that with her left foot, and skipping and hopscotching she made her way into downtown Mill Valley.

* * * * *

It was a small place, a fraction of the size of Beelzebul's city, far less grand than Pandaemonium. No gold, no bronze, no visible gemstones. But it was far more colorful. A yellow building sat beside a deep brown one which in turn sat beside a greyish blue one. They all had brightly-colored signs, some with images and some with letters, and for the first time in her millennia-long existence, Baphomet wondered what it would be like to know how to read. Why had God given writing to humans and not to his own angels? If Satan's forces had

146

known how to write and read, might the rebellion have triumphed? At first the squiggles and lines on the signs fascinated her, but then they started to make her angry. It felt like Satan's meetings with his aides back at Pandaemonium: important things were taking place behind closed doors, and she was stuck outside.

Nasty signs, nasty feeling of being left out. Baphomet wanted to fly up, rip a sign away, and drop it off a cliff. Watch it shatter. But she had no wings, so instead she picked up a small stone lying near the trunk of a tree and hurled it at the writing on one of the windows near her path.

She might have the flimsy-looking body of a human girl, but her arms still had the strength of a devil. The window shattered with a crash. Shards of glass flew everywhere. An unnatural screech pierced the air and started to repeat itself, over and over. What had she done? Baphomet glanced around, terrified, and took off running down the street, around a corner, down an alley, as fast and as far as her now-human legs could go.

* * * * *

She crouched behind bushes, heart pounding.

Wait. Don't move. Be sure no one has followed you.

Gradually she calmed down. There seemed to be no police, no army, no humans "going nuts." The street was quiet, the patch of grass around the bushes deserted.

She fingered a leaf of the bush and was swept with memories of picking flowers in heaven. It had been her destiny. It was why she'd been created. Baphomet didn't regret spurning it, not with her mind, but her

147

fingers were a different matter. They felt at home on the leaf, the first plant she'd touched since the fall to Hell. Of course it would never pass muster for a garland: the green was too dark, more like Earth's night than the silvery green of heaven. But simply being close to it made her happy. Baphomet pulled the leaf off its branch and twirled it in her fingers, ran its waxy surface across her lips, inhaled its tangy, gossipy scent. Could she take a leaf back to Hell? She sniffed it again and tucked it in the pocket of Annie's pants.

After a long time, she ventured out of her hiding spot and back down the alley to the main street. A human man was hammering flat pieces of wood over the broken window. Otherwise everything seemed quiet and unchanged. She made sure to stay far from the window and picked her way down the street.

For the rest of the day, she kept a tight rein on herself. No show of force. Nothing abrupt or noisy that might attract people's attention. She stared at the ground and let herself sag down inside Annie's large jacket whenever a human approached, and amazingly no one seemed to notice her.

At one point she went into a building that sold food. Annie had given her green pieces of paper to exchange for such things. A group of human girls clustered in front of a glass counter, chattering and pointing at vats of different colors. (Yes, more colors! This place was overflowing with colors.)

She followed their example, and the human behind the counter scooped two small spheres—one pink, the other brown and white—into a dish for her. They looked like the consistency of congealing lava, but once he handed her the dish, she realized they were cold, almost as cold as the winds of the crossing.

She took the dish outside and sat alone on a bench. The human girls were gathered around a table, eating and giggling. Foolish humans. How could they be so happy when they had only a few score years of life? When cells in their bodies were dying every minute? She felt contemptuous of them but also a little lonely, so she started picturing them in the fire.

That girl with long red hair: *Ha! See how that hair will look when it's red with unquenchable flames!* Or the girl with a sack filled with books on her back: *Feel that sack in the fire, dragging you down, dragging you under...*

Baphomet poked at her food with a small, scoop-like tool she'd been given and cautiously tasted it. Her mouth exploded.

Ice! Snow! Frozen! Freezing!

She'd only heard these words, never experienced them, but she instinctively knew that this was what she was feeling. Take the cold winds of the crossing and concentrate them, mine them for their essence like ore from rock, and this is what you'd get. Her tongue tingled. Her lips numbed. And then all that cold was knocked aside by the taste.

Sweetness. Smoothness. The sweetness sprinted to the corners of her mouth, leaping up and down. Sweet as fresh grass. Warm breeze. Earth sun. Smooth as new petals, as angel skin. It started out thick and mucousy but almost before you could notice, it melted away and left you wanting more. Barely an echo of the sweetness of heaven but so much more vibrant, intense, fleeting. Pow! A plunge of flavor and then it was gone.

She took another bite, and another. The pink ice cream had an echo of tartness inside the sweet. It seemed to be made from fruit, perhaps the same fruit that Eve had eaten in Eden. For the first time Baphomet understood the allure. Was it worth giving up immortality? No, but still, so amazing on her tongue...

By the time she paused to let her mouth warm up, the girls had left. The sun was lower in the sky, almost hidden behind the trees and buildings.

A creature sat before her.

An animal, four-legged and shaggy, smaller than one of her wings. It stared up at her with large brown eyes that seemed too big for its head. Baphomet surmised it was a dog or a cat: the only animals she'd ever seen were the winged horses of Heaven and Hell.

It wanted something from her, and Baphomet realized those big eyes were not in fact staring at her but at her dish. Without thinking, she dipped her tool and reached it out.

The animal stretched towards her and with one curl of a long pink tongue took all the ice cream. It licked its lips and smiled at her. She offered a second glob and it ate that one too. She took another mouthful herself and felt torn: the ice cream was so good, but it was also delightful to watch the animal enjoying itself. She took one big, final taste and then put the rest of the dish on the ground.

When the animal had lapped it all up, she reached out a hand and it licked that too. Its tongue was rougher than her own, sand come to life. She reached into the thick tangle of its fur and felt the small, pulsing body underneath. Those big eyes stared up at her. Could you take an animal through the crossing?

"Quincy!"

A human woman strode down the path, holding a cord.

"There you are! Bad dog." She turned to Baphomet. "I'm sorry. Was he bothering you? He's quite the beggar."

"No, he wasn't bothering me."

"Quincy! Come." The dog bounded away from Baphomet without a glance back, and the woman fastened the cord to a collar around his neck. She smiled at Baphomet, told her to have a good day, and walked off.

A good day. The sun was well below the trees and rooflines now. Lights were appearing on tall poles and in windows. Baphomet thought it would be supremely frustrating to have time broken up like this: you'd barely begin an activity when the day would end and you'd have to stop. It would be a constant on-and-off, start-and-stop. How did humans get anything done? On the other hand, it offered constant new beginnings. *Have a good day.* If today wasn't good, you could just wait until the next day and that might be better.

Time to fetch Annie. Baphomet reached into her pants pocket to make sure her leaf was still there and headed back the way she'd come. She felt vaguely sad and regretted not having more time with the dog. So that was a pet: you could stroke it, feed it, have it come when you called. You could make it happy. She thought of Pandaemonium's giant hall and how she felt alone even with hundreds of devils there and wondered if, when she returned, Satan might let her take a human soul as a pet.

She turned off the main street back onto the smaller road towards Annie's house. Leaves still dotted the ground but they were different from this morning—dryer, more dispersed, crackling when you stepped on them. Everything on Earth seemed to be constantly changing—the sun, the leaves, even the melting ice cream. Satan had wooed her away from her bouquet-gathering with promises of change. But nothing in Hell ever seemed to truly change.

Ahead of her a group of human males leaned against a fence talking and laughing. They were drinking something out of a bag. She briefly wondered if she should cross to the other side of the street but decided it wasn't necessary: so far none of the humans had paid her the least notice.

"Hey! New girl!"

They were calling to her but she didn't know how to respond.

"You just move here?"

"Where you from?"

Several of them were calling. They moved off the fence as one, a swarm, and into the center of the path.

"You at Tam High?"

"Where you going?"

She froze. They had no swords or flaming arrows but there was menace here.

"Aww, come on, tell us your name."

"Cute girl like you, want to party?"

She understood there were words that would defuse the menace, but she had no idea what they were.

Be careful. Not like earlier with that rock. Don't call attention.

"Whatsa matter, too good to talk to us?"

"Hey baby. Let's party!"

They tightened ranks in the middle of the path. She tried to veer into the street but they outflanked her and moved in close. One of them made little sucking sounds with his lips.

"Nice ass."

"Hey baby. Give us a kiss!"

One of them reached towards her. She pushed him away, trying not to use more force than a human girl, but he still went flying across the path.

"What the fuck!"

"Stupid bitch!"

They crowded in, faces distorted with anger, hands grabbing, torsos pushing. She couldn't breathe. She couldn't think. Fear mixed with rage.

Don't touch me! How dare you! Stupid humans! Stupid mortals!

Without thinking, she jerked her consciousness into itself and transformed into the creature that had been the nemesis of humans since the Garden of Eden. Writhing body as thick and legless as a tree trunk. Long as three cars. Eyes blazing like rubies and fanged mouth wide enough to swallow any of their heads.

Baphomet coiled and reared and hissed down at them. Now they were properly small and puny. And she was queen of the fallen angels, Satan's chosen, Satan's beloved.

"Never touch me! Never touch me!" she hissed as the boys fell and scrambled and scattered, terrified, into driveways and gardens.

153

CHAPTER TWENTY-TWO

Annie

Annie launched into action as soon as Baphomet left. She called a nanny service and signed up at an astronomical price for daytime babysitting, starting the next day. She gave Mary breakfast and sent her father off to work as if nothing were wrong. Then she called a meal delivery service and ordered a pre-cooked dinner to be dropped off for her father each afternoon. She bundled Mary into the car seat and dashed to the supermarket, where she bought so much baby food and formula and diapers that the cashier asked if she were stockpiling for an earthquake. She hoped to be gone for only a few hours but needed to plan for longer. If she stopped moving for even a single moment, she would break down entirely.

Unloading the diapers and formula, though, Annie realized she needed more than a babysitting service. Someone had to be *in charge* of Mary—to make sure the babysitter was competent, to feed and bathe Mary in the evening, to be there at night if Mary woke up. Her father couldn't handle that stuff, at least not in his current state. The only person she could think of was Melanie.

"Mel," she said on the phone. "I have a super-huge favor to ask."

She didn't mention Hell. She told Melanie that a cousin in Indiana had been in a car accident and she needed to go there for a few days. Amazingly, Melanie said yes: she'd come after work and stay as long as needed. Annie flew into another round of preparations. She picked up her father's dry cleaning, paid her credit card bill, and typed up a sheet with Mary's daily routine and the pediatrician's phone number. She pumped and froze breast milk to supplement Mary's formula. She thought of writing a letter to Mary—to be delivered sometime in the future, in case she didn't return—but the prospect was too grim to contemplate. She'd be back in hours, or maybe a day. She *had* to come back.

Melanie showed up just after 4 p.m., earlier than Annie had expected.

"You sounded stressed," she said. "What's going on?"

"My cousin. This accident—"

"Cut the b.s." Melanie sat down with assertion in the middle of the couch. "You never mentioned any cousins in Indiana before. What's really going on?"

Annie was silent.

"It's not a guy. You look freaked out, not excited." She peered at Annie appraisingly. "Is this about the concussion? Those Hell fantasies again?"

Annie had to nod.

"Girlfriend." Melanie shook her head in frustration. "I thought you'd gotten over that...Wait. Are you going into some kind of treatment? And you don't want anybody to know?"

Annie melted with relief. "Something like that."

"Good. I guess your father doesn't know either, right? Well, I can keep a secret. But I need a better story than a cousin in Indiana. Should we make up a secret lover in Paris? How long will you be gone, anyway? Hey, Mary, honey!"

Melanie called up the stairs to the nursery, grinning at Annie.

"Auntie Mel's here! We're about to have some fun. Girls gone wild!"

* * * * *

It was almost dusk. Annie showed Melanie how to change Mary's diaper and mix formula and they gave her some supper. Luckily Annie's father was staying at school for a teachers' union meeting. Annie kept glancing at the door and windows for Baphomet, while hoping against all odds that the girl devil had given up and gone back to Hell.

The doorbell rang. Even expecting it, she startled.

"Take Mary upstairs," Annie whispered. "Give her this bottle. Close the door and don't come down until I'm gone. No matter what."

Melanie shot her a skeptical look but complied. Alone in the living room, she opened the door.

It wasn't Baphomet.

Ben stood there, wearing a business suit that was too formal for California and holding the handle of his small, wheeled suitcase.

"What—"

"Good. You haven't done anything crazy." He pushed past her into the living room, his bag rolling behind, and dumped his jacket on the couch.

156

"You're supposed to be in New York."

"You're supposed to be over your accident. Since you won't get help for yourself, I'm here to get it for you."

Annie clenched her jaw and glared. At the same time, she listened for sounds of Baphomet outside. "I don't need help. And I don't need you taking charge of my life."

"You certainly sounded like you needed it yesterday. So I'm taking you to see Dr. Emily Fishkoff at UCSF. Tomorrow at 10:45. World-renowned specialist in PTSD—"

"Shh. Mary's sleeping. You have to leave." She needed him out of the house before Baphomet showed up, or before Melanie heard their voices and came downstairs. He removed his tie and tossed it on top of his jacket.

"Where's dad?"

"Out. You really need to leave—"

"Is there any dinner? I haven't eaten."

"No! Just leave! Stay somewhere else! Get a motel!"

"Annie, chill out—"

Now there was a scrabbling sound at the front door, like somebody trying to turn the locked knob, somebody who didn't know about keys and doorbells.

"Get in the kitchen!" She shoved him but he only moved about a foot. "Go! It's Satan's assistant. I'm serious. She's come to get me. Go!"

Ben didn't budge. More scrabbling. Now banging—hard, insistent.

No alternative. She took a breath and opened the door.

It was indeed Baphomet. Annie saw her as Ben, standing near the couch, must be seeing her: a slight,

157

gamin-like teenage girl in clothes that were too big for her. Her hair was rumpled. Her pants—decade-old jeans that Annie had outgrown but refused to toss—were barely held up by a belt on its tightest notch. The sleeves of a worn denim jacket draped halfway down her hands.

Her eyes glowed with excitement.

"It's...wonderful," she said. "I fed an animal. I changed shape." She seemed to swell with pride. "I became a serpent."

Ben dropped down onto the couch and stretched his arms along its back. "Satan's assistant," he said with amusement. "Apparently there's a labor shortage in Hell."

Baphomet suddenly noticed him. She narrowed her eyes.

"Who's that?"

"My brother. Don't pay attention. He's about to leave."

"No human tricks. It's time to go."

"Go where?" Ben said. "To the mall?"

"Stupid human," Baphomet hissed.

"Or maybe junior prom?"

"Ben, stop," Annie said urgently.

"I said one day only. It's time to go."

Baphomet stepped into the middle of the living room and closed her eyes in concentration. In the space of a heartbeat, she transformed into her leather-winged, red-eyed devil self. Annie's old clothes lay on the carpet.

"Whoa." Ben gaped.

"Let's go," Baphomet said, ignoring him. "I'll carry you. Although you're very heavy, you know. It's not easy."

158

"Wait!" Ben jumped up. "How'd you do that?"

"Stay back, human!" Baphomet flapped her wings. "No tricks."

"I just want to know what you did. Seriously."

The girl devil paused. "You've never seen anyone change form?"

"No. Is it holography?"

"I don't know what that is."

"Light. Sculpture with light. That's not it?"

"Stupid human. It's..." She glanced at Annie as if to confirm the right phrase. "Shape shifting."

"Yes, but how?" Ben was sounding more excited by the minute. Annie needed to get Baphomet out of here before Melanie wandered downstairs.

"Ben, stop—"

"No, I need to know. And those wings. They're beautiful. I've never seen anything like them."

Baphomet cocked her head. "You think my wings are beautiful?"

"Stunning. They're both sculpted and alive at the same time. Beyond anything they did in *Avatar*. May I touch them?"

He stepped forward. Baphomet tensed her whole upper body and pulled her wings tight, and Annie braced for an explosion. But then she nodded and let them fall back. Ben gingerly touched one. "Warm yet cold," he murmured. "Powerful but light. And the circuitry is invisible. Incredible."

"Enough!" Baphomet jerked away from him. She gave a powerful flap and the wind knocked Ben backwards onto the floor. "Annie-human. We need to go."

"I'm coming too." Ben jumped onto his feet. "Take me too."

159

"No!" Annie lowered her voice. "Ben, you don't get it. This is real. It's not technology."

"Whatever it is, I need to understand it." He looked at Baphomet. "Whoever you are—whatever you are—I've never seen anything like you. You're amazing. Take me with you. Please."

"Baphomet, no," Annie said. "Satan wanted me. Just me, remember?"

The girl devil considered. When she spoke it was to Ben, not Annie. "You think I'm beautiful?"

"Very. And unique. Extraordinary."

"No tricks." She glared at him. "The Great Satan can decide what to do with you."

Baphomet wrapped an arm around Annie, opened the front door, wrapped her other arm around Ben, and lifted off. The house, her mother's garden, the streets of Mill Valley and the Golden Gate fell away below as they flew towards open ocean. Wind slapped Annie's face and tossed her hair, and a hollow ache filled her gut.

Mary remained behind. Each flap of the devil's wings took Annie further from her daughter. In her panic at the doorbell, she had shoved her at Melanie and ordered them upstairs. No kiss, no cuddle, no whispered words of love and farewell.

This might be the start of Mary's life as an orphan, and she hadn't made the time to say goodbye.

PART TWO

Abyss

CHAPTER TWENTY-THREE

Trua

Trua continued the wraith training out of loyalty to Haisheng, but also because he didn't know what else to do. He tromped dutifully between the safe houses, hoping Haisheng would change his mind and return. Occasionally he got the wraiths to respond just by raising a fist. Other times he brandished one of the iron batons. Trua had trained wild horses when he was alive, but these creatures were more skittish than horses, more timid than rabbits, stupider than sheep. He walked around with a roiling anger in his gut.

One of the wraith houses was particularly bad: the wraiths seemed to melt into the floor whenever he arrived. If he made the slightest progress, they backslid by the time of his next visit. They refused to say the names that Haisheng had given them. They refused to say anything.

"Take this!"

He'd managed to coax one wraith out of the huddle. Now it stood there trembling. He proffered an iron rod—a small one, the lightest he could find—but the creature didn't move.

"Hold it. You don't need to do anything else, just hold it."

The folds of grey rippled in place.

"Take it. That's an order." He raised his voice. "Take it."

A veil-like arm emerged and Trua pushed the baton at what passed for a hand but it clattered to the stone floor. The wraith jerked away, quivering.

"Son of a motherless goat," he muttered. Could these creatures never learn anything?

He retrieved the baton and pushed it at the wraith again. Again it clattered to the ground. "Take it!" He shoved the baton at the wraith, hard. This time he felt something grip the other end of it. Finally!

He let go and the baton crashed onto the floor.

"Damn you! I said to take it!"

Trua grabbed the baton and slammed it against the gauzy folds. The wraith collapsed into a quivering mound. It didn't push back, didn't shout, didn't even try to flee. "Fight back, damn it," he growled and kicked the pile of grey. Its passivity made him even more furious. He kicked it a second time. When it still didn't respond, he hammered it with the baton. Again. And again. And again...

Gauzy grey bits scattered across the room. Grey flakes drifted at his feet like ashes of an abandoned cookfire.

Trua stared at the fragments, hurled the baton away, and fled into the streets.

* * * * *

He sought out a corner of the city where he'd never been before. The familiar places held ghosts of Annie and Haisheng and the others. No one should see him. No one should see what he'd become.

He clambered through debris and curled into a nook created by fallen stones. At least he hadn't done it for fun like the marauders in the canyon. He wasn't that bad, yet. But would he get to that point, alone in this city with nothing but wraiths?

His hands were shaking. He used to have steady hands that could send arrows into a target at full gallop. He'd hunted. He'd fought. He'd killed men before, but it never felt like this.

There was the marauder Falc, who would have murdered him: no regrets over that bastard. Or the men he'd killed when he was alive: one Goth fighter during a short tribal war, but that had been necessary to defend his clan. One man from an unknown tribe who'd tried to steal his flock when he was alone on the plain. Beyond that, he'd taken occasional shots at Roman villagers during raids, but he'd never killed any...

Except the Syrian farmer and his servant.

Two of the last people he'd encountered while alive, and he'd killed them. It hadn't bothered him at the time but now it fed the curdled feeling in his stomach. They were fellow humans. They were from the same land as Ishaq, maybe even ancestors of Ishaq. They'd done nothing wrong. He was the one who invaded, who instigated.

And he'd told Annie about it.

Shame flushed through him. He'd sat with Annie in the mountains outside this city and told her the story of his death, including those two killings. She hadn't spoken a word of judgment. But he knew how she must have seen it—Annie, who trusted everyone, who took care of strangers, who didn't differentiate between tribe and outsider. All that time they spent together in the city and the desert, she had known and said nothing.

Thank the gods she wasn't here.

Thank the gods he'd never have to look her in the eye again.

* * * * *

Trua hunched in the nook until his legs cramped.

He considered staying in the nook forever. He never wanted to see another wraith. Plus they'd just watched him kill one of their own: what if they attacked him like a swarm of angry bees? But Haisheng was counting on him. Trua pushed himself up and headed back, the dark street mirroring his mood. He needed to find light.

Think of little Manka at home with her rabbit. Think of horses. Think of Annie alive, playing with her baby in a patch of sunlight—

Something moved in a doorway.

He tensed into fighting posture but felt none of the skin-prickling chill that signaled a devil. More wraiths? Maybe a human? An animal from Earth that had strayed through a portal?

He moved forward cautiously. Whatever it was, it had withdrawn too deeply into the doorway to see. Trua approached the door, halted, leaned forward and peered into it.

A shriek exploded at him and he leapt back. A human woman crouched in the doorway—long hair strewn every which way and a wild expression on her face—he knew her somehow—

"Oudine!"

"Don't kill me!" she shrieked. "Leave me alone! Don't kill me!"

Trua raised his hands to show they were empty of weapons. He let out a long slow breath and felt his limbs relax. Even with Oudine's madness, it was wonderful to see her—human, alive, familiar. One of her legs jutted strangely to the side, perhaps broken.

"Calm down. It's me, Trua. From the safe house."

"You!" Her voice was high-pitched and frantic. "You did it! You killed her!"

"What?"

"You killed her! You evil, evil man!"

Those gauzy bits of grey, scattered like ash. His guilt. How did she know?

"I didn't mean to—I was angry—"

"Evil man! You killed her with the flying fire!"

"What?"

He was fogged with confusion. Then it struck him: she was talking about Eiko.

They'd all been trapped in the plaza during the devil battle, fireballs plummeting around them. He was trying to shove Eiko to safety when Baphomet swooped down, grabbed him and Annie, and carried them away.

Eiko was killed. He'd been beside her one moment and gone the next. In a crazy way, Oudine's accusation made sense.

"That's not—"

"Liar!" she shrieked. "You and the Arab and the Chinaman! All of you! Liars! Killers! Eiko was the only one who cared! And you killed her!"

"I didn't—"

"But you won't kill me. God won't let you. I won't let you."

167

She reached into a fold of her tattered dress, pulled out a jagged piece of iron, and brandished it at him.

"Get away from me," she said, her voice now low and menacing. "God means for me to find my angels. And I'm not letting any lying, killing, evil man get in my way."

"Oudine," he began, reaching out a hand. The situation was almost laughable. But she lunged and sliced a deep gash across his palm.

"Get away from me!"

She reared up, waving the iron shard and shrieking like a prophetess in the grip of the gods. Trua turned and fled, his hand stinging and bloody, but her voice followed him down the echoing street.

"Killer! Evil killer! Run! Run away and never come back!"

CHAPTER TWENTY-FOUR

Ben

Ben couldn't decide which was more amazing—the girl-devil avatar or the background graphics of this simulation. "Graphics" wasn't even the right word for it; there were visuals but also tactile sensations.

Wind blasted his forehead as they flew through a wracking maelstrom. When they emerged into a desert landscape, the heat felt so heavy that he found himself sweating. He inhaled black dust. Black dust stuck to his sweaty forehead.

Brilliant, all this sensory detail. What tech genius had come up with this?

Baphomet—as Annie called the avatar—flapped towards a massive structure that looked like a black stone version of the Parthenon. Giant iron doors opened into a pillared hall dimly lit by sconces and chandeliers of lava. A wave of bone-chilling cold overtook him. (*More of that sensory detail!*) His eyes adjusted to the dimness and he saw that the hall was filled with hundreds of mottled, splotchy devils.

Near the entrance, devils played a noisy game with polished stones. Across the hall, dozens of devils surrounded a pair of devil wrestlers and egged them on. One devil massaged another's wings with an oily substance. Others sharpened and buffed their talons. Devils flapped, devils argued, devils chortled. It was like the bar scene in *Star Wars* but a thousand times more realistic, beyond anything Ben had seen on VIP tours of Google and Microsoft labs.

Tarnished heads turned and gemlike red eyes stared as the Baphomet avatar carried them through the hall and past an empty golden throne. She ferried them into a series of dark corridors, deposited them in a cell with a barred iron door, locked the door, and flew away.

"Wait!" Annie called, but Baphomet didn't look back. Ben brushed black dust off his white shirt. "Do you believe me now?" Annie asked in a bitter voice.

He smiled at her. At least she wasn't completely hallucinatory. Mistaking a digital simulation for reality was bad, but it was nowhere near as worrisome as making the thing up altogether. When they finished the game, he'd get his phone and look up treatment programs for people with video game addictions.

"So what's the goal?" Every game had a goal—to find treasure, or build an empire, or corner the market on commodities of some sort. "We start by trying to get out of this cell, right, like an escape room?"

Annie shot him a dark look and slumped onto the floor. She gave up too easily, always had. As a kid, Annie came to him for help with math problems she could easily have solved on her own. Then dropping out of Brown: he'd never understood that. Now having this baby and not even trying to get the father, whoever he was, to pay child support...Annie had so much potential and at every opportunity threw it away. Even here, inside her own Hell fantasy game, she was giving up.

"Come on," he said. "Check the walls. Don't just sit there."

The cell was lit by a single lava sconce, which made it hard to see seams and textures. Ben patted his hands along the wall systematically, looking for a secret exit or hidden control panel. There was always a way out, the designers made sure of that, you just had to think like a game designer.

"The bars," he continued when Annie didn't move. "Try the bars. There could be a loose one. Or a section that twists, and you have to align it to open the lock."

She stood up and listlessly fingered one of the bars. "You don't get it," she muttered. "This isn't a game."

"Well, if it's not a game, there's even more reason for you to try, isn't there? Now come on, do all the bars, like you're really trying. Like this isn't an escape room. Like you're really stuck in a prison cell in Hell and need to get out."

* * * * *

There were no panels in the walls. There were no trick bars. Ben directed Annie to stand in various places in case her weight tripped a switch to open the door. (It didn't.) His excitement grew as the challenge grew. It was like being part of a giant Rubik's cube, more engaging than anything else he'd done recently. Over the past few months his TV appearances had started to feel rote, and he was spending the rest of his time updating essays for an anthology, which was necessary but tedious.

Face it: he hadn't had this much fun since he and Natasha broke up.

Natasha had challenged him on so many levels. Her intellect, her curiosity, her willingness to play devil's advocate and then reverse herself just for the fun of it. She was unpredictable, not least of all in bed. All of his dates since Natasha—and he'd been on a lot since they ended the engagement a year ago—felt drab. Their relationship had been like a chess game, only with sex.

No sex here. But the game certainly was afoot.

"So it's not a physical key," he told Annie. "Not something here in the cell. To win, we need to strategize our way out. We need to outplay the devil."

"Impossible," Annie said.

"Challenging, yes. Impossible, no." He grinned at her. "It's a good thing you insisted I come along with you."

CHAPTER TWENTY-FIVE

Annie

Annie could barely think with Ben barking out all those cheerful, useless instructions. She needed to figure out what to do, and fiddling with cell bars was not the answer. If only he would shut up! She was relieved when Baphomet returned.

"The Great Satan will see you now," the girl devil said curtly and flew them back through the maze of corridors.

Satan—unmistakable, unforgettable—lounged with casual ownership on the golden throne at the front of the hall. No longer the listless figure she'd first met in the palace, this was the electric Satan who'd silenced hundreds of devils in mid-battle with his mere presence. He emanated command. He was marble in a pile of slate, a glistening salmon in a pond of catfish.

A half-dozen lieutenants gathered by the throne and eyed the humans with suspicion. In fact, Annie realized, the whole hall was watching them. It wasn't just Baphomet: all the devils could see her this time.

"Miss Maple Tree," Satan drawled lazily. "So you found your way back to life. But you didn't like it enough to stay there. Now who is this other specimen you've brought?"

Ben jumped in before she could respond. "Benjamin J. Maple, writer and commentator," he said assertively. "Who are you?"

Satan's mouth widened into a delighted smile. He glanced across the hall. "He wants to know who I am." The crowd responded with a spreading, snakelike hiss.

"Fool!"

Satan abruptly lifted off his throne and whipped a wing across Ben's face. He tumbled backwards.

"Don't waste my time on questions with answers you already know."

Ben picked himself up. Annie touched his arm in caution.

"Now, Miss Maple Tree. You survived the passage. That's interesting."

Annie quailed. As terrifying as the flight was, she hadn't doubted Baphomet would get her there. Apparently that hadn't been a sure thing. "What do you mean?" Her voice sounded small and tremulous in the great hall.

Satan shook his head in mock disappointment. "You haven't learned a thing since our time together. I'm the one who asks the questions. I understand you want a favor from me."

"I do...your highness. I think my mother's in the fire. Can you get her out?"

"Ah. Filial piety. The fifth commandment, or is it the fourth? You humans can't agree on even the most basic things. In any case, a commendable sentiment. God should be pleased with you."

Low snickers traveled across the room.

"God hasn't commended you?"

Annie didn't answer.

"I see. God hasn't been exactly...chatty?" He looked out across the hall. "Such a sad old story. Humans spurn us until they too are spurned. And then they come running to us for all the gifts that God won't grant."

"She doesn't want gifts!"

Ben's voice rang out in his most combative Fox News tone. Under the tough talk, Annie heard a thrill: he was having a very good time.

"She wants your respect. That's a human right, not a gift. And now, isn't this the point where you tell us that humans are miserable creatures who don't deserve respect or even survival? And we call forth Daniel Webster for the defense, or Captain Picard? Shall I give a Patrick Stewart speech?"

Ben looked as if he'd like nothing better than to give a speech. How could someone be so brilliant and so dense at the same time?

"No speeches," Satan said with a shrug. "No games. Sorry to disappoint you and your captain, whoever he may be. But you're not even supposed to be here. I wanted *her*."

The brilliant red eyes seared into Annie. The lazy amusement in his voice sharpened into accusation. "You returned to Earth. How?"

She described the portal. Satan listened and nodded, thoughtful. The devils around him murmured buzzily. Annie tried to turn the conversation back to Callie.

"About my mother—"

Satan had turned away and was talking to a lieutenant.

"My mother—"

"Enough about your mother!" His gaze snapped back on her with irritation. "Your mother is the least of your problems."

"She doesn't deserve—"

"What about your other 7 billion fellow humans? What do they deserve? Do they deserve annihilation?"

The lieutenants snickered. Annie wasn't sure she'd heard right.

"I don't—"

"No, you don't. You don't know anything. You don't understand anything. So let me explain. There's a foolish upstart devil named Zarphan who thinks he can conquer Heaven through technology. There are rumors that he's using portals to bring human weapons from Earth, including some of your so-called 'nuclear' ones. He may or may not be able to damage Heaven with them. He certainly won't destroy it. But there's a good chance that in trying, he'll pulverize your mortal section of the cosmos. There, does that seem any more significant than your dear mother?"

Annie's stomach pitted. Devils with nukes? Earth as collateral damage? Before she'd been to Hell this would have sounded like bad science fiction. Now it was completely plausible. "Can you stop him?" she blurted.

"*Can* I," Satan said, pleasure sliding across his face. "Or do you mean, *Will* I? Either way, it's the first intelligent question you've asked. *Can* I stop him? Possibly. But not without risking thousands of my beautiful brothers and sisters. The only ones who could reliably stop him are the forces of Heaven, under that fool Michael, who has no idea what's happening.

"*Will* I stop him? Of course not. It will be delightful to watch Zarphan ambush Heaven. Let them maim

176

each other. If Earth suffers, so be it. Your people stopped being amusing a long time ago."

"But—"

"Enough." He waved a hand. "You were helpful about the portals. We'll save a ringside seat for you when Zarphan blows up Heaven and Earth. Now, Baphomet, take them back to their cell."

The girl devil flapped over, wrapped an arm around Annie's waist, and reached for Ben.

"Wait," Ben said loudly before she could tighten her grip. "You'll want to hear this."

* * * * *

If anyone could talk their way out of this situation, it would be Ben. Annie had no idea what his plan was, but she welcomed it. Baphomet released both of them as hundreds of red eyes swiveled from Satan to the humans.

"Send us back to Earth," Ben said with authority. "We'll alert the government to secure all nuclear material. I have contacts at the State Department, the Pentagon. Zarphan won't be able to get his hands on a thing. He'll be humiliated. Weakened."

Satan smirked. "And you'll be home free."

"Of course. But you said it yourself: we don't matter. We're inconsequential."

"No."

"Then send us to infiltrate Zarphan's camp. We can report back on his plans. He won't expect humans to be working for you."

"So you can play double-agent or escape? No."

"Then another option—"

"So many options!" Satan smiled happily at his followers. "Humans are superb at coming up with options. Then they invariably choose the wrong one."

"Tell Heaven," Ben said.

The lieutenants around Satan fell silent. The whole hall fell silent. The edge of Ben's mouth lifted slightly in a way that Annie recognized as pleasure at owning the room.

"Tell God and the angels that Zarphan's planning an ambush. They can disarm him. No nuclear war, which is good for Earth, and Zarphan is defeated, which is good for you. You neutralize Zarphan without sending a single one of your fighters into battle. Who knows, Heaven might even reward you."

Satan slapped his wings together in a single, echoing jolt of contempt.

"Heaven? Reward *me?* And here I thought your sister was the naïve one. You actually think the Archangel Michael would listen to a warning from me? If I told him lava was hot, that idiot would decide it was cold. If I told him Earth's sky was blue, he'd decide it was red."

The circle of devils guffawed.

"Then send *me*," Ben declared.

Satan pulled back a wing as if to slam Ben but halted. His gaze traced the contours of Ben's face. He waved to the other devils.

"Go. Everyone. Back to your business."

Wings rustled, talons clicked against the stone floor. Satan waited for them to clear away and turned back to Ben.

"Michael *would* listen to a human," he said, musing. "And it would guarantee Zarphan's defeat. For once, a decent idea from a mortal."

Annie's gut relaxed. She didn't care if Ben still thought this was a game. He would win, as always. Ben would take care of everything—save Earth, bring them both home, maybe even save their mother.

"Not a bad idea," Satan continued. "But..."

He glared at Ben.

"I'm sending *her*, not you. You're too sly for your own good. You'd come up with some kind of double-cross. But her? She couldn't lie to save her own soul. No worries about trickery with that one."

He turned to a large, heavyset devil. "Belial, take her to the gates of Heaven."

"No!" Annie exclaimed. "I don't—"

"Master!" Baphomet spoke over her. "Let me do it! I carried them both here from Earth. I can do it!"

"Ha!" Satan looked to the devils nearest him. "Bathmat couldn't find her way to Heaven if God laid out a trail of angel feathers."

"Let me follow them, then. To learn. The more I learn, the better I can serve you."

Satan rolled his eyes. "Fine," he said. "Go with them. Or not. It doesn't matter to anyone."

The Belial devil hoisted Annie up and flew her out the hall's front entrance with Baphomet winging close behind.

CHAPTER TWENTY-SIX

Ben

Ben shouted and threatened but it made no impression on the devil who hauled him back to the cell.

The room felt airless and constrictive and wrong without Annie there. This wasn't how things were supposed to go. He should be the one negotiating with Heaven—him, the debater, the analytical one, the fast-thinking one.

He checked again for hidden panels. Nothing. He listened for sounds of other prisoners. Nothing. He pulled out the tiny memo pad and pen that he always carried in his pocket and jotted a note to Satan demanding release from the cell.

He wondered about the game.

There were things that couldn't be accounted for by even the most advanced virtual reality. His bladder, for instance. He hadn't needed to urinate since they left Mill Valley. Hadn't eaten anything or had any bowel movements either. Perhaps the game simulated the passage of time. It was possible they'd only been playing for a few hours, although it felt like days.

Or perhaps it wasn't a game. Perhaps it was real.

It certainly felt real—the hot, dry air he was breathing, the warm stone of the cell wall under his palms.

But Ben had studied enough accounts of supernatural visitations to know that *feeling* had nothing to do with reality. Every day people claimed to have been visited by God or kidnapped by aliens. They all insisted that their experiences felt real. Did that mean they actually had coffee and donuts with Jesus or E.T.? Of course not.

Still, Ben had built his life on questioning assumptions. And when you question assumptions, if you have any intellectual integrity, you have to include your own. So he let himself wander down the path. Perhaps this place was real. And if Hell were real, the Bible must be real. Jesus must be real. God must be real...

Impossible. All these sensations were just neurons misfiring, some kind of biochemical phenomenon. There was always a rational explanation for things, even if science hadn't yet progressed to a point of recognizing it. The key was to avoid taking refuge in comforting, easy bullshit.

But was it bullshit to believe that he was in Hell? Or was it bullshit to deny that he was in Hell? Alone in the cell, his sniper-sharp debater's mind turned its guns on itself.

Proposition: Hell is real.

Arguing in the affirmative, Benjamin J. Maple.

Arguing in the negative, Benjamin J. Maple.

He went round and round, building argument on top of elaborate argument, ending back where he started but hemmed in by higher walls. The cell grew smaller and more confining. That was just his imagination, though; he was sure of it.

Wasn't he?

Game versus reality. Senses versus logic. Science versus religion. When it got too circular, he veered off to thoughts of Defoe in the pillory, Galileo under house arrest, Solzhenitsyn in the Gulag, and how those great minds had borne up under duress. Now he too was in a prison cell, but he was not managing very well. And what was the revolutionary idea that had earned him this punishment? For all his celebrity, had he ever done anything that would change history? Was self-doubt one of the obstacles to overcome in this game? And why did Annie get to fly off to negotiate with Heaven when it had been his idea?

He paced the cell. He shook the bars. He yelled into the hallway—"Hey! Somebody! Anybody there?"—and no one answered.

Ben's thoughts jangled like a car radio stuck between stations. So much static: he wondered, for the first time in his life, if he might shake himself apart.

CHAPTER TWENTY-SEVEN

Annie

Belial smelled like warm, curdled swamp water. He clearly had nothing but contempt for Annie and held her as far away as possible while they traveled.

They flew directly up towards what on Earth would have been the stratosphere. The palace and clifftop and orange sea receded. Soon she could see nothing but hazy grey, save for Baphomet's small figure winging frenetically behind them.

"How far is it?" she asked.

Belial didn't answer.

His wings were wider and strokes more powerful than Baphomet's, and Annie sensed they were traveling further and faster than on the journey from Earth. There was none of the turbulence of the passage from Earth, just the all-encompassing grey that was like flying through a can of house paint.

If only Satan had chosen Ben instead of her. If only she were home with Mary. And what was Mary doing right now—was she hungry, wet, crying? Annie's whole body ached with longing but, weirdly, her breasts didn't feel the sore heat that came after hours without nursing. It made sense in a bizarre Hellish way: no one got

183

hungry or thirsty in Hell, they didn't need sleep, they didn't pee. Apparently breasts didn't lactate either.

They flew for hours, maybe days. Had Satan and his followers plummeted through this same space after losing their rebellion? More hours passed, perhaps more days, with nothing but grey and the trailing speck that was Baphomet. Finally the grey haze seemed rosier. The sky itself seemed to thicken. She felt increased effort in Belial's wingbeats, and the air around them rippled the light like a coating of Vaseline. Belial heaved upwards like a swimmer doing the butterfly stroke.

"The boundary waters," he muttered.

Flashes of yellow light appeared through the grey. Then the haze vanished altogether and the air turned golden and a spit of land emerged like a silver island floating in the sky. They were castaways surfacing from the depths, paddling for their lives, and she was ecstatic to see the shore.

Belial heaved himself up to the spit, dropped her, pivoted and started flapping down and away.

"Wait—" Annie called, but he didn't look back. Below, as his dark shape disappeared into grey distance, she saw Baphomet turn back too. Both gone.

So this was Heaven? Or boundary waters, whatever they were? The air seemed thin and normally breathable. Annie examined the ground beneath her. From a distance it had looked like silver sand, but those grains of sand were in fact tiny translucent spheres with refracted rainbows like soap bubbles. She shifted a foot and the spheres rippled. She took a step and pushed forth widening circles of rainbow waves. It was like walking on a waterbed. It held her weight, but she had to move slowly and constantly adjust her balance.

If only Trua were here.

He'd been at her side throughout Hell. She felt incomplete entering this new strange place without him—his defensive instincts, his sharp eyes and ears.

Another step. The spheres rippled.

Which way? There didn't seem much of a choice. Behind her, the spit dropped off into air. So, slowly, rocking from foot to foot on the fluid sand, she headed up the slope and away from the shore.

* * * * *

Annie hadn't gone far when she saw the fence. A procession of gold pillars and bars, it was tall as a three-story building but obviously no barrier to winged beings. Perhaps, like the walls around the devil city, it was for show—a symbolic or psychological boundary.

The bars were spaced too tightly to slip through. Far above, they were capped with gold leaves and flowers like the perimeter of an oversized Versailles. Beyond the bars, the ground continued its gentle upslope and the spheres gave way to silvery-green grass. Distant slim trees sported golden trunks and leaves of that silvery green. On the horizon, faint hints of hills.

She followed the fence, looking for an entrance. The silvery lawn beckoned with the soothing allure of a baked apple, a turned-down hotel bed, a sunlit patio. She felt none of the unease that had been a constant in the deserts of Hell. The only frisson of anxiety came from remembering the drop-off behind her—the halt of firm ground, the days of freefall below.

There.

Far ahead, beyond the gate, something was moving.

185

Large, silver, winged—an angel.

It was flying slowly along the gate towards her, peering across without any urgency. The hairs on Annie's arms stood up. She felt a breath-sucking sense of lightning about to strike.

Stay calm.

Angels were friendly to humans, weren't they?

"Hello!" Annie shouted. She waved her arms. "I need to talk to you!"

Even from a distance, she could see the angel's surprise. It jerked to a halt in mid-air, peered in her direction, then gave a single determined flap. It landed across from her, just beyond the fence.

"A human? Embodied? What are you doing here?"

The creature was a day-versus-night version of the devils. Human-featured and larger than life, its skin was a glassy, almost translucent, silver. It sparkled like a stream in the sunlight, but with no sun here, the angel seemed to be both a source and a reflection of light. Silver feathered wings unfurled from its shoulders like royal banners. It wore a short silver linen tunic with a braided gold belt and carried a golden sword. No talons on these feet; instead, small secondary wings protruded from its heels like the Greek god Hermes.

"I need to talk to someone in charge, maybe the Archangel Michael. Can you help me?"

The angel peered past Annie to where the land dropped into sky. It had unsettling golden eyes and thick golden hair that radiated like a divine Afro. It was undeniably real and solid, yet also light and ethereal.

"You're alone?"

"Yes."

"How did you get here?"

186

"It's complicated. A devil brought me, but I'm not part of them. I'm trying to protect Heaven. And Earth."

"Wait here." The angel looked past her, nervous. "Stay close to the gate. I'll bring Michael."

"Thank you. Your name is—" Annie attempted, but the being had already turned and was winging uphill across the light green meadow.

* * * * *

A group of angels armed with gold swords and shields peered through the fence at Annie. One, presumably Michael, stood ahead of the others with a longer sword and a golden breastplate over his tunic. Gold curls meandered below broad shoulders. His eyes were an even brighter shade of that inhuman gold, and a cleft in his chin suggested a Hollywood-casting Superman. Like the first angel he exuded airy lightness, but his voice was dark with suspicion.

"Who are you and what are you doing here?"

Annie explained. Michael listened intently through the bars but did not invite her in. As she spoke, more angels fluttered down and formed a crowd, whispering to each other. When she was done, Michael frowned.

"Your whole story is impossible," he said. "The Fallen shouldn't be able to bring objects from Earth into Hell. Souls of the damned can't spontaneously leave the fire, and they certainly can't return to life. Nor can they be transported from Earth to Hell again." The golden eyes peered accusingly at her.

"I don't understand it either. I'm worried—"

"These could all be lies planted by the Adversary."

"I'm telling the truth."

Michael stepped away to confer with some of the angels. While they huddled, another angel inched close to the golden bars.

"When you were down there..." The angel hesitated, then spoke in a whisper. "Did you happen to meet a devil named Rimmon?"

Annie shook her head.

"One named Mastema?"

"No."

"Sariel? She was a wonderful seamstress, weaving tunics..."

Annie shook her head again. The angel sighed and slipped back into the crowd. Michael returned from his huddle.

"Your claims are too worrisome to ignore. These rivals to Lucifer: are they powerful?"

"I...think so." In the battle in the devil city, Beelzebul and Zarphan had more combatants than she could count. Plus fireballs, cavalry, cannons. Now maybe nukes.

"And Zarphan is the one with the human weapons?"

"Yes. Tell me, if he uses a nuclear bomb, would it harm the Earth?"

"I don't know. In the past, the borders between realms were impassable except to divine beings. Now, perhaps not."

"Can you stop him?"

"Of course. All is possible through the Lord."

"And you will? You'll stop him from using the bomb?"

"It's our duty to defend Heaven and Earth from evil. From those traitors." A murmur of assent ran through the crowd. "Our Lord should have eradicated them after the rebellion. His mercy is great, but their perfidy is greater. So yes, we'll destroy any of their weapons that could harm Earth. First, though, we need to return you to the mortal world, where you belong—"

"Wait! My brother's here too. Imprisoned in Satan's palace. We have to rescue him."

Michael narrowed his eyes. "That's more difficult. Not every angel can cross into Hell, let alone penetrate Pandaemonium." He turned away from her again, conferred with the others, then turned back.

"We'll free your brother as part of the operation against Zarphan. Meanwhile, you need to wait there, on your side of the gate." He smiled at her for the first time, a smile more golden than his hair. "We look forward to having you join us on this side someday, Annie. But not just yet."

Gratitude swamped her. Gratitude to Michael for believing her. Gratitude to the angels for protecting Earth, for agreeing to retrieve Ben and take them both home. Michael had even suggested she was destined for Heaven! All the frustration of her earthly attempts at prayer fell away. She would never complain about God's silence after this. She would be thankful and worshipful for the rest of her life. She would ask God for nothing...

Except maybe one thing.

"If it's okay to ask...can you tell me if my mother is in the fire? And if she is, can you get her out?"

Silence draped the silver beach and grass. "Annie," the archangel said solemnly. "There are billions upon billions of human souls in Heaven and Hell, so many that even we angels can't keep track of them. Only our Lord knows who's here and who's down there. And we can't alter God's judgment."

There had barely been time to hope but she still felt crushed. Michael turned away, ready to leave.

"Michael? Please? Just one more thing?"

He swung around sharply, golden eyes flashing. Full-blown anger? Or just annoyance?

"If it's going to be a while before you can take Ben and me home…and if it's not too difficult…there's a friend I'd like to see. Just briefly. He's another shaken-loose human, but he stayed in Hell when I went back to Earth. He may be in the city that Beelzebul built."

"Not afraid to press your luck, eh?"

Her stomach clenched; she'd gone too far. But then his mouth twitched in a way that might have been a smile.

"You've proven yourself a loyal servant of our Lord, Annie. You've aided the forces of light. So yes, you can visit your friend while we work the rest of this out." He glanced at his cohorts, then back to her. "He's in Beel-zebul's city, you say? I've wanted to see what that greedy worm is up to. I'll take you there myself."

CHAPTER TWENTY-EIGHT

Baphomet

Baphomet trailed Belial down through the abyss. He was a braggy, lazy devil who never deigned to say a word to her, so why bother keeping up with him? She let Belial wing out of sight and drifted downwards, flapping just enough to keep moving.

With each flap, she felt more powerful and proud. She was strong enough to fly to Heaven and back! Strong enough to travel to Earth too, hauling those heavy humans. She deserved respect, but what did she get?

Couldn't find her way to Heaven if you laid out a trail of angel feathers.

You can go. Or not. It doesn't matter to anyone.

It was Belial's fault, she decided. Belial and the other senior devils. When they were around, Satan had no use for her. She wished they'd never come back to the palace. Things were better when it was just Satan and her. No, that wasn't true. Things were better now. Baphomet was so happy—explosively, deliriously happy—to see Satan emerged from his torpor, back in the fullness of his glory.

She just wished he would be happy to see *her*.

Drifting down, she peered into the unrevealing grey and wondered at the depth of the abyss.

God must have really hated us to banish us so far away.

Baphomet would never forget the fall: cataclysm of bodies, armor, horses, and weapons crashing down, down, down. Wings flailing and legs kicking, angels climbing onto each other in desperate efforts to halt their fall, arms grabbing for purchase but only pulling each other down faster and more heavily into the depths. Swords fell like windmills, blades over handles, slicing through angelic flesh. Loosed shields crashed from body to body. Horses screamed. Angels cursed. At some point in the fall, their bodies started changing—darkening, solidifying. And when they crashed into the sea of fire, the change was complete. Feathers burned away. Inner light melted away. They emerged as tarnish and leather and talon—the hard fire-tested beings they were today.

Baphomet had wandered shell-shocked amidst the smoldering throng on the shore until *he* emerged.

He brought her back to herself, brought them all back to themselves.

"Coal under pressure becomes diamond," he'd said. *"You are diamond. I swear to you with the light and power of the morning star that we will never submit."*

Now, far below, she glimpsed orange in the grey. The fires of Hell. Home.

Baphomet heaved her wings and veered away from the sea of fire and towards the clifftop plain surrounding Pandaemonium.

* * * * *

Satan and Belial were ringed by the usual clique of senior devils, laughing, when she arrived in the great hall. No one greeted her. She flapped quietly out the door that led down to the dungeon.

In his cell, the human male sat against the wall, looking down at the floor. Nothing had changed in the cell since she'd last been there, but he seemed more...ragged. She alit next to the bars and he jerked his head up. He looked as disoriented as if he'd just come out of a cave into the light.

"Hello. Your sister arrived safely at Heaven. I thought you might want to know."

The man regained his bearings. He recognized her. He gave his shoulders a shake and sat up straighter.

"It's a long trip. But we got her there safely."

The "we" was a bit of a stretch. But the man wouldn't know the difference, and she liked the look of gratitude in his eyes.

"Thank you."

His voice scraped like a rock that hadn't been moved in a long time. There was really nothing else to say to him, but on Earth he'd called her wings beautiful. She didn't want to leave just yet.

"How'd it go?" he asked. "Did she talk to God or Michael?"

"I don't know. I didn't stay to see."

"What happens now?"

Uncomfortably, she had no answer. She shifted from foot to foot, wings rippling.

"Say." The man's eyes widened as if he'd just remembered something. He stood up stiffly, reached into his pocket, and pulled out a white piece of paper that was smaller than his hand. "Would you take this to Satan?"

"No!"

She pulled back. The paper was covered with inscrutable black marks—more of that writing she'd seen on Earth. It could be a trick. It could be dangerous.

"It's just asking to see Satan. Nothing more—"

"I said no!"

"Here. Read it for yourself—"

Was he taunting her? She felt shut out and furious. She seized the piece of paper, glared at it, and threw it into the dust.

"Stupid human with your stupid writing. I don't care what it says. The Great Satan doesn't care what it says—"

"Wait." The man was looking at her in an intent way that made her uncomfortable. "You can't read English? No, that's not it. You can't read at all?"

"Shut up, stupid human," she said, and spun away down the corridor.

* * * * *

She returned later to pick up the crumpled paper. It was evidence that she'd been talking to the human prisoner; no other devil should see it.

"Give me everything in your pockets," Baphomet ordered the man. She'd make sure there were no other hidden surprises. He handed over more small pieces of paper, bound together by circles of wire, and a writing tool. She turned to go but the man called her name.

"Baphomet, wait! Would you like to learn to read?"

"What?"

194

"I can teach you. Even without my notebook."

"No. Absolutely no."

"We can use the walls like a blackboard. Do you have any rocks that could make a white mark? Like chalk?"

"No!" Anyone could see human marks on the walls. She would be ridiculed, punished, maybe even exiled.

Still, learning to read...

The man seemed to be thinking. He was a smart one, for a human. In some ways he reminded her of Satan. A puny, diminished, mortal Satan, almost unrecognizable, but still there was a tiny spark of Satan's command.

"Sand, then." He gestured down at the floor of his cell, which was bare rock. "Bring in some sand. We can spread it out and draw letters in it."

After they drew the letters, they could wipe them away. Scatter the sand. Who would notice some extra sand in a dungeon?

"All right," she said. "I can get sand. But no tricks, human."

* * * * *

Ben—she had started thinking of the human by his name—traced a vertical line with an attached semicircle in the black gravel on his side of the iron bars. She copied it on hers.

"The letter 'b,'" he said. "Sounds like 'buh.' Like in Baphomet."

"B," she repeated quietly. "Buh." How elegant—the simplicity of the line and then the fullness of the curves. It was thrilling to think that this was the start of her own name. It was thrilling to hear him speak it.

195

"And this is the letter 'a.'" He drew another figure, a circle with a small vertical line clinging to it. "It's trickier. It can sound like a lot of different things. Ah. Aw. Ay. *Cat. Awful. Baseball.*"

She knew about cats. They were like that animal, the dog, she'd fed on Earth. Its sand-rough tongue, its big eyes.

"Baseball?" she asked.

"Never mind. 'A' as in *name.*"

"Oh. I get it." She traced a 'b' and then an 'a.' "So this could be *bah.* Or *baw.* Or *bay.*"

"Yes!" The man beamed at her. She liked that.

"Almost...*Ben*," she said.

He beamed even more. She'd known he would. She was delighted by her power to make him happy, like the dog.

"You're really smart, Baphomet, no matter how those others treat you. You are. Now, this is a 't.' The sound is 'tuh.'" He drew a vertical line, then an intersecting horizontal line, and she froze. A cross!

"Stop it! No tricks! I told you, no tricks!"

If anyone saw it, she'd be exiled for sure. She reached through the bars and smashed his designs, scattering sand across the cell. She withdrew her arm and smashed hers too. The 'b.' The 'a.' All gone.

"No tricks. You broke your promise."

Baphomet flapped up and away without another look.

* * * * *

She couldn't stay away, though. She went around mouthing *bah* and *tah* and *bay* and *tay* to herself. She needed to learn more letters.

When she returned, Ben looked relieved. Before Baphomet could issue any threats or warnings, he was apologizing. Or explaining. Although it had looked like a cross, he said, it wasn't *the* cross.

"Letters are different from pictures, in the Latin alphabet at least. They represent sounds, nothing more. But even with pictures, a cross doesn't always represent Christianity. There are plenty of cross-shaped things on Earth that have nothing to do with Jesus. Telephone poles. Hanging scales. The molecule laminin. The hilts of daggers."

Daggers she understood. Devils carried daggers into battle. So maybe his cross-shaped 't' was okay after all. She palmed the floor on her side of the bars, gathering some of the scattered gravel back into a pile. She would make a 't.'

Ta. Tab. What if you reversed those letters to make *b-a-t*?

"Bravo," he said. "Then you have *bat*, which is a small, winged mammal on Earth. With wings like yours, only much smaller. Or a bat for hitting things, like in baseball."

There it was, that damned baseball again.

There was so much she didn't know about Earth. About the universe.

* * * * *

She asked him questions. About himself, starting with the way he looked.

"Are all male humans so scrawny?" she asked. "And do they all have such skimpy hair? The way your scalp is bare near your forehead and up at the top...it looks like something's missing."

Ben flushed. "It's called male pattern baldness. Some people get it earlier than others."

She asked about family. What did it mean that he and Annie were brother and sister?

"We have the same mother and father. The word for that in English is siblings."

"Yes, I know," she said impatiently. "In Heaven, all the angels were siblings. God created all of us. But what does it *mean*? Do you treat her better than the humans who are not your siblings? Is she your second-in-command?"

"Our families aren't military hierarchies. Annie was born second, but she's not second-in-command. She doesn't follow my orders. Although sometimes I wish she did." Ben flashed her a grin. She guessed this was supposed to be funny, though she didn't know why. He continued.

"People don't necessarily treat their siblings better than non-siblings. In fact, many people treat their family members worse than strangers they'd meet on the street. So it's more about shared experience and emotional intensity. The affection is more intense, *and* the anger is more intense. Then there's the genetic component. Siblings share a lot of inherited traits, from hair color to musical ability. But human personality is a mix of nature and nurture. And genetics don't determine the character of family relationships..."

Baphomet lost track of what he was saying. It sounded terribly complicated and made her glad she didn't have human siblings. But what was even more confusing was when Ben told her that he didn't believe in God.

"What do you mean?" she said. They had moved on from b's and t's to complicated letters like c, which could sound like a hiss or a crackle or a crunch. "God isn't something you choose to believe or not believe. God just *is*. Can you choose not to believe in your foot? In your male pattern baldness?"

"You can *see* those things. Touch them. You can't see or touch God. There's no scientific evidence supporting the existence of a god."

"I couldn't see Annie either the first time she was here. But I knew she existed. I heard her. I *smelled* her."

Ben leaned forward over the 'ca's and 'ch's in his pile of sand, an intent look on his face. His forehead almost touched the bars.

"Baphomet. Before the fall, when you were in Heaven. Did you see God? What was God like?"

She was stumped. For millennia, a purple rage had risen up whenever she thought of God. God the victor. God the punisher. God the rigid. God the unfair. It was almost impossible to remember what she'd known of God before that.

"God was..."

She remembered angels singing to God. Praising God. Weaving tapestries to honor God. She remembered the flowers she had picked for garlands to honor God.

She couldn't remember God.

Stupid human with his stupid questions!

Baphomet was about to shout at Ben—to curse and fly away and leave him alone in his stupid cell. But something stopped her.

"I don't know," she said quietly. "I don't...remember."

For a while after that, he became strangely gentle with her. He asked her questions about her old life. Not big unanswerable questions about God, but little questions like what were her favorite places for picking flowers. It made her happy to talk about that, so she told him more. She told him about meeting Satan and joining the rebellion and the long millennia since then. Satan's depression and recovery. The devil civil war and Satan's plan for a mass suicide. Her one-day visit to Earth.

The last person she'd talked to like this was Annie, during Annie's first visit to Hell. But she told Ben even more than she'd told his sister.

"Baphomet," he murmured, turning the syllables over on his tongue the way she had tongued that smooth, cold food on Earth.

And one by one, he taught her all the letters in her name: b...a...p-h that together sounded like f...o...m...e...and, at the very end, the letter that wasn't a cross, t.

T as in talk. T as in try. T as in touch.

"Baphomet, may I touch your wing again?" he said during one of their sessions.

Her breath caught. There was that reflex again to flee down the hall. But she gingerly extended the edge of a wing through the bars.

"Thank you," he said. "Like I remembered. Warm yet cold. Extraordinary."

He didn't let go immediately, but stroked the edge of her wing ever so gently.

Nothing bad happened.

They went on with the lesson.

CHAPTER TWENTY-NINE

Annie

Michael deposited Annie at the foot of the mountains near the devil city. "I'll meet you here once we're done with Zarphan," he said. "Don't take risks. Stay hidden. This won't take long." He launched himself upward and vanished into the grey sky.

Annie stretched her arms. The flight with Michael had been as soothing as nursing Mary, and a warm well-being flowed through her. She was sufficient, she was whole, she was part of a larger golden wholeness. She'd done what was needed to protect Earth, and Michael would take care of the rest.

And now she would see Trua! The flight's serenity had dissolved her fears that he might be lost in the desert or back in the fire. He was here and she would find him. She glanced around, noted the location so she could return, and set off across the plain to the city walls.

Black gravel under her feet. Dry sulfurous air in her lungs. It was as if no time had passed since her first visit to Hell. But Mary was seven months old. Her mother was dead. Ben was trapped in Satan's palace.

The devils could see her now too.

That liquid well-being ebbed. Annie glanced around nervously. This time she had good comfy sneakers and sturdy jeans. She was grateful not to feel every pebble under her feet, but on the whole she'd rather be invisible.

What if she couldn't see Trua?

It was possible. She didn't understand all these different iterations of being alive in Hell. What if *he* couldn't see *her*? What if they walked right past each other in the city and didn't notice?

And what did she want to do when she saw him anyway? They couldn't hug. They couldn't touch. *I've missed you so much.* She could tell him that.

I love you. I miss you. I wish you could see how Mary is turning into a little person.

Come back with me, if Michael lets you.

Entering the city, she was taken aback by the damage. The fallen buildings made it difficult to slink along walls, and debris turned the streets into an obstacle course. Annie had been terrible at navigating the city even when it was intact, and this was worse. What had she been thinking? Why had Michael agreed to bring her here? She was risking everything—home, Mary, life—on an emotional impulse.

The street ended in a mass of rubble. She backtracked and took another street. She was doing it all wrong. The first rule of not getting lost was to pick a path and stay on it. She couldn't help herself, though, and each turn increased her panic.

Another turn. Still no sign of the plaza.

And another turn. Nothing.

No, wait. A door near the corner looked familiar. Her heart lifted: the street of the safe house.

She broke into a jog, hopping over chunks of fallen stone. Halfway down the block she spotted the familiar building. When she was barely a house away, the door opened. Someone was pushing it, coming out. It was Trua.

She stopped short. He stared at her. She wanted to cry and laugh and hug him, to shout her relief so loudly that even Heaven would hear.

"Annie?" Trua said. His face fell dark. "Didn't the arch take you home?"

She nodded.

"Then what in the name of the gods are you doing here?"

* * * * *

Trua refused to let her into the safe house. Instead, he led her around the corner into an empty building on the next street. He looked terrible—new lines across that long forehead, his scars barely visible under all the black dust. His body was as compactly muscled as ever but his face seemed hollow.

Annie asked about the others. He told her that Eiko was dead, Ishaq was gone, and Haisheng had left on a foolish mission to find Satan.

"Henry?" she asked, and he shook his head.

"Oudine?"

He didn't answer, just looked away.

She babbled an explanation of her return to Hell, hoping for a smile, a word of welcome, anything to reestablish their connection. "I missed you so much," she said, but now that she could actually speak the words to him, they sounded artificial, even robotic.

She'd forgotten his silences and his sullenness when displeased. Over the past year there'd been so many things she'd wanted to tell him, and now he didn't want to hear any of them. They sat there. Eventually Trua stood up.

"I need to go."

"Where?"

"Haisheng left me in charge of some freed wraiths. I was on my way to see them."

"I'll come with you."

"No."

"Please?"

"No."

"Please! Don't leave me here alone! I'm...afraid." It wasn't true, but she would say anything to stay near him. He frowned, then shrugged, which she took for assent.

Following him down the empty street felt so familiar, as if time had looped back on itself. Could her entire return to life have been a dream? Or maybe she was in bed in Mill Valley, and this was the dream?

She wished it were a dream.

She wished Trua were happy to see her.

Her sneakers made shushing, squeaking sounds on the stone. She was audible as well as visible. Trua stopped before another intact building.

"I'm training them," he said stiffly. "If I don't show up regularly, they backslide. Wait for me here."

"Can't I come in?"

"No."

"Please?"

He stared at her for a long time, then shrugged. He knocked a short rhythmic pattern on the iron door and pushed it open. Annie just saw dimness; then her eyes adjusted and settled on a shifting grey mass in a corner.

"Three of you, it doesn't matter who," he said gruffly. "Come out here."

The mass rippled like a department store rack of gauzy scarves but no one came forward.

"That's an order." He shot Annie a quick, hard look that was almost a dare. Then he picked up a long piece of iron, and brandished it.

"Come out here. Or else."

Finally a wraith stepped forward. Then two more. They huddled together.

"Line up." He reached down to a pile of rods and proffered one to each of the three wraiths.

"Take it. Form a circle facing out. Remember? Now what if someone comes at you like this? What do you do?"

He took a few steps back, raised his baton, and leapt towards them. The wraiths dropped their rods with a loud clang and collapsed into a shapeless huddle.

"Get up. GET UP. That's an order. Now."

The wraiths didn't move.

"Get up." Trua prodded them with his baton until they rose. Annie's chest tightened with horror. Trua thrust the rods back into the wraiths' hands.

"Raise your rods and hammer them down. Do it right or I'll call the demons. I swear it. Now try again."

He stepped back, lifted his rod, and leapt. Once again they collapsed.

"Blast you. Blast all of you." Trua shook his baton at the wraiths, who cringed in their pile. "Get up. Blast all of you, get up and fight like men."

He turned to Annie. "There. Are you happy now that you came in here?"

* * * * *

Annie trailed him to another empty building, where they sat in dim silence. She didn't know what to say.

Trua was a monster. The year in Hell had made him someone she no longer recognized. Or perhaps the brutality had always been there and she'd refused to see. Billie had warned her. Billie was a liar and a murderer, and nothing Billie said should matter, but there it was, lodged in her mind, as stubborn and uninvited as a tick: *I told you so.*

Trua stared at the ground.

"How could you?" Annie blurted. "They're traumatized. They need respect, and kindness, and care—"

"You don't understand."

"That was like the overseers—"

"You don't understand."

"I thought I knew you! I *loved* you! I came back here for you!"

Her voice quavered. Trua exploded in rage.

"You came back! You came back!" His eyes were wild and his scars bulged through the dust. "What about Mary? What about your life? You were alive and you threw it away! You should have just stayed there—"

The building trembled.

It was a faint tremble, but they both leapt up. Trua pushed open the door and they peered at the empty street. Whatever caused it was far away. Again, the ground shivered.

"Another battle?" Trua murmured.

"Michael," Annie whispered. "His attack must have started."

"The wraiths." Trua glanced up the street and broke into a run towards the house where they were hidden.

CHAPTER THIRTY

Kezia

Kezia heard trumpets.

They were far off, muffled by layers of rock, but the brass summons was unmistakable. Under her feet, the stone floor of her cell vibrated. What kind of trumpet could make a mountain vibrate?

She lurched over to the door. Somewhere beyond the empty corridor, she heard shouts and the clatter of metal. The trumpets sounded again.

"What's going on? What's happening?"

The corridor remained empty. The shouts continued but were too distant to shape into words. Suddenly her cell—the whole corridor, maybe the whole mountain—shook with an explosion. Then another one.

"Help! Ardat!"

More explosions. The mountain could collapse on top of her. She reached through the bars and waved frantically.

"Help! Anybody!"

More trumpets, explosions, shaking. Could it be the forces of Heaven? The end of days?

"Jesus! Help me. Save me." It was a breathless, staccato, machine-gun of a prayer.

The cell shuddered from continued blasts. Stones clattered outside in the corridor. A shoebox-sized chunk of rock dislodged from the ceiling and shattered on the cell floor, and she leapt back against the wall.

Closer than the shouting now, she heard the rush of pumping wings. Ardat appeared and unlocked the door, and Kezia ran to her. The devil scooped her up and flew through the rubble-strewn corridor, panting. Devils with armored breastplates and swords crowded the passageway and pushed towards the fortress entrance. Other devils hauled what looked like cannons and cannonballs. Some were shouting; others were cursing. Ardat veered away from the throng, down several faceless corridors, and hauled her through a narrow gate into open air.

"Stay here. I'll come back for you." Ardat lowered Kezia onto a shelf behind a rock outcropping and flew off.

Battle convulsed the mountain. Devils hurtled past Kezia's ledge, pursued by—yes—angels. Silver wings and golden breastplates streaked through the air and swords of gold sliced the grey sky. The devils had cannons, but the angels launched swirling projectiles of golden fire from their swords. They outnumbered the devils, or perhaps they'd managed to surprise them; in either case, the devils were being routed.

Above, an angel commander hovered over the scene, directing troops. Another angel flapped nearby holding a banner with a golden cross on a field of white. Kezia's heart leapt. She shoved aside her fear of heights, moved to the tip of her ledge, and waved frantically.

"Help me!"

They didn't notice. She shouted but it was no use. The rock under her feet jolted as a nearby arm of the mountain exploded into flame. Three angels swooped away from it towards a lower section, pointed their swords to hurl fireballs, and it exploded too.

The devils were scattering towards distant ridges. The angels seemed to have captured the immediate area. A rough arm jerked Kezia's waist, and Ardat pulled her up. Bizarrely, the devil hauled a wooden harp under her other arm.

"Retreat," Ardat panted, and they joined the flock of devils fleeing across the plain. Kezia flailed—*so close! if they would just notice her!*—but the angels were dueling with their last remaining opponents. As Ardat carried her away, her potential rescuers dwindled to tiny, glistening sparks.

* * * * *

They regrouped in a canyon. Ardat deposited Kezia and the harp on a ledge high in the rock and settled below with Zarphan and some other devils. Looking down the canyon, Kezia saw a long river of devils, thousands, more than she could count, sprawled, tending their wounds, commiserating.

She heard enough to piece things together. The devils had been surprised and overwhelmed by the Archangel Michael. Their guards were ambushed, their weapons stored too deep in the mountain to access quickly. And apparently the storerooms were Michael's target. He hadn't tried to take prisoners, hadn't seemed interested in wounding or crippling. His forces captured the main entrance and searched the mountain. They obliterated the storerooms and manufactories and left. No pursuit of the fleeing devils: the angels let the vanquished trickle away across the plain, turned their gaze upwards, and returned to Heaven.

If only they'd seen her.

In the canyon below, the devils were sniping at each other. She glimpsed snarling faces, heard angry voices. Zarphan remained surprisingly calm and unflustered. At one point he reached down and, smiling, held up a pile of...papers? All this fighting, and he was hoarding *paper*?

She sank back against the rock and let the devils' bickering fade into background noise. She needed a plan. If she could get off this ledge, maybe she could hide in the desert. Maybe she could find one of those angels...

A shriek jolted her upright. No, not a shriek—a flock of shrieks, layered together like thousands of screaming hawks. She glanced up at a sky filled with wings.

A new horde of armed devils hovered over the canyon.

These weren't wounded and fleeing. They flapped boldly, heads high and swords raised, waiting for a command to attack. Zarphan and his followers scrambled, reaching for swords, lifting slightly off the ground, forming defensive circles. But even Kezia, with no military expertise, could see they were trapped.

Above the canyon, one devil moved to the front of the attacking army. He could have been a superhero from one of Jeremiah's old comics—gleaming dark body with hints of silver, sculpted muscles, and red eyes that beamed command.

Satan. *The* Satan—the one who had tempted and doomed Jeremiah. Who had doomed so many people. If she could get off this ledge, she would throttle him with her bare hands. *Jesus, give me wings. Give me a sword.* But she remained grounded and trapped.

"The game is over," Satan said, his voice gentle as a caress yet ringing through the canyon. "Michael has vanquished you. Again. As he always will. We've spent eternity playing a game where the rules and winner are predetermined by God. It's time to abandon those rules. End the game."

Murmurs spilled up the canyon. Zarphan and the fighters around him formed a tight circle, conferring.

"You were just crushed by Michael," Satan continued. "We could put you through that again. But we're giving you a choice. Join us to end this rigged game and show God that we are masters of our own destiny. Or resist and be crushed, and join us anyway in shackles."

The murmurs grew louder. The masses in the canyon seemed fluid, like water sloshing right then left as you tilt the bucket.

"What will it be?" Satan said. His voice rang louder, demanding. "Will you join us and end God's sham of a game?"

Zarphan raised his sword. He looked puny and ordinary next to Satan. He held the weapon awkwardly, a child tilting with a broom.

"Never!"

A hum of assent rose from the devils around him, who brandished swords too. But up the canyon, Kezia saw devils cradling injured arms and leaning unevenly on injured legs. They weren't ready for another battle. Wings rustled. Feet shuffled.

"I'll join you!" A male devil near Zarphan launched himself up from the canyon floor. Kezia recognized the stocky frame, the blunt features.

"Welcome, Turael." Satan looked pleased.

"Me too!" "Yes!" "I'm coming!"

Throughout the length of the canyon, devils shot skyward. Some carried their swords; others let their weapons clatter onto the rocks. The sky darkened with the combined mass of Satan's forces and Zarphan's deserters.

The canyon broke into chaos. Devils staying behind grabbed for weapons dropped by those taking off. Some rushed toward Zarphan and milled around, trying to form combat units, while others flapped frantically through the ravine, searching for paths of escape.

"All right then." Satan sounded mournful. "You've made your choice. Brothers and sisters...attack!"

Kezia threw herself back against the rock. Winged bodies coursed past. If the angel battle had been a rout, this was a massacre. Satan's forces plunged dark swords into tarnished bellies, lopped off wings and legs. Black blood spurted and streamed through the canyon.

Jesus, be my protector.

Before, she had prayed to be noticed. Now she prayed to be overlooked. She closed her eyes and hoped it would end soon.

Shrieks. Clash of metal. Crash of devil bodies and crack of devil bones. And through the clamor, a stench of burnt metal and curdled milk—

Ardat's rough arms grabbed her yet again and jerked her upwards. Kezia choked. Eyes shut tight, she lurched one way and another. Somehow Ardat was dodging through the mayhem, holding both Kezia and that harp. Finally they broke free and flew a straight line, the sounds of battle growing fainter.

"Where are we going?" she managed to croak through her terror.

"Away," Ardat snapped. "Somewhere they won't find us."

CHAPTER THIRTY-ONE

Ben

Ben stopped trying to figure out if this Hell place were real or a game. Great minds, he told himself, were able to live with uncertainty: he'd resolve the nature of this place when he had more facts.

Really, though, he was preoccupied with Baphomet.

The girl devil was extraordinary. She embodied such contradictions—self-absorbed yet curious, childishly impatient yet also dogged when there was something she wanted. She was whip smart. It was just a matter of time until she challenged Satan's demeaning treatment. Her curiosity was like a vine, tendrils slithering into cracks in a wall and slowly jimmying them wider.

Between their visits, he planned lessons for her— spelling, punctuation, sentence structure. Had he ever been this fascinated by a girl or woman?

Naomi Eisenberg in fifth grade. She asked him for homework help and gave him a box of English toffee for Valentine's Day. Ben liked the toffee, although it got stuck in his teeth. He set up an experiment to see how long it would take to dissolve a piece of toffee in a shot glass of saliva versus Coca Cola. He remembered that the cola won handily; he didn't remember anything else about Naomi.

Francie Blackwell. Long blonde hair and blue eyes, she was living proof that it wasn't just nerds who excelled at high school debate. They made out one night during a debate tournament in San Diego. The next day, she messed up a super-easy round on capital punishment and he was embarrassed to be seen with her.

Eve Anthony and Marla Graham. Physics majors and roommates at Princeton. Ben got involved with Eve, then decided he liked Marla better, and didn't understand why they both cut him off.

Nancy Wesolowska. Just a fling at Princeton.

Eve Ferber. A fling in New York.

Eve Crittenden. Did he have some subconscious obsession with Eves?

Masha Volkov. Three-night-stand at a conference in London, although they had terrific email exchanges about Russian politics for several years afterward.

*Columba Hayes. Winnie Chappel. Amy Marks...*There were quite a few others as he became famous. Ben prided himself on remembering every name—*shame on men who treat women as objects!* But there were none that he could honestly classify as relationships until Natasha.

Natasha was his equal, even when it came to height—six feet to his six-two. They met at a Cornell Medical Center fundraiser where he was speaking on the ethics of genetic screening. From the podium he'd noticed the billowing red hair that stood inches above the other female heads in the audience; when she approached him afterwards, he was delighted to find she was a post-doc biologist rather than the vapid trophy wife of some Wall Street donor.

They went to theatre. They went to concerts. They went to lectures on scientific topics that neither of them knew anything about. When she accompanied him to a conference in Geneva, he arranged a private tour of CERN for the two of them. He remembered her in the hotel room there, her silhouette against the floor-to-ceiling window, the glacial lake sparkling blue behind her. She wore only a bathrobe. She dropped the bathrobe.

Ben scorned romantic claptrap, but he went so far as to admit that Natasha might be "the one." He bought her a ring, although they decided to delay the wedding until she finished her post-doc.

Then she called it off.

She was completely rational about it. No tears, no blame. She said that he was distant and unavailable and that she needed someone more "present," which he assumed referred to his extensive out-of-town travel. He respected her level-headedness and that she wasn't trying to change him. They agreed to stay friends.

Annie showed up the following week expecting him to moan and wail. That's what she might have done, but not him. He was focusing on his work, moving forward, moving on.

Still, when Annie left, the apartment felt empty. There was a vacant shelf on the fridge door where Natasha's yogurts used to sit. The shower drained more smoothly without long red hairs clogging it, which should have pleased him. One evening, wrestling with a stubborn essay, he lay down on the living room rug and spotted a shiny metal hair clip under the couch. He held it to his nose and inhaled.

It gave no whiff of her. Organic compounds like those that create scent wouldn't adhere to a metal surface. Of course he knew that.

It was an inexpensive hair clip and he threw it away.

That night he dreamed he was shooting pool in a dive bar, where everyone else was drinking and talking and laughing. He was invisible. Alone. No one saw him pocket all the balls, including a masterful shot from behind his back that was worthy of a Hollywood movie.

Ben doubted he would ever again find someone as compatible as Natasha.

* * * * *

It was wrong, though, to compare Baphomet to Natasha. It was wrong to compare her to any of his girlfriends.

For starters, Baphomet was a child. And then she probably wasn't even a real person, just an avatar. During their lessons, Ben tried to figure out her function in the game, if this was in fact a game. Did she guard a valuable talisman like a map or a key? Was she keeper of some essential secret? Should he cajole her into setting him free?

"Homophones," he said. "Those are words that sound the same but have different meanings and different spellings. If you're saying 'hear' like what we do with our ears, you spell it H-E-A-R. If it's 'here' like a place, it's H-E-R-E."

The girl devil eyed the sandy floor as he traced the letters. She looked up at him and beamed.

"*Where* and *wear*. *There* and *their*."

"And *they're*."

She looked perplexed but when he started to spell it out in the sand, she grasped it at once, with pleasure.

"There are so many! *Haul* and *hall*. *Ball* and *bawl*. *Sun* and *son*. *One* and *won*—"

Her wings twitched and she wiggled back and forth as if about to dance from the rhythm of it all.

"*Red* and *read*. *Know* and *no*. *Sew* and—" She halted abruptly. "Is that poetry?"

"What?"

"*Know* and *no, sew* and *so*. Is that poetry?"

"It's a rhyme."

"Is that different from a poem?"

Ben wasn't listening. He'd noticed a seam on the shoulder of her tunic that looked unusually thick, like a pouch that could hide a talisman.

"There's something on your tunic—a wrinkle—may I straighten it out?"

Baphomet craned to look at her shoulder. She peered at him, suspicious. "All right. Fix it. Then tell me about poetry."

She leaned her shoulder up close to the bars. He reached through and touched the seam, patted his fingers up the ridge of her shoulder. It was just a seam. No pouch, no hidden clue. But as he lifted his hand from the fabric, it brushed against her hair.

From a distance, her hair looked thick and wiry. He'd assumed it would feel like a wire grill brush. But in fact it was soft—smooth as silk, soft as a rabbit.

"*Hair* and *hare*," he murmured.

He slid his thumb and forefinger along a length of hair. It was beyond silk. She stared at him, unreadable, but didn't flinch. He reached again, slightly higher, and let his hand rest on the side of her head. So soft. She

220

leaned into his touch and he felt an urge to stroke her neck. Natasha used to shiver when he touched her neck, but Baphomet was a child. She was an avatar. He should focus on clues for the game.

Far down the corridor, something clanged. They both lurched away from the bars.

"Clean it up," Baphomet said sharply, gesturing at the floor. Ben scattered the sand and erased the words. "Next time, you'll teach me about rhymes and poetry," she snapped, and flew off.

CHAPTER THIRTY-TWO

Kezia

Ardat's wings slammed the air, her jaw clenched and grim. Kezia felt the devil struggling to haul both her and the harp, and knew she shouldn't bother her with more questions. After perhaps an hour of flying, though, curiosity overcame her fear.

"The devil who led the attack. Was that Satan?"

"Miserable worm." Ardat spat the words and pumped her wings harder. "I curse the day he was created."

"What'll he do to Zarphan?"

"He can't kill us. But he can cripple us, imprison us. The worm! Using Michael to soften us up, then coming in for the final blow. Coward."

"Whoa. Satan was working with Michael?"

Ardat craned her neck to glare at Kezia with contempt. "You think it was coincidence he showed up right after Michael's attack? Even humans can't be that stupid."

Kezia fell silent. Angels partnering with the devil? Things weren't supposed to work that way. Below, the mouth of a small volcano glowed a hungry red. Clouds of black sulfurous steam swirled and Ardat veered to avoid them. Kezia's gut clenched: if Ardat tired and decided to let something drop, would it be the human or the harp?

Her body pulsed with the devil's powerful flaps as they left the volcano behind and churned across the desert.

* * * * *

They landed in the middle of a city—an empty, ruined city built entirely from black stone. Ardat flew low through the streets, glancing cautiously down each alley, and finally touched down in front of what looked like a large row house. She pushed open the iron door, peered inside, and lowered Kezia and the harp onto the floor. She was gentler with the harp than with Kezia.

The room was dim and empty except for a stone bench.

"It will do," Ardat muttered.

"Where are we?"

"The city of Azazel. Beelzebul's city until we routed him. It's abandoned now."

"What are we doing here?"

Ardat cast another of her "you idiot" looks.

"Hiding, of course."

"Wouldn't it be safer out in the desert?"

"Hiding under rocks like some human hermit? No thank you." Ardat paused, and when she continued her voice had lost some of its authority. "No one's living here now. Hopefully they won't think to look for us here."

Kezia peered around their shelter. It was better than her cell, but not by much. She assumed Ardat had brought her here as some kind of hostage or bargaining chip. She took a step toward the front door.

"Don't." Ardat glared. "If you try to escape, I'll put you in chains."

Kezia retreated. Ardat centered the harp in front of the bench, sat down, and ran her fingers lightly across the strings. Kezia's breath caught.

The sound was from another world—a place of light, beauty, and joy. It was like the first green shoots of crocus in Prospect Park after a long, slushy New York winter. It was like sunlight refracted through a crystal vase. It was nothing like Hell.

Ardat stopped and wiped dust from the frame. She spent a long time doing something with knobs that was probably tuning. Finally she played again—first a brief touch on the strings, then a series of single notes, then a scale.

Joy, fullness, light: the music was more beautiful than anything Kezia had ever heard. She imagined Ardat's blotchy skin and rough wings peeling away like the skin of a snake to reveal, inside, a gleaming angel. Ardat moved on from scales to bits of melody and then songs. Devil battles and Jeremiah's torment and the fight with George all vanished in the shimmer. Kezia had no words to express what she was hearing, only images.

A trip to the Botanical Gardens as a little girl: profusions of brilliant pink blossoms. The bush was bigger than she was. She couldn't see the top. Pink blossoms, all the way up to the sun.

Jones Beach in the fall: empty beach stretching for miles, sand cold and damp on her soles, sneakers in one hand and George's hand in the other. Two birds skimmed the breaking waves, wings moving in tandem like dancers.

Jeremiah's room on a Saturday morning: dust motes floating in lazy golden light. Her month-old son a sleeping caterpillar in his crib. She stood in the cracked door, careful not to wake him. From down the hall, the smell of George's buttered toast.

Ardat played and Kezia listened. Her captivity was transformed. Perhaps they were both captives. Perhaps neither was. Time broke like a geode into two sparkling pieces, music and silence. Ardat played and Kezia wandered paths of melody and memory. Ardat rested and the silence was a cool drink on a hot summer day.

"Your songs," Kezia said after a long time. It was hard to pull herself back to the world of language. "Do they have names?"

Ardat too seemed to return from a distance. "They did," she said slowly. "But not in any language you would understand. They used to be all about God but now I call them what I want. If you can't understand it by listening, I don't know how to explain it to you."

They went on like that, playing and listening and resting. Sometimes Kezia emerged from the music long enough to wonder if Ardat had any plan beyond hiding out and playing the harp. Then, while Ardat was playing an intricate piece that evoked the geometry of snowflakes, Kezia heard a scraping sound beyond the front door.

It might be an enemy devil. It might be a rescuer. If this were Brooklyn, she would have said it sounded like a very large rat.

Ardat didn't seem to notice. Before Kezia could decide whether to say something, the front door cracked open and a human woman peered in.

She was a wreck. She dragged herself along the floor, hair wild and tangled, her face a dusty, pale moon cratered with pockmarks. One of her legs trailed behind, seemingly broken.

"My angel," the woman whispered, staring at Ardat with wonder.

Ardat stopped playing, balanced the harp on the ground, and flapped up into the air. "Who said that?" she barked. "Who's there?" She glanced fiercely around the room but apparently couldn't see the woman.

"Don't stop playing. I beg you, don't stop!"

The woman sounded desperate. Ardat stared in the direction of the voice, then glared at Kezia.

"Is this a trick? I swear to you, if this is a trick—"

"No trick! It's a real person—over there by the door—"

"Then why can't I see her?"

"How am I supposed to know? I don't understand anything about this place."

Ardat glanced angrily between Kezia and the doorway. She propelled herself to the door with a single flap and groped for the woman, who seemed happy to be found.

"I'm here. Thank you. Oh, thank you! May I touch you?" The woman stretched both arms out and grabbed Ardat's hand. Ardat jerked away.

"Fool! Be careful!"

The woman beamed. "My angel. At last you've come! Please, keep playing. It's the most beautiful thing I've ever heard."

Ardat glared.

"Please. It's so beautiful. Just play. Please."

The devil flapped in place, as if weighing what to do. Finally she lowered herself back onto the bench and resumed playing. The woman dragged herself over to Kezia and propped herself against the wall, positioning her bad leg with her hands. She stared at Ardat and swayed in time with the music.

"So beautiful," she murmured when Ardat stopped to rest. "My angel."

"Are you blind?" Kezia hissed. "Can't you tell a devil from an angel?"

"Oh, I know devils." She turned to Kezia with a frown. "Father Adelbert was a devil. The Arab was a devil. He said my angels wouldn't come. But now they have!"

Jesus, give me patience. All this time in Hell without another human being and now that Kezia finally found one, she turned out to be crazy.

"What's your name?"

"Oudine."

"How'd you get here?"

"I don't remember. It's been so long. But now I've found my angel!"

"Why can't she see you?"

"Oh, they can't see any of us. But they can still hurt us. They have fireballs and swords and fire."

"Wait. There are more of you? More humans?" Kezia's heart lifted.

"Oh yes. Eiko's my friend. And Annie. But the men aren't so nice. Especially the Arab."

Kezia gave up. She would only get nonsense from this woman. But the possibility of other humans…

"Keep playing. Please!" The woman clapped her hands together and stared at Ardat, her face bright with devotion.

* * * * *

Kezia weighed her options. She could stay in this house with the amazing music. The harp constantly revealed new textures of notes like unexpected, delicious flavors of ice cream—raspberry chocolate, orange mint. George's harmonica was never like this. And Ardat had grown friendlier since the arrival of the crazy woman, beaming at Oudine's applause and letting Oudine touch her wings and sometimes even telling stories about the meadows of Heaven.

So she could stay. It was better than being in a devil war zone. Or she could try to escape and find those other humans that Oudine had mentioned. But what if she couldn't find them? What if she were obliterated by a fireball or thrown into the sea of fire?

Kezia wavered. Then George spoke to her. She didn't see him, but his voice emerged through Ardat's arpeggios, rich and full and 34 years young.

Kee, girl. Ain't no fire truck coming to save you. You need to get your own self out of that house. Right now.

The message was clear. Only a fool would disregard it.

"Oudine," she whispered. "I bet she'd show you how to play a note if you asked. Wouldn't that be amazing? To touch the harp and make music?"

Oudine didn't answer. But, some time later, she timidly asked Ardat to show her how to play a note. Ardat was silent and Kezia held her breath. After a long pause, Ardat nodded.

"Your hands must be completely clean. Wipe them on your garment."

Oudine squealed with excitement and set about rubbing her hands in the tatters of her dress. She dragged herself across the floor and up onto the stone bench beside the devil. Kezia stood, trying to look casual, and strolled across the room as if stretching her legs. Oudine nestled in close to Ardat, who groped for her hands and wiped them again on her rags. Kezia edged towards the door. Ardat took one of Oudine's hands and placed it on the strings. Kezia stepped closer to the door. Ardat was preoccupied, staring at the invisible hand to make sure it didn't violate her instrument. Devil hand and human hand together plucked a string and the sound reverberated through the room—buzzy, harsh, mortal.

Kezia pushed the door and ran. Creaky middle-aged knees and bad back be damned, she ran like a teenager, like Jeremiah when he used to run in Prospect Park, down the street and around the corner and then around another half dozen corners. She didn't stop and she didn't look back and her feet pounded a prayer that God would show her a path through the rubble and ruin of the devil city.

CHAPTER THIRTY-THREE

Annie

Annie waited for Michael at the rendezvous spot for what felt like days. She hunched against a large rock for cover and tried to relax. The angels must have won their battle: the sky was empty except for an occasional ragged-looking devil wobbling out of the mountains towards the city.

But what was taking Michael so long?

And Trua. They'd had a bleak farewell. Annie had followed him in silence to the city wall after they'd checked on the wraith houses. She couldn't afford to miss the rendezvous, and Trua seemed eager to have her gone.

"Good-bye," she'd said tentatively, almost a question. If he showed the slightest warmth, she'd ask him to return to the Bay Area with her. Michael could take them both; of course he could. But she needed to hear that this brutal, cold man was not the real Trua. She waited.

"Don't come back," he had said. "Not ever."

The words were like shutting a box. They were like the seal on the urn—tucked high on a living room shelf—that held her mother's ashes.

Now, waiting on the empty plain, Annie wondered if she'd been more upset by Trua's brutality to the wraiths or his coldness towards her. One of the things she had loved about him was his loyalty—the knowledge that, no matter what, he'd stand by her.

Loved. She'd just used the past tense.

He wanted nothing to do with her.

He wanted to play at being lord of the wraiths. Well, let him then.

Annie glanced at her wrist. She'd made a point of wearing a watch on this trip but it had stopped working during the flight from Earth. Now it sat there like a relic from Pompeii, eternally proclaiming 6:49 p.m.

Where was Michael?

What if the archangel had been injured or captured? Would any other angel know to come get her? How would she get home?

She couldn't pray aloud for help because the devils could hear prayers. She was no longer invisible. She was alone.

Please, Michael, she begged silently. But she knew that if he hadn't shown up by now, something terrible must have happened to him.

* * * * *

Finally she decided to return to the city. It had devils but also places to hide and figure out a plan. Out here she was just too exposed.

She sprinted back across the plain. The ruined streets felt more dangerous now. She heard—or did she imagine?—the scrape of leather wings. At one point a devil flew directly overhead and she held her breath, crouching. She heard a clatter somewhere behind her and broke into a run.

Turn here. No, here.

She rounded a corner and nearly screamed.

A middle-aged Black woman in jeans and a sooty, fraying blouse stood in front of her, holding her back and panting.

"Help me!" the woman gasped. "Hide me!"

Annie glanced around. Somehow she'd ended up on the street of the safe house. A blast of cold. No time for questions.

"Come on." Annie raced to the house and pushed open the door. There, massed in the back of the room, was a gaggle of wraiths. Beside them sat Trua, talking quietly to them. He leapt up.

"The angel didn't come?"

"No—"

"And you!" Trua shifted his gaze to the woman. Strangely, he seemed to recognize her. "You were—"

"Angel? What angel?" The woman stared at Annie.

"The Archangel Michael." Annie slumped down against the wall.

"Michael is coming for you?"

"Supposedly." Her panic had subsided enough to let hopelessness take over.

"To take you to Heaven?"

"To take me home. Back to Earth."

"Where's he going to get you?"

"Outside." Annie gestured wearily towards the street. "Beyond the walls."

"Why didn't he come?" Trua frowned.

"You mean to tell me"—the woman, excited, spoke over him—"that Michael is coming here, now?"

There was a stirring and a hum among the wraiths in the corner.

"The angel Michael himself?" the woman repeated when Annie didn't answer. "Here? To carry you back to life?"

The wraiths' murmurs grew louder. The mass of bodies swelled and heaved. And then—just as the woman said the word "life"—the huddle exploded and the wraiths hurtled across the room toward the door in a shadowy, frenzied stampede.

Annie lurched out of their way. The woman didn't move quickly enough and was shoved to the ground. Trua reached to grab them but they were too fast and too fluid. They pushed open the door and pulsed through the entryway like a gauzy tornado.

"Stop!" Trua lunged after them.

Annie trailed him out. There in the street the wraiths were cavorting—running back and forth, leaping, waving grey filmy arms in the air. They were chaotic and expectant and joyous.

"Inside!" Trua barked. "Back inside!"

They paid no attention. The woman joined Annie in the doorway. Trua lunged for the wraiths, but they twisted and spun out of his grip: it was like watching a child chasing dandelion fluff in the breeze. They pirouetted and leapt and reached for the sky.

"They're kind of beautiful," the woman murmured. "What are they?"

Before Annie could respond, the familiar cold descended. "Get back!" she urged in a low voice. "Inside!"

The wraiths kept dancing. Over the line of shattered houses, a dark winged silhouette emerged. Then another one, and a third.

Trua ducked back to the doorway, panting. Annie pushed the woman back inside and he stumbled through too. Outside, a devil plummeted to pluck a wraith like an osprey taking a fish. Another devil swooped for another one. Annie shrank back from the doorway, trying not to make a sound, and listened to wheezy shrieks and scuffling from outside.

After barely a minute, the scuffling stopped. There was one lone shriek, then a second, cut short. Flapping of wings, then silence.

Inside the dim room, the woman looked to Annie with worry, and Annie raised a hushing finger to her lips.

Trua slumped to the floor with his head in his hands.

* * * * *

Eventually Trua stood up and said he needed to check the other wraith houses. His face was closed and weary.

"We'll come with you," Annie said.

He glared. "You haven't done enough damage?"

"I—"

"First you come back. Now this. Why'd you have to talk about angels? Blurting it out in front of them—"

The woman raised a hand to silence him, her forehead lined with concern. "That's my fault. I'm so sorry. I am truly, truly sorry."

Trua grunted. "I don't know who you are. But *she*"—he shrugged towards Annie—"should know better."

"I'm sorry too," Annie said. "I wasn't thinking..."

"No, you weren't thinking. Not about this. Not about anything—"

"Please. Don't argue," the woman said. "I'm responsible. And here you were being so kind and taking me in. And you"—she looked at Trua—"you tried to warn me in the desert, didn't you?"

Trua nodded.

"I should be thanking you, and instead there I go messing things up."

"Mm." Trua gave a softer grunt, which sounded like acceptance of the woman's apology. "Who are you? How did you get here?"

The woman told them her name, Kezia, and how she'd been imprisoned by devils. "You did your best for those creatures and now it's in God's hands," she said. "Surely he'll protect them. Now let's go find Michael."

The woman was so hopeful. So confident. Kezia was decades older than Annie, but Annie felt ancient in comparison. She shook her head.

"I don't think he's coming."

"Patience. God doesn't work on our schedule."

"I waited a long time. Am I supposed to wait there forever?"

"If that's what the Lord wants, yes. I'll wait with you."

"Yes, go," Trua said. "I'll take you to the walls."

Annie was silent. He truly didn't want her around. She remained silent as Trua led them back to the city's edge. At the wall he made eye contact with Kezia but not with her.

"Good luck," he said.

"You sure you don't want to come?" Kezia looked concerned. "Michael could take three people for sure."

"I'm not a Christian," he said awkwardly. "Anyway, I need to stay with the wraiths. The ones that are left."

"All right, then." Kezia turned to Annie. "You lead the way."

Annie started across the plain towards the meeting spot, forcing each step. Trua stayed by the wall, arms folded over his chest. Leaving him over and over again was its own kind of Hell. She pushed back tears. They were halfway across the plain when the cold hit her again.

Shit. Not more of them.

Annie glanced toward the city, expecting to see a devil or two emerging, but the sky there was empty. Trua's small figure remained by the broken wall. But now, rather than watching stolidly, he was waving his arms and pointing toward the mountains.

There—pouring over the peaks as thick as coastal fog but darker, much darker—was a cloud of devils. There were hundreds, all armed with swords. A turbulence of dark wings converged on the city.

Kezia gripped Annie's arm. "Satan's army," she murmured.

They were both visible. There was no shelter nearby. Kezia started running back to the city wall. Annie took off too and quickly drew ahead. She glanced over a shoulder and saw a half dozen devils break away from the main force and wing towards them.

She kept running but heard the swelling churn of wings. Ahead, Trua beckoned them to run faster. Behind, Kezia screamed. Annie hurled her body on, hoping that something would intervene, maybe Michael, maybe other devils, maybe—

A rough arm grabbed Annie's waist. She pulled against it but the arm held tight. It was a large male devil with a dark metal breastplate and a long sword in his other hand. He shifted to steady his hold on her, then gave a powerful flap and her feet left the ground.

She thrashed and he hovered, adjusting his grip. Something yanked her left leg and Annie gasped in pain. It was Trua, pulling. The devil launched himself upward but Trua held on. Pain shot from her hip down her thigh.

Catching an updraft, the devil soared up the face of the mountains with Annie tucked under his arm and Trua wrapped tightly around her leg.

CHAPTER THIRTY-FOUR

Haisheng

More mountains, more basins, and Haisheng still hadn't found Satan's palace. He hadn't found Ishaq. Through this whole trek, he'd seen nothing but rock and gravel and perhaps a half dozen devils passing high overhead.

Afoot and lighthearted.

The words mocked him now. His leg remained tender; any scrape started it bleeding again. He descended into yet another basin and followed its wall of black cliffs. The endless desert was numbing. It was easy to let the mind wander and get careless. But was carelessness a greater threat than paranoia? Was despair a bigger danger than both of those? What if Trua's directions were wrong and he was moving further away from Satan's palace with every plodding step? Haisheng reminded himself to stay alert: keep an eye on the sky, check the side canyons—

He halted.

Ahead of him, near the cliff wall and almost as high, the air was shimmering.

It could be one of those gateways to Earth that Trua had talked about. Possibilities ignited like sparklers: a return to life, to his family, Xinghua, the revolution. He

238

tensed with both wariness and hope. But the shimmer was high in the air and far beyond his reach. And it seemed bigger than Trua's description, the size of a house.

He picked a sheltered spot beside a boulder and sat down to monitor it. The shimmer felt portentous, as if he were meant to learn something from it. Nothing moved, nothing happened; the shimmer simply hung in the air. He felt increasingly certain it held a message for him. He sat for more hours. When he heard a faint hum, he thought it was his imagination. But the hum continued—real, not imaginary—slicing the desert silence and swelling into a rumble and a roar. It was louder than ten automobile engines, loud as the printing presses of Shanghai.

The shimmer became a shake. The air itself was vibrating. And then two devils abruptly emerged from the shimmer, flapping frantically as they veered away from the cliff. The roar intensified—Haisheng covered his ears—and something monstrous and unthinkable shot out of the shimmer. It was huge and silver and cylindrical, a giant bullet with wings, but before he could make sense of it the thing slammed into the cliff and exploded in a giant ball of flame.

Haisheng tumbled back. Bitter black smoke choked him. He pulled his shirt over his nose and mouth and hid behind the boulder.

Finally the smoke cleared and he ventured forward. The thing had been reduced to a pile of melted, smoldering metal. From some future Earth, maybe—from Annie's time, some advanced kind of airplane? Beyond the charred mess the two devils lay sprawled on the desert floor, felled by the explosion. No movement, no sound. Carefully he circled the wreck and approached them. One of the devils lay in a smear of black blood, a shard of metal protruding from its singed torso. Its eyes were closed but its chest rose and fell.

"Help," it murmured faintly. "Zarphan..."

The other devil wasn't breathing. There were ragged stubs where its wings used to be. Its body was charred, its eyes a dull black instead of glittering red.

Devils were supposed to be immortal. Haisheng had never seen a dead one. But Satan had said things were changing—that devils now could die, that they could even commit suicide. And this one was clearly dead.

"Help," the other, wounded devil repeated weakly.

The creature was suffering. But it was an oppressor, an enemy. Haisheng stared. He'd failed as a militia leader when he was alive but he wouldn't fail now. He reached for his dagger, took a deep breath, and plunged it into the devil's gut. It was no harder than cutting into a melon. He stabbed it again.

This one for the wraiths in the plaza. This one for the wraiths in the factory. This one for Eiko.

Black blood spurted across his dagger and slicked his arm. The devil convulsed and fell still.

Above, the shimmering vanished and the air returned to its usual dusty haze.

* * * * *

Haisheng almost skipped across the plain. *Devils could die, and he could kill them!* The doubts of the desert trek fell away. He could lead an army of wraiths. He could negotiate with Satan. He could free the souls of Hell. All he had to do was reach the palace—

That familiar cold swept over him but he no longer cared. Two devils winged across the plain with unswerving determination. Clenched under their arms were two smaller humanlike figures. One seemed strangely elongated, is if it were two linked bodies. The devils clearly had a destination in mind—perhaps the palace?

Haisheng followed, running to keep them in sight, more excited with each step. *You want to kill yourself?* he'd tell Satan. *Then make the wraiths your heirs. Set them free and they'll fight your enemies. They'll honor you forever. You'll be immortal in your mortality.*

He pictured the wily demon sitting back and weighing the offer. History was shaped by unlikely allies. Now he—Chen Haisheng, son of a grocer, failed poet, second-level cadre never invited into the party's higher circles—was on the verge of an alliance that would shape not just history but eternity.

If only Xinghua were here to see.

Haisheng no longer noticed the pain in his leg. He hurled himself at the next range of hills and scrambled to the ridge, barely winded, bright-eyed.

Another plain stretched before him, but this time not empty. Far away, the land dropped off to an orange sea of fire. And across the plain, black as oil but beckoning like the brightest of lanterns, rose the thick walls and pillars of Pandaemonium.

CHAPTER THIRTY-FIVE

Trua

Trua let himself drop from Annie's legs when the devil swooped towards the palace: better a few bruises than capture by Satan. Now he hunched against the building's wall, wondering how to make his way inside.

The main entrance was impossible. Devils lounged on the portico and gathered on the dusty plateau in front of the palace—talking, showing off swordplay, comparing weapons. There must be other, less busy doors. Crouching, he moved along the side of the palace.

The wall stretched further than any Roman building he'd seen. There were no windows; he reached an iron door but it wouldn't budge. Even a king would feel like a prisoner in this accursed place. And the real prisoners: how could Annie and Kezia be freed? He felt too jagged to plan—still shaky from the flight, relieved at being back on the ground, and confused about Annie.

The damn woman should never have come back to Hell. He'd stayed here to protect her, and she threw that protection away. She didn't respect his decision. She didn't respect what he'd gone through for her. She showed up blithe as a child on a spring day, expecting him to be happy she'd thrown her life away.

242

And then, on top of all that, she insisted on following him into the wraith house.

He hated her seeing him like that. He hated her for judging him. Who was she to judge—she who'd spent all this time basking in the sunshine and starlight of Earth? He was furious with her. And yet his heart had leapt when she magically appeared outside the safe house, which made him furious with himself.

Damn her.

Trua halted. Two devils writhed against the wall ahead, rutting like goats or dogs. One pushed the other's face into the dirt. Wings slapped and tongues hissed. The smell of rancid meat assaulted him. He left the shelter of the wall and made as quick and generous a circle around them as possible.

The back corner of the palace arrived without any more entrances. Trua turned and kept moving. Far ahead, a low black stone wall marked off some kind of roofless enclosure holding indistinct, shifting dark shapes.

Another group of devils passed overhead. The movement in the enclosure continued—not wraiths, he hoped. He edged further along the wall. The darkness in the enclosure took shape and his breath caught.

Horses.

They looked like the winged horses that had carried generals in the devil city—dark, massive, powerful. Trua couldn't resist. He forgot all about keeping cover and sprinted to the enclosure.

The wall came up to his chest—not high enough to keep the horses penned, but then no wall would be high enough to pen flying horses. Instead they were tied to iron posts with leather-looking cord. An entire herd, maybe twenty or thirty creatures, nuzzled each other and nickered and tossed their giant heads.

They were magnificent. They were like gods. Their coats were the same muddy brown and green as devils, but the specks of silver were so bright as to seem illuminated. Their flanks were twice the girth of Hun horses, necks arched and muscled, tails proud as banners. And their wings! The wings of devils always seemed monstrous to him, but here the wings were an organic extension of the beast, and suddenly all the flightless horses he'd known seemed incomplete and stunted. Even penned, the wings danced in tandem with their bodies—graceful, sensitive, powerful.

His thighs ached. His stomach tightened. He needed to ride.

Trua leaned over the paddock wall. The horses closest to him shrank back and snorted. Their nostrils were cavernous. "Shh," he murmured. The horses beat their wings and danced away from him, their fear rippling across the corral.

He reached a hand across the wall and they shimmied further away. "Come," he whispered, but none came. The need to mount one was physical—in his legs, his gut, his chest. He pulled himself up onto the wall, but one horse shrilled a warning and he dropped back. If he could ride one of these gods for even a moment, just a quick ascent with those powerful haunches, those wings...

With a horse, he wouldn't be alone. With a horse, he could hide in the desert forever. No devils. No wraiths. No human women making reckless decisions and getting themselves captured.

He forced himself back to the palace wall. Long ago, when he was alive, he would have leapt into that corral without a second thought. Back then he would have killed a stranger without a second thought too. Behind him, the horses nickered to each other faintly. He listened with longing and eventually resumed his circuit of the palace walls.

* * * * *

The rear wall of the palace had no openings. On the fourth side, he found another iron door but it wouldn't budge. This wasn't going to work. Approaching the front of the building, he froze. Two devils flew jerkily towards the palace with a third devil clamped between them in iron chains. Trua pressed against the wall. The devils flew past and hauled their prisoner into the great hall.

He waited and assessed. Even invisible, they might hear or smell him. Could he mask his scent? He reached for a handful of black dust and rubbed it on his arms and legs.

"Trua!"

The shout came across the plateau, from the direction of the ridge. It was low and hoarse, but on the open plain it carried like the blare of a ram's horn. A figure jogged towards him—human, not devil—too distant to distinguish at first, but then it took shape. A man, short hair, slim build: Haisheng.

What in the gods' names was he thinking? Trua edged back along the wall, away from the entrance. Haisheng, oblivious, ran directly towards him and then stopped, panting.

"Are you mad?" Trua hissed in a low voice. "They're everywhere!"

Haisheng grinned with triumph. And Trua realized he *was* mad, the way he himself had gone mad alone in the desert. Haisheng's right leg had a gash like the wound Trua had sustained on his trek. His arms were caked with dry black blood that he hadn't even tried to wipe off.

"Trua! Comrade! I have great news!"

"Sit down. Not here." Trua ushered Haisheng back along the wall, the way he would lead an over-excited child. "Rest. Keep your voice low."

"They can be killed! It's true! I killed one! And now you're here! We'll open negotiations together, the two of us. An even stronger position."

Madness. Trua had no idea what to say.

"We'll play roles. The tough one and the compromiser. We— Wait." Haisheng stared as if he had just noticed Trua. "The wraiths. If you're here...who's looking after them?"

Trua's face heated with shame. "No one."

"You were supposed to watch over them! Protect them! Train them!"

"They were not...capable."

"Of course they're capable! They just need training! And you were supposed to do that! I got them started. All you had to do was keep it going—"

"Shut up," Trua said gruffly.

"There were enough for a militia. If you'd trained them—"

"Shut up."

"You said you'd protect them!"

"Shut up about the wraiths! Just shut up!"

Trua hurled himself on top of Haisheng but Haisheng pushed back and managed to shove him off. The two rolled and pummeled. Trua forgot about the devils and lost himself in the hammering. *Curse Haisheng—curse the wraiths—curse everything about this accursed place.* He landed a punch in Haisheng's gut and felt him buckle. Haisheng rebounded with a lucky kick to his groin and Trua fell back. Haisheng tried to pin him but Trua pushed him off balance. The city dweller was no match for him. He pushed him down, knees on Haisheng's thighs, hands pressing his wrists into the dirt. Haisheng glared, sweat now smearing the dust on his face. Trua wanted to smash Haisheng's head against rock like he'd done to the marauder Falc. But Falc was an enemy. Haisheng was a friend, the closest thing to a brother that he had here.

No more killing.

Trua released Haisheng, who rolled over onto his side and moaned.

No devils had noticed.

Trua sank against the palace wall, holding his aching crotch and fighting off nausea. Haisheng just lay there. His leg wound had re-opened, red and raw. After a while Haisheng sat up and wiped his face with his shirt. Another squadron of devils appeared above the plain, hundreds of them, winging towards the palace.

"Annie's back and they've captured her," Trua said stiffly. When Haisheng didn't respond, he continued. "Another woman too. We need to rescue them."

He couldn't tell if Haisheng heard him. Finally Haisheng spoke.

"We'll negotiate their release," he said. "That's the best chance. It'll be one of the conditions for our alliance."

Trua stared.

"Along with freedom for the wraiths. Of course that's our first demand. But freeing Annie can be our second."

"Don't do this."

"It's why I came here."

"He won't listen. He'll destroy you."

"He won't. He needs my help. The wraiths' help. I just have to persuade him. And then we'll free the wraiths—and the souls in the fire—"

Trua thought of tackling him again and tying him down like the devil horses. Haisheng seemed to read his mind.

"I need to do this."

Haisheng stood and brushed off his legs, careful not to touch the wound. He nodded formally to Trua and stepped unsteadily toward the front of the palace. Reaching the corner, he called out.

"Hello! I'm here to see Satan. I want an audience with Satan!"

Trua heard murmurs and the scraping of wings around the corner, near the front entrance.

"Here I am! Right here! Take me to Satan!"

Dark wings descended, honing in on the source of the invisible human voice, and carried Haisheng away.

CHAPTER THIRTY-SIX

Annie

The devils ferried Annie and Kezia through the dim corridors of Pandaemonium and deposited them in the cell with Ben, who slouched against a wall. He leapt up when he saw them.

"Are you okay?" he blurted.

"Mostly," Annie said. She felt a spurt of pleasure that Ben was worried about her—*had he finally accepted this wasn't a game?*—but then realized with dismay that he was still here. Michael hadn't rescued him, hadn't even made an appearance. Something bad must truly have happened to the archangel.

In the stillness of the cell, there was nothing to do but talk. Kezia and Annie shared their stories and Ben peppered Kezia with endless questions about devil politics. Annie closed her eyes and imagined Mary waking in her crib. Mary would coo and kick. Sunlight would filter in between the curtains. The earthy smell of her father's coffee would waft up from downstairs. Just an average morning—so beautiful in its averageness—but without her there.

Would Mary care that it was Melanie opening the curtains and giving her a bottle? Would it be worse if Mary cared, or worse if she didn't care?

Everything was a mess. The only bright note was Kezia's account of the angels ransacking Zarphan's fortress: the nukes must have been destroyed and Earth saved. Annie knew that was infinitely more important than her own puny problems, but it still felt like thin consolation.

A series of thuds reverberated in the corridor. A devil flapped into sight dragging another human, unlocked the door, and shoved him into the cell.

It was Haisheng, and he looked terrible. His face was plastered with black dust. His limbs were scratched and bloody. He pulled himself up to a seated position and wiped his face with his shirt, revealing a swollen, bloody cheek.

"Annie," he murmured blankly. "Trua said you were back."

"What happened? Did the devils do this to you?"

Haisheng looked at himself as if noticing his wounds for the first time. He thought for a moment, then pointed to the scratches on his arms and legs. "This was the devils." He waved dismissively at an open gash on his leg. "That was the desert." He grimaced and wiped the blood from his cheek. "This was Trua."

Goddamn Hun! As if brutalizing the wraiths wasn't enough, now he'd attacked Haisheng. Annie requisitioned a sleeve of Ben's shirt—he had the most intact clothing of any of them—and bandaged Haisheng's leg. He leaned back against the wall and rested. After a while he looked up and told them, haltingly, where he'd been.

The devils had hauled him to a windowless chamber and left him with a lieutenant named Belial. Haisheng demanded to see Satan, but Belial just laughed.

250

"I tried arguing but he wouldn't listen," Haisheng said. "He said Satan had no time for humans. He said I was lucky he didn't drop me in the lake of fire. He *laughed*. Then he told the guards to bring me here. These"—he gestured at his scrapes—"aren't from being beaten. They're from being dragged down the hall. They didn't even think I was worth beating."

"No, but Trua did," Annie muttered.

Haisheng stared at the floor. After a long time he looked up at Annie.

"It wasn't his fault. He was right. He told me not to look for Satan. I left him with an impossible task. I knew it but couldn't admit it. He was right on all counts."

"But he was terrible to the wraiths—"

"He was right. Ishaq was right. The only thing the wraiths understand is fear. They'll never be an army. They'll never be able to govern themselves. They're no longer really human."

"I don't know if that's true." Annie remembered the wraiths leaping in joy in the street, dancing like banners in a breeze at the prospect of Michael's arrival.

"I was a fool," Haisheng said, and then was silent.

* * * * *

Kezia prodded Annie for details of Mary's rescue. "If you saved your daughter, I can save my son," she declared. Ben paced the room, looking impatient and bored. Eventually he dropped down beside Haisheng and asked about his life.

"Shanghai in 1927," he repeated musingly when Haisheng told him where he was from. "The Shanghai Massacre."

Annie glanced across the cell: there was no limit to the obscure information Ben knew. Haisheng cocked his head.

"Shanghai Massacre? What's that?"

"The decimation of the Shanghai Communist Party by Chiang Kai-Shek. Wasn't that how you died?"

Haisheng looked puzzled. "General Chiang freed Wuhan from the warlords. He has bourgeois tendencies, but he's part of the nationalist alliance. He didn't massacre anybody."

"When exactly did you die?"

"Late February...I think. It's gotten harder to remember. I know it was after the New Year celebrations."

"Then you died before. The massacre started in April. Chiang and the right wing of the Kuomintang arranged for criminal gangs and the police to attack the communists. They disarmed the workers' militias and executed the communist leadership. Union leaders too. Some sources say they killed as many as 10,000 people."

"Ben!" Her brother had zero tact: Haisheng had suffered enough without talk of massacres in his hometown. But Haisheng didn't seem perturbed.

"You're wrong," he told Ben. "The unions were well organized. The people were with us. My friend Xinghua analyzed the objective conditions and proved that revolution was inevitable."

Ben folded his arms. He looked bored, like a student reciting multiplication tables for the fifth time.

"The communists did launch an armed uprising that captured most of Shanghai. But then Chiang allied with the foreign interests, the gangs, and anti-communist army commanders to suppress the left. They call it the April 12 tragedy or the Shanghai Massacre. He went on to kill hundreds of thousands of leftists throughout China over the next year. The party had to go underground. It fought a civil war with Chiang until the late 1930s, when Japan invaded China."

Haisheng's brow furrowed as Ben talked. "You know this?"

"It's history. Everyone in China knows it."

Now Haisheng looked at Annie. "You told me the revolution succeeded. That China is united and led by the Communist Party."

"It is!"

"So what about this?" He gestured towards Ben. "What he says? A massacre?"

"I don't know," Annie said helplessly. Her knowledge of China was based on news headlines. Ben's was based on books and policy papers and conferences in Beijing and Shanghai.

"Did it happen?" Haisheng snapped at her. "A massacre?"

"I don't know!"

"What happened after I died?"

"I don't know!"

He turned back to Ben, his mouth grim. "Tell me more. Tell me everything."

Afterwards Haisheng sank against the wall like a man who'd just lost his best friend. Probably, Annie thought, he had.

"How does he know all that stuff?" Kezia whispered.

"It's who he is. Who he's always been."

Just because Ben knew stuff, though, did that mean he needed to broadcast it? When it would do no good? When it would crush someone?

"Ben." She motioned him over to her side of the cell and tried to keep her voice low. "*How dare you!* Look at what he's been through. And you go out of your way to tell him all his friends were killed? Just to show off how much you know? What is wrong with you?"

Ben shrugged. "It was the truth."

"People don't need the truth all the time! Sometimes they need"—she struggled for the right word—"tenderness. They need to be taken care of. They need—"

"Lies?"

"You always have to be smarter than everyone else. You always have to prove you know more—"

"Not always."

His voice was level but there was something dangerous in it. She didn't care.

"Right," she snapped. "Tell me one time. Just *one time* where you didn't show off your goddamn knowledge. One time where you kept it to yourself. One time where you shut up to protect someone's feelings—"

"Zarphan didn't have any nukes," he said quietly.

She stopped. "What?"

"Baphomet told me while you were gone. If you'd bothered to think about Kezia's story, you'd know it too. Zarphan didn't have any nuclear weapons, Annie. He didn't have any functioning electronics at all, and Satan knew it. You were played by Satan. Royally played."

She glanced around the room for help. But Haisheng was staring at the floor, lost in his own disasters. Kezia was listening but said nothing.

"You were manipulated, Annie. We both were. Satan got you to go to Michael with this non-existent threat. He knew that Michael would jump at any excuse to punish his enemies. Michael weakened Zarphan, and then Satan came and captured him. It was all a ruse to destroy his rival. There were never any nukes."

"You don't know that. They could have been hidden—"

"Honey." Kezia spoke up, her voice gentle, almost apologetic. "I was in Zarphan's headquarters. That place was low-tech. They were happy when they got *pencils*. He knew about nuclear weapons, for sure, but he didn't have any of that stuff."

Nausea rose from Annie's gut. Calling on Satan to save her mother had been more than foolish; it was a gift to him. She was the perfect bait. And Michael had taken that bait. Perhaps the archangel had been captured or destroyed because of her. Or perhaps he realized what she'd done and cast her off.

She'd screwed up yet again, and this time it was on a cosmic scale.

CHAPTER THIRTY-SEVEN

Kezia

All those months jailed by Zarphan and Ardat, Kezia had longed for human companionship. Now she had it and things weren't much better. The young Chinese man was in a royal funk. He sat by himself and refused to say a word. Annie had also withdrawn, except to hurl dark looks across the cell at Ben.

Brother and sister fighting like that: they should be ashamed, adults acting like eight-year-olds! They needed to pull together, all of them, to get out of this place—to get Annie home to her baby and Jeremiah out of the fire.

And where was this girl devil who had rescued Annie's baby? Would she be willing to save Jeremiah too?

Now that Kezia had learned it was possible to rescue souls from Hell, every minute of delay felt like a month. She prayed silently for God to open the girl devil's heart. She begged George to forgive their fight and watch over Jeremiah. She prayed for patience and for the wisdom to know what to do. The wisdom didn't seem to come but eventually a numbness settled into her chest, so perhaps that was patience, or close enough.

"Psst."

Kezia spun around. Trua stood on the other side of the cell door, his scarred cheeks pressed up against the bars. The others heard his whisper too and were staring.

"Who—" Ben began, but Annie hissed at him to shut up. Trua put a finger to his lips and gestured them to come close.

"I've been looking for a way out. The building is full of devils. Devil prisoners too, not in this hallway but other ones." He fingered the latch on the door and frowned. "Do you know where they keep the key?" Annie shook her head. "See if you can learn about the key. Meanwhile—"

Far down the corridor, Kezia heard the sweep of wings.

"Get back," Trua whispered. He slipped past the doorway and flattened himself against the wall. Kezia and the others dropped back to where they'd been sitting.

The wingbeats grew louder and a slight female devil—*was this Baphomet, the one who'd helped Annie?*—landed by the door. She wrinkled her nose and looked into the cell with distaste.

"Such a stink," she said. "It's not so bad when there's just one of you, but it multiplies. It's even spread into the hallway."

She stared directly towards Trua. Kezia forced her own gaze to the floor, to Annie, to Ben—anywhere that was not Trua.

Baphomet shrugged. She unlocked the door, pulled her wings tight to enter, and carefully closed the door behind her. She proffered a pile of paper to Ben.

"Look what I found." She beamed at him, ignoring the rest of them. "It was confiscated from Zarphan's fortress. No one wanted it so I took it!"

Ben thumbed through the papers. Kezia could see they were blank—plain 8-by-11 sheets, like you'd find in any photocopier.

"And this!" Triumphantly the girl devil displayed a handful of ballpoint pens. "We can do real writing now. Not just in the dust."

"That's great," Ben said guardedly.

"I'm tired of words and sentences, though. I want to write poetry. Let's start on poetry."

"Sure. But..."

"You don't think I'm smart enough to write poetry?"

"No! Of course not!"

"You don't want to teach me with these other humans around?"

"No—"

"I don't like all these other humans either." Baphomet's mouth curved down in a pout. "I don't want to write poetry with them here. We need to get rid of them."

"You can't just get rid of people!" Kezia blurted. She couldn't help herself: this devil looked like she belonged in a junior-high lunchroom.

"Stupid human. We can get rid of you any time. All of you. Drop you in the fire. Any time we want."

"Baphomet!" Annie exclaimed.

"Shh!" Ben hissed at Annie.

"I could do it right now," Baphomet continued. "Drop you all in and watch you burn. Your stupid human skin. Your stupid human hair—"

"Stop it—" Annie said

"Your stupid human eyes. Your stupid human teeth—"

"I was a poet," Haisheng said quietly. They all turned. "Or...at least someone who studied poetry. I can teach you."

Baphomet cocked her head toward the voice she couldn't see. "Maybe. Who are you? Were you friends with John Milton?"

"Milton?"

"The greatest human poet. Everyone knows that."

Haisheng looked embarrassed. "I...don't know of him."

"Then what *do* you know?"

"Du Fu. Li Bai. Guo Moro..."

Baphomet glanced to Ben. "Who are they? Have you heard of them? Are they like Milton?"

"Hard to say. Earth is different from Hell that way, we have hundreds of languages and cultures. People don't necessarily know the literature of other cultures. Much of it isn't even translated. Du Fu I've heard of, he's a classical poet from the Tang Dynasty, but can't say I know his writing, while those others—"

"What about my son?" Kezia couldn't sit through any more jabber about poetry. "Look, he's barely older than you are but he's suffering in the lake of fire. And Annie and Ben, their mother's in there too. Help us. I know you can do it. Just fly out there and rescue them. What are two little souls when you've got billions? Just rescue them, and then take us all back to Earth—"

"Stupid human, with the stupidest idea ever!" The girl devil clapped her wings like slamming a book closed. "I don't care about any of you. I don't want to learn your poetry. I don't care about stupid human cultures—"

"Baphomet." Ben stepped forward. Gently, he touched his hand to her arm. His voice was almost too soft for Kezia to hear.

"You can be a poet. You can do anything you set your mind to. No one in this palace will ever tell you that, but it's true. You're smarter than they think you are, and your mind is more open than theirs will ever be. You can be whatever you want. You can be a poet, you can be a writer, you could write plays or epic poems or novels..."

Baphomet sank into Ben's touch, her wings drifting lower like the tail of a cat being stroked.

"You're better than all of them. You deserve a better life, a real life. Help us escape, and then come back to Earth with us—"

She jolted upright.

"Tempter! Second-rate tempter!"

She snatched the pile of papers from Ben and hurled them across the cell. Then she launched herself toward the cell door, jerked it open, and slammed it shut. "Stupid humans! I hope you all die!"

She winged furiously down the hallway.

* * * * *

They gathered by the cell door with low voices. "You should have tackled her," Trua muttered from the other side of the bars. "Held her down and forced her to give you the keys."

"You tried that once, remember?" Annie said. "It didn't work out so well."

"There are more of you. You could have done it."

"And then what?"

"Stop it," Kezia said. Did she always have to be the grown-up in this group? "We need to pray," she continued. "Look, I know some of you don't believe, but we need God's help right now. He's the only one strong enough to help us."

Ben exhaled loudly. Haisheng looked away.

"It won't help," Annie said gently. "You've been praying since you got here, right? And look where we are."

"If we could just travel to Heaven," Trua mused. "Like you did, Annie. You got help from Michael once. He might do it again—"

"Oh sure. Just fly to Heaven. With whose wings?"

Kezia stepped away from the others and sat down on the floor. Annie thought prayer had no effect, but Annie hadn't felt George by her side all these years. Annie hadn't heard God telling her through George to escape from Ardat.

Jesus, thank you for the love you've shown me. Help me discern your will and carry it out. I can't imagine you want us all stuck in this cell forever. Help us escape so we can do what you need us to do—

Darn it. The others were bickering so much that it was hard to concentrate. Ben was lecturing Haisheng. Annie was sniping at Trua. Now Trua lost his temper: he raised his fist and slammed it down on the handle of the door, which swung ever so slightly open.

Not locked?

God, you heard me!

Electric energy propelled her up and over to the group. They would need to move fast. The warm, stale air filled with their whispered questions: *Did she leave it open on purpose? Is this a trick? Trua, do you know how to get out of the palace? Where do we go if we make it out of the building?*

"I have an idea," Trua said.

CHAPTER THIRTY-EIGHT

Trua

Trua led them through the labyrinth of Pandaemonium. His aim was one of the iron doors. During the hubbub of Haisheng's capture, he'd darted into the palace and found they were bolted from the inside by bars the width of a sapling. Heavy, but with a group of five people liftable.

He chose a roundabout route to avoid busy areas. Finally the corridor started sloping upward, a sign they were nearing the exit. To reach it, they'd have to pass a stretch of cells with devil prisoners. Any one of them could raise an alarm.

"Act like you belong here," Trua whispered. "The ones of you who they can see. Walk slowly. Act important, like you're guests of Satan."

Annie's brother led the way. The role seemed to fit him. He took long, measured strides and glanced with casual condescension at the cells lining the walls. Annie and Kezia followed, engaged in a mock conversation.

Invisible, Trua had freedom to peer into the cells. Here a massive male devil sat hunched in a corner, wings folded, morose. There a short scrawny devil paced and mumbled to herself. Their ruse seemed to be working. The prisoners stared, and one muttered something that must have been a curse, but no one challenged them. Then they passed a cell that held a tall female devil. She sat against the wall, seemingly lost in thought, her fingers moving in a strange, quick way that was more than a fidget, almost a dance. She glanced up.

"You!" She stared at Kezia. "Traitor! You were working for Satan after all!" Her wings snapped open and she hurled herself against the bars of her cell. "I'll kill you! Maim you! Everyone—here's the traitor! A runaway human! Who we coddled! Who we treated like a guest—"

Other devils threw themselves at their doors, shouting and shaking their bars. Trua panicked. *Guards would come, they'd be caught, hurled into the fire—*

Annie's brother took charge. He drew himself up to his full height, which was at least a head taller than Trua, and crossed his arms.

"Shut up," he said to the female devil, loud enough for the whole corridor to hear. "You think solitary confinement is bad? Satan can do much worse. You know that. He's looking to make an example of someone. Disrespect us and you're the perfect candidate. So if you value your miserable wings, you'll shut up and treat the ladies with respect."

The cells fell silent. The tall female devil stopped shaking the bars. She curled her lips and bared her teeth like a wild beast but didn't make a sound.

They resumed their slow walk. They passed out of the cell area, through another short corridor, and reached the door. Straining together, they lifted the bolt.

Outside, Trua felt lighter. They weren't out of danger, but at least they were no longer entombed in all that stone. He hurried them along the back side of the building and stopped across from the corral. Dark wings and bodies shifted; dark heads lifted and ears stiffened.

"Annie. Can you find the way back to Heaven?"

"I guess so. It was pretty much just straight up—"

"Good. We're going to ride." He stepped forward, but none of them followed. "Come on. Before they see us."

Still no one budged. In the corral, the horses whinnied.

"What?" he asked. Then he realized: *they don't know how to ride.*

Of course. They were city dwellers. He'd heard of Romans who hadn't ever touched a horse, but he'd never met anyone like that. It simply hadn't occurred to him.

"Okay. We'll ride together." He glanced over to the corral, assessing how much weight the devil horses could carry. "I can take one or two of you with me. But we need someone else on a second horse."

No one spoke up.

"Annie. You've never ridden?"

She shook her head.

"The rest of you? No one?"

The whinnying from the corral got louder: the horses were getting nervous. Devils could show up at any moment.

"Maybe a little."

The voice was Kezia's, still breathless from their dash.

"When I was just married. At my husband's family in Alabama. He tried to teach me but I wasn't any good. That was thirty years ago..."

Trua nodded. It would have to do.

"Annie, you ride with her. You others, come with me. Fast."

They sprinted to the corral. The horses were snorting, jostling away from him, twitching their wings. Magnificent creatures. He leapt the low wall and walked purposefully, calmly, toward one of the smaller ones. Hopefully it had been ridden before. Hopefully it would respond even if the rider on its back were human.

He kept his voice low and his gaze averted. When close enough, he reached up the broad shoulders to grab a fistful of mane: full fist, tight grip. It was larger than any horse he'd ridden and he felt like a child again, barely able to reach a flank. With sheer will he pulled against the mane and launched himself, feet higher than his head, up onto its back.

The horse reared. It spread its wings but he pressed in with his legs and stroked its neck. "Calm down. Yes. Good. Hold still now."

The horse settled. Trua beckoned Kezia to mount behind him. She edged over, eyes wide, and Haisheng boosted her up.

"All right. See what I'm doing? Grip tight with your legs. Yes, like that. You can use your arms too, but it's mostly the legs. If you lean, it'll respond. You're in charge. Remember that. Its legs are your legs. Don't think about it. Just follow its rhythm. I'll be close by. They're herd animals. They like to stay together."

He didn't give her time to protest, just slid off the horse and boosted Annie up behind her. He handed his stone dagger to Haisheng.

"Start cutting the tie-down. Don't cut it completely loose until we're ready to go."

266

The next horse was more challenging. He approached several that reared and struck out at him. Finally he spotted one at the edge of the pack that seemed less agitated. He grabbed a fistful of mane, swung himself up, calmed the animal, and hoisted Ben up behind him.

"Give me the dagger." Trua sawed through his horse's leather-like cord, then handed it back to Haisheng to finish Kezia's tie. "Okay, come on! Up!"

He gestured at the spot behind Ben, and they took off.

* * * * *

It was everything Trua had imagined and more.

His horse surged into the sky with the power of a half dozen Hun horses. Wind gushed past his ears in a torrent that made the Great Plain wind seem like a trickling brook. His horse seemed to have forgotten he was a stranger and answered the slightest pressure of his legs.

On a horse like this, he could go anywhere, do anything. He could be a king, an emperor, a god. It was both the same and different from riding at home. Same: the mingling of human and beast that turned you into something more than yourself. The sweating, heaving life between your legs. The propulsion. Different: the verticality. They were flying straight up, with Ben and Haisheng gripping him desperately so as not to slide off. Also the smoothness. There was none of the pounding impact of riding on Earth, no percussive beat of hooves on dirt. It was strange to feel such power but also such smoothness.

And the wings.

A whole new section of horse was in play. Yes, front legs still pawed and powerful haunches beat the air, but the beast's shoulders churned with unfamiliar muscles. Trua couldn't reach all the way around the neck but he gripped the mane and leaned in to the shoulders and came to breathe in tandem with the wingstrokes. He no longer noticed Ben's arms cinched tight around his waist.

They traveled up and up. Annie and Kezia's horse flew alongside his, facing skywards, pumping those powerful wings. There was nothing to see, just hazy grey everywhere, so his other senses took over. The warm, damp coat under his hands. The rushing sound of wings against air. The ripe scent of sweating horse— different from home, no hay and earth smells, but a metallic tinge like the taste of water from a copper cup. A little sulfur too. It wasn't foul like the devils' smell, just different. Thinking about the horse's scent led him to wonder how it had ended up in Hell. Surely horses hadn't chosen to rebel? They must have been captured, ridden into battle like any horse, and then thrown down into Hell with their devil riders. It seemed grossly unjust, but it was only one of the injustices committed by this Christian God.

Trua feared he was going to have a difficult time in this Christian Heaven.

They continued to ascend. Behind him Haisheng, anxious, asked repeatedly how long it would take. Trua maneuvered his horse closer to the other, and Annie called out to be patient: it would take days.

Trua was fine with it taking days. Months, even. This ride was his version of a heaven. He wished Damla were here to share it, crouched low against the neck of her own winged horse. She wouldn't be a tentative, nervous rider like Kezia. She'd kick her horse and shout and the two of them would take off, racing across the sky.

He couldn't resist. Thinking of Damla, he gave his horse a kick and it jumped slightly and hurled itself into a sprint.

"Hey!" Haisheng called.

"You wanted to get there quicker!" he shouted back with glee.

He gave the horse some leg and they veered left, then right, then left again. Trua zigzagged and circled, ignoring the protests behind him. And then he needed to try a descent.

"Lean forward, both of you," Trua called, and he worked his hands up the neck, straining forward and looking down, and his stomach lurched, and now they were hurtling down, faster than an avalanche, faster than a falling star, the horse's ears plastered back and its great wings gusting.

"Eehah!" Trua shouted, and they plummeted on until he remembered they were heading back to Hell.

"Lean back now, but hold tight," he called to Haisheng and Ben, and it took a couple of tries but the horse turned around and surged skyward again. They caught up with Kezia and Annie and passed them, wings roiling, and the grey ether blurred and the wind rushed by so fast that Trua's ears hurt and they flew like reverse lightning, striking up, up, up.

His horse was slowing down. Was it fatigue? They'd been riding far longer than any mortal horse could have sustained. He'd heard stories of Roman soldiers who rode their horses to death. He didn't want to think about what would happen to them, suspended in nothingness, if the horses stopped winging and died.

Kezia and Annie veered towards him.

"It's close," Annie said. "You can feel the air thickening."

She was right. It wasn't exhaustion slowing down his horse, but the strain of pushing through heavier air. Now that he noticed, he could feel its resistance. "Go easy," he murmured to the horse, stroking its neck. "Slow. That's fine."

Flashes of yellow appeared in the grey haze. It was like the Great Plain in the morning, when sunlight chiseled cracks in the fog. Here too the grey began breaking up. His horse gave a quick, small buck and flared its nostrils. Suddenly the haze was gone and the air was thin again and everything was bathed in warm, golden light. The horse leapt and pranced through the open air.

"Look," Ben said.

Land stretched ahead of them—a long strip of silvery sand.

"We made it," Haisheng breathed.

Both horses were ecstatic. They shook their heads and capered and pranced. Trua grinned with them. Kezia—pressed tight against her horse's neck from all the prancing—glanced at him with wide, relieved eyes.

The horses whinnied and sprinted onto the sand. Trua jumped down to help the others off. The horses were prancing on land now like earthly horses. Then he heard a distant sound of fluttering—lighter than his horse's flaps, almost a whisper.

The horses heard it too. They turned and called out shrilly and started galloping up the sand. Without thinking, Trua followed. There, far ahead of them, rose a fence—brilliant golden pillars, taller than any trees he'd ever seen. On the other side of the fence a herd of horses was gathering. They had wings too, but made of a million feathers rather than rough leather. They were unmarred silver. Their eyes were glistening gold.

The silver horses gathered by the fence—flying down, trotting over. They whinnied and nickered and pawed the ground.

They were waiting. Welcoming.

The devil horses reached the fence and whinnied. It was like returning to his tribe's herd after days of riding alone. The dark horses shook their heads and stuck their noses up against the fence openings. The silver horses nuzzled them back, breathing into each other's nostrils. Then the devil horses gave an enormous flap and launched themselves up towards the top of the fence. Trua braced for something horrible to happen: clearly this fence was a magical border, a line you couldn't pass. And something did happen as the horses topped the fence, but it wasn't horrible.

They turned color. It started with a lightening of the mane, a fading of the hooves. Then, as the horses topped the fence, the changes cascaded. The tarnish of their coats melted into foam-green and then grey and then silver. Rough leather wings softened and sprouted feathers. Red eyes turned brilliant gold.

The horses touched down in the middle of the herd. The others crowded around, nuzzling and nickering. They were pure silver now, the transformation complete. Trua's breath caught. As well as he knew horses, he could no longer tell which two in the herd had brought them here.

The entire flock took off, winging out of his sight into the pastures of Heaven.

PART THREE

Above

CHAPTER THIRTY-NINE

Annie

Annie watched from a distance as the herd lifted off. Trua was a small, dark silhouette before the golden posts. In the light that suffused everything here, he looked dense and earthbound, a lead toy soldier on a playing field of linen and glass.

The silver spheres rippled under her feet as she made her way up the slope. Behind her, Haisheng and Kezia were sifting handfuls of the spheres through their fingers. Ben was in full lecture mode, probably explaining away the spheres as mercury or ice crystals or some chemical compound she'd never heard of but he knew intimately.

Ahead of her, Trua slumped. His shoulders drooped and he stared into space where the horses had been. Riding had transformed him. In Hell, he'd been cold to her and brutal with the wraiths, yet on horseback he glowed with joy. He barely moved and his horse responded. It was the furthest thing from brutality. Watching him as they rode up through the grey, she'd felt his gentleness meld with the power of the horse and she'd flushed with desire, then embarrassment: here she was, traveling to Heaven, consumed with feelings of lust.

Now, standing by the golden fence, Trua looked bereft. But she was probably the last person he wanted to see right now. Back at Pandaemonium, he'd ordered her onto the other horse.

"They're beautiful," she said softly.

He didn't answer but neither did he tell her to leave, so she stayed there, behind him, watching the grasses wave a silvery green where the horses had been.

* * * * *

"Look!"

Haisheng's voice rang out. Annie felt it even as she turned—that breath-sucking, hair-standing sense of lightning about to strike. An angel flapped towards them on the other side of the fence. She was female, her golden hair braided with flowers, and enormous, perhaps half again as tall as Ben. Her fleshy arms and broad chest exuded power. She landed just beyond the golden bars.

"Help us!" Annie called, running towards her. "We escaped from Hell—can you let us in—"

The angel stared in ferocious silence. This wasn't like meeting Michael. Did God now view her as an agent of Satan? The angel's gaze seemed to strip them all bare. What if none of them were deemed fit for rescue—a pagan, a communist, a professional atheist, and a tool of the devil? Of all of them, at least Kezia should get in. But maybe not even her?

"I'm sorry—I wasn't trying to trick anyone—" She was babbling, frantic. "Let the others in. Please. It's not their fault. Leave me out if you want, but save them—"

"You."

276

The angel's voice was deep and accusatory. Annie readied herself to be smited, pulverized, vaporized.

"You're the one."

"I was trying to help—"

"The embodied human."

The voice now held wonder along with accusation.

"Yes—I guess—"

"But others too." The angel glanced darkly across the other humans. "You shouldn't be here. You are unprecedented."

"Exactly! Things are happening that shouldn't be happening. I told Michael about it. If you can just take us to Michael—"

"Don't talk about Michael!" Spikes of light shot forth from the angel. Annie lurched back. The spikes vanished and the angel eyed them coolly.

"Michael is otherwise occupied," she said. "I am Urielle, and I'll take you to the Celestial City. This is a matter for the Lord."

* * * * *

Urielle carried them, one at a time, over the golden fence. She explained that it wasn't just a matter of crossing a physical boundary: they needed to be lustrated, or purified, in order for their mortal senses to tolerate Heaven.

Annie went first. With a single effortless flap, Urielle crossed the fence and lifted her up. For a moment she felt the same soothing warmth as with Michael. Then she was pierced by sharp, crystalline light. She smelled light: lemony, pungent, clean. She tasted light: crisp and steely as sauvignon blanc. She heard light:

277

translucent chimes, like rims of glasses being tapped with a knife. The light thrust itself into the far corners of her body. Her sensory organs—eyes, ears, nose, tongue—felt simultaneously tougher and more sensitive. She was changing. Membranes thickened, receptors multiplied exponentially. Her eyes expanded so much she thought they might burst from her head. She reeled with a sudden fear of being stuck in-between— neither human nor angel, living nor dead.

Then firm ground beneath her. The air was sweet with the scent of cherry blossoms, like the tree outside her bedroom window at home. So Heaven smelled like Bay Area springtime? With a rush of wings, a half dozen angels descended. Urielle nodded at one of them.

"Anael," she said. "Take her to the city. I'll continue with the others."

CHAPTER FORTY

Haisheng

Haisheng stood on the wrong side of Heaven's gate, waiting his turn. Annie, Trua, and Kezia had each been carried over. Now the archangel lifted Ben high above the gate and Haisheng was alone.

Not just alone by the fence, but alone in the world.

The terrifying, exhilarating flight to Heaven had temporarily displaced his despair. Now it returned. They were dead—Xinghua, Liang-li, all of his old comrades.

Ben clearly knew what he was talking about when he explained the suppression of the left in Shanghai. Secret meeting houses would have been ransacked, printing presses smashed. Union leaders, left-wing professors, sympathetic newspaper editors—all of them would have been imprisoned or killed.

Xinghua most likely killed.

Those slim cigarette fingers—burning. The mouth that curled down when reading the capitalist newspapers—burning. The arms that wrapped around Liang-li and pulled her tight in the dark—burning.

The knowledge was unbearable. Xinghua must have been in the fire all those decades that Haisheng was also there, maybe even close by, and Haisheng never knew. Why had he of all people—not Xinghua, not any

279

of the more deserving millions—been granted a return to life?

Everything he touched turned to failure. He'd spurned Ishaq, he'd failed the wraiths, his plan to ally with Satan was pure folly. His parents were right: he should have become a clerk. Or sold vegetables like his father. How much damage could you do selling beans and onions?

I grow old, ill and tired, blown hither and yon;
I am like a gull lost between Heaven and Earth.

Du Fu understood loss better than any of the modern poets. *I was a poet*, Haisheng had told Baphomet. Still more hubris and folly.

"Your turn," Urielle's deep voice intoned, and great silver arms wrapped around him.

* * * * *

The air was fragrant with the fruity scent of osmanthus. So Heaven smelled like Shanghai in autumn? A silent angel named Katmielle ferried Haisheng over green meadows dotted with pastel wildflowers and manicured gardens with crystal gazebos. They passed copses of trees but no wild forests, gentle hillocks but no jagged peaks. It was like earthly nature, only more deliberate and harmonious: palace grounds for an infinite and controlling emperor.

Below them, a group of angels danced in a silvery circle, arms raised in joyful tribute. Other angels flitted above a stream and gathered crystals from the sparkling current. They looked up at Haisheng, pointed, and stared.

"You are something new," Katmielle murmured, coasting over a tree with pale pink flowers.

Such beauty here and such suffering in Hell. Haisheng's gut clenched in refusal. He cramped; he needed firm ground. Katmielle apparently knew and flapped down beside a tall circular hedge.

He knelt and pressed his forehead into the damp earth, willing the stomach pains to stop. Blades of grass tickled his cheeks. The last time he'd lain in grass like this was by the pond on Xinghua's estate. Eventually he sat up.

"This is really the Christian Heaven." He said it, but it was a question.

Katmielle nodded.

"Why am I here?"

"That is not for me to know."

Branches rustled. Silver wings fluttered around the curve of the hedge—another angel, this one a young man holding a golden basket and shears. His calves were smooth and slender. His shoulders were glazed porcelain. His eyes were golden gems set in the silver of his face. Those eyes went wide when he saw Haisheng.

"Is he...?" the angel asked Katmielle. "Is it...?"

"A visiting human. On his way to the Celestial City."

"I am honored." He bowed formally to Haisheng. "You're most welcome here, visiting human. Are you a prophet?"

Haisheng held back a bitter laugh. "No. Far from it."

"I'm sorry." The angel looked stricken. "I only asked because I've always wanted to meet a prophet. I didn't mean to offend you. My name is Esor."

"You didn't offend at all." Haisheng had never met such a beautiful being. He felt both shy and bold.

"I'm…Chen Haisheng. From Shanghai, on Earth. May I ask what you're doing?"

"Trimming. I'm a hedge angel." Esor nodded at his basket, which was half-full with twigs and leaves.

"What's the hedge for?" Haisheng didn't care about hedges. He just wanted to keep this beautiful creature near him, talking.

"A tribute to God. Come inside. I'll show you." Esor's luminous face shone even brighter. Katmielle nodded permission and lifted Haisheng over the hedge onto a slightly curved path bounded by tall leafy walls. "It's a circle. The most holy shape: no beginning and no end, like God. We can walk here when we want to feel especially close to God. Or flying overhead, we see it and remember God's perfection."

Haisheng trailed Esor slowly. It was peaceful walking the circle—immersed in green after so much time in black dust, following a path with no forks or choices. He ran a hand along the precisely squared-off hedge. "It *is* perfect," he said. "You never make mistakes?"

"I do." Esor smiled. "But God is forgiving."

Utter crap! The angel clearly knew nothing of Hell. But Haisheng didn't want to contradict this stunning being.

"So is God your boss?"

The angel looked puzzled. "I don't know what that is."

"Your supervisor? The person who tells you what to do? The owner of the hedge?"

"Oh. That doesn't happen here. No one owns the hedge. No one owns anything. And we all understand our missions so there's no need for anyone to direct us. For instance, myself." Esor gestured at the green walls.

282

"I know which parts need trimming. I work as much as needed to highlight the beauty of God's creation. I love trimming, but when there are no more branches to trim, I'm free to enjoy other parts of creation."

How bizarre. Christian Heaven was like communism: no wage labor, no private property, people working for their own fulfillment and the common good.

"We should go," Katmielle said.

Esor reached his shears into the hedge, snipped off a leafy twig and proffered it. His slim fingers held the twig like Xinghua used to hold his cigarette.

"For your journey," he said.

The air was thick with the scent of tobacco smoke and printer's ink. Impulsively Haisheng grabbed Esor's hand and pressed it violently against his lips. He wanted to hold it there forever. He wanted to devour it. He wanted to pull the angel's beautiful slender body against his. He didn't know what he wanted. The angel's hand was glassy and cool and inhuman.

"Come," Katmielle said, enfolding Haisheng under a wing and lifting up.

"Peace be with you, Chen Haisheng," the hedge angel called as they flew off. "Be patient and faithful, my friend, and perhaps someday God will make you a prophet."

CHAPTER FORTY-ONE

Annie

The Celestial City was all crystal and gold and light. Its wall was a low, sparkling band of light that conveyed welcome—*rejoice! you have arrived!*—rather than exclusion. The streets glistened like an ice rink lit from below. The buildings were made entirely of glass—not the dark mirror-glass of suburban office complexes, but the delicate clear glass of a conservatory.

Annie waited with the angel Anael in a small square surrounded by structures that rose the equivalent of four or five floors, sparkling with sourceless light. She could see everything inside, which was basically angels. Angels dancing. Angels playing musical instruments. Angels carving, or weaving, or stretching their wings and limbs in some angelic version of yoga. The Celestial City seemed to be a place of communion—joining together in common activity—and of transparency, where everything about you was known. For the first time she understood the devil city: its dark empty houses and meaningless walls were what you would get if you tried to copy Heaven with no materials but volcanic rock and no purpose other than spite.

Annie seated herself on a golden bench that was slightly larger than human scale, her feet dangling above the ground like a toddler. The air was moist with the scent of redwoods and loam.

"About Michael," she ventured. "Urielle said he was 'otherwise occupied.' Is he...all right?"

Anael looked at her with what might have been pity. "He is on retreat," she said and, though Annie tried to follow up, wouldn't say any more.

A rush of wings brought another angel into the square. He deposited Trua on the luminous pavement, nodded to Anael—apparently the designated angelic babysitter—and left.

Trua stood staring at the gleaming buildings. He looked small and scared. If this city felt alien to Annie, who came from a world of glass and steel skyscrapers, what must it be like for him?

"It's just a city," she said, although of course it wasn't. "You did great in the devil city. You found your way around better than I ever did."

He didn't seem to hear her. She tried again.

"We're safe here. This is probably the safest place in the universe. There's no way Satan will get us here—"

Now he looked at her.

"Not Satan. God. Your Christian God. What will he do to me?"

The enormity of his fear slammed her. He was a pagan. He'd killed Christians. He'd looted and pillaged. He'd scorned people who were not of his tribe and treated them as less than human. He had already spent 1,600 years in the fire; what new torment would God devise for him now?

But Trua had also just rescued them all from Pandaemonium. He'd sacrificed his own second chance at life to protect her and Mary. Alive, his values might have been tribal and narrow but in Hell he'd risked himself for so many strangers—Dev in the canyon, Haisheng and the wraiths, even Kezia when she was completely unknown to him.

He didn't deserve more punishment. But where in Hell had she seen any evidence that God cared about what people truly deserved?

"I won't let him hurt you," Annie said fiercely, feeling the absurdity of the claim even as she made it. She had no control over God. She'd never even felt God's presence. And wasn't she just as rigidly judgmental as God in her puny, mortal way?

"I'm sorry," she said to Trua in a low voice. "I'm sorry for judging you. For not thinking about what you'd been through. You were right. I shouldn't have come back here. I was stupid. I abandoned Mary and brought Ben here and took you away from the wraiths. I should never have called on Satan—"

Trua had been looking at the ground but now he turned to her.

"I'm glad you came back," he said.

The world seemed to stop. Her eyes filled. She wanted to hurl herself into his arms—to kiss him, hold him, never let him go. And then it occurred to her that they were no longer in Hell. Perhaps different rules applied. Annie stepped closer, reached a hand to Trua's cheek and, when he didn't move away, leaned in and put her lips to his.

He reached his arms around her and pulled her tight.

She'd imagined this for so long. Annie braced for nausea and retching to set in, but they didn't. The muscles of his back were firm and taut under her hands, and his mouth pressed against hers with the urgency of a drowning man finding breath.

* * * * *

The air was crisp with the scent of clean sheets and new books.

One by one, the others were delivered. You'd think that people arriving in Heaven would be ecstatic, but they all looked uneasy. Even Kezia: as soon as the angel released her, she turned anxiously to Urielle.

"When can I see my husband?"

"Patience," the archangel said.

Ben launched into a joke as his angel set him down—something about the quality of the taxi service improving—but stopped in mid-story when he saw Annie and Trua. They'd pulled out of their embrace but remained leaning into each other, hands clasped.

"What the Hell?" Ben mouthed, staring, but Annie ignored him. She bent in to Trua's neck and inhaled his wonderful, sweaty smell. She needed to feel him, again and again. He was here. They could touch. He'd forgiven her.

"Where's my husband?" Kezia repeated. "Where are my parents? My grandparents?"

She had a point. Where were all the human souls? Annie wasn't sure if the angels filling this city were former humans, or if the humans were busy with divine duties elsewhere in Heaven, or if they took some completely different form here.

"Sit down," Urielle said, gesturing to the golden benches. "We can talk more freely here in the city. Of course Heaven is secure, but considering what you say is going on, it's prudent not to discuss certain things near the border. You asked about Michael...Michael is on retreat, reflecting. I'm filling in while he makes amends."

"Amends?" Annie asked.

"He acted rashly. Michael is zealous for God, which is a beautiful thing. He loves God perhaps more than any of us, which is like saying there's a number beyond infinity. But sometimes his love of the good and his hatred of evil leads him to make errors."

"That was my fault," Annie murmured.

"No. You tried to protect others, which is laudable. And you're hardly the first human to be manipulated by Lucifer."

Urielle used Satan's original name, her voice wistful. Once he had been an angel too. Perhaps the two of them had danced side by side in one of those sparkling halls. They would have worshipped, conferred, planned together; they would have trusted each other almost as much as they trusted God.

"But Michael's mistakes are not the issue." Urielle's voice turned hard. "The issue is this news of yours. Souls released from the fire, portals opening up to Earth. All unprecedented. And then Lucifer's call for the Fallen to destroy themselves. That shouldn't be possible, but with these changes—"

"Wait!" Kezia interrupted. "You promised to bring me to my husband—"

Urielle flared.

Her body stretched and morphed into a looming pillar of light—blinding, terrible, enraged light. Daggers of light spiked and arced across the courtyard. Shards of light shot skyward like glistening razor blades. Annie gasped. They all cringed. Annihilation loomed. And then, just as instantly, the light dissipated and Urielle was once again a figure with arms and legs and wings.

Trua wiped his forehead. Ben and Haisheng rubbed their eyes. Kezia looked like she'd been slapped.

"Of course," Urielle murmured, as if nothing had happened. Her tone was tolerant, benign, even warm. "Your loved ones. Humans through the millennia have wanted to see their loved ones even before they wanted to see God. It's the human way, ever since Adam chose to follow Eve into mortality. Well. Let's take care of this and then we can return to the business at hand."

The angel rose and fluttered a few feet off the ground. "Follow me. You can walk; it's not so far. And it's appropriate to approach the Lord as pilgrims."

CHAPTER FORTY-TWO

Annie

The palace rose ahead of them, a gleaming mass of prisms like a giant crystal beehive.

"We've got the iceberg, now where's the Titanic?" Ben quipped. He'd been cracking jokes ever since arriving in Heaven. Annie wanted to slug him.

The palace radiated such bright light that it was impossible to see anything inside. Gold bas-reliefs of flowers and trees climbed the entry doors. Urielle led them into a giant crystal hall that was devoid of furniture or adornment. Rows of angels lined each glass wall, heads bowed, facing the far end of the room where a mass of light pulsed and sparked on a crystal pedestal.

It wasn't a particularly large or interesting mass of light. It could have been an oversized disco ball or a Christmas ornament designed for a very big tree in a public square. There were no heavenly choirs, no haloed celebrity saints. There were none of the angelic musicians or dancers or garland makers who filled the rest of the city. It was, frankly, underwhelming.

"The great and powerful Oz," Ben said.

"Shh," Annie whispered.

"Pay no attention to the man behind the curtain—"

"Shut *up*."

She was remembering the moment when Mary changed from an abstract idea into something real. Annie had been sprawled in the dust of Hell, dizzy from her latest descent into the fire, when she realized there was something in her lap. It didn't glow like this mass, but it too had been round and pulsing.

"Anyone got a stick? We can roast marshmallows—"

"Shut up." This time it was Trua who snapped at Ben. Why did her brother have to be such an arrogant ass? Then she realized: he was afraid.

"Approach," Urielle said. "The Lord is waiting."

"George?" Kezia's voice was hesitant. The mass of light kept pulsing and sparking.

"Oh, come on," Ben said. He pushed past Annie and strode towards the throne. "If her dead husband is here, let her see him already. And if you're really God, you can do better than a '70s party decoration—"

The world turned inside-out.

The floor rose and the walls folded in on themselves, then out again into a different shape. It was like that moment in origami where, after a half dozen incremental folds, a flat, scrunched wad of paper opens up into a spread-winged crane.

The palace and its throne and crystal walls were gone. Annie floated in mid-air near the center of a bowl with tiers that radiated up and out like the petals of a giant rose. It stretched higher and farther than Annie could see—a rose big enough to encompass a planet. The petals were comprised of a warm, dawn-like light that was fed by a more powerful light at the stamen— that pulsing glow from the throne, magnified a million-fold.

White dwarf star? Pulsar?

God.

This was peace. The wildflower meadows and silver fountains were only a hint; Michael and Urielle's embraces were the removal of a pebble from a shoe. Everything was full. Everything was complete. No pain, no loss, no conflict, no lack. All was well. All was as it was meant to be. The universe fit together in a single perfectly-designed whole and she was part of that beautiful whole and she belonged and she was perfect.

That moment when you place the final jigsaw piece in the puzzle.

Berry pie emerging from the oven, golden crust and purple bubbles.

Mary asleep on her breast, nipple in mouth. No sound but breath.

All of that and more. Fearless wren in the Steep Ravine mist. Neon sign in the laundromat window in darkening twilight. Take every moment of beauty and peace from your life and melt them together with every moment of beauty and peace from a billion different, unknown lives. Bowl of steaming rice on a rainy night. A single lily stem in a clear glass vase. Flash of red through the jungle green and then sixty crimson parrots feeding at a clay lick. All this is now yours. All this your inheritance. All this your dowry.

Hills covered with gladness, valleys mantled with grain.

Boundaries dissolve and borders vanish. *I, you, they*—all gone. You bloom with the beauty of others and they bloom with yours. You guzzle each other's souls like college students in a beer garden; you're drunk on each other's beauty. You are known, treasured, loved. You are all one.

Eternal weight of glory far beyond all comparison.

And now she heard music. Angels and saints, a million harmonies and a million counterpoints, all blended perfectly. Voices and instruments, strings and brass. She heard them and also played them, Annie who had never blown a penny whistle or keyed a piano in her life. Music conveying wonder and gratitude, and music kindling wonder and gratitude. It said everything she had ever wanted to say—the things she groped to say when alive but never quite articulated—and said it all in one word: *hallelujah.*

Praise God with the sound of the trumpet
Praise God with the harp and lyre
Praise God with timbrel and dancing
Praise God with strings and pipe
Praise God with the clash of cymbals
Praise God with resounding cymbals

God the creator, God the sustainer, God who makes possible. Magnificent wholeness. No more *I* or *you* or *they*, only a great *we*, and even that great *we* can't express the oneness and ubiquity and beneficence of God...

Annie floated.

In Hell, she had struggled to stay above the flames. Here God held her and she floated in a still pond of peace. The water knew each dip and sag of her body—no matter how blemished, no matter how mortifying—and filled it, accepted it, held it. Light. Music. Oneness.

Praise God with timbrel and dancing
Praise God with strings and pipe

She could float there forever. There could be nothing better.

Then a pinch on her waist, like someone tugging the belt of a bathrobe.

No. Let me stay.

Her chest hollowed. She felt cold and empty, a drained glass. Now the palace floor returned under her feet. Her body was heavy as armor, clanking and immobilizing. Already her experience of the light and music was starting to fade. *Remember it!* she thought fiercely, but she couldn't put it into words, even to herself.

She would have stayed in that place—that vast, billion-petaled rose—without a second thought. Without even a thought for Mary.

"Now do you understand?" she heard Urielle ask, faintly, as if from a different universe.

CHAPTER FORTY-THREE

Ben

Ben was having a heart attack. He was sure of it.

Clammy hands and sweating. Tightness in his chest. Palpitations.

"Are you all right?" someone said. He didn't know who, but he couldn't let them see. Somehow he managed to mutter *yes*. Must shut it down. Stop the sweating, dry the hands. But you couldn't make a heart attack go away. He needed a hospital. He needed to be left alone. Aspirin! He needed aspirin. There was aspirin in his bathroom, aspirin in the emergency box at the studio. Defibrillator in the studio. Epi-pen in the studio for peanut allergies. Nothing like that here. And where the hell was here. He knew and didn't want to know. Where the *hell*. Ha. But make the tightness stop. The palpitations. He needed a doctor. He needed self-control. Like that first TV gig when he was 23: the lights made him sweat, the make-up felt like a death mask, but he held it together. He shut down the palpitations then and he could do it now. No one should know. *Yes I'm all right*. But it's not all right. Arteries blocked. Oxygen stopped. Heart tissue dying—

"Ben—"

Annie touching his arm. *No.* She'll feel the sweat. Time to leave, back to the airport. Need a taxi. Should never have come. Better alone.

When Natasha left, she said that too: *better alone.*

"Ben!"

People were fussing around him. Annie had one arm, the Chinese guy had the other. Leading him somewhere. Sitting him down on a bench. Sweat still pouring off him, sweat like a sauna, a hothouse, like getting too close to a fire—

No.

Long cool fingers touched his forehead. Whisper of feathers, scent of eucalyptus and camphor. The sweat dried up. The clamminess vanished. His chest opened up and his heart relaxed to its normal, unremarkable rhythm.

"Was it his heart?" Annie asked anxiously.

"No." This was the throaty voice of the large female angel. "It was what I think you call...a fear attack."

"Panic attack?" Annie asked.

Humiliation washed over him. He wanted to sink through the bench. Worse, now that the sweat and the palpitations were gone, he was thinking clearly again.

A panic attack was the least of his problems.

* * * * *

He'd been wrong. Utterly, completely wrong.

God existed.

God created the universe. God reigned over everything. God sent prophets to convey God's rules, and scriptures to codify them, and churches to reinforce them. Follow the rules, and you get to experience what

296

he had just experienced, forever. Spurn them and you go to Hell.

Ben was going to Hell.

No doubt about it. He'd spent his entire adult life denying God in repeated and extremely public ways. How many people had he taken with him? The cable shows he appeared on had millions of viewers. Top ratings: he wouldn't waste his time on anything less. Say there were 5 million viewers and one percent of them started questioning the existence of God because of him. That would be 50,000 people. Say half of those questioners decided to reject God entirely: 25,000 people. Enough to populate a public university, a small city. And was it arrogant to think that one percent was a conservative estimate? Ben was popular. People were always coming up to him in restaurants saying how much they appreciated his perspective, his wit. Even on this last trip to check up on Annie: a woman had approached him in the Admirals Club at JFK, a matronly woman with silver hair and a Gucci handbag, and told him to "keep giving those holier-than-thou hypocrites what-for." So it could easily be more than 25,000 or 50,000. It could be hundreds of thousands. Maybe millions when you added in his articles and books, translated into 17 different languages. An entire metropolis going to Hell because of him! He was more than a false prophet; he was an industrial-scale propagator of blasphemy. A Henry Ford of heresy. A Sam Walton of wickedness.

Until now, he would have been proud of that.

But it wasn't the prospect of all those millions of people going to Hell that appalled him, not if he were being honest. It wasn't even the prospect of himself in Hell.

Hell was an abstraction: he now accepted that it existed, but all he had personally experienced was that jail cell in Satan's palace, which was hardly eternal torment.

What appalled him—what socked his gut in a way nothing did before, not even Natasha leaving—was the loss of Heaven.

Those few moments when he had been one with God. Ben never had occasion to use the word "bliss" before, but that summed it up. The unity, wholeness, perfection. The most beautiful human constructs—Newton's *Principia*, Einstein's relativity, the Constitution of the United States—were shabby rags next to that.

Benjamin J. Maple the individual had vanished for those few moments and it didn't matter. It was shocking! His knowledge, his verbal acumen, his achievements—everything that made him *him*—had dissolved but he didn't care. All of that individuality was like an abandoned cocoon. It wasn't that he had emerged as a butterfly—after all, there was no more *him* to emerge—but that he had become part of a much bigger butterfly. An infinite butterfly. A butterfly that fluttered the tiniest tip of an infinitely beautiful wing and the whole universe fluttered too.

Fullness. Unity. Totality. Bliss.

And now it was gone. He'd been hurled out like a deadbeat drunk who couldn't pay his bar tab.

Take my limbs. Take my kidneys, my heart, my lungs. Just let me back.

A wild thought arose: all those alien abduction stories he'd ridiculed, where the aliens extracted people's organs. Were they in fact true and the victims were people like him, bargaining away their body parts to get back to Heaven?

Now he understood addiction. He'd paid lip service to the idea that addiction was an illness, but inside he'd always condemned it as a failure of will. *Just say no.* But this craving for paradise was stronger than words or will. He *needed* to return to that oneness with God. He would crawl across nails. Eat broken glass. Tear his throat open with his own hands if that would help.

It wouldn't help. He had been an arrogant, stubborn denier. He had done the devil's work. He had doomed himself, forever.

"Ben, talk to me."

Annie. Damn her. She'd been right and he'd been wrong. Just one time in their lives she was right, and it had to be about this?

Ben hid his face in his hands. He tried to shut his ears to his sister's voice.

If he couldn't see that perfect, all-consuming light again—if he couldn't hear that universal harmony—he didn't want to see or hear anything.

CHAPTER FORTY-FOUR

Kezia

The first time Kezia saw George was at a New York Phil-harmonic concert in Central Park in 1985. Those were the days when she was game for anything, anywhere, as long as it was free—Italian street fairs, roller skating marathons, the mermaid parade at Coney Island. She met two of her girlfriends and they maneuvered through the hordes of picnickers, found a little triangle of grass, and spread out their blanket. Kezia's friends had brought lasagna but forgot forks, so they ate it with their hands. She would always remember the lasagna because of the embarrassment of meeting such a hand-some man when she had tomato sauce all over her face.

Classical music in the park drew a white crowd, so of course they noticed the good-looking brother sitting by himself a few blankets away with a box of Chinese take-out. Kezia smiled at him. (This was before she re-alized about the tomato sauce.) He smiled back. And the next thing she knew, he was standing beside their blanket, offering to share his fortune cookies.

They talked until the music started. All of them talked, but really it was him and her. They joked about the fortunes in their cookies. They joked about the con-ductor, whose name was something Polish and unpronounceable. "I've got a hard name too," George said. "P-a-r-k-e-r. That's Polish for Parker." When George told them he was a firefighter, Kezia felt her friends swoon. She tried not to stare at his big, calloused hands. When the music started, George tapped a chopstick in time and afterwards told her that, yes, he played an instrument too. Not a symphonic one, though: harmonica.

Kezia wanted to slap herself when they joined the throng filing out of the park and she hadn't gotten his phone number. He hadn't asked for hers, either, so maybe there was nothing to it. She imagined walking through the five boroughs from firehouse to firehouse, asking if anyone named George Parker worked there.

The next Sunday, he showed up at her church. *Felt in need of a little spiritual uplift,* he said. *What a nice coincidence to see you.* But then Kezia remembered talking with her girlfriends about church in front of him. So she knew.

When George died, Kezia had the church play a recording of the piece from that concert—Beethoven's Egmont Overture—at his memorial, along with his favorite harmonica solo, "Blue and Lonesome" by the Charles Ford Band. She'd dug through George's stacks of cassette tapes to find that song. After that, she didn't touch the tapes again for ten years, by which time cassettes were ancient history.

She bagged them and put them out with the trash while Jeremiah was sleeping, and wept.

* * * * *

Now dread coated the hollow of her stomach. Where was George?

The others were all gathered around Ben, who was having some kind of panic episode. Kezia walked away, hoisted herself onto a golden bench, and slumped over.

She had been waiting for George—worried that he'd be angry or disappointed with her, yes, but certain she would see him. Along with her parents, her grandparents, George's parents. For decades, she'd counted on seeing all of them.

She'd felt no trace of any of them.

It had been wonderful, there was no denying that: peace and joy beyond anything she'd imagined, communion with billions of other souls as well as with God. But all those souls were a big mishmash, like pea soup after you cook it in the crockpot all day and the individual peas break down into thick green puree. She couldn't find George. There was no "George." There was God and oneness and transcendence but no identifiable, individual soul that used to be her husband.

How could that be? George's spirit had talked her through all those years raising Jeremiah. George had kept her sane during the endless hours in the devil prison cell.

In my father's house are many mansions.

She didn't need a mansion, didn't need a room. All she wanted was a triangle of grass with him like that evening in Central Park. Not even grass! Let her find him in a crowded subway car among sweaty strangers pushing and shoving. Let her find him in a grocery store checkout line or the trash-strewn alley behind her apartment building. Even for just one minute. Just one touch. She had been *promised*. All these years, suffering, sorrowing, and waiting for this promise.

God! How can you do this!

Rage welled up. She wanted to rip things. It was more than a promise, it was a covenant, and this time it wasn't the children of Israel who broke the covenant, it was God. She hated the golden bench underneath her. She hated the crystal buildings and luminous streets. George's soul was lost to her and her own soul would be lost too. She used to imagine a heavenly reunion someday between George and Jeremiah—father and son getting to know each other for the first time—and now that would never be. Orphaned in life, orphaned in death. *Don't be blasphemous,* a small part of her said. *God is everyone's father. There are no orphans in heaven.* But she had been promised George. She had been promised her loved ones. She had been sold a bill of goods, and even all the transcendence and joy that came with joining the great green pea soup of souls didn't make up for that.

She didn't want to love people in a perfect divine mass. She wanted to love specific, imperfect individuals.

George tracking mud into the house on rainy nights after a jam session. When she scolded him, he would pull out one of his harmonicas and blow a big fat fart noise at her.

Kezia stood and raised a fist towards the palace and the throne. "I don't want your Heaven! I want my husband!"

The others, still clustered around Ben, turned and stared. Several angels passing overhead halted and hovered in shock. Urielle shot into the air and landed, grim-faced, in front of Kezia.

"Stop this nonsense about your husband right now. You, and him"—she nodded towards Ben—"and all of you. Stop all this nonsense. We need to hear what you know about Satan's plans—"

"Give her a minute!" Annie dashed over. "She's grieving!"

"Yes, give her a minute," Trua echoed.

Urielle flared again—towering, immense, blinding. She arced white sparks and pulsed with enraged power. Kezia cowered. She had sinned, she had blasphemed, they would all be destroyed.

"Forgive me, Jesus," she whispered.

"JESUS!"

The shout came from across the courtyard. It was Annie's brother, and he didn't sound terrified; he sounded amazed.

There, walking serenely down the steps into the courtyard, was a tall tobacco-skinned man with wavy hair down to his shoulders, a trim beard, and a beige tunic belted with a dark brown cord.

He was as familiar to Kezia as her son, her husband, her own face in the mirror.

CHAPTER FORTY-FIVE

Annie

Yes, Jesus was walking down the steps of the palace.

Annie knew it could only be Jesus. He looked like every greeting-card, picture-book image of him she'd ever seen—skin pale as a white peach, blue eyes, and long straight hair.

"My Lord." Urielle morphed back into her winged form and dropped onto one knee. Three angels who had been passing overhead dove to the ground on their knees also.

"Down," Trua murmured, tugging on Annie. She lowered herself but before she could settle, Jesus gestured her to stop.

"Please. There's no need for that," he said. His voice held olives and sesame, coarse wool and smooth balm. "Come with me. Yes, you, Urielle, too." He glanced at the other angels. "The rest of you, go about your business. I'm sorry to interrupt you."

The other angels flapped up, hovering for a moment, and Annie got the sense that something unusual had just happened. She followed Jesus into a smaller courtyard with a set of gold benches that seemed designed for intimate conversation. In the far corner, a crystal fountain gushed chimes of water. A single vine of pink roses climbed a crystal wall. The air was buttery with the scent of just-baked cookies.

"Not just God? But you too?" Ben said. His panic seemed to have given way to fascination. "You're real too?"

Jesus nodded.

"Virgin birth? Crucifixion? Resurrection?"

He nodded

Annie's shoulders loosened with relief. All those times she'd failed to find Jesus in prayer, and now here he was. He would fix everything. He would take her home to Mary and deal with Satan and save Kezia's son from the fire—maybe he would even save her mother—and everything would be fine. She wanted to throw herself in his arms like a child.

It was strange, though, that he looked so much like those greeting-card Jesuses. "What does he look like to you?" she whispered to Trua.

"Roman, of course."

She leaned towards Haisheng, seated on her other side. "What does he look like?"

"English. Smartly dressed. Young, but with eye-glasses for reading..." He halted, surprised. "He looks like Master Crowley!"

"Who?"

"The Bible teacher in my childhood school."

Jesus—*her* Jesus, the greeting-card one—smiled at her. He'd heard every whispered syllable. "That's right," he said. "Each of you sees me as you are accustomed to seeing me. It's easier for you and it makes no difference to me."

"Is *anything* real here?" Annie blurted. She was still unnerved by Urielle's transformation.

"It's all real." Jesus looked slowly at each of them. "But you perceive it in a limited, earthly way. My apostle Paul called it 'through a glass, darkly.' Your modern thinkers might call it metaphor. No human can view the divine and live, not even Moses, not even Paul. Do you understand? Because now there are things I need to know. Tell me about your release from the fire."

* * * * *

Annie had never felt such focused listening before. Jesus questioned them about their emergence from the fire and about the portals and about two dead devils that Haisheng had apparently found in the desert. His expression remained calm throughout, but Urielle fluttered in growing agitation.

With a chill Annie realized: *he didn't know about this.*

The boundaries between Hell and Earth—between life and death, between the mortal and immortal—were breaking down. Secure for billions of years, they were now cracking. It wasn't just her own release from the fire: Hell's entire structure was being shaken loose.

And Jesus, who supposedly saw everything, hadn't been aware of it until this motley group of humans showed up outside the gates of Heaven.

"You can close the portals, right?" Annie asked. "You created the system, you can fix the problems—you can save my mother—you can save Kezia's son—"

"Annie. Listen carefully," Jesus said. "God the creator set up this universe and its rules, and one of the rules is that there *are* rules. God chose to limit himself to the rules that he created. To limit *us* to those rules. Think of a bride or groom vowing to be faithful. They

307

have the power to stray at any moment, but they choose not to exercise it. Thus God chose to live by the rules he created for this universe. So I can't turn off gravity or make time run backwards. And I can't remove people from the destiny they earned in their lifetime. No matter how beloved they are. No matter if they have many wonderful qualities. No matter if it doesn't seem fair."

"You can't or you won't?" Annie said cautiously.

"Listen again. Perhaps this way will be more clear. There once was a master clockmaker who made the most beautiful, elaborate clocks—"

"It's a parable, right?" Ben interrupted. "And not just any parable. The classic watchmaker analogy—"

Jesus raised a hand and Ben fell silent. He turned back to the others and continued.

"This clockmaker made the most wonderful clocks. All kinds: cuckoo clocks, grandfather clocks, precise mechanical marvels where small figurines would emerge and parade in a semicircle in front of the clock every hour. He made one immense chiming clock for the center of the town, mounted on the town hall, and all the villagers relied on it to know when to wake up each morning, when to start work, when to break for their noonday meal. And then he went away. Far away, across the sea, never to return. He left his son to oversee the clocks. And everything was fine—the chimes, the moving figurines—until one day the clocks began to slow down. They were old. The mechanisms were wearing out. Soon they chimed only every two hours, and then only once a day, even the grand clock in the center of the town. The villagers staggered around, exhausted, arguing over who was late and who was early, while crops rotted in the fields and loaves burned in the ovens. They sent a delegation to the clockmaker's son. 'Help us!' they cried. 'Fix this!' The son knew the clocks inside out—he knew each screw, each spring, each jewel—but he hadn't known they would wear out. He was not sure that he could fix them. More crucially, he was not sure that he *should*. 'When the clocks chimed, you praised my father's thoughtful handiwork,' he told the villagers. 'Now, when the clocks fall silent, is this not also part of his design?'"

Jesus halted. A breeze riffled the courtyard with the toasty scent of stir-fried garlic and sesame oil.

"That's all?" Kezia said. "That's the end?"

"God is gone?" Haisheng asked.

"Parables." Ben shook his head. "They obfuscate more than they illuminate."

"I don't think I need to explain again," Jesus said to him. "They understand."

CHAPTER FORTY-SIX

Jesus

One of the things he missed about being human was water.

Those immersions in the Jordan River. Hot wind and dust from the Judaean Hills, then the crashing shock of cold and wet. Every pore in his human body shouted with glee. He would toss his head back, droplets careening from wild hair, and then splash water on his face all over again. The prophet John had introduced him to river baptism and dressed it in the language of godliness—a rebirth into holiness, a renewal of God's covenant with Israel—and yes, it was all of that, but for him at the core it was the water. The sensory slap. The sudden chill. The thrill of a different way of physical being—suspended, limbs moving through thickness, refracted vision. And afterwards the very human pleasure of a clean body, skin tightening as it dried in the sun and tingling with the slightest breeze or touch.

The Jordan was best, but any water would do. The formal Temple baths run by the corrupt Sadducees. The spring-fed, algae-edged *mikvot* of the Galilee. Even the buckets of water his family had drawn for washing: he remembered waiting his turn, volunteering to go last, selfless but also secretly eager for the chance to lift the bucket and dump the gritty, greyish remains over his seven-year-old head.

Coursing down his forehead, tickling his neck, causing him to gasp and choke and laugh. It was always surprising, always new.

As God, he could see water—the rivers and oceans of Earth, the seas of other planets. But he couldn't experience it. It wasn't the same.

* * * * *

He missed other things too. The arrival of these dislocated humans reminded him. It was one thing to watch humanity from the distance of Heaven, or to absorb the souls of the worthy dead. It was another to be around living humans—the musky smell of their nervous perspiration, the rhythmic draw of their breath, the multitude of ways they unthinkingly glanced at or touched each other.

Touch: the man Trua gripping the woman Annie's arm. He thought he was doing it to steady her, but there was so much more. Possessiveness. Fear. Affection. Desire.

Glance: Annie's eyes darting onto Ben with his cheeky comment about parables. Mortified by her brother, furious at him, proud of him. None of the angels of Heaven displayed such shifting, contradictory emotions.

But touch. He kept returning to memories of touch. How he had loved healing people with his hands! The warmth of their skin, the way it bowed so far but no further to his fingertips, like a couple negotiating a dance. Then the electric charge as his divinity pulsed

311

into them, the exhilaration of their body as bones mended and bacteria shriveled.

And human desire, like Trua's. He'd never let himself pursue that when he was alive: the Magdalene would suffer enough losing her teacher without also losing a lover. Of course he had experienced perfect communion, billions of times, with each human soul that arrived in Heaven. It was the imperfect communion he lacked—the yearning, the sparks from downed wires, the triumph of even a badly spliced connection across the void.

Admit it! He envied Annie and Trua! But of course he did. Even as God he wasn't immune to emotion. Even his father hadn't been immune, although his father's weakness most often was wrath or jealousy. "I am a jealous god," he had admitted to the Hebrews with remarkable honesty before he went away.

He envied them and yet he sorrowed for them. Weigh that flash of imperfect intimacy against everything else that was human—their limited, self-bound perspective, the misunderstandings and conflicts, the bodily decay that began the moment they were born—and divinity would win every time.

* * * * *

And while he was thinking this, he was also watching and noting:

A migrating yellow-rumped warbler flew into the reflective glass wall of an office building in Minneapolis, Minnesota, broke its neck, and died.

Melia Ortiz of Jalisco, Mexico, gave birth to her fourth healthy child and first daughter. Her husband Javier wept and thanked God.

A small volelike vertebrate on a planet in the Canis Minor constellation sniffed its dead mate and had the unprecedented understanding that it, too, would some-day die, starting its species on the long upward climb to self-consciousness.

Jessica Chen of Bethesda, Maryland, realized that Jason Carlisle would never love her and used her fa-ther's razor to cut a long, shallow notch on her left arm.

A street cat in Kristiansund, Norway, discovered a loose board that allowed it into a warehouse where bar-rels of salt cod sat uncovered.

Lichens on a planet in the Cygnus constellation colo-nized a new rock.

Bruno Freund of Goppingen, Germany, flew to Spain with his wife's best friend after withdrawing all 227,000 Euros from their marital bank account. He bought a bot-tle of cava and toasted his new life and how he was done with "that castrating bitch."

An asteroid hit a planet in the Andromeda constella-tion, causing a massive explosion that wiped out all ver-tebrate life.

A small creature in the Marianas Trench was eaten by a larger creature. The small creature: terror. The large creature: delight.

Nguyen Hai Giang of Hanoi, Vietnam, age seven, fi-nally learned how to ride a bike.

And while he was witnessing these things and so many more, he worried about the portals. They swam upward through the ocean of his consciousness, pushing aside the churning mass of plankton and krill that represented all the lives of this universe.

This beautiful universe created by God.

Abandoned by God.

Now, perhaps, coming apart.

* * * * *

In the beginning was his father, the creator.

God was an inventor. It was his nature. He delighted in creating universes, and he was very, very good at it. Maintenance, though? Not as interesting to him.

God created the universe. Heaven and angels first. Then Hell, when Lucifer and the rebel angels were vanquished and required a place of exile. After that, the realm known to humans—matter, and stars, and galaxies, millions upon millions of galaxies. Scientists called it the Big Bang, but it was really just God doing his creation thing. And then, in a kind of compensation for the loss of his beloved Lucifer, humans. The Garden of Eden, free will, the fall. Milton summed it up pretty well. Human society was born and history began, twinned perpetually with strife, suffering, death. Hell's lake of fire became the repository for human souls who flouted God's edicts or didn't pay appropriate homage to their jealous, demanding, perhaps overly punitive creator.

And God was engaged, for a while. He marveled at Noah's ingenuity in carrying out those cryptic ark directions. He wreaked chaos upon the Babylonians for their presumptuous tower. He buddied with Abraham, argued with Moses. And when he despaired of humans becoming what he wished them to be, he sent a version

314

of himself—his son, so to speak—in human form to spread his Word.

It was some time after that when God lost interest. Perhaps the lure of new creation was too strong to resist, or perhaps humans grew tedious, making the same mistakes over and over. But God moved on. He left his son in charge and went on to create other universes. Jesus remembered him musing about the prospect of universes without linear time, and universes that doubled back on themselves, and universes with one, two, or ten dimensions. And those were just a few of the ideas. God the creator saw infinite possibilities and he wanted to explore them all. He refused to be limited or tied down. He was Pytheas setting sail for lands beyond the Pillars of Hercules, Huck Finn lighting out for the territories.

That was a very long time ago.

No one had heard from him since.

But Jesus remained. He witnessed. He listened. He loved. No sparrow fell on Earth that he didn't see, no soul cried out in the depths of Hell that didn't move him to weep, but he followed God's rules and didn't intervene. He refused to wave a hand and grant wishes like a fairy godmother. He didn't descend in luminous, raging glory to halt unjust wars or depose brutal dictators. He watched and listened in sorrow and in joy. And all the time he was the force holding and feeding the vast heavenly rose. He was calyx and stem, xylem and phloem. He couldn't help the living but he could hold the fortunate dead—unite them in one body with God, provide that golden warmth, fullness, and communion. It was his role; it was what God had intended. He was the gravity that anchored those countless souls, the

315

fissile reaction fueling light and connection and eternal life. They were billions upon billions, the number constantly growing, all feeding on his love like so many puppies at the teat. It was exhilarating and exhausting. He couldn't leave. He couldn't pop off on a quick jaunt through the stars, couldn't descend to wander, nostalgic, through the limestone-stubbled hills of Galilee. Even now—*this*—talking with these out-of-place humans just dozens of yards away from his throne, was a strain. He held Heaven together but it took effort. Sometimes it overwhelmed him and he faded. The Celestial City flickered. Just for the slightest moment, though. Then he would pull himself together (God's only son, failure was unthinkable) and tighten his grip and hurl love—LOVE, LOVE, LOVE—out through the throbbing, needy, worshipful billions that relied on him for eternal life, the petals of the rose.

* * * * *

And now this beautiful, heartbreaking universe was apparently faltering like the handiwork of that absent clockmaker. (It was a good parable. Despite Ben's carping, it really was.)

"Why us?" Annie had asked. "Why were we shaken loose and other people weren't?"

He didn't have an answer for her. He felt an emotion he hadn't felt in 2,000 years—inadequacy. And fear. Even when God the father had left, he hadn't felt fear. He had been confident of his own divinity, his ability to fulfill his mission.

"I don't know," he'd told her. It would have been easier to move a dozen galaxies than speak those words.

"You can fix it, right?"

Her voice had quavered with hope and fear. Perhaps he could. But perhaps these cracks were part of God's design. Thousand-year-old giant sequoias tired and died; rocks cleaved with water seepage; suns burned themselves out. Decay, like linear time and physical matter, was built into this universe.

Of course it would be Lucifer—the shining one, the prodigy, the tragedy—who would have figured this out and chosen to test it.

Anthony Robbins of Johannesburg, South Africa, pulled a knife but the other guy had a gun.

A stray dog in Santiago, Chile, had puppies.

Lindy Marshall found a $20 bill on the sidewalk and gave it to the homeless man standing by the I-17 off-ramp in Phoenix, Arizona.

12,537 sentient jellyfish-like beings were killed in a tribal war on a planet in the constellation Leo Minor.

A chicken laid an egg.

Usually when he remembered his human life he thought of the good things—sharing warm flatbread with the disciples around a firepit at night, his mother's generous laughter when Joseph told another bad joke, those skin-shocking immersions in the Jordan. Now, though, sitting in the crystal courtyard of his heavenly kingdom, he thought of Gethsemane.

Dead leaves underfoot. Earthy smell of fallen, rancid olives. No blossoms or new fruit yet—he would not live to see that—just tangled branches and silver leaves in the moonlight.

Take this cup from me, he had prayed to his father then.

And now.

His father was gone. Yet his will still had to be done.

CHAPTER FORTY-SEVEN

Kezia

Kezia's legs barely held her. She felt like a sack of potatoes balanced on a post: the only question was whether it would tumble this way or that. She managed one step after another until she was out of the small courtyard and away from the others.

Please, Jesus, don't be offended.

She pulled herself up onto yet another oversized golden bench, this one under a shimmering tree with long, draping branches. The air was rich with the scent of roasting chicken and freshly-chopped wood.

George was gone.

Worse, God was gone.

How could God just up and leave? How could He create this universe—its skies and oceans, its billions of souls, many of them with faith in him—and then forsake it? This world was like God's child. It was God's baby. And He had abandoned it.

She felt bereft. She felt betrayed. She felt alone.

She felt like Jeremiah.

The understanding struck her like a brick. She had never seen it this way before. A boy with only one parent, but that parent doted on him as if he were a universe that she'd created. She hugged him when things were bad, promised they would get better, told him he was her perfect child. She wrapped him in love. And then she withdrew. It didn't matter that she was doing it for his own good. She had withdrawn. So he must be wrong, inadequate, a disappointment. And as he grew older and became more obviously himself, he was told that he was not just a disappointment but a sinner, a pariah, an abomination.

No, Kezia wailed silently to herself. *Never an abomination, not you. It was all from love, all to help you. Couldn't you see that?*

She withdrew. She condemned. She saw where he was most vulnerable and sliced him there. And then she sent him away. He must have hated her. He must have hated himself. There were times he must have believed he was an abomination. But the memory of being a perfect child had been baked into him so deeply that he knew it wasn't true. He was Jeremiah, still.

So he ran.

Jeremiah, forgive me.

She hadn't seen. And George never told her. All those years of consoling and advising and he'd never said anything until that argument in Zarphan's cell. Well, she'd never really been talking with George's spirit, had she? Those conversations were a fiction sprung from her own neediness, a rippled mirror of her own assumptions.

No George. No God.

Jeremiah lost to her forever.

Her son might be in the fire or he might be hidden in some unknown corner of the Earth but either way he was alone. Either way he must believe that she'd abandoned him. Either way he was lost to her.

Better she had died at birth than lived this life. Better to vanish forever in a cloud of dark. If God didn't care enough to stay in this world, why should she? Maybe if she begged and pleaded, Jesus would let her remain in Heaven—would blend her into the soup of souls and she wouldn't have to know anything ever again.

Above her, the tree dangled long strings of leaves like it was fishing. Maybe some kind of weeping willow. The leaves swayed in the breeze, which was spiced with hints of baking lasagna and summer grass.

Lasagna in a grassy field. Was the whole universe mocking her?

"Um..."

Kezia startled. There at the entrance to the courtyard stood Haisheng.

"Can I come in?"

She wanted to snap at him to go away, but this wasn't her house. She shrugged. "It's a free country."

He looked perplexed but inched forward. She didn't know much about him; on the ride up from Hell, he'd been on the other horse, and since their arrival in Heaven he'd barely spoken. He approached her bench and climbed onto the far corner.

"I wanted to make sure you were safe."

He was so earnest. She rebuffed him, but only half-heartedly. "What'd you think would happen to me? That I'd be mugged in Heaven?"

He pressed his lips together. It struck her that coming from the past, from China, he might have no idea what a mugging was. After a while he spoke, looking at the ground.

"I'm sorry about your husband."

321

"Thank you." She didn't want a conversation but had to be courteous.

"I've lost people too. Many people."

Kezia bristled. If this was his way of consoling her, it wasn't working. People never knew what to say. At work, after George died, they'd said meaningless things like "at least he didn't suffer." How in the world would they know whether or not someone had suffered? Her church friends had been better: they assured her that George was in Heaven, and that Jeremiah would come home safely, and they would all be reunited someday. That had helped, then. Now it no longer did.

"There was a boy," Haisheng said. "My best friend. I used to think I was in love with his girlfriend. But now I think maybe it was him. I'm sure they killed him. Her too. Basically, all my friends are probably dead. Shot or beaten to death. Maybe tortured. There was a militia unit that I was in charge of and they're all dead too. It was my fault. I was careless. Sloppy. So much time has passed, my father and mother must be dead now too. I disappointed them. They sent me to school to become a clerk and have a secure life and I threw that away. And then in Hell there was an old man named Ishaq who saved my life. I threw that away too. I turned my back on him and he went off into the desert and I don't know what happened to him. And there was a girl, a Japanese girl, an amazing person, so strong and brave. She's dead now too. From a fireball. I don't know why I survived and she didn't."

Kezia had barely been listening when he started. But as Haisheng went on, she understood he wasn't trying to console her at all. He was unburdening himself.

"You have no one left?"

He shook his head. "My sisters. They were born in 1915 and 1917. But it's 2015 now, right? They'd be dead by now too, wouldn't they?"

Poor child. Not a soul left alive on Earth who knew who he was. At least she had Donna and the pastor and her other church friends. She might never have grandchildren of her own, but at least she was Auntie Kee to Donna's grandchildren.

Haisheng was looking at her sadly. She hadn't noticed this before, but his eyes were brown like Jeremiah's. His hair was needle-straight while Jeremiah's was curly, but they both had a little crescent moon behind their ears where no hair grew. Haisheng looked too young for all this revolution and death. He should be shooting hoops or playing video games or whatever teenage boys did in his China. In another world he could have been a high school friend of Jeremiah's. In another world he could have been her son.

Haisheng kicked his legs back and forth and stared at the ground. He'd given up on a response from her, or perhaps he'd never expected one to begin with.

"Let the dead bury the dead," Kezia said. She spoke slowly to be sure he was listening. "You're alive. You've got time to make new friends, to do things that would make your parents proud. You'll find a girl to love, I promise you. Or a boy, if that's what you want. It's okay. It's up to you. You can figure it out. But you've got to look forward, not back."

He was so young. Kezia reached for his hand and pressed it between hers. His hand was icy, here in this eternal springtime of flowers and crystal, and she rubbed it to warm him up.

"You listen to me, and let the dead bury the dead," she repeated.

CHAPTER FORTY-EIGHT

Annie

Jesus asked Urielle to summon the other archangels. Waiting, Annie marveled at his unhurried calm. If she were a deity whose universe was starting to fracture, she'd be rushing around with celestial duct tape and spackle, shouting for the heavenly equivalent of the Army Corps of Engineers.

But she was human and he was God. So he didn't look perturbed when Kezia fled the courtyard; he thanked a shy angel who flew by and offered him a garland; he responded with patience when Ben started peppering him with questions about particles and antimatter and a unified theory of physics.

Two unfamiliar angels flapped into the courtyard, and Jesus introduced them as Raphael and Gabrielle. Raphael gave off a deliberative calm that reminded Annie of her childhood pediatrician. Gabrielle was quicker, twitchily alert.

Michael trailed Urielle into the courtyard. The last time Annie had seen him, he'd been aglow with righteous anger at Zarphan. Now he flew low to the ground, his golden hair faded to a pale flax. When he saw Annie his eyes widened.

"She's human after all?" he murmured to Jesus, who nodded. He dropped down onto one knee before Annie. "I beg your forgiveness. I erred. I abandoned you."

Urielle grimaced to Annie. "When there were no nuclear weapons, he concluded you were Satan's agent. So he never returned for you."

"Please, get up, you don't need to apologize," Annie said. Having a divine being at her feet felt intensely awkward.

"Come." Jesus beckoned the four archangels. "I want your counsel on this."

* * * * *

At first, Annie knew everything that Jesus was relaying to the archangels: souls shaken loose from the fire, portals between Hell and Earth. But then he got to the repercussions.

"The portals may expand," Jesus said. "Not just the occasional human passing through, but whole streets or even cities sucked into Hell. Matter may travel the other way too, with Hell's fire pouring onto Earth."

He spoke as evenly as a teacher explaining a homework assignment. But the scenario was something from a Hollywood apocalypse—cities flooded with infernal fire, live humans slipping into Hell, thousands of devils free after millennia of imprisonment, looking for amusement and power and revenge.

That wasn't all. If devils were now mortal and Satan's mass suicide plan succeeded, it would doom more than the devils themselves. Hell had been created as a place of exile for the fallen angels: it had no independent existence. If devils ceased to exist, Jesus said, Hell would cease to exist too.

"All of Hell? Gone?" Gabrielle asked. She was vibrating like a high-tension wire.

Jesus nodded.

"Its human souls too?"

He nodded again.

Annie reached for Trua's hand. Her mother was one of those souls in the fire. So was his father, the man honored in the scars on his cheeks. Billions of human souls would vanish with no chance for redemption or rescue.

"It mustn't happen," Urielle said firmly.

"We will stop him!" Michael declared, clenching his golden sword.

Annie felt a wash of relief. The angels would stymie Satan and protect Hell's human souls; perhaps there'd still be a way to free her mother. But Jesus spoke again, cutting off the others.

"It's time we heard from the fifth archangel."

* * * * *

A torrential wind engulfed them. Water from the fountain sprayed across the courtyard. The climbing rose came loose from the wall and whipped back and forth from its roots. Annie gripped the bench to anchor herself. Even the archangels were straining to stay in place, their wings clamped tight. Only Jesus seemed untouched. He sat placidly in the maelstrom, hair lapping his shoulders, robe draped in loose folds over his knees.

The wind swelled into an even more powerful gust, dropped a large, dark shape in front of the fountain, and ceased.

The stillness was unnerving. Had the wind deafened her or was the courtyard really this silent? Satan pulled himself to his feet, shook out his leather wings, and looked from the humans to the archangels with scorn. Amidst the city's shimmering crystal, his tarnish swallowed light like the entrance to a cave. His beautiful red eyes gleamed.

"Consorting with mortals. You *have* reached a new low, haven't you."

Urielle's jaw was tight. Michael looked ready to attack. The courtyard was charged with something stronger and more turbulent than any wind. It was bigger than Annie could comprehend; it had been going on for ages. She was a small child hearing unimaginable things beyond her parents' closed door. She was a novice sailor on the open ocean, waves swelling, lightning on the horizon, water deeper than she could know.

"It's good to see you again, Lucifer." Jesus's voice was steady but not warm.

"Ruling the roost?" Satan straightened his tunic and nodded sardonically in the direction of the palace. "And now you're summoning people hither and yon? Daddy letting you try on his shoes?"

"'Daddy' is gone."

"Gone fishing." He sneered. "For men."

"It's true. He's left our universe and moved on to other creations."

"Lies."

"You know me, Lucifer. Do I lie?"

"This summoning." Satan sounded bored. "Was it really necessary? You could have sent an errand boy." He gestured at Michael, who bristled. "Or you could have paid a visit yourself. It's been a while since you dropped in on the poor relations. What's your angle? More to the point, what's *his* angle?"

"There is no angle. Our father is gone. You don't need to fight him anymore. Push all you want, but there's no one to push against. No one to anger and appall. You're playing to an empty house."

Jesus paused. Satan was as unreadable as stone.

"Let the old battles go. We can mend the breach. Lucifer, the doors of Heaven are open for your return."

"No!" Michael flapped violently into the air. His silvery face was now tinged a muddy red—the color of rust, of blood. "It's the prodigal son all over again, but worse! You're going to welcome him back—*him*? After he ruined so many of our brothers and sisters? After he doomed humankind? It's not right. It's unworthy."

Urielle nodded emphatically. Gabrielle wasn't quite nodding, but her wings twitched in agitation.

"Lord," Michael continued. He lowered himself to one knee. "I've been rash in the past, and you've been merciful to me. But Lord, sometimes mercy can go too far. Lucifer's sins weren't only against you. They were against all of us, humans too. You may forgive him for his rebellion against you, but is it right for you to forgive his crimes against others? Think how many angelic souls fell because of him, how many humans are in Hell right now because of him. Would *they* want to forgive him? Think of Eden. Think of what Earth could have been. Think of what it became—"

329

"Michael," Jesus said firmly. "I know all that. Don't you think I feel those losses all the time?"

"Yes. Of course—"

"You mentioned the prodigal son. He regained a home and a fresh start. His parents regained a son, and his brother a helpmate on the farm. The only damage was to the brother's pride. Isn't that a worthwhile trade-off?"

"Of course, my Lord. But the prodigal son was just a human—fallible, tempted. All he did was lose human money. While Lucifer—"

Annie stared. Unbelievable, that she was here listening to God and angels debate happenings from the Bible. But something about the discussion bothered her. It was like a single off-key instrument in an orchestra: something was wrong but she couldn't identify exactly what.

"That's enough now," Jesus said to Michael. His tone was calm but forestalled any further argument. He turned to Satan.

"Lucifer, the offer stands. Come home. It's a new era. You've seen the changes that are happening. There are challenges we can all face together—"

"You mean the portals. And *them*." Lucifer gestured at Annie and the other humans. "So you've finally found something you can't control. Besides us, of course."

"Come home," Jesus repeated. "You and the others will be welcomed with open arms. You don't need to fight anymore. You don't need to prove anything."

"Lord—" Urielle began.

"Oh, save your perfumed breath," Satan hissed at her. "I wouldn't want to come back here anyway." He turned to Jesus. "Come back for what? To worship you on daddy's throne? To live in debt to your great magnanimity? You're a cheap, pathetic knock-off of your father. I should have been the heir all along. And for the record, I have no regrets. One day of freedom in Hell is better than eternity under the chains of Heaven. And yes"—he turned and stared at the humans—"know that they are chains. No matter how much crystal and gold they use to tart them up. *Do God's will. Sing his praises. Deliver his messages.* You're better off in the muck of Earth where you can do what you want. So no, Urielle darling, there's no need to tie your tunic in knots. I would not choose to come back here, ever."

"What *do* you want to do then?" Jesus said evenly.

Satan rolled his eyes. "You know already. You know everything, don't you?"

"What is it you want?"

"It's no secret. We're going to destroy ourselves. With the changes going on, I believe it will work. I'm quite looking forward to it."

"No!" Michael's voice was urgent. "He wants to evade God's justice—"

"He mustn't destroy Hell!" Gabrielle exclaimed, wings fluttering.

"Send him back below," Urielle said gravely. "Close the portals, return the humans to the fire where they belong. Return everything to the way God ordained it."

There! With Urielle's words, Annie grasped what had been bothering her: the angels wanted to maintain Hell as it was. They saw nothing wrong with Hell.

"And you, Raphael?" Jesus was asking. "What do you think?"

331

The quiet angel nodded. "I agree with the others. Hell is holy and beautiful because justice is holy and beautiful. We must preserve God's justice."

No! Annie wanted to scream a denial. Hell wasn't holy or beautiful: it was cruel and hopeless and dehumanizing. It was arbitrary and unfair. But the words wouldn't come. These were immortal beings older than the Earth, while she was just a human, and not a particularly articulate one. She glanced to Ben for help but his eyes were fixed on Satan and the angels.

Trua's hand gripped hers so tightly that it hurt. She glimpsed movement at the courtyard entrance: Kezia and Haisheng returning. Kezia's hand rested on Haisheng's back as if guiding him. She froze when she saw Satan. Her knees buckled and she started to wobble, but Haisheng reached for her and propped her up.

"Come, Kezia," Jesus beckoned.

His serene face had taken on a gentle sadness. He looked at the humans as if waiting for them to say something. When none did, he spoke quietly, as if to himself.

"So it is decided. My archangels have spoken. We will not let them destroy themselves."

"Wait," Annie said. Her voice echoed off the crystal walls and filled the courtyard. Barely a croak, it was the loudest sound she'd heard in her life.

"Let them do it. Help them, even. It's the right thing to do."

CHAPTER FORTY-NINE

Annie

It was a weekday evening shortly after Annie had finished her maternity leave and returned to work. She ate dinner with her parents and afterwards took Mary upstairs to nurse. Eyes closed, she let the world slip away and sank into the counterpoint rhythms of Mary's suckling and the chair's rocking.

The nursery door creaked. Her mother peered in, then took a seat on Ben's old bed, which was piled with packages of diapers.

"You're so beautiful there. Like one of those European paintings of madonna and child."

"Hardly. But thanks."

Callie made herself busy straightening the diaper packages. Then, abruptly, she looked up at Annie. "Sweetie, do you feel socially isolated?"

"What?"

"Living here. You gave up your apartment. You spend every evening at home with Mary. You don't go out with people. I was wondering if you feel lonely."

"Of course not!" Annie was truly surprised. "Mom, this afternoon I was in charge of 28 fifth-graders. I spent all morning in planning meetings. I *like* having quiet nights with Mary."

"Can I ask what happened with you and Melanie? You never see her anymore. Are you still friends?"

She didn't answer. It was classic Callie to intuit that there'd been a falling-out, although there's no way her mother could have guessed it was over Hell. Annie felt a sudden, cavernous need to tell her mother everything.

Tell her. She was worn down by keeping secrets—isolated, but not in the way her mother thought. How wonderful if she could talk to someone about Hell and Trua and Mary's real origin.

Don't tell her. It would be Melanie all over again: disbelief, concern, exhortations to see a shrink.

Tell her. She'd been surprised by her mother's support so many times these past few months. Wasn't it worth giving her a chance?

Annie teetered back and forth, craving connection but fearing judgment. It was one thing to announce you were single and pregnant; it was another to insist you'd visited Hell. She would become the problem child again, the failure. Her mother took such pride in the orderly perfection of her garden—how the lantana was bushy rather than leggy and how the petunias lined up in color-coded rows. Annie would return to her old role as the scraggly lantana, the aphid-riddled petunia. *Oh sweetie*, her mother would sigh, disappointed yet again.

Fear won. She stayed silent.

"We just went separate ways," Annie said. "Her being single and me having Mary. It happens to a lot of friendships. But I'm not lonely. Not at all."

Weeks later, her mother was in Hell.

* * * * *

This time she would choose voice over silence.

Sitting on the golden bench, surrounded by the luminous glass of Heaven, Annie tried to figure out how to communicate the reality of Hell to the archangels. *The tormenting fire, the traumatized wraith-slaves, the injustice.* It was too much to put into words. She wasn't a debater like Ben. But no one else was speaking up so she'd do her best. She felt terribly, icily exposed.

"Hell isn't holy or perfect." she said. "It's terribly, horribly unfair. Good people are condemned for following the wrong religion or for not following any religion at all. And even people who've done bad things—the punishments don't fit the crime. Adultery doesn't deserve a billion years in a sea of fire. Theft and lying don't deserve that. Even murder doesn't deserve eternal fire. And there's no chance for people to change, or reform, or do better. It's not justice, it's only torment—"

"It's like a tribe."

Trua's voice rose harshly from beside her and she pivoted in surprise: Trua, critical of tribes?

"A tribe made up of Christians," he growled. "Members of the tribe are admitted here, to Heaven. They get protection and light and..." He struggled for words. "That thing in the palace. That happiness. They get everything. And outsiders get nothing—worse than nothing, they get the fire. Tribe members win and outsiders lose. Outsiders don't matter. Their suffering doesn't matter. I used to think like that too, I admit it. But I was wrong. There are no tribes. There are only human beings."

He paused and stared accusingly at Jesus.

335

"Doesn't God know that? Don't *you* know that? How can you be the son of God and not know that?"

"Blasphemy, human!" Michael lifted up with a great slap of wings but Jesus grounded him with a glance. Annie placed a cautioning hand on Trua's arm.

"Please," she said to Jesus. "He wasn't trying to insult you. But he's right. If there's a way to fix Hell and make it more just, I'd say to do that. But if the only choice is destruction of Hell versus eternity in the fire, then let it be destroyed. Even if it means the end of my mother's soul. Of my own soul someday—"

"My son's in that fire too, Lord." Kezia spoke softly but firmly. "Better if he's gone entirely than to keep him suffering like that."

Annie had run out of words. Across the courtyard, Satan smirked. "Bravo for the little orator," he said. "She can't hold a candle to her brother, but she gets the prize for Most Sincere."

"Shut up!" Ben lunged towards Satan, but Haisheng pulled him back.

Raphael smiled at Annie. "The fires of Hell are indeed terrible," he said gently, as if instructing a child. "But they burn away sin and leave souls pure. And God judges righteously. God doesn't give souls more than they can bear."

It wasn't true. The angels didn't understand. Satan was right: her brother was the master persuader. But Ben had never experienced the fire. You couldn't truly understand unless you'd experienced the fire—

Later Annie would try to remember which happened first—the idea or the heat. They arrived together like leaves in a gust of wind. She had the idea and heat rushed to her head. Red and orange flames swarmed her vision. She started to dizzy.

No. Not now. Not yet.

Trua saw and reached an arm around her. "Annie, stay with me," he murmured.

stay here stay here stay here stay here

She anchored herself to Trua and to her idea. The heat subsided. The dizziness retreated. Orange flames gave way to the gleaming crystal light of the courtyard. Annie took a deep breath and looked across to the archangels. Michael was glaring at Satan, Urielle and Gabrielle looked impatient, Raphael seemed placidly assured. She didn't know how to do this. There must be a way, but she didn't know what it was.

Jesus answered her question before she could ask.

"All four of you," he said. "Gather around Annie. Lay hands on her."

The angels' touch was firm and cool on her head. She had never tried this before. She was afraid of failure and afraid of success. She glanced another question at Jesus—*if I go, can you bring me back?*—but he gave no answer.

"Don't let go," she said to Trua, who tightened his grip.

Annie closed her eyes and willed herself into the fire.

* * * * *

burning

burning

*burningburningburningburningburningburningburningb
urningburningburningburningburningburningburningbu
rningburningburningburningburningburningburningbur
ningburningburningburningburningburningburningburn
ingburningburningburningburningburningburningburni
ngburningburningburningburning—*

You are floating in fire. Sinking in fire. Drowning in fire.

Sea of pain that you never left. No before and no after. No shore and no sky. No Heaven or Earth. Only fire above and fire below, each vying for the greatest agony. Push yourself up and your lungs inhale fire. Let yourself sink and the flames take you down, into pain into pain into fathomless depths of pain.

stop stop make it stop

Flames wrap your body and dress you in pain—hairshirt of fire, corset of fire, leggings of fire. Claw them away and rip your own flesh, more fuel for the flames. Tender and raw, you burn. Bloody and oozing, you burn. Contrite and pleading, defiant and outraged, confused and lost, you burn you burn you burn you burn—

help me help me help me help

Skin chars to ash. Hair sizzles like wire. Veins pulse with lava and fire and pain. Fire was, fire is, fire will be, world without end. Burning but not consumed. Over and over. Burning but not consumed. Over and over. Over and over. Over and over—

But now something worse. The flames, somehow, *know.*

They feel your hubris, your intent to destroy them. They swarm. It's no longer enough to torment you, no longer enough to string you along for eternity in a delirium of pain. They aim to erase you, burn you to a point where the cycle stops and there no longer is a *you* to sense the pain. They may do it through incineration. They may do it by driving you mad. They've never faced this before so it's all unknown but you are an existential threat and you will burn like no other soul has burned before.

burningburningburningburningburningburningburningb
urningburningburningburningburningburningburningbu
rningburningburningburningburningburningburningbur
ningburningburningburningburningburning—

The tips of your fingers are screaming.

The tips of your fingers are ash. Like the charred end of a fireplace log, they crumble and fall away. No more fingers.

The palm of your hand scorches. Once a soft cradle for fresh plums, for a baby's head, it blackens to bone and then slag. No more palm.

On to your wrists: you writhe and scream, but writhing just roils the flames and your voice is lost among the screaming billions. Your wrists crumble. No more wrists.

Flames swarm your arms.

Flames swarm your shoulders.

You're sinking now. You're giving up. Blackness swirls, blotches of black in a sea of fire. You know nothing of sin. You know nothing of life. You know nothing of God. You toggle between pain and oblivion, no longer caring where the dial will land. Lights blink off. Radio silence. Droplets of red on a curtain of black.

you are nothing but pain

you are nothing

but pain

you are less than nothing

CHAPTER FIFTY

Trua

Annie felt like a dead thing in Trua's arms. He dropped to the ground with her as her eyes rolled into her head, her body dense and still against the glistening pavement.

What if she truly dies? What if she's trapped in the fire? Could that happen here, in the heart of Heaven, with the Christian god looking on?

The archangels towered over him, hands still on Annie's head, their eyes closed. He heard a faint hum like swarming flies. The air was ripe with the scent of wild blackberries and warm horse.

Damn those blackberries. Damn the horse.

Annie had returned to Hell for him. Yes, she'd come back for her mother but he knew it was also for him. He couldn't lose her again.

"Jesus..."

The name was hard for him to speak.

"Lord..."

That was even harder. But what he'd experienced here left no doubt that this god was the ruler of all. Trua's absorption into the petals of that flower was beyond anything he'd ever imagined. Sunsets on the Great Plain, nights around the cookfire, flying with the winged horse...the flower was a thousand times all of that.

He didn't know how to reconcile the god of the flower with the god who created Hell. He didn't know how to reconcile the Jesus sitting across from him with the Jesus of the Roman Empire.

He needed to make sure Annie came back.

"My Lord," he repeated quietly. "I'm sorry for disrespecting you just now. I'm sorry for things I did when I was alive. I didn't know. The Romans treated us—the Romans said—"

"My child." The other humans didn't seem to hear anything, but the voice was clear and firm. "Challenging injustice is not disrespect. I will never take it that way. And you don't need to apologize for your life. Some things you've taught yourself since then, and others you couldn't have known." The voice took on an edge. "Not everyone who assumes my name walks in my steps."

"Will she return? Can you protect her?"

Jesus didn't answer. Trua forced himself to trust. He waited.

Annie awoke.

Her body shifted and her eyes returned, blinking. He pulled her close. The angels drew back.

Raphael wept silently, tears proceeding in regal restraint down his cheeks. Gabrielle keened and rocked while Urielle, hands tented, whispered a prayer. Michael stood aloof but his thin lips turned down and spider threads of sorrow radiated from the corners of his eyes.

"Annie," Jesus said. "Thank you." His face opened into a broad smile like Trua's father when Trua was a boy and had just ridden home with his first stag. Amazing: God was proud of Annie! But now a new fear struck him—that he might lose her to Heaven rather than the fire. He held her tighter.

Across from them, Gabrielle stopped rocking.

"We didn't know," she said to Jesus, her eyes lowered.

"No," Jesus said. "But now you do."

He gazed at the four archangels, his smile turned sad.

"And now you understand, don't you? This is why we must allow them the freedom to carry out their plan."

* * * * *

Satan watched from the far side of the courtyard, arms crossed, with a bored expression. He'd stood like that the whole time Annie was in the fire. Trua wanted to throttle him.

"We're supposed to be grateful now?" Satan said. "Bow down and praise your magnanimity in allowing us to kill ourselves?"

"No," Jesus said.

"Of course. Still Mr. Humility. Never asking for praise. But perfectly willing to accept the adulation of billions of devoted Christians. How many paintings of you are there on Earth by now? Plus the sculptures? All those ghastly crucifixes."

"Lucifer, the decision is yours. If you choose to destroy yourself, I won't stand in your way. I'll even help if you want. However, there are two conditions."

Satan looked suddenly alert. He'd always liked bargaining, didn't he? The devil eyed Jesus appraisingly,

343

and Trua knew he was witnessing something momentous.

"First condition," Jesus continued, "No other living beings can be harmed by your destruction. No humans, no animals, no life of any sort. The second is that every fallen angel must be given a choice."

"A choice?"

"They can repent and be welcomed back to Heaven. Or they can follow you to destruction."

"Hardly a choice. Repent or die? Is that the only way you can get new acolytes? On Earth, they'd call that a shotgun wedding."

"Very well. Three choices. Follow you, repent and return to Heaven, or become mortal. They would be born as ordinary humans, with no memory of Heaven or Hell, to live a normal human life and die a human death."

Across the circle, Gabrielle slapped her wings together. Michael's mouth was tight with disapproval. Trua didn't like the idea any more than the archangels did: thousands of devils being reborn on Earth. His home.

But was it even his home anymore?

It struck him that he belonged nowhere. Dead and condemned to the fire like all his ancestors, somehow he'd ended up here in God's courtyard. He was an accidental visitor, alive only because of mistakes and malfunctions. If Hell and all its souls were destroyed, would he be destroyed with it?

Satan was still weighing Jesus's offer. Annie had recovered and was watching beside him, intent.

"All right," Satan finally said. "It's a deal." He stepped forward and proffered a hand to Jesus, but Jesus didn't move to shake.

"One more thing," Jesus said. "How do you plan to do it?"

The two entered into a back-and-forth that Trua couldn't follow. Satan seemed to want to fly his forces into the sun, but Jesus forbade that. They were tossing words at each other that Trua had never heard before.

"What's a 'supernova?'" he whispered to Annie.

"A star that kind of explodes," she whispered back. "Jesus won't let them fly into the sun because it would blow up and destroy Earth. They can't use any other suns either. So they're settling on a black hole."

"Black hole?"

"Region of spacetime." Ben jumped in, excited, quick. "Gravity so strong that nothing can escape. Not light, not radiation, nothing. Einstein hypothesized it in general relativity, it deforms spacetime so that particles bend toward the mass—"

Gravity? Relativity? Spacetime? More things from Annie's era that were foreign to him. He belonged nowhere. He felt as lost as when he'd stumbled, delirious, across the desert.

"Agreed, Lucifer?"

Jesus was looking steadily at the devil, waiting for a response. The archangels fluttered in agitation. "Don't trust him, Lord," Gabrielle begged, flapping her wings in small urgent motions. "He's a liar, a schemer—"

"Don't believe a word he says!" Michael echoed.

The angels were right. Trua might not know what gravity or spacetime were, but he knew better than to trust Satan.

"All right," Satan said. "A black hole. Agreed."

The angels sagged like wineskins that had sprung a leak. Satan stepped forward again with an outstretched hand, and this time Jesus rose and took it. Trua stared in confusion. God and his nemesis shaking hands? This bizarre compact between enemies might mean his own death. He felt a surge of longing for home, where things made sense.

Satan pulled his hand away first, shaking it as if dirtied.

"Send me back down." he said. "I need to muster my people."

CHAPTER FIFTY-ONE

Ardat

They were herding the prisoners out of Satan's palace in small groups of five or ten.

Ardat heard the commotion from inside her cell. It started far away, in some other corridor of Pandaemonium's sprawling dungeon, but sounds echoed loudly against the stone walls. Barked commands. Clank of iron doors. Muttering, cursing, and shouts—some exultant, some threatening. All of it was welcome. Any diversion was welcome.

Ardat had no idea how much time had passed since Satan's forces captured her in the empty city. The only break in the monotony was when that wretched human Kezia had sauntered by like a royal guest. Now she pressed herself against the bars and tried to decipher the shouts. Was this a revolt? Led by whom? Zarphan would punish her as a deserter, and she certainly didn't want to see Satan. For any other devil commander she'd grovel, swear loyalty, whatever it took to get out of here.

The commotion sounded closer. And now shapes were approaching through the dim corridor. Guard devils, a mass of them. Satan took no chances. They stopped in front of a cell down the corridor and she heard the scrape of keys and iron. Lowered voices, no sounds of struggle. Now they were moving towards her cell, crowding in front of it. A small devil whispered in the ear of a large devil, one of Satan's lieutenants, whose name she couldn't remember.

"Ardat," the lieutenant said.

"Yes."

"The moment is here. We rebel angels can finally determine our destiny. All of us, both the loyal and the treasonous."

Ardat almost laughed. *Who are you to call yourself loyal?* she wanted to taunt. *You abandoned Satan like everyone else. You simply returned when it was opportune.*

"Torture me if you want. I'm still immortal, as far as I know. And I won't join your suicide game."

The lieutenant grunted. "You'll have a choice. We all will have a choice. The great Satan has decreed it."

"What choice? What kind of choice?"

"Come. You'll find out."

He jiggled a rough key into the lock, which rasped open and released her into the crowd of guards.

* * * * *

The line trailed outside the gates of Heaven, farther than Ardat could see. There were no longer any guard devils, but they were unnecessary: there was nowhere to flee. She'd been carried there with thousands of other devils in a sudden whirlwind. On her right were the unbreachable gates. On her left, the abyss with its plummet back to Hell.

"Hey. You were with Zarphan?" the devil behind her asked. He was short and round and looked useless; in Heaven, he might have been one of the scheduling angels who arranged when choirs and orchestras would perform.

"Yes." She spoke curtly. She didn't want to talk politics, or anything, with him.

"Is Zarphan here too?"

"I wouldn't know." Ardat pivoted away and stared at the line stretching ahead.

Truly, she hadn't seen so many devils in one place since the original rebellion. No one seemed to know what was going on, but there was a buzz of nervous anticipation. She felt it too. Had Satan triumphed? After all this time, were they finally about to inherit the kingdom?

A cool breeze wafted through the gate—a shock after eons of hot desert air. It carried a hint of fresh grass, and Ardat thought with a pang of the woody scent of that human harp. It was gone, smashed to pieces when Satan's forces captured her in the city.

But here was Heaven. And, beyond its gates, countless angelic harps.

Did her old golden harp still exist? Had it been given to some other angel? If Satan's forces were now in command, she might be able to reclaim it and punish its usurper. Or she might have her pick of all the other harps—yes, even the one belonging to (don't say his name), the buffoon who'd stolen her solo.

If Satan had won.

But if he'd won, how would he treat defectors?

It seemed like a good sign that she was here in line with all the rest. She glanced around for familiar faces.

349

The line inched forward and, far ahead, she thought she recognized a sentry from Zarphan's fortress. Near him, a devil she'd known long ago at Pandaemonium.

And there—ahead and to the right, beyond the gates—movement.

She peered past the golden bars and saw, above the grassy slope, a half dozen angels fluttering towards the gate. The silver of their tunics and the light of their faces were almost blinding after so much time below.

That had once been her.

Purity. Virtue. Holiness.

Obedience.

Ardat pursed her lips. If they were still flitting around so freely, Satan must not have triumphed. So why was she here? Surely Satan wouldn't try his suicide plan at the front door of Heaven? The queue moved slowly forward. The group of angels gathered in a cluster by the gate and called out names—*Jetrel, Auza, Asbeel*. How charming: they were looking for their friends. As if they cared about anyone besides God!

Ardat knew none of them. She wouldn't want to know them—sycophants, cowards, mediocrities. Still, there were a couple of angels she wouldn't mind seeing again. Pahaliah was one, a flautist who used to play in the same orchestra as Ardat. Paha was an adequate musician who occasionally produced transportive, astonishing phrases. She appreciated Ardat's playing, although she changed the subject whenever Ardat criticized the orchestra leadership. Sometimes after a rehearsal the two of them would sit on the edge of a fountain, dangle their feet in the sparkling water, and improvise melodies—one of them humming a line, the other humming a response, until they had composed a complete song.

Nakir was another angel she wouldn't mind seeing. He was a smith who provided sheets of gold to the instrument makers. He lived in a perpetual state of awe at the musicians and the sound they coaxed from his metal. He'd seemed especially fond of Ardat.

"Let me see your beautiful hands," he used to ask her, examining them as intently as if he were working filigree.

"The secret is only partly in the hands," she would tell him. "The rest is in the heart."

"Ah, but I can't see your heart, can I?" he would smile. He was right: he had never seen the frustration building there.

Ardat hadn't thought of either Nakir or Paha in ages. If they showed up at the gate calling her name, what would she do?

Heaven was so close. Ardat stared at the devils ahead of her, at the glistening spheres under her feet, even at the abyss—anything other than the silvery grass beyond the fence, which raised too many confusing emotions.

* * * * *

So many devils, so little movement: the line was going to take a millennium. But then another miracle happened and the vast crowd in front of her vanished. Ardat was in a much shorter queue, with maybe 50 devils ahead and another few dozen behind, and they were standing in the courtyard of God's palace in the Celestial City.

She had no idea how they'd crossed the gate or where all the other devils had gone. This was definitely not Satan's work.

"Do you know—" the short, round devil behind her began.

"I do not," she snapped, which shut him up.

The palace: God's abode. Ardat had performed in courtyards, amphitheatres, and plazas throughout the city but never the palace itself. She peered at the golden doors, wishing for a glimpse inside. What treasures there must be, gold and gems beyond imagining. Perhaps secret stores of knowledge. And the acoustics: what would it be like to play music in God's own hall?

Her fingers twitched. Forgotten words rose in her throat. "Blessed are you, my Lord, our God, sovereign of the universe—"

She pressed them back down.

The line moved slowly, in fits and starts, into an adjoining courtyard. Finally Ardat neared the opening and shoved the devil in front of her aside. She gasped.

There, on two golden benches, side by side, sat Satan and Jesus.

Jesus! She had only glimpsed the son of God once, during the great battle when he descended upon the grappling hordes with his flaming fierce chariot and his terrible eye-winged cherubs and his bow of ten thousand thunderbolts, routing the rebels and driving them over the precipice into the abyss.

That had been a cataclysm, an apocalypse. And now here he sat, like a brother, with Satan.

There were others too. The four remaining archangels stood behind Jesus's bench. All mindless lackeys.

352

And nearby, also watching, was a cluster of humans, including—*no, was it possible?*—the human Kezia.

Not good.

In fact, very, very bad.

Ardat had rebelled against Jesus, deserted Satan, and imprisoned Kezia. No matter who was the judge, she'd be condemned.

She pivoted, looking for escape. If she flew up and out of the courtyard, could they catch her? What if she ducked out of the line and snuck down an alley? If she found Nakir, would he take pity and hide her in his workshop?

He wouldn't.

Ahead of her, a devil stepped forward into that next courtyard. Ardat pressed forward to hear and see better.

"Barbiel, it's good to see you again," Jesus was saying. "You understand your choices?" There was some quiet back-and-forth that she couldn't hear. Then Barbiel raised his head defiantly.

"I choose the Lord Satan," he said, as Satan's tight mouth widened into a triumphant smile. The archangel Rafael ushered Barbiel out the far side of the courtyard.

"Come," Jesus said.

He was talking to *her*. Ardat's pushing had landed her in front of the opening. She forced herself into the courtyard.

"Her!" Kezia gasped. "She's the one. In Zarphan's mountain—"

Jesus raised a hand ever so slightly and Kezia fell silent.

"Ardat," he said. "We've missed your music."

353

Satan caught her gaze and rolled his eyes. She knew exactly what he was saying: *Missed your music? When did he show the slightest interest in your music? He doesn't care about you; he just wants to deprive me of another follower.*

"What are you offering?" she said.

Jesus explained. The archangels watched her sharply. Kezia shifted, agitated, on the bench. Ardat stalled for time, asking questions, pretending she didn't understand. But of course she understood.

She could follow Satan to non-existence. Fat chance of that: he'd botched the rebellion and then done nothing for millennia. She would never follow him anywhere again. And she didn't want to die. She wanted to live.

Heaven. For eons, she would have rejected this too. But waiting in line she'd felt Heaven's pull—the grassy breeze, her old friends, her harp. Ardat's fingers twitched. Perhaps things would be different now. Jesus had noticed her, even missed her; perhaps she would finally get the recognition she deserved...

Or Earth. Most pathetic of the options. Why would anyone choose to be frail and mortal? A lifespan barely longer than a moth. If you were doomed to die, better to plunge into it with the vigor of Satan than mope around and watch your body decay on Earth.

So Heaven it would be. She'd retain her immortality and reclaim her harp. Perhaps they'd let her solo but if they didn't, she'd swallow her pride. She'd live as one of a thousand anonymous harpists, but at least she would live.

Ardat took a breath and steeled herself to speak. Satan narrowed his eyes and glared. He knew.

"Lord!" Kezia burst out, unable to contain herself. "She makes beautiful music but she's evil. She'll make trouble. She'll—"

"Quiet!" The bootlicker Michael snapped at Kezia. "They're all evil, not just her. Don't you think our Lord knows that? Don't you think he has ways to keep them in line?"

Kezia dropped her gaze, abashed. But Ardat kept hearing the arrogance in Michael's voice—the righteousness of the victor. Eons had passed but it all came rushing back. This was the same arrogance with which he enforced decrees in Heaven, the arrogance with which he'd slashed his golden sword through rebel wings.

Of course. She knew it now. She could never return to Heaven—to toe the line, bow to the powerful, restrain her own will for the sake of the collective.

"I choose Earth," Ardat said, standing tall and proud and spreading her wings.

She would never have wings again. She'd age and sicken and die. She'd forget the music of the spheres and be consigned to feeble, diminished human harps.

But she would play. Oh, would she play. Nothing could stop her—not mortal bones and muscles, not loss of all memories of Heaven, not starting out in the disgusting form of a mewling infant. Through all of it she would remain Ardat and she would find her instrument and play and solo and reach the top. Fame. Fortune. Immortality of a sort. No one would stop her. No one would silence her. She would be a god of the musical world.

"Earth, I said," she repeated, as if none of them had heard her the first time.

355

CHAPTER FIFTY-TWO

Baphomet

Baphomet strained for a glimpse of Satan but all she could see were the wings and shoulders of larger devils, both ahead and behind her in line. She felt unseen and trapped at the same time. The brawny male devil in front took a step back and nearly knocked her over. The female devil behind her, busy exchanging snide comments about Heaven with her friends, grabbed one of Baphomet's wings and shoved it to the side.

"Stop it," Baphomet protested, but the devil didn't even look at her.

It wasn't fair.

(*Fair* and *fare*. Ever since that lesson with Ben, she'd been noticing homophones. Usually it gave her pleasure but now she was too frustrated.)

She was the only one who'd stood by Satan in his bad times. Why hadn't he taken her with him now? Why was she stuck in the middle of this rude, pushy horde?

(*Horde* and *hoard*.)

The thought of Satan was the only thing that made the line bearable. He'd won the devil civil war, he'd negotiated with Jesus himself, he was about to achieve his ultimate dream. She imagined triumph blazing in his red eyes, power surging through his wings and shoulders. She wanted to flap up, just a little, to catch a glimpse. Behind her, the female devil gave her a shove and a pinch.

"Move forward."

"There's nowhere to go!" Baphomet snapped, but the nasty creature had turned back to her friends.

Stay in line, the guards had ordered them. *No flying allowed.*

(*Allowed. Aloud.*)

Baphomet stood on her tiptoes but saw only shoulders.

* * * * *

Finally she reached the courtyard entrance and stepped inside. There was Satan—as princely as she'd ever seen him, enthroned on a gold bench that highlighted the shifting, textured darkness of his limbs. And there, nearby, was Jesus. She'd expected him too.

She hadn't expected the humans.

Annie. The older woman who'd been thrown into the cell with Annie. Two men she'd never seen before. And Ben.

This felt intensely wrong. She didn't want Ben to see her with Satan. She didn't want Satan to see her with Ben. She was unsure which way to look, so she looked at her feet. They seemed bleary and filthy next to the luminous crystal paving of the courtyard. For the first time in eons, she was ashamed of her talons. Crude, rough, graceless. Angels didn't have talons.

"Baphomet," Jesus said. "Welcome back. The garlands of Heaven haven't been as full since you left."

She stared. God had been aware of her garlands?

Satan snorted. "The garlands of Heaven are always full. Full of flattery and servility." He turned to Jesus. "I have some nice nicknames for her. Do you want to know them?"

Know and no. Not Bathmat. Please not Bathmat in front of God. In front of Ben.

She waited for Jesus to take Satan up on his offer—they were civil with each other now, maybe even friends?—but his gaze remained steady and warm on her.

"We've missed you, Baphomet. Do you understand the choices? We would welcome you back here."

She straightened her shoulders and raised her head and puffed out her wings. She refused to look at the humans.

"I stand with Satan."

She'd wanted to sound defiant but her voice came out wobbly and thin. Jesus leaned towards her and reached out a hand.

"My child. You don't need to be alone anymore."

"Alone!" Satan snorted. "She's underfoot all the time. Pokes her nose in everywhere. That's hardly alone."

"Baphomet."

Jesus's voice hung suspended in the courtyard air. In it she heard the swishing of flowers in barely-remembered breezes, and the giggles of girlfriends sharing bouquets they'd just picked. She heard the layered breath of ten thousand souls united in work, worship, love. His hand remained outstretched, just a few paces away. With one flap she could fly over and take it.

"I'm going with Satan. Now let me go."

Jesus sighed and nodded.

"Good girl!" Satan said brightly.

She swelled with pride. Finally he recognized her devotion! But then the memory of that dog on Earth popped into her head. The female human striding down the path, holding a cord for the dog's neck. The creature had turned from Baphomet and bounded over to the leash.

Bad dog. Good girl.

She had a sick feeling in her stomach. She looked pleadingly at Satan. He detested pleading; she knew that. But had he nothing more for her?

He had nothing more.

"Wait!"

Ben leapt up from the bench. She looked directly at him for the first time since entering the courtyard.

"You, sir, are a shithead," he said to Satan. "Do you know what you're throwing away here? Can't you see who she is?"

Satan shrugged. "Apparently someone you want very much."

Ben turned to her. "Don't do it. Come to Earth. Live with me. We'll read together every day. We'll read everything. We'll read Milton! I'll show you the world. We'll go to Paris, London, Africa. The rain forest! The Antarctic! You can be whatever you want to be. A writer. A poet. Damn it, you can even be a florist and make garlands! You'd be wonderful at any of it—"

She couldn't move. She couldn't breathe. Long ago she'd heard stories of God turning humans to pillars of salt and wondered if that had just happened to her. She didn't understand how Ben dared say any of this, or why he was saying it.

"Come with us. If they send you back as a baby, I'll adopt you. I'll take care of you, raise you, teach you everything. Reading and writing are only a start. You've got such a drive to learn—such tenacity—you could be a scientist. A journalist. Whatever you want! And Annie's got a daughter too. We'll raise you together. Like sisters. You wanted to know about siblings? Come back to Earth with us and you'll have a sibling. A family. People who love you, who value you—not like that asshole—"

Her breath caught at his audacity. Puny human with a body that could be shredded more easily than one of Heaven's blossoms. She braced herself for Satan's wrath—Ben's blood, his splattered human guts, she couldn't bear to see it—but nothing happened.

"All yours if you want her," Satan said casually. He leaned back on his bench, arms folded. "You know there's no return policy, though."

Worse than splattered blood and guts. Even the dog had an owner that wanted to keep it.

"Baphomet, listen to me," Ben said to her. "You're too young to die. Too smart. Too strong. Too..."

He halted, at a loss for words. For the first time in her millennia of existence, Baphomet had an intimation of her own power. The human wanted her. What the Great Satan was to her, she was to Ben.

Vistas of possibility opened. If she wanted to learn poetry, he would teach her poetry. If she wanted to eat ice cream, he would bring her ice cream. She could make him happy, like she did with the dog, like she did during their lessons. It was so simple—a few carefully chosen words, a joke, a private smile. She could transform his world. It was power, magic, the work of a god.

But even more stunning: she could make him un-happy. Every trick of Satan's could be turned on him. Ridicule, disregard, dismissal, temper. She could weave his life into a garland of misery, bind it in a bouquet of new and sparkling torments.

"Baphomet." Ben had regained his voice, but just barely. "Come with us. I...I love you."

"I...don't know," she said in a tiny voice.

"Go," Satan said, waving a hand. "He wants you, for reasons I can't discern. Have fun on Earth. Ride roller coasters. Go fishing. Do whatever it is they do down there for fun. I've got plenty of followers without you."

She didn't know, truly. It was all a jumble.

Her single day on Earth: the trees throbbing with liquid life, the soft textures of Annie's bedroom, the words and writing everywhere. She could have ten thousand days like that. She could have a sister. She could have a dog. She would be able to read all those words. She could have a garden all her own with flowers just for her...

And Ben wanted her. Satan didn't want her. Surely she should go where she was wanted. And Ben compelled her—his knowledge, his authority, even his male pattern baldness. But he was nothing next to Satan. The world was nothing next to Satan. Her insides turned liquid at the caresses in his voice, even though the caresses were always for others. How could she leave Satan alone at the time of his death? Or—even worse—how could she let him die with some other devil at his side, some rude, grabby devil who didn't love him the way she did?

She didn't understand death. She couldn't imagine non-existence. Death was as impenetrable as those human scritch-scratches before Ben taught her to read. She knew it must be terrible because humans feared it so. But either way she would die—with Satan soon or with Ben someday. *Too young to die.* Ben had said that. But she had already lived for eons. What difference would another seventy or eighty human years make?

The trees. The dog. Satan. Ben. Death now. Death later...

It was too much, such a big choice. The last time she made such a choice it hadn't felt difficult at all. She had been swept up in Satan's vision, his passion, his justice. She had decided as swiftly as a wingstroke and never regretted it. But now she was torn. She didn't know how to decide. She was just a small devil, a weak devil, a girl, she had never asked for this responsibility, it was all a mistake, if only she could hurl herself off the cliff of Heaven and fall down, down, down, back to Pandaemonium and spend her days polishing the throne, burnishing the door handles, that was where she belonged, that was all she was suited for—

"Baphomet," Ben said again. His voice was low. It cracked, and in that crack she heard mortality—the snapping of branches, the breaking of ice. "Please. I love you."

She flashed another pleading look at Satan: *Decide for me. Give me a sign.* But he gave her nothing. He glanced away, up the walls of the courtyard, across the shining pavement.

She understood that this was how it would be: he would give her nothing, and then they would die.

"I follow the Great Satan," she said in a choked voice, and ran out of the courtyard into the dark throng of waiting devils.

CHAPTER FIFTY-THREE

Annie

"You shithead!" Ben shouted at Satan. He launched himself after Baphomet but Michael flapped down and blocked his way. Then he lunged towards Satan but Urielle intervened. Annie grabbed his arm, pulling him back toward his seat.

"Ben—let it go—you can't—"

Finally he slumped onto the bench. Kezia tried to speak to him but he shrugged her off. He slouched, staring at the ground. Then he jerked his gaze up at Jesus.

"How can you let them do this?" he snapped.

Jesus looked at him steadily. "Did you listen at all to your sister?"

The devils kept coming through the courtyard, though after Baphomet Annie felt too drained to watch. She reminded herself that the ultimate result would be an end to Hellfire, but it still felt like a bad business all around. She just wanted to go home. She yearned to feel Mary dozing on her shoulder, to watch Mary pucker at a spoonful of new food. She wanted to be back in a world where the most momentous choice was between pureed peaches and pears, between cloth and disposable diapers.

And then the final devil passed through the court-yard.

Annie didn't know how Jesus had managed to process tens of thousands of them in such a finite amount of time, but it was done. The flock of angels that had gathered overhead to welcome the returnees to Heaven dispersed. Raphael closed the gate that led out of the courtyard. Silence rang in Annie's ears. It should have been twilight—the end of a day, the end of an epoch, the end of a huge chunk of God's creation—but the sky remained bright and the crystal walls glistened as crisply as ever.

"Well," Satan said. "That was efficient." He drew back and looked at Jesus with grudging respect. "I didn't think you'd actually go through with it. God never would have. Maybe you're your own man after all."

"Maybe I am," Jesus said. He sounded as drained as Annie, too tired to argue or reprimand.

"Then let's get on with it. You'll let me take my people?" Satan waved beyond the courtyard. "I assume we can fly directly from Heaven to the mortal universe? That we don't need to waste time going back through Hell?"

"Yes, you can go from here. But first there are some things I need to do. We need to return these mortals"—Jesus glanced towards Annie and the other humans—"to their homes. And I need to convene the angels and let them know what is happening."

"Why not." Satan seemed strangely accommodating now that he was on the verge of getting his way. "It's been an eternity; what's another few hours? Go. Do whatever you need to do." He strolled to a corner of the courtyard and stretched out on a bench like a cat in the sun.

Jesus turned to Annie and the others.

"Thank you," he said solemnly. "For your warnings. Your presence. Your witness." He looked directly at Annie. "Your courage." He gestured for them to approach. They all did—even Ben, still grim and angry—and Jesus raised his hands. "May God bless you and keep you. May God's face shine upon you. May God grant you peace."

"Amen," Kezia murmured.

"You've witnessed a lot, and later you may realize that you witnessed more than you knew. I ask you to remember. I'm not asking you to be a prophet like Moses or an apostle like Paul, but to be true to what you've learned here. Love our father the creator and honor his creation. Protect his creation, all of it, the large and the small, the grand and the homely.

"I suppose I could tell you a parable that would make this all clear—or—" He gave a sad smile to Ben. "More obscure. But the hour is late and there's much to do. So all I will say is: bear witness. Protect creation. And now we'll take you home."

A bittersweet sorrow descended upon Annie. She didn't completely understand what Jesus was trying to tell them but knew she'd never be this close to God again while alive. The harmony of the rose, the golden warmth of his presence, the sense of wholeness and sufficiency. She would grope for those feelings on Earth and they would be elusive as shadows. They'd be hidden in the clutter of daily life—the gridlocked commutes and youth soccer matches, the laundry loads and vacation plans, the celebrations and illnesses and farewells.

The consolation was that Heaven would be waiting for her if she managed to follow his ways. No more fear of Hell after death; only the chance to earn a return to Heaven.

"Annie. Ben. Kezia," Jesus said. "You all came directly to Hell from present-day Earth. So Urielle, Gabrielle, and Raphael can fly you back to your homes.

"Trua and Haisheng, it's more complicated for you since you died a long time ago. We can use one of the portals to return you to the moment of your death. Michael will carry you back to Hell and find a portal."

Trua shifted, frowning. Annie's gut hollowed. She was about to lose him again, this time forever. This was worse than her previous return to Earth, when she could imagine him shaken loose in the deserts of Hell. Now—in her era—he would have been dead for 1,600 years. Not even bones or dust left. Not even the grandchildren of his grandchildren. She clasped Trua's hand, tried to memorize the short, thick fingers and calloused palms. It had felt like a miracle when they arrived in the Celestial City and could actually touch each other. She hoped Jesus would allow them a few minutes alone to say goodbye.

"Sir, excuse me," Haisheng said.

He'd spoken barely five words this whole time in the courtyard. Now he looked awkwardly at Jesus, like a student approaching his professor with a question he knew was basic and dumb.

"If I may be so bold? There are other humans who were shaken loose. Besides us. They're still down there. One is a man named Ishaq—"

"A woman named Oudine," Kezia added.

Trua nodded. "A fat man. A cook."

"Yes, and probably more," Haisheng continued. "What will happen to them when Hell is destroyed? Can you save them?"

Jesus smiled. "We can. The souls that you call 'shaken loose' are *in* Hell but no longer *of* Hell. I'll send some other angels with Michael. They can seek them out and return them through the portals."

Now Kezia leaned forward.

"Lord. If you can save those people...can you save some of the souls in the fire too? Just a few? My son— I failed him before but if you brought him back, I would hold him so close—he's a good boy, he would do you proud—"

Jesus shook his head.

"Not even one person? He was just a boy—"

Jesus looked into Kezia's eyes. Annie didn't know if it were an embrace or a battle. After a long time, Kezia bowed her head.

"Yes, Lord. I understand. Those souls will no longer suffer. They'll be gone but they won't suffer. That's enough of a blessing. Yes. Thank you, Lord."

* * * * *

Michael flew off to gather his lieutenants. Annie was about to ask for time alone with Trua when Satan started complaining about delays—the time it would take Michael to search for portals, the time it would take to round up all the other shaken-loose souls. For the first time, Jesus ignited with rage.

"No one flies fast enough for you? No one retrieves souls fast enough for you? Does this entire universe revolve around you, Lucifer? You'll have your freedom when everything is ready, and not one moment before. You never learned patience in your lifetime, so learn it before your demise."

Jesus didn't explode into light like the archangels, but his voice was an icepick. Satan lurched back as if slapped. Annie feared having such anger directed at her. Still...just a few minutes alone with Trua? Was that unreasonable? She was steeling herself to ask when Haisheng spoke up again.

"Sir. If I may request something else? For me this time. I've been thinking about it...I don't want to return to the time of my death. Ben told me what's going to happen. My city will be taken over by reactionaries and gangsters. My friends will be killed. I don't want to return to a time when I know what's going to happen. I would foresee the disaster, and try to prevent it, and fail. I'd be haunted forever."

"What is it you wish then, my son?" Jesus's voice was gentle again.

"Perhaps...could I go to Shanghai in the present day? When these people are alive?" Haisheng nodded towards Ben and Annie. "He tells me that the revolution triumphed. That China has become prosperous, not just the factory owners but many millions of people."

"Do you really wish that?"

"I think so...I don't know..."

Ben looked up in caution. "I said the revolution triumphed, but I also said it's not a revolutionary society anymore. Greater material wealth but tight restrictions on speech and dissent—"

Haisheng gestured him to stop. "I know. It's not a paradise. But the future is open. In 1927, the future is written already. It feels like anything I could do with my life would be meaningless." He turned to Jesus. "So...yes. I think I want that."

"Very well. It can be done."

"Contact us," Ben said to Haisheng. "I'm on the web, Benjamin J. Maple. We can help you. If you go back to university and want to study abroad, I've got connections—Fulbright, the State Department, Princeton—"

"My Lord," Trua said to Jesus. "I too have a request..."

No. Don't leave yet. She knew how much Trua missed his world—his sister Damla, his brothers, the Great Plain. He'd been away from them for so long. She was afraid he'd be sent off before they could say goodbye.

"What is it you request?" Jesus smiled as if he knew already.

"I wish to go to the present-day world. With her."

Annie's breath caught.

"Do you understand what you would be giving up?" Jesus asked.

"I understand."

"Don't," Annie whispered.

He glared at her. "You don't want me?"

She couldn't lie. She wanted him desperately.

"I'm not sure you do," Jesus continued to Trua. "That world is very different from yours. The traditions will be different. The values will be different. The things that you are good at...you will probably not be able to do those things there."

"I know."

"You may love each other now. But that doesn't always last for a lifetime. You would be giving up everything you cherish for something that can be as fragile as a leaf."

"I know."

"But you don't know this: you understand each other here because you are in the realm of God. On Earth, you will speak Hunnic and she will speak English."

They both fell silent. Annie had never considered this. Of course learning a language wasn't impossible. People did it all the time: a friend of hers had fallen in love with a Roman tour guide on a trip to Italy, although she knew barely enough Italian to order meatballs. She and Trua could teach each other. It would be fun, a game, a secret intimacy between the two of them...

But on top of his having to learn about 21st century America? With its computers, automobiles, job interviews, conference calls?

Her friend's Italian affair lasted 18 months.

He had only ever lived in a tent.

He didn't know how to read or write.

"I understand," Trua said.

But he didn't. He couldn't. A future opened up before Annie and it wasn't a cozy routine of Sunday mornings in bed together. It was Trua adrift, and she his only lifeline. She would have so much—family, language, job, home, skills—while he'd lost everything. He would be dependent on her. She would try pathetic ruses to compensate him—vacations at dude ranches, roasted lamb dinners, feigned helplessness at fixing a fence or opening jars. He would come to resent her. She would come to pity him. And they would be bound together.

371

She would stay with him, no matter what—through sickness and health, of course, but also through anger, depression, silence, his bursts of physical rage. Divorce would never be an option. She had loved his loyalty; she would have to learn that from him.

"Let love cast out fear," Jesus said, looking at her.

Annie's cheeks were wet, and she wiped them with her sleeve. The world was all before them. She groped for Trua's hand.

All right. She would try.

CHAPTER FIFTY-FOUR

Kezia

The goodbyes felt surreal, everyone hugging and promising to stay in touch as if they were leaving a dinner party. Jesus beckoned Kezia aside and gave her one final instruction.

"Wait until the summer before contacting Annie and Ben, no matter how urgent it feels," he said. "You left Earth in October and will return in October. They left in June and will return in June. If you contact them too soon, they won't know who you are. It could alter everything that has happened here."

"Yes, Lord." He didn't need to seek her promise: of course she would do what he asked.

Kezia's trip to Hell through the portal—it felt like a century ago—had taken only a second. The journey home let her glimpse how vast the distance really was. Raphael gathered her close and leapt skyward before she could utter a final thanks. They flew through the silvery nimbus around Heaven for what felt like hours, then entered a tunnel in the sky that held a crystal staircase. The steps were made of air that, icelike, took form and held weight. The angel leapt from step to step, the stairs growing further and further apart so they came to be soaring across gaps the size of continents and solar systems and galaxies. It was resplendent and transfixing and wondrous, but there was a limit to how many miracles a human mind could take in. After a while, Kezia let it all blur past and sank into a stew of clashing emotions.

Relief at going home. Sorrow at leaving Heaven. Amazed gratitude that she—*Kezia Parker, an accountant from Brooklyn!*—had been given a chance to visit Heaven and feel Jesus's embrace. Continued heartbreak that she would never see George again. But also an exhausted thankfulness that Hellfire would be brought to an end. Jeremiah was lost to her but that torment would cease—both for him and for countless other undeserving souls.

Undeserving, yes. Because God shouldn't punish people for being true to how they were created. If only she'd realized this years ago. But she hadn't, and Jeremiah had paid the price. She now understood his running away. What she didn't understand was how to reconcile God's laws with God's love. Or with justice. God was just and loving—she had always believed that, and Jesus's embrace conveyed its truth to every cell of her body—but his laws were not.

Things are always changing, George had told her, back when she believed he was speaking with her. So perhaps some of God's laws hadn't kept up with the evolving world he'd created. Perhaps God's views had changed over the eons too, and he now regretted aspects of creation like Hell. She didn't know. It was all a muddle.

"We're almost there," Raphael murmured, and Kezia realized the staircase was gone and she could see the blue and green marble of Earth from space—*from space!*—and then she was enveloped by dense, moist clouds—

And then she blacked out.

* * * * *

Kezia was in a chair.

Not a hard kitchen chair but a forgiving, bucket-like chair. The seat cupped her bottom, and fabric shaped itself to her back. Woozy from the voyage, eyes closed, she floated in the dark. Her right forearm rested on fabric with a small circular gap—*a hole? a well? a cupholder!*—and she realized this was a picnic chair.

She was back at the picnic.

She didn't want to open her eyes. Nothing could replace the gleaming light of Heaven. And it was cold here. People had piled jackets on her, even a small blanket, but still it was cold. She suddenly recalled that she was supposed to leave the picnic for the cemetery, and then return to her apartment with its empty second bedroom, and everything felt even colder.

"Is she okay?"

"Must have been the shock."

"Should I call 911?"

Voices filtered into her consciousness. "Kee," she heard her friend Donna say, and felt Donna's warm hands around her own. "Wake up, Kee. Come on, girl."

She opened her eyes just a bit. Donna was squatting directly in front of her. Just to her left was Donna's son LaQuan, looking more scared than any eight-year-old should look. Ivy Washington was there too, and Shawna Cook. Warmth streamed through Kezia's stiff limbs. Forget God's justice or injustice; forget Heaven

375

and Hell. This, here, was her holy community. This was where she belonged.

"I told you not to do it like this," Donna snapped at Young Pastor, who was standing behind her. He looked worried. They all looked worried. But behind Young Pastor, was that—?

Yes, there in the crowd was Pastor Ron, her real pastor, leaning on his cane, also looking concerned. *All these men of God, worried about little old me,* Kezia thought with wonder. But no one had told her Pastor Ron would be coming to the picnic. He didn't get out much these days. Maybe it was spur-of-the-moment. Maybe he'd remembered it was George's birthday. Maybe he was the "fellow" that Young Pastor wanted her to meet—

"Get over here! She's awake," Donna called, and another face pushed itself forward through the crowd.

Familiar broad cheeks and big ears, but the sculpted face of a grown man.

Trim beard and mustache of a grown man.

A grown, handsome man with more than a passing resemblance to George, and another handsome young man close beside him, touching his back and giving him the strength to meet this moment.

"Mama," Jeremiah said.

"Baby boy. My perfect child," she murmured and folded him into her arms.

They gripped each other as if a single hug, held long enough, could make up for a decade.

CHAPTER FIFTY-FIVE

Annie

Urielle lifted Annie and Trua as easily as kittens while Gabrielle took Ben. A group of angels flapped past them towards the palace. Other larger groups trailed behind, filling the silvery sky, all heading toward the gathering called by Jesus.

"Like cranes over the Great Plain!" Trua called out. It was as if he'd read Annie's mind: she too had been picturing flocks of cranes and geese, but hers were in California's Central Valley, winging over stubbled fields at sunset with Sierra Nevada peaks in the distance.

The palace and city shrank to the scale of doll's houses. The angels became specks. Annie had an unsettled feeling of having lost something important without being sure what it was. She could still see the meadows of Heaven so she focused on those. *Remember that silvery green.* Someday, when her life had run its course, she would return to these meadows and join the rose.

"Peace be with you," Jesus had said as a farewell, placing a hand on each of their heads.

Satan had just stretched and yawned on his bench. "Goodbye, little Miss Maple Tree," he'd said. "You were hardly original. But you had a knack for being in the right place at the right time."

Now silvery light gave way to deep black. Space became stairs. Suns and galaxies passed like headlights on a late-night freeway. Then the black was gone and they were standing in Annie's bedroom in Mill Valley.

Ben shook his head in wonder. Trua peered around warily. The room was dim, the world outside the window dark, the only light trickling under the closed door from the hallway.

Mary.

Annie shoved through the door and raced down the hall.

The door to Mary's room was half-open. Melanie sprawled in the rocking chair, fully dressed, head listing to one side and mouth open, lightly snoring. Mary lay in the crib in her bunny-print pajamas, asleep.

Annie scooped her up, careful not to wake her, and pressed Mary to her chest. So warm. So compact. So right. *Honor his creation.* She closed her eyes, swayed back and forth, and let herself feel those familiar small breaths, Mary's silky hair against her neck, her own beating heart.

* * * * *

Eventually she set Mary down. There would be more time in the morning, and on many mornings. Let her sleep. Let Melanie sleep, too, as uncomfortable as she looked.

Annie stepped back into the hall. At the far end, her parents' bedroom door remained closed, her father asleep behind it on his side of the queen bed. Annie felt a stab of grief at the thought of the half-empty bed but let it go. She hadn't been able to bring her mother back, but she'd freed her from the fire. That was an accomplishment. That was a miracle. It was all she could do, and it was enough. She was enough.

But her father?

A good man who wasn't religious. Annie no longer had to fear he'd go to Hell, but now she wondered whether he'd be allowed in Heaven. Why hadn't she confronted Jesus about this? In her exhaustion from guiding the archangels through the fire, then the hubbub of sorting the devils, she'd never asked if Heaven would still be limited to members of the Christian tribe. She should have asked! She should have argued! And what about Earth? There was so much injustice here too, with good people suffering tragedies they didn't cause. Earthquakes that leveled cities, children with cancer, wars launched from ornate palaces and paid for with the lives of teenagers from slums and villages—the list could go on forever—

Regret stung her. She should have challenged Jesus. She should at least have asked him to explain God's intent. No one in millennia had been given the privilege of speaking with God. But Annie had, and she let it slip away.

There was still a chance, though: Urielle.

The archangel could carry a message to Jesus, and maybe he'd answer. It couldn't hurt to try. But she'd need to reach the angels before they left. They might even have gone already while she was dawdling with Mary. Annie pivoted and, newly urgent, raced the few steps down the hall to her room.

The lights were still off. Ben sat on the bed and Trua stood near him. Both looked disconcerted, awkward.

Urielle was weeping.

Annie had thought Gabrielle was the emotional one. The only emotion she'd seen Urielle display, other than that terrifying anger, was when she'd shared Annie's experience of the fire. Now the archangel's cheeks were wet and she gripped Gabrielle's hands in silent grief.

"What...happened?" Annie asked cautiously.

Trua shook his head. She approached the two angels.

"Urielle...?"

They paid her no attention. She waited and tried again.

"Urielle? What is it?"

Finally Gabrielle dropped Urielle's hands and turned to her.

"It is the end."

"The end? Of what?"

Gabrielle turned back to Urielle questioningly.

"Yes," Urielle said slowly. "Perhaps they should know." She drew herself up to her full, imposing height and nearly touched the ceiling. She started to wipe her face with her tunic but Annie pulled a tissue from the box by her bed and offered it.

"Thank you." She fingered the tissue distractedly, patted it on her cheeks, then looked back to Gabrielle. "Perhaps that's why he sent us with them. So they can know."

Gabrielle nodded. Urielle placed the tissue down. She didn't seem able to do anything more; her wings were limp as sails without wind.

"Here. All of you. Place your hands on mine. Annie, you shared the experience of the fire with us...Now it's our turn to share something with you."

They gathered. Urielle's hand was cold as window glass on a winter day. Trua's overlapped hers, warm and reassuring.

The room disappeared.

* * * * *

She was somewhere high, hovering over a great space similar to the rose, some kind of heavenly amphitheatre. Instead of souls, it was filled with hundreds of thousands of angels. Jesus stood at the center—Annie's image of Jesus, the long-haired white man, although even as she saw him she knew that was not remotely what he was—speaking to all the beings of Heaven.

The time has come for change, he told them. He didn't know if this were a fulfillment of God's plan or a modification of God's plan but it needed to happen. Satan and his followers were undertaking a journey that would destroy Hell forever. There would be no more suffering for the damned—merely sleep. Hell would not seep through cracking walls into the human world. The mortal universe and all God's creatures in it would be preserved.

Appreciative murmurs rippled through the amphitheatre. Light glistened and reflected from a million quivering, excited feathers.

But that is not all, Jesus continued. The devils require an escort. To honor and witness their self-sacrifice, yes, but also to ensure they do what they have pledged. He himself would lead the escort, and all the children of Heaven would join him.

More murmurs, now unsettled.

There are risks. They know the risks. And so he offers them a choice. It's similar to the choice he'd given the fallen angels: stay with him and form the escort, or choose rebirth and life as a mortal human on Earth.

A crescendo of murmurs, then silence.

"All who wish to choose Earth, feel free to go. There is no shame. You will carry out God's will in a new way. My love is with you."

Not a single angel stirred.

* * * * *

"Is that happening right now?" Annie asked. Her bedroom had re-materialized. "Or did it happen already? Or in the future?"

"Already," Urielle said. "Shh. There's more."

The room disappeared again and now Annie felt herself suspended in space. Floating like that David Bowie song. Darkness all around, cold beyond cold, tiny pinpricks of light like holes in a sieve. She no longer felt Ben or Trua's hands but knew they were there too and rejoiced for her brother, the teenage astrophysics nerd, finally getting a chance to experience outer space.

Her eyes adapted to the void and the pinpricks multiplied. She could see nearly to infinity. Stars emerged behind stars like seeds of a dandelion. Colors too: reds and yellows and blues, scraps and shards and discs. The stars were gems of sparkling sea glass like she used to collect at the beach. The stars were confetti hurled up in an unceasing New Year's celebration, riotous joy, chemicals churning and matter colliding into new life, changed life, new chances. It was God's creation happening over and over. It was fireworks with meaning, not just spectacle but generation, her own miraculous second chance on an intergalactic scale. Annie could have hung there forever, her vision extending as the universe extended, seeing deeper and deeper, understanding more and more...

Far off in the corner of her peripheral vision, something moved.

This was abrupt movement in human time, not the steady rotation and expansion of galaxies across millions of years. At first it was only a ripple in dark water. But as it came closer, she made out shapes: thousands of discrete dark forms traveling in a mass like birds migrating at night. And trailing them an even larger mass of light—thousands of luminous winged figures.

The procession had a regal rhythm. It was stately and intentional. Annie thought she could discern one particular figure at the very front, giving off a dark glow, but it was far away and she couldn't be sure. The procession arced slowly through the void. Stars vanished behind it as it passed. Would astronomers on Earth pick up any of this? And where were they anyway—how many millions of light years from Earth? Where was the black hole that was their destination?

The procession continued. Awe budded and flowered within her. The three of them were bearing witness to the end of Hell. It was an incredible honor. She felt unexpected respect for the devils, even for Satan. As vain and vicious as the devils were, it took self-possession to fly to your death. Their destruction would transform the universe and eliminate infinite suffering. If God—

wherever he'd gone—were watching, perhaps he was proud of them. Had Urielle been weeping from a similar pride in her fallen siblings? Or from grief that now they'd truly be lost to her forever?

Annie pivoted to follow the river of devils and angels as it flowed through space. She peered beyond them for familiar constellations but everything was strange. Was there a prayer she should say to honor the devils' passing? Baphomet with her petulance and curiosity, taciturn Belial, foul-breathed Jomjael—all soon gone. Above and below the long procession, stars glittered. Were any of the devils having second thoughts? Did they see the beauty of the cosmos and regret their decision?

Chaos erupted.

Before her eyes, the front of the procession broke apart. Dark winged shapes shot into empty space like noiseless shrapnel. As the front of the line disintegrated, the middle exploded too. The procession zippered open, devils flying every which way. This wasn't a few regretful individuals breaking ranks; this was organized insurrection. And it was all eerily silent—tumult and riot without a sound. From the rear, masses of angels surged forward to contain the disruption. Individual angels swooped after individual devils; groups of angels formed cordons to rope the devils back into line. Dark and light forms careened through space, dodging, zigzagging.

Golden swords flashed. Leather wings pumped. Annie stared. There were no discernible battle lines. The devils seemed bent on sheer escape, angels chasing behind them like luminous contrails. Then, in a section of space near where the head of the line used to be, a new dark mass gathered and swelled. Dark bodies raced towards it like metal filings pulled to a magnet. Too far away to distinguish individuals, Annie nonetheless knew the center was Satan. The dark mass pulled itself into a compact, disciplined column and veered away from the procession route.

"Stop them!" Annie shouted but her voice made no sound. Was this the silence of space, or was she trapped inside Urielle's vision? Without fully understanding what was happening, she knew this was not the plan. This was bad.

A bloc of angels launched itself in pursuit of Satan's column. More devils joined the mass, which swelled into a dark cloud and receded at an astonishing pace. Closer to her, angels continued wrestling with devils— grabbing them, pinning their wings, holding their flailing forms in place. Battling figures somersaulted in silence, locked together, their wings a black and white blur.

They were going to the sun.

Jesus had banned it, so that must be where they were heading. Another battalion of angels swarmed past her in pursuit of Satan's column, and then another. The angels had numbers but the devils had the benefit of surprise and a head start. Barely yards in front of her, the limp form of an unconscious angel drifted through empty space. Another angel flapped frantically after it.

Annie's heart pounded. *Satan the liar. Satan the traitor.* Above her, angels had started corralling devils into a cordoned-off area. They linked wings and arms, shoulders and feet, to create a shimmering white enclosure in space that stretched dozens of angels high and dozens more across. As pursuing angels dragged more devils into the corral, still other angels added their bodies to expand the walls.

Far away, Satan's column had vanished. Annie could see the glow of angels chasing it but not the devils themselves. Streaks of light arced across the void like flares. *Catch them. Stop them. Don't let them get away.* The glow chasing Satan's column faded into black. Angels and devils alike were lost in the distant dark. Could Jesus have miscalculated? He hadn't known about the portals or souls being shaken loose; perhaps he couldn't stop this. It was Satan's ultimate revenge, his spit in the eye of God. Annie glanced around wildly for Urielle, groped for the touch of a reassuring arm or wing, and found nothing.

Then, to the left, where the tail of the original procession had been, she heard a new sound—a keening whistle like a teapot working itself up to a full boil. The world around her exploded in white light. Her eyes jerked shut and she covered her head. A frenzy of cross-blasting winds hammered her with heat that could only be fury. A moment later it was all gone. The white light vanished, leaving her with the afterimage of a blazing chariot. The heat dissipated and renewed silence throbbed in her ears.

Dark space, pinpoints of stars.

Everything seemed muted and flat after the explosion of light. The corral of angels was still there, fluidly stretching and morphing to contain more devils—one moment a giant sphere, the next a tunnel-like cylinder. This section of space was calming down. Angels tackled the few remaining devils and hauled them within the cordon. In the indistinguishable distance, lights still arced and flashed. Annie waited. She listened. She peered into the void, trying to discern what was happening, but saw nothing. Where was Urielle in all this? Where were Trua and Ben? Would someone tell her what was going on?

Then they returned—the angels, the devils, the light. It began as a bright smudge against the dark distance, then clarified into figures. Here too the angels had formed a bodily cordon, but it was enhanced by a diffuse white light that filled the gaps between wings and limbs. The cordon rolled forward through space like a train; as it came closer Annie could make out flashes of dark bodies caged within the light.

The near and far cordons met and merged like cells fusing. Angels shifted positions and the light shifted with them. They become a single long cylinder, uniform and tight.

The cordon paused as if to take stock or draw a breath, and then it started moving—deliberately, slowly, regally again—along the path of the original procession.

* * * * *

She was back in her bedroom. They all were.

"So it's all right?" Annie asked Urielle. "They didn't get away?"

Urielle looked at her for a long moment. She didn't seem happy.

"They didn't get away."

Annie glanced at Ben and Trua to see if they had shared the vision. Ben looked furious; Trua looked confused.

"Were they trying to capture Heaven?" Trua asked.

Urielle pressed her lips together and pulled her feathers tight. It was Ben who answered. "They were going to the sun."

"But why? Wouldn't that destroy them too?"

"Spite!" Ben blurted. "Pure destruction and spite. They wanted to destroy the Earth, the whole solar system, maybe more. Just to spite God." He glared at Urielle. "Isn't that correct?"

"Yes."

"But they were stopped, right?" Annie asked. "You said they didn't get away."

"That's correct."

"So everything's okay?"

Urielle didn't answer.

"Tell them," Gabrielle said. "It's why we're here."

Urielle looked at Annie sadly. "The Lord understood this might happen. Would happen. It's why he convened the escort. We are accompanying them to the black hole—not just *to* the black hole, but *into* it. So they can't escape to harm the mortal world."

The house was silent—no sound from Mary's room, from her father's closed door, not even the usual rustle of cherry branches outside. Annie didn't want to understand. Angels were immortal. Weren't they?

"At one point we were," Urielle said. "But the universe has changed. Is changing. You've seen that. You were part of that."

"So they'll die? The angels as well as the devils?"

"Yes."

"All of them?"

Urielle nodded.

"What will happen to Heaven?"

"God created Heaven as his abode. If God no longer resides there, it loses its reason to exist."

"But Jesus will still be there. Even if the angels are gone—"

Urielle didn't answer.

No. Not him too.

Panic welled and overflowed. She was drowning in it; she couldn't breathe. "He can't! He's God. He's immortal. He's *God!*" Annie stopped. Urielle's silence was worse than any answer she could have given. "The souls?" she asked quietly. "The rose?"

Urielle shook her head.

No heaven. No rose. No homecoming into God's presence. She reeled under the enormity of the loss. Instead of eternal bliss—nothing.

"So there will be no Heaven, but also no fire," Trua said, frowning, trying to puzzle it out.

This was the price. Jesus had known it would happen. He was sacrificing himself again, and this time he was giving up more than his mortal body. The angels were sacrificing themselves too. All out of love for God the creator and his creations, the brambles and lichens and sparrows and the stubborn species called humankind. Hell would never spill into Earth. Hell would no longer punish people with eternal torment. But neither would Heaven be there to reward the elect with eternal bliss.

"When people die, they'll be nothing," Trua said, still thinking out loud. "Not in Heaven, not in Hell. Just nothing. That's not bad."

Annie thought of her mother in the fire. She would give up her own future in Heaven without regret if that were the price of releasing Callie from pain. She thought of Kezia's family—husband in Heaven, son possibly in Hell, an even more daunting calculus. But Kezia would do it too.

"We'll be alone then," Annie said. A year ago, she never thought about God. Now she felt orphaned. "No God. No Jesus. No Heaven."

"You still have a piece of God," Urielle said with a sad smile. "Inside each of his creations. That will never leave you."

Annie looked down at her hands. Knobby knuckles, bitten nails, and a wrist that would snap like dry wood if bent too far. Hands that changed dirty diapers and cleaned the kitchen sink and pried open cartons of ice cream. It was hard to believe that a part of God rested in there. But apparently it did.

"And maybe..." Gabrielle said softly.

Annie glanced up. Urielle was frowning.

"No," the archangel said.

"Urielle, they should know," Gabrielle continued, almost petulantly. "Our Lord is the son of man as well as the son of God. We don't know because this has never happened before. But it could be that he'll return as a human. A full human this time, mortal. To live one human lifetime and share God's word as a human prophet."

"We don't know that," Urielle said sharply.

"But there's a chance."

"Don't raise false hopes."

"Urielle," Gabrielle said, "when is hope ever false?"

* * * * *

The angels were silent. Annie wanted to shake them into admitting this was all just a story. Maybe another parable? But they were unapproachable—withdrawn into themselves, their light dimmed. Then Urielle straightened and turned to Annie and the other humans.

"Here," she said brusquely. "Give me your hands again. It's beginning."

They gathered around. Again the room vanished and Annie hung suspended in space. Again Annie saw the long white cordon of angels and light, snaking through the dark cosmos with the devils penned inside. The column seemed longer than before; perhaps she had seen only a section of it earlier. Like before, the void beyond was filled with pinprick stars.

But now there was one spot beyond the column that was starless—a silky unmarred black.

The head of the column was so distant as to be a bright blur. It crawled forward, a white chalked squiggle moving across a blackboard. It neared the silky spot. And then it wasn't there.

The rest of the column remained. It was as if someone had wiped a classroom eraser across the tip of that chalk drawing. Then erased a bit more, and a bit more.

The column was still a brilliant river of light across the cosmos. Unhurried, disciplined, it seemed like it could inch along forever. Annie stared at the light, trying to sear it into her eyes and preserve it.

"Can't we—isn't there—" she said but no sound came out.

Bit by bit it vanished until nothing remained but space and stars.

* * * * *

In Annie's bedroom, the angels' glow provided enough light to glimpse shadowy versions of the familiar furnishings—bed, night table, dresser, desk. Everything was grey and blurred after the stark black and white of space.

The angels withdrew their hands from hers. They stepped away towards the window.

"Now," Urielle said. "We must join them."

"Peace be with you," Gabrielle said gently.

Urielle pushed the bedroom window further open, and the two of them flapped past the cherry tree into the night. By the time Annie reached the window to call, they were gone.

CHAPTER FIFTY-SIX

Annie

She felt drained and nauseous at the same time. There was nothing left inside her and yet her body seemed on the verge of retching itself up. Annie sank onto the bed and buried her face in her hands.

Eventually she lifted her head. Ben was pacing back and forth, muttering in a voice too low to make out. He looked like a professor preparing a lecture, like he was rehearsing for one of his goddamn speaking gigs.

Rage welled up in her. She didn't try to stop it.

"Happy now?" she snapped. "You got what you wanted. No God. No Heaven. No Hell. Isn't it great? You can go on TV and tell everyone that God is dead. How many books can you get out of this? Maybe a PBS special? *Exclusive! Ben Maple proves that God is dead!* You'll blast all those Christian talking heads right out of the water. *God is dead and Ben Maple is right and everyone else in the world is wrong.* I bet you can't wait to go on TV and show everyone how right you are—"

"I can't." He stopped pacing and looked at her sadly.

"Of course you can. Here." She grabbed the cell phone she'd left on her night table and shoved it at him. "Call CNN. Fox. Whoever."

"Annie."

393

She refused to look at him. She glared at the floor.

"Think about it, Annie. What would I tell them? *A devil flew me to Hell and then I rode a winged horse to Heaven and met God but now he's dead?* I'd sound like one of the Jesus-in-a-tortilla people. I'd sound crazy, like I thought you were when you died and came back. I've spent my whole life debunking irrational bullshit and advocating for logic. Scientific method, controlled experiments, replicable results. What do I have here? A vision. A story. Nothing."

His voice broke on the word "nothing," and she understood he wasn't just talking about TV opportunities.

He dropped onto the bed. "Here." He reached into his pants pocket and pulled out the small spiral notepad that he carried around for taking notes. Annie hadn't realized it had traveled to Hell with them. He shoved it at her, arm straight as a yardstick, as if he wanted it as far from him as possible.

She took the notepad and flipped it open. It held page after page of Ben's familiar scrawl, indecipherable at the best of times, let alone in a dim room. She could make out a word here and there—NRA, Syria, climate—but mostly it was chicken scratch. She turned more pages and came upon something different—the letter 'b,' printed over and over like a first-grade writing exercise.

She continued to the next pages and peered through the dimness.

ba ba ba ba
bat bat bat bat
ban ban bad bad bad
beg beg beg beg
ben ben ben

The lines of the letters were precise and aligned, crafted with determination and care.

They threw their arms around each other and rocked back and forth together on the bed.

* * * * *

When they finally pulled apart, Annie realized Trua was gone.

No.

On top of everything else, to lose him? Had Jesus's death undone his miracles? What if Trua had been hurled back to the 4th century? What if he'd been obliterated along with the angels and devils and every other piece of the divine world? That was a galaxy-scale loss, a universe-scale loss, but this was the loss of a single person. It would mean nothing to anyone except her. It was worse.

"Ben," she gasped, pulling at his sleeve. "Where's Trua?"

Ben looked around too, taken aback.

"He was here," Annie blurted. "Before the angels left. I know he was. But after that? I don't know, I was so upset, I didn't notice—"

Didn't notice! Careless! Self-absorbed! Had she learned nothing from Hell?

"Calm down," Ben said but his voice echoed her fears. "He must be here somewhere—"

Annie ran to the open window and peered frantically into the dark yard. Could he have fallen? Climbed out? Flown off with Urielle and Gabrielle?

"Come on," she urged Ben, who was still sitting on the bed. "I need your help. Come on—"

Before she could finish, the hall floor creaked. Trua appeared in the doorway. He was backlit and silhouetted, the hall light forming a halo around him. He held Mary close to his chest and rhythmically rocked her up and down. He knew how to hold babies! Mary gave a snuffle and a wiggle but stayed asleep.

He saw Annie and his scarred cheeks lifted up in a wide smile.

"Kizin chok guzul," he said, or something sounding vaguely like that. "Kizin gordugum en guzul cochuk."

"What?" Annie blurted.

They stared at each other as if across a river.

"You really can't speak English anymore?"

"Beni daha fazla anlayamiyor musun?"

Outside the window, the night sky was an impenetrable black. A breeze riffled the tree. The rustling leaves were more comprehensible than Trua's words.

They were lost. Stranded. Alone.

No. She would not accept that.

Annie pointed a finger at herself. "I," she said.

She placed two hands over her heart and extended them towards him. "Love." She pointed at him. "You."

He seemed unsure. She tried again.

"Mary," she said, pointing at her daughter. A nod: at least he recognized the name. "Baby," she continued, still pointing.

"Ba-by," Trua repeated carefully.

"Mother," she said pointing to herself.

"Mo-ther."

Now she pointed at him. "Father."

Beyond the window, the cherry tree stirred. The moon emerged from behind branches and cast silvery light on the sill. Mount Tam was a dark sleeping mass

396

waiting for dawn. Steep Ravine lay out there with its ferns and redwoods, and the city with its neon laundromats, and the coast with her students and their sand-filled sneakers, and it was all enough. It was more than enough. It was, even without a god or a heaven, a blessing.

In the room, Trua jiggled Mary up and down and she made a little whuffy sigh.

"Father," he said, and smiled.

Acknowledgments

People often describe writing as a lonely process, but throughout a decade of writing about Hell I never once felt as isolated as Annie did during her return to life. So many people were supportive and helpful: I'd be justified in repeating all the thank-yous from *Shaken Loose*. But in the interest of space, let's focus on people who played a key role in *Shaken Free*.

The team at Hypatia Press—David McAfee, Rae McAfee, and Rob Johnson—bravely committed to this sequel even before they knew how the first book would fare. My writing group—Lindsey Crittenden, Audrey Ferber, and Monica Wesolowska—walked every mile in Hell with Annie and Trua and made their journey, if not more pleasant, more readable. Diane Glazman reprised her role as a fantastic developmental editor. Insightful beta readers included Nanette Asimov, Deb DeBare, Sue Fishkoff, Susan Ito, Carolyn Said, Sam Schuchat, Krista Vossekuil, and Nicholas Herold. (Nick gets double thanks since I inadvertently omitted him from the acknowledgments in *Shaken Loose*.)

Shelly Simon, Destiny Muhammed, and Monica Moore shared their knowledge of horseback riding, harp playing, and the Black church respectively. Do check out Destiny's wonderful jazz harp performances at destinymuhammad.net! Simon and Chris Schuchat provided background on Shanghai, and Jim Mayer was my go-to source on olive harvests. Joe Albanese was a great help in learning how Hell has been portrayed in art through the centuries. Of course mistakes in any of these areas are my responsibility, not theirs.

The translations of Du Fu poems are by Mark Alexander, used with permission from his website, chinesepoems.com. The starlight poem read by Ben is my own very rough translation of "Kochavim" by Hannah Senesh from the Senesh Family Archive (National Library of Israel), with thanks to Ori and Mirit Eisen.

For helping shepherd *Shaken Loose* and *Shaken Free* into the real world, I can't say enough good things about Kathleen Caldwell, owner of A Great Good Place for Books, who is a fairy godmother to Oakland writers. Every author should have a such a supportive local bookstore. Also thanks to Jim Richardson, who helped bring *Shaken Loose* to Beer's Books in Sacramento, and Leah Garchik, who helped me launch it at Green Apple Books in San Francisco.

I'm grateful for my daughter Rebecca Schuchat, a talented cartoonist (rebecca-schuchat.com), who designed the covers for both *Shaken Free* and *Shaken Loose*. And more than grateful for my husband Sam— cheerleader, sounding board, steady keel, and mixer of strong gin and tonics when they're most needed.

Finally, thanks to all the readers of *Shaken Loose* who shared their enthusiasm, brought it to their book groups, sent me funny Hell cartoons, etc. I've been eager to get this sequel to you and hope it lives up to your expectations.

Acknowledgments

People often describe writing as a lonely process, but throughout a decade of writing about Hell I never once felt as isolated as Annie did during her return to life. So many people were supportive and helpful: I'd be justified in repeating all the thank-yous from *Shaken Loose*. But in the interest of space, let's focus on people who played a key role in *Shaken Free*.

The team at Hypatia Press—David McAfee, Rae McAfee, and Rob Johnson—bravely committed to this sequel even before they knew how the first book would fare. My writing group—Lindsey Crittenden, Audrey Ferber, and Monica Wesolowska—walked every mile in Hell with Annie and Trua and made their journey, if not more pleasant, more readable. Diane Glazman reprised her role as a fantastic developmental editor. Insightful beta readers included Nanette Asimov, Deb DeBare, Sue Fishkoff, Susan Ito, Carolyn Said, Sam Schuchat, Krista Vossekuil, and Nicholas Herold. (Nick gets double thanks since I inadvertently omitted him from the acknowledgments in *Shaken Loose*.)

Shelly Simon, Destiny Muhammed, and Monica Moore shared their knowledge of horseback riding, harp playing, and the Black church respectively. Do check out Destiny's wonderful jazz harp performances at destinymuhammad.net! Simon and Chris Schuchat provided background on Shanghai, and Jim Mayer was my go-to source on olive harvests. Joe Albanese was a great help in learning how Hell has been portrayed in art through the centuries. Of course mistakes in any of these areas are my responsibility, not theirs.

The translations of Du Fu poems are by Mark Alexander, used with permission from his website, chinesepoems.com. The starlight poem read by Ben is my own very rough translation of "Kochavim" by Hannah Senesh from the Senesh Family Archive (National Library of Israel), with thanks to Ori and Mirit Eisen.

For helping shepherd *Shaken Loose* and *Shaken Free* into the real world, I can't say enough good things about Kathleen Caldwell, owner of A Great Good Place for Books, who is a fairy godmother to Oakland writers. Every author should have a such a supportive local bookstore. Also thanks to Jim Richardson, who helped bring *Shaken Loose* to Beer's Books in Sacramento, and Leah Garchik, who helped me launch it at Green Apple Books in San Francisco.

I'm grateful for my daughter Rebecca Schuchat, a talented cartoonist (rebecca-schuchat.com), who designed the covers for both *Shaken Free* and *Shaken Loose*. And more than grateful for my husband Sam— cheerleader, sounding board, steady keel, and mixer of strong gin and tonics when they're most needed.

Finally, thanks to all the readers of *Shaken Loose* who shared their enthusiasm, brought it to their book groups, sent me funny Hell cartoons, etc. I've been eager to get this sequel to you and hope it lives up to your expectations.

Ilana DeBare is a former newspaper reporter for the *San Francisco Chronicle* and *Sacramento Bee*. Before *Shaken Free* and *Shaken Loose*, she was author of the non-fiction book *Where Girls Come First: The Rise, Fall, and Surprising Fall of Girls' Schools*. Ilana lives in Oakland, California, with her husband, Sam. Learn more at ilanadebare.com.

Ilana is available to visit with your book group via Zoom! See ilanadebare.com for contact information and sample discussion questions.

www.ingramcontent.com/pod-product-compliance
Lightning Source LLC
Chambersburg PA
CBHW021126260626
47169CB00005B/1465